SANDRA BROWN

SMASH CUT

SIMON & SCHUSTER
New York London Toronto Sydney

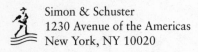
Simon & Schuster
1230 Avenue of the Americas
New York, NY 10020

First Simon & Schuster hardcover edition August 2009

SIMON & SCHUSTER and colophon are registered trademarks of
Simon & Schuster, Inc.

For information about special discounts for bulk purchases,
please contact Simon & Schuster Special Sales at
1-866-506-1949 or business@simonandschuster.com.

The Simon & Schuster Speakers Bureau can bring authors to your live event.
For more information or to book an event contact
the Simon & Schuster Speakers Bureau at 1-866-248-3049
or visit our website at www.simonspeakers.com.

Designed by Jaime Putorti

Manufactured in the United States of America

10   9   8   7   6   5   4   3   2   1

Library of Congress Cataloging-in-Publication Data
Brown, Sandra.
    Smash cut : a novel / Sandra Brown.— 1st Simon & Schuster hardcover ed.
        p.   cm.
    1. Trials (Murder)—Fiction   2. Rich people—Georgia—Fiction.   3. Atlanta
(Ga.)—Fiction.   I. Title.
    PS3552.R718S64   2009
    813'.54—dc22   2009019430
ISBN 978-1-4165-6308-2
ISBN 978-1-4165-6321-1 (ebook)

SMASH CUT

PROLOGUE

A DELICATE *PING* ANNOUNCED THE ARRIVAL OF THE ELEVATOR. The double doors opened. Inside were three people: two middle-aged women who chatted in the manner of established friends, and a thirty-something man with the stressed-out bearing of a junior executive. He shuffled back to make room for the man and woman waiting to board.

They smiled pleasantly as they stepped in, then turned to face forward. The elevator started its descent to the hotel lobby, the five passengers reflected in its brass doors.

The couple stood elbow to elbow in companionable silence. One of the two women in the back hadn't stopped talking, but out of politeness, she was keeping her voice low. Her friend covered her mouth to stifle a laugh and was overheard to say, "Oh, my. And she was so proud of that darned thing."

When the elevator slowed and a chime announced a stop on the eighth floor, the young businessman glanced at his wristwatch and winced as though reconciling himself to running late.

The elevator doors opened.

There stood a person wearing a navy blue tracksuit, wraparound opaque sunglasses, and a ski mask. Around the mouth hole, the yarn had been woven into the pattern of a shark's open maw with jagged, pointed teeth.

Even before the occupants of the elevator had time to register their surprise, he reached into it and banged his gloved fist against the Door Open button. In his other hand, he brandished a pistol.

"Kneel. *Now! Do it!*"

His voice was high and singsong, which made it all the more creepy coming from the open jaws of the shark. The two lady friends immediately dropped to their knees. In a whimper one pleaded, "Don't kill us."

"Shut up! *You.*" He jabbed the pistol toward the businessman. "On your knees." The young professional raised his hands and dropped, leaving only the couple standing. "Are you deaf, or what? Get down!"

The woman said, "He has arthritis."

"I don't care if he's got polio. Down on your fucking knees! Now!"

One of the women in the back wailed, "Do as he says, please."

The gray-haired man clasped the woman's hand as he went down on his knees with evident discomfort. Resentfully, the woman did likewise.

"Watches and rings. Put them in this." The assailant thrust a black velvet bag at the businessman, who dropped in his wristwatch, the timepiece that only moments before had caused him consternation.

The bag was passed to the women behind him, who quickly placed their jewelry into it. "The earrings, too," the thief said to one. She hastily complied.

Last to get the velvet pouch was the gentleman with the arthritic knees. He held it open for the woman with him, who added her jewelry to it.

"Hurry up!" the thief ordered in that hideously girlish voice.

The gentleman placed his Patek Philippe into the bag, then extended it toward the robber, who snatched it and tucked it into the pocket of his zippered hoodie.

"All right." The gentleman's voice carried a ring of authority. "You've got what you wanted. Leave us alone."

The pistol blast was deafening.

The two middle-aged women screamed in terror.

The young businessman cried out an expletive in a shocked, raw voice.

The woman with the gentleman gaped in soundless horror at the blood spatter on the elevator wall behind his crumpling form.

CHAPTER
1

CREIGHTON WHEELER STORMED ACROSS THE BLUESTONE TER-race, whipping off his sun visor and making a swipe at the sweat streaming down his face, then without breaking stride, angrily tossed the damp towel and visor onto a chaise. "This better be damn important. I was about to break his serve."

The housekeeper who'd summoned him from the tennis court was unfazed by his temper. "Don't you take that tone with me. It's your daddy wants to see you."

Her name was Ruby. Creighton didn't know her last name and had never bothered to ask, although she'd been in the family's employ since before he was born. Any time he got out of sorts with her, she reminded him that she'd wiped his butt and his nose, that both had been nasty, and that she hadn't enjoyed doing either. It rankled to think of her being that familiar with his person, even when he was a baby.

He brushed past her three-hundred-pound bulk and crossed the industrial-size kitchen to one of several refrigerators, yanking open the door.

"Right now, he said."

Ignoring her, Creighton got a can of Coke from the Sub-Zero, ripped off the tab, and took a long drink. He rolled the cold can across his forehead. "Take one of these out to Scott."

"Your tennis coach's legs ain't broke." She turned back to the counter and slapped her large hand on the hunk of beef she was preparing to go into the roasting pan.

Something ought to be done about her sass, Creighton thought as he pushed through the swinging door and made his way toward the front of the house, where his father had a study. The door was ajar. He paused outside it, then knocked once on the doorjamb with his Coke can, nudged the door open, and strolled in, twirling the tennis racquet against his shoulder. He looked every inch the aristocrat called away from a session of healthy exercise. It was a role he was perfectly suited to play.

Doug Wheeler was seated behind his desk, which was presidential in proportion but much more pretentious than anything inside the Oval Office. The desk was flanked by mahogany flagpoles, one for the Georgia state flag, the other for Old Glory. Ancestors glared from oil portraits hanging on opposite walls, which were paneled in stained cypress meant to last till the Second Coming.

"Scott's time is money, and the clock is ticking," Creighton said.

"I'm afraid this can't wait. Please sit down."

Creighton took a seat in one of the cordovan leather chairs facing his father's desk and propped his tennis racquet against it. "I didn't know you were here. Weren't you scheduled to play golf this afternoon?" He leaned forward and set his Coke can on the polished surface of the desk.

Frowning, Doug placed a coaster beneath the can so it wouldn't leave a moisture ring. "I dropped by here to change before going to the club," he said. "But something urgent—"

"Don't tell me," Creighton interrupted. "The paper clip audit exposed an embezzlement. Damn those sneaky secretaries."

"Paul is dead."

Creighton's heart gave a bump. His smile collapsed. "What?"

Doug cleared his throat. "Your uncle was shot and killed in the Hotel Moultrie about an hour ago."

Creighton continued to stare at him, then finally released his breath. "Well, in the immortal words of Forrest Gump. Actually his mother. 'Life is like a box of chocolates. You never know what you're gonna get.' "

His father lurched to his feet. "Is that all you can say?"

"I think that says it fairly well."

Creighton had never seen his father cry. He wasn't crying now, but his eyes looked suspiciously moist and he was swallowing too often and too hard. In an attempt to hide the emotion about to overwhelm him, he stepped from behind his desk and moved to the wide window. He looked out over the grounds of the estate, where Mexican laborers were hand-picking weeds from colorful beds of impatiens and caladiums.

Quietly Creighton asked, "Did I hear you correctly, Father? Uncle Paul was *shot*?"

"In the forehead. Almost point-blank range. During an apparent holdup."

"A holdup? Like a robbery? At the Moultrie?"

"As unheard of as that seems."

Doug ran a hand through his hair, which was thick and gray like that of his brother—now late brother—who had been his senior by only eleven months. He and Paul went to the same barber and used the same tailor. Of almost identical height and weight, they were often mistaken for each other from the back. Their sibling relationship had been almost as close as that of twins.

"I don't know any details," Doug continued. "Julie was almost too distraught to speak."

"She was notified first?"

"Actually, she was with him when it happened."

"At the Hotel Moultrie. During the middle of a weekday."

Doug came around and gave his son a hard look. "She was almost hysterical. According to the policeman. Detective actually. He took the phone from her when she could no longer speak. He told me that she had insisted on calling and telling me herself. But she managed to get out only a few incoherent words before she began crying .to the point that I could no longer understand her." He paused to clear his throat.

"The detective, Sanford I think he said his name was, seemed decent enough. He extended his condolences and told me I could come to the morgue if I . . . if I wanted to see Paul's body. There'll be an autopsy, of course."

Creighton looked away. "Christ."

"Yes," Doug said on a weighty sigh. "I can't come to terms with it either."

"Did they catch the guy?"

"Not yet."

"Where in the hotel?"

"The detective didn't say."

"One of the shops?"

"I don't know."

"Who would rob—"

"I don't know," Doug snapped.

A taut silence followed. Doug's shoulders settled heavily on his tall frame. "I'm sorry, Creighton. I'm . . . not myself."

"Understandably. It's astonishing."

Doug massaged his forehead. "The detective said he would give me a full account when I get there." He glanced at the open door but made no move toward it, clearly reluctant to leave on that errand.

"What about Mother? Has she been told?"

"She was here when Julie called. Naturally she's upset, but there are arrangements that must be made. She's upstairs making preliminary calls." Doug went to the bar and poured himself a shot of bourbon. "Want one?"

"No thank you."

Doug tossed back the drink and picked up the decanter again. "As difficult as this tragedy is to absorb, there are practical matters that must be addressed."

Creighton braced himself. He disdained anything with the word *practical* attached to it.

"Tomorrow morning, I want you to go to the offices and make a personal statement to our personnel."

Inwardly Creighton groaned. He wanted nothing to do with their personnel, which amounted to several hundred people, each of whom held his uncle Paul in the highest esteem while most demonstrated nothing but contempt for him whenever he graced the corporate headquarters with his presence, which was as seldom as possible.

Wheeler Enterprises manufactured and sold building materials of some kind. Whoopee. Fascinating.

His father looked over his shoulder at him. Obviously a response was expected.

"Of course. What should I say?"

"I'll write something out tonight. I'll call for a companywide assembly in the auditorium on the third floor at ten o'clock. Deliver your statement, then perhaps a minute of silence should be observed."

Creighton nodded solemnly. "Most appropriate."

Doug downed the second drink, then decisively set the empty tumbler on the bar. "You may be required to take up some of the slack while we're sorting through all this."

"All of what?"

"The funeral, for starters."

"Oh, of course. That'll be an event."

"No doubt," Doug said with a sigh. "I'll keep it as dignified as possible, but your uncle was involved in—"

"Bloody everything. He was the undeclared king of Atlanta."

Doug pressed on. "Yes, and now the king is dead. To complicate matters, his death was a homicide." Thinking about the brutality of it, he winced and dragged his hand down his face. "Jesus." He glanced toward the bar as though considering pouring one more shot of Kentucky's finest, but didn't. "The police will need our full cooperation."

"What can we do? We weren't witnesses."

"But Paul's killer must be apprehended. You will cooperate and do so willingly. Do we have an understanding?"

"Of course, Father." Creighton hesitated, then said, "Although I hope you'll act as the family's official spokesperson. The media will flock to us like vultures to carrion."

Doug gave a brusque nod. "I'll see to it that you and your mother are sheltered. Although I'm compelled to make the funeral a public observance, I'll insist on it being as low-key as possible.

"We must set an example to our employees, and keep the company running smoothly, which is what Paul would want us to do. To that end, I want you to be prepared. I've left some materials in your room. You should review them tonight, bring yourself up to date on new products, where we rank in the market, our projections for next year."

"All right." *As if.*

His father seemed to read his mind. He gave him the full-on, American eagle, hard-ass treatment. "It's the least you can do, Creighton. You're almost thirty years old. I've been remiss and take partial responsibility for your lack of interest in the company. I should have given you more responsibility, involved you more in the expansion of the business. Paul . . ." He stumbled over the name. "Paul encouraged me to. Instead, I've spoiled you. No more. It's time you stepped up to the plate. Now that Paul's gone, you'll take over when I retire."

Who was he kidding? Himself maybe, but certainly not Creighton. His father was delusional if he thought Creighton planned on jumping into the corporate cauldron. He knew nothing about the business or management thereof, and didn't want to know. All he wanted out of the family business was revenue. He loved his life exactly as it was and had no intention whatsoever of changing it by taking on responsibilities that any yes-man could do.

But now wasn't the time to replay the scene he and his father had played a thousand times before, when his shortcomings and misplaced priorities were paraded for his review, when he was reminded of duty and what it meant to be a grown-up, a man, a Wheeler. Bullshit like that.

Changing subjects, he asked, "Has it made the news yet?"

"If not yet, it will soon." Doug moved to his desk and picked up a sheet of paper, passing it to Creighton. "Would you please call these people and notify them? They deserve to be told by a member of the family, rather than hearing it on the news."

Creighton scanned the typewritten list, recognizing most of the names as personal friends of his uncle Paul, stockholders in Wheeler Enterprises, city and state officials, other prominent businessmen.

"And would you also break the news to Ruby?" Doug asked. "She knows something's up, but I didn't have the heart to tell her, especially considering the horrible circumstances. You know how much she loved and admired Paul."

"Yes, I'll do that." *And I'll enjoy it,* Creighton thought. That was one way to get back at her for sassing him. "Would you like me to go to the morgue with you?"

"Thank you, but no," Doug said. "I wouldn't ask that of you."

"Good. I can't think of anything worse." Creighton pretended to ponder it a moment, then shuddered. "Maybe a Carnival cruise."

CHAPTER

2

"JULIE?"

She'd been staring into near space, unaware of the ringing telephones, the busywork being done, the people passing by, the curious looks cast her way. At the sound of her name, she turned, then stood up to greet the man walking toward her. "Doug."

When Paul's brother saw the bloodstains on her clothing, he drew up short, the features of his face collapsing with grief. Using the strong-smelling disinfectant soap in the police station ladies' room, she'd washed her face and neck, her arms and hands, but she hadn't yet had an opportunity to go home and change clothes.

For Paul's sake, she and Doug were friendly but never entirely comfortable around each other. But her heart went out to him now. It must have been shocking for him to see his brother's blood on her, indelible proof of the violent act that had taken his life.

She closed the distance between them, but it was he who reached out and hugged her. Awkwardly. Leaving a wide gap between them. The way a man would hug his brother's girlfriend.

"I'm sorry, Doug," she whispered. "You loved him. He loved you. This has to be horrible for you."

He released her. The shine of tears was in his eyes, but he held himself together admirably, as she would have expected him to. "How are you?" he asked. "Were you hurt?"

She shook her head.

He looked her over, then scrubbed his face with both hands as though to remove the sight of the bloodstains on her clothing.

Standing deferentially apart from her and Doug, allowing them this private moment, were the two detectives who'd introduced themselves to Julie when they arrived at the hotel to investigate the crime scene.

Detective Homer Sanford was a tall black man, wide in the shoulders, having only a slight paunch to give away his age, which Julie guessed was just past forty. He looked like a former football player.

Physically, his partner was his polar opposite. Detective Roberta Kimball stood barely over five feet and tried in vain to camouflage the extra twenty pounds around her middle with a black blazer worn over gray slacks that were stretched tight across her thighs.

The first responders to the Hotel Moultrie had been uniformed policemen from the local Buckhead office. But immediately they'd requested a CSI unit. It and the two homicide investigators had been dispatched from the main police headquarters.

Sanford and Kimball had impressed Julie as being wholly professional but human. At the scene they'd treated her with kid gloves, apologizing numerous times for having to launch their investigation immediately by asking her questions when she was still shell-shocked over the crime that had left Paul dead.

Now, Kimball addressed Doug gently. "Do you need a few extra minutes before we begin, Mr. Wheeler?"

"No, I'm all right." He said it briskly, as though trying to convince himself.

The detectives had escorted him here straight from the morgue. A distinctive odor clung to the three of them. Julie was still chilled, body and soul, from her visit to that grim domain.

"I hope you don't mind if Mr. Wheeler listens in while we go over your statement," Sanford said to her.

"Not at all." Doug would want to hear her account of the shooting at some point. It might just as well be now.

They entered the violent crimes unit, and Sanford herded them toward a cubicle, apparently his. Julie had guessed right. There was a photo of him in a Bulldogs jersey and scratched helmet, crossing the goal line with the football tucked under his arm. Other photos were of a pretty lady and three smiling children. He wore a wedding ring. Roberta Kimball didn't.

Sanford held a chair for Julie. "Ms. Rutledge." She sat. He brought in an extra chair for Doug. Kimball said she preferred to stand. Sanford sat down at his desk and reached for a ring-binder notebook labeled with the date, Paul's name, and a case number. He had died barely five hours ago but already he was a statistic.

Sanford turned to Julie. "The other witnesses have given their statements. The one you recorded earlier has been transcribed. Before you sign the transcription, I'd like to talk you through it, see if you've remembered something else, see if you want to add or change anything."

Julie nodded. She crossed her arms and hugged her elbows.

Noticing the gesture, Kimball said, "We understand how difficult this must be for you."

"It is, yes. But I want to help. I want the culprit captured."

"So do we." Sanford picked up a ballpoint pen and clicked it several times while he scanned one of the typed sheets in the binder. "Prior to the incident, you and Mr. Wheeler were occupying room 901? That's a corner suite, correct?"

"That's right."

The detectives were looking at her in silent query. Doug was staring down at his shoes.

"Paul and I met there around one-thirty," Julie said.

"You went straight to the suite. You didn't check in."

"Paul had checked in for us. I was a few minutes late. He was already in the suite when I got there."

The detective and his partner communicated silently with a quick glance at each other, then Sanford looked back down at the notebook. Julie didn't think he was reading from the typed page. She didn't think he needed to. By now he would know that she and Paul had a confirmed reservation for that suite each Tuesday, rain or shine, fifty-two weeks out of the year. She wasn't going to elaborate on their arrangement. It wasn't relevant.

"You ordered lunch from room service," Sanford said.

Followed by Kimball, who added, "We have that from the hotel staff."

No doubt they also knew what she and Paul had eaten. They would know that Paul had ordered champagne today. What, if anything, would they make of that? Since they didn't address it, she wasn't going to make anything of it, either.

Sanford asked, "Other than the room service waiter, no one else saw you in the suite?"

"No."

"You were alone the whole time?"

"Yes."

After a significant and awkward gap, Sanford said, "You told us earlier that you left the suite at approximately three o'clock."

"I had an appointment scheduled for four."

"At your gallery?"

"Yes."

"The 911 call came in at three-sixteen," Sanford said.

As though completing his sentence, Kimball said, "So the robbery would have occurred a few minutes before that."

"Then I guess it was several minutes after three when we left the suite," Julie said. "Because we walked straight from the suite to the elevator and we didn't have to wait long for it."

Doug, seemingly impatient with the timing details, spoke for the first time. "The killer got away?"

"That's what we're trying to determine, Mr. Wheeler," Sanford said. "Every guest of the hotel is being questioned. Every employee."

"He couldn't have walked around the hotel wearing that ghastly mask," Julie said.

"We figure he got rid of it immediately," Kimball said. "But a thorough search of the hotel hasn't turned up anything. Not the tracksuit, the mask—"

"Nothing," Sanford said, finishing for her.

"There are a lot of hiding places in a hotel the size of the Moultrie," Doug said.

"The search is ongoing," Sanford said. "We're also searching trash receptacles, manholes, culverts, any place in the area where he could have stashed the stuff if he carried it out with him."

"He simply walked out?" Doug asked incredulously.

Kimball seemed reluctant to admit it, but she said, "It's a possibility."

Doug swore beneath his breath.

Sanford clicked the pen a few more times as he read from the material. "Let's back up a minute." He looked at Julie. "There was no one in the corridor when you left the suite?"

"No."

"Housekeeper, room service—"

"No one." She remembered making that walk to the elevator. Paul had laid his arm across her shoulders. He'd been such a solid presence beside her. Strong, warm, vibrant. So different from the form beneath the sheet in the morgue. He'd asked her if she was happy, and she had told him she was.

Kimball asked, "Did you speak to the other passengers when you got into the elevator?"

"No."

"Did Mr. Wheeler?"

"No."

"Did any appear to recognize either of you?"

"No."

"None of them spoke to you? Acknowledged you?"

"Not really, no. The two women were talking and paid no attention to us at all. The young man didn't say anything, although he politely moved back so we could get in. He seemed lost in his own thoughts."

"He was here from California for a job interview at three-thirty. He was afraid he wouldn't make it in time," Kimball supplied. "We've checked that out."

"The two women are from Nashville," Sanford said. "They're in town for their niece's wedding this weekend."

"How awful for them," Julie murmured.

Certainly everyone in the elevator had been traumatized. But those three hadn't lost someone like she had. Beyond sharing that brief elevator ride, they had no connection to Paul Wheeler. He was nothing more to them than a name, an unfortunate victim. Undoubtedly they would be affected by the incident, and would think of it each time they got into an elevator, but it hadn't left a vacuum in their lives. The consequence to them wasn't irreparable.

Sanford dropped the pen onto his desk. "Why don't you talk us through it from there? For Mr. Wheeler's benefit as much as for ours." He laced his long fingers and settled them on his belt buckle in an attitude of listening.

Kimball propped herself against the corner of his desk. Doug had one hand cupped around his chin and mouth, his eyes steady on Julie.

She related the short descent to the next stop, on the eighth floor, the doors opening, the robber reaching into the elevator and pressing the button to keep the doors open.

"Your first impression?" Kimball said.

"The mask. The shark's mouth."

"You couldn't distinguish any of his features?"

She shook her head. "No skin or hair was exposed. Not even his wrists. He had the sleeves of the tracksuit pulled over the gloves. The mask went into the neck of the hoodie, which was zipped up high under his chin."

"Height, weight?"

"Taller than me, but not by much. Average weight." The detectives nodded as though that was how he'd been described by the other witnesses.

Sanford said, "In the next day or two, we'd like you to listen to some recordings, see if you can pick out the voice from some used in other crimes."

Mention of the eerie voice caused the hair on Julie's arms to stand on end. "It was awful."

"One of the ladies said it was like fingernails on a chalkboard."

"Worse. Much more frightening."

She experienced a disturbing flashback to the wraparound sunglasses. "The sunglasses were very dark, making his eyes as black and unreadable as a shark's. But I felt his eyes on me."

Sanford sat forward slightly. "If you couldn't see his eyes, how do you know he was looking at you?"

"I just do."

No one said anything for a moment, then Kimball prompted her. "He told everybody to kneel."

She continued uninterrupted until she reached the part where Paul addressed the robber. "He said, 'All right. You've got what you wanted. Leave us alone.' I could tell by his tone of voice that he was more angry than afraid."

"I can believe that," Doug said.

"I turned my head and was about to urge him not to provoke the thief. That's when—"

An involuntary and unexpected sob issued out of her throat, stopping the words. She lowered her head and placed her hands over her eyes in an attempt to blot out the image of the bullet's impact.

No one spoke, creating a silence interrupted only by the ticking of someone's wristwatch. It served as a reminder. Julie lowered her hands from her face. "Why did he rob us of jewelry and wristwatches only? Why not wallets? Wouldn't that be more practical? Jewelry has to be fenced or pawned, but wallets have cash, credit cards."

"We speculate he wanted to travel light," Kimball said. "He didn't want to be burdened with wallets or handbags he'd have to rifle through and dispose of before leaving the hotel."

"After shooting Paul, what did he do? Where did he go?" Doug asked.

"I can't tell you," Julie replied. "I was . . . I really don't remember anything past the gunshot."

Sanford said, "The other three in the elevator were also too horrified to notice where he went, Mr. Wheeler. The young man says when he recovered some of his wits, the gunman had vanished. He punched the buttons for the elevator to descend. He didn't know what else to do."

"He could have tried to chase the man down."

"Don't blame him, Doug," Julie said softly. "I'm sure he was afraid. He'd just witnessed Paul being shot in the head."

Again no one said anything for several moments. Sanford clicked his ballpoint. "Well, unless you remember—"

"I do," Julie said suddenly. "He wasn't wearing shoes. Did anyone else notice that?"

"One of the Nashville women," Sanford said. "She said he was in stocking feet."

"Again it's a guess," Kimball said, "but he probably knew that shoes, especially athletic shoes, leave tracks that can be imprinted."

Julie asked, "Did he leave footprints?"

"Our crime scene unit checked. No."

Doug exhaled a sigh. "It seems he thought of everything."

"Not everything, Mr. Wheeler," Sanford said. "There's no such thing as a perfect crime. I'm confident we'll catch him."

Underscoring her partner's optimism, Kimball said, "Count on it."

Sanford waited to see if anyone else was going to add anything, then said, "That's all for now then, Ms. Rutledge. Are you ready to sign your statement?"

She did so with dispatch, and the two detectives ushered her and Doug out. As they walked down the hallway toward the elevator, Kimball touched her arm. "Would you rather take the stairs, Ms. Rutledge?"

Julie appreciated her sensitivity. "Thank you for asking, but no, I'm fine."

Sanford was telling Doug that he would be notified when the ME had completed his work and the body could be released to the family for burial.

"As soon as possible, I would appreciate knowing when that may be," Doug said. "We'll have a lot of arrangements to make."

"Of course. We'd also like to talk to the other members of your family. Your wife. Your son. Tomorrow if possible."

Doug stopped and faced him. "What for?"

"Routine. If your brother had any enemies—"

"He didn't. Everyone loved Paul."

"I'm sure. But someone close to him may know something that they don't even know they know."

"How could they know anything? It was a random robbery."

Sanford glanced at Kimball, then came back to Doug. "At this juncture, we believe so. However, we must cover every eventuality."

Doug seemed on the verge of responding to that, but thought

better of it. He said, "I assure you that Julie and I, my family, will do whatever we can to assist your investigation."

"You've suffered a tragedy and you're grieving, Mr. Wheeler. We're intruders on your grief. I understand, and I'm sorry for it." Despite his apology, Sanford told Doug he would call him in the morning to arrange a meeting time. "Ms. Rutledge," he said, turning to Julie, "we may also be calling on you again."

"I gave Ms. Kimball my contact information. I'll be available whenever you need me."

If she survived the night, she thought. Her exhaustion was such that she could scarcely move, yet going home alone, getting into bed, and turning out the lights wasn't an appealing prospect. With the memory of Paul's gruesome death etched in her mind, how would she ever sleep again?

As though reading her mind, Kimball asked if she had someone to stay with her. Julie shook her head. "We could have a police-woman—"

"No thank you," Julie interrupted. "I'd rather be alone, actually."

The female detective nodded with understanding.

The elevator arrived. Julie's heart clutched, but she entered the enclosure and turned to face out. Doug joined her. Sanford divided a remorseful look between them. "Please accept my deepest condolences."

"Mine as well," Kimball said.

Then the doors closed, leaving Julie and Doug alone. She said, "To spare the family embarrassment, I'll keep a respectable distance." She hoped he might argue that decision. He didn't. "I have only one request, Doug. Will you allow me to choose the spray for Paul's casket?" Her throat seized up, but she refused to weep in front of him. Her gaze remained fixed on the seam between the elevator doors, her head held high, her posture straight. "Please."

"Of course, Julie."

"Thank you."

He made a choking sound, and out of the corner of her eye, she saw that he was crying silently, his shoulders shaking in an effort to control himself. Her instinct was to extend him a comforting hand, to make some gesture of compassion. But, unsure of how he would receive it, she didn't.

"I still can't believe it," he said huskily.

"Nor can I."

"He's really gone."

"Yes."

"Jesus." He sighed heavily and rubbed his fists across his eyes. "Such a shockingly violent act. And the audacity of it. Only a guy with nothing to lose would dare it."

"Or someone who was certain he could get away with it."

She turned and looked him straight in the eye. Then the elevator doors opened, and she walked through them without looking back.

CHAPTER
3

It was decided midway into their second Bloody Mary. At least his mind was made up, and gauging from the signals she was sending, hers was, too. The conditions weren't ideal. It would take some tricky maneuvering, but he happened to be extremely good at tricky maneuvers, and where there was a will . . .

Right now, his *will* was making his seat belt uncomfortable.

Fortunately they were flying first class and not coach. A first-class ticket was almost worth the fortune the airline charged for a transatlantic flight. The leather seats were cushy and roomy. With push-button convenience, the passenger could configure the chair almost any way he wanted it, even recline it flat. It wasn't a Beautyrest, but it beat coach seats, no contest.

Each passenger had his own video system, although he hadn't utilized his yet. The food, for airline fare, had been better than passable. According to his body clock, it was time for breakfast, but the meal he'd been served was lunch. During the numerous courses, he'd read the European edition of *The New York Times,* which he'd picked up at a newsstand during his rush through de Gaulle Airport.

He never arrived early at the airport. Instead, his habit was to get there with barely enough time to check his luggage if need be, get through security, and reach the gate just as boarding was announced. He gambled on not making it. The risk added an element of fun to an otherwise tedious process and made air travel tolerable.

The flight attendant had wheedled him into eating a hot fudge sundae, made just for him with his choice of toppings. He'd congrat-. ulated himself for the restraint it took to pass on the whipped cream.

From the warm nuts to the rich dessert, lunch service had taken up the first two hours of the flight. With eight more to go, he lowered his window shade as requested to darken the cabin so others could sleep. He switched on his task light, settled more comfortably into his seat, and began reading a new fiction thriller that was number one on the bestseller list. He'd been five chapters into it when the woman in 5C walked past his row on her way to the lavatory.

That wasn't the first time he'd noticed her.

As the two of them had shuffled toward the forming line when the first-class passengers were invited to board, they'd made chance eye contact. They'd glanced away as strangers do, but then each had come back to take a second look. Once onboard, while they were storing their carry-ons in the overhead compartments, he had happened to catch her looking in his direction.

He was aware of her going into the lavatory. He was aware when she came out. He was watching her as she made her way back toward her seat, and was delighted when she paused at his row, leaned across the empty aisle seat beside him, and indicated the novel. "I noticed earlier what you're reading. It's good."

"Starts off that way."

"It gets better as it goes along." She smiled again and was about to move on when he sat forward and detained her by asking, "Have you read his others?"

"I'm a fan."

"Huh. Interesting."

"Why?"

"Call me a sexist, but isn't his writing directed toward a male readership? It's edgy. Gritty."

"You're a sexist."

He grinned, liking that she was so quick on the uptake.

She added, "Some women enjoy edgy and gritty."

"You?"

"I confess."

He motioned toward the empty seat beside him. "Can I buy you a drink?"

"I just finished lunch."

"Can I buy you an after-lunch drink?"

She glanced toward her seat two rows away and across the aisle, then looked back at him. "Bloody Mary?"

"That'd be my choice."

She sat down and crossed her legs toward him. Good legs. High heels. No stockings and none necessary. She caught him looking where her hemline stopped just above her knee, but it didn't seem to make her self-conscious. She met his gaze levelly when he raised it back to hers. Very pretty eyes, he noted. Gray. The color of storm clouds above the ocean.

He reached up and pressed the button to summon the flight attendant. "I'm Derek Mitchell."

"I know."

He went warm with pleasure, believing she'd recognized him, until she reached across the armrest they shared and touched the boarding pass sticking out of his shirt pocket. His name was clearly legible.

She laughed softly at his chagrin, then asked, "Is Atlanta home?"

"Yes. You?"

"Yes. What were you doing in Paris? Business, pleasure, or just connecting there from somewhere else?"

"Pleasure. Sort of. It was my mom's sixty-fifth birthday. She'd never seen Paris, so she twisted my dad's arm to hold the celebration there, and a whole slew of Mitchells descended on the city."

"Large family?"

"Large enough. At least we left the Parisians thinking so."

Again that soft laugh that was akin to a purr. He wondered if she realized how sexy it was and decided that she did. Of course she did.

"Did your mother enjoy herself?"

"She had a ball." He glanced toward the front of the cabin. The flight attendant was taking her sweet time.

As though reading his mind, his companion stood up and stepped into the aisle. He was afraid she was leaving, but she whispered, "Spicy?"

"Roger that."

As she walked up the aisle he had an excellent rear view. Not just good but pretty damn great. Her black three-piece suit was tailored but feminine. The body-conscious fit bespoke a designer cut. Her dark hair was pulled into a ponytail, which ordinarily wouldn't have attracted him. But somehow, on her, that classic look worked. She had taste and class as well as a sharp wit and sex appeal. And she wasn't wearing a wedding ring.

She returned, followed by the flight attendant carrying a small tray. The flight attendant leaned across her to serve him his glass of ice and Bloody Mary mix and a small bottle of Ketel One. Her drink had already been mixed.

"Check back with us," he told the flight attendant.

"Will do."

He poured the vodka into his glass, gave it a quick stir with the swizzle stick, then raised his glass. She did likewise. They clinked glasses but held them touching for several moments while they looked closely at each other. Then she glanced up at the task light.

Acting on instinct and without consulting her, he depressed the button on his armrest that turned the light out. "Better?"

"Yes. The glare . . ." She spoke in a much lower voice then, as though the absence of the light invited whispering, and she didn't finish whatever it was she was about to say. Instead, she took a sip of her Bloody Mary, a bit nervously he thought. Keeping her head down, she stared into her glass and nudged the floating lime with her swizzle stick. "What do you do?"

"About what?"

She raised her head and gave him a look.

He smiled. "Attorney."

"Corporate?"

"Criminal."

That got her interest. Turning more toward him, the toe of her shoe brushed the leg of his trousers, and suddenly his calf was an erogenous zone.

"Which side?" she asked.

"Defense."

"I would have guessed that."

"You would?"

"Um-huh," she murmured as she took another sip of her drink. She'd looked him over. "You dress too well for a man who earns a civil employee's salary."

"Thank you." And because she was still appraising him, he'd said, "And?"

"And you don't look . . ." She tilted her head, considering. "Righteous enough to be a prosecutor."

He laughed, loud enough to cause the man across the aisle to glance at them and adjust the volume on the earphones bridging his head. Taking the hint, Derek leaned closer to her, bringing his face to within inches of hers. She didn't move away. "I don't think anyone would use *righteous* as an adjective to describe me."

"So the derogatory lawyer jokes don't offend you?"

"Hell no. In fact, I'm the basis of most of them."

Mindful of the man across the aisle, she clamped her teeth over her lower lip to keep from laughing. Straight teeth. A plush lower lip barely glossed. An overall sexy mouth.

"Why criminal law?" She was fiddling with the top button of her blouse, and for a moment, the motion of her fingers distracted him.

"Criminal law? That's where the bad guys are."

"And you defend the bad guys."

Again he grinned. "Profitably."

They continued to chitchat through those first Bloody Marys. They touched on their favorite restaurants in Atlanta, the serious traffic problem, this and that, nothing personal or consequential.

Then out of nowhere she said, "I take it you're not married."

"No. I'm not. What made you think so?"

"Deductive reasoning. If you were married, even unhappily, your wife would be with you. No woman would pass up a trip to Paris, not even if it meant suffering through the celebration of a mother-in-law's birthday."

"My wife could have come along but stayed behind in Paris for some extra sightseeing."

She let that lie a moment, then looked down into her glass and swirled the ice cubes with the tip of the swizzle stick. "I doubt a wife would trust you to travel alone."

"I look untrustworthy?"

"A wife wouldn't have trusted other women."

His ego spun drunkenly. He leaned maybe an inch closer. "You're traveling alone, too."

"That's right."

"Business or pleasure?"

She drained what was left of her drink, then looked down at her left hand, which was noticeably without a wedding band. "I went all the way to Paris to catch my husband in bed with his girl-friend."

Bingo, Derek thought. He'd just won the lottery. Her pride had suffered a blow. She, of the cloud-gray eyes, kissable mouth, great legs, and shapely ass, had been dumped for another woman. She was vulnerable, in search of validation, in desperate need of reassurance that she was still an attractive, alluring woman.

He nodded toward her empty glass. "Another?"

Her eyes stayed on his, and he could tell she had reached a cross-roads. Thank him politely but decline and return to her seat? Or stay and see where this went? She dragged that delectable lower lip through her teeth again, then said, "Sure. Why not?"

The flight attendant responded more quickly to the summons, and they ordered another round. While they waited, he noticed that the other passengers in the cabin were either already sleeping or deeply engrossed in the feature on their private video screens. The cabin lights had been extinguished except for those marking the exits and lavatories. On the other side of the cabin, an elderly woman was reading by her task light, and it provided only a pin-point of light.

The flight attendant returned, serving the drinks the same way she had before. "How come she's pouring yours?" he asked.

She ducked her head shyly, fiddled with the top button on her blouse again. "I asked her to. When I went up front, I asked her to pour me doubles."

"Foul!" he cried in a stage whisper.

"I didn't want you to think I was a lush." That was when she pulled the elastic band from her hair and gave her head a shake. Her dark hair fell into a sleek cape around her shoulders. Sighing, she leaned her head against the headrest and closed her eyes. "I needed to relax, to let go, to . . . to block my mind from thinking about . . . it."

"Tough scene in Paris?"

She swallowed with difficulty, and a tear slid from between her eyelids and down her cheek. "On a scale of one to ten?"

"Ten?"

"Twelve."

"I'm sorry."

"Thank you."

"He's an idiot."

"Thank you again." Leaving her head on the headrest, she turned it toward him. "I don't want to talk about him."

"Neither do I." He paused for a count of ten, then reached out and wiped away the tear on her cheek with the tip of his index finger. "What should we talk about?"

Never breaking eye contact, she counted to at least twenty, then asked in a husky voice, "Do we have to talk?"

Her gaze had moved to his mouth, where it remained for several seconds before she looked into his eyes again. And that's when he knew. It was a sure thing. They were going to have sex. And not when they got to Atlanta, either. Right here. Right now.

He'd had friends who boasted of doing it on an airplane. He'd heard the urban legends about in-flight couples being caught in flagrante delicto, but he hadn't given those stories much credence.

From a practical standpoint, it was dicey. For one thing, you had hundreds of chances of being caught, depending on the size of the aircraft and the number of passengers onboard. Venue was another factor, and space was limited no matter where you did the deed.

But the possibility of it had his whole system pumping testosterone.

Especially since his potential partner was looking at him with such naked need, and her eyes hinted at a hot, sexual nature smoldering inside the classy exterior. Maybe she was thinking that her husband had cheated because she'd been too reserved in their marriage bed, that she should have let her hair down sooner, acted on impulse, said to hell with inhibitions.

Whatever.

He looked around. The reader had turned off her light. The man across the aisle was dozing through his movie. When Derek's eyes came back to her, they transmitted his willingness with the intensity he used to communicate innocence to a skeptical jury.

She sat her glass on the armrest, then touched his hand with her cold fingertips. It was just a brush across his knuckles, but it was an unmistakable invitation. In an instant she was gone, moving silently up the darkened aisle toward the lavatories at the front of the cabin.

A curtain had been pulled across the galley on the other side of the cabin. No one, neither passengers nor attendants, was looking. Nevertheless, his heart was thudding. Was he nuts? Had he lost his mind completely? Was he really going to do this?

You bet your ass I am.

Because he thrived on high-stakes situations. Because he had a hard-on to beat all hard-ons. Because if a woman ever wanted and needed to be fucked, it was this one. And because of the most fundamental reason: He wanted her.

He unbuckled his seat belt, then painfully stood up and squeezed himself into the aisle, trying not to attract anyone's attention or disturb the dozing passengers.

She'd left the lavatory door open a half inch. He slipped into the impossibly small enclosure, then reached behind him to pull the door shut. He made sure it was securely locked.

She was practically sitting in the basin. She'd taken off her suit jacket. The first three buttons of her blouse were undone, giving him a glimpse of cleavage above lacy bra cups.

They looked at each other for maybe ten seconds, then came together like cymbals. Their lips fused in a kiss that was as amorous as any in his recent memory. She took his tongue into her mouth with an eroticism that made him groan from a surge of lust unequaled since adolescence.

His hands went straight to the fourth pearl button on her blouse, undid it and the one below it. He pushed his hands inside her blouse, and placed them on her breasts, squeezed gently, caressed the tight centers. She gasped into his mouth.

Holding the kiss, she fumbled with his belt and fly while he slid his hands down the outsides of her thighs, then pushed up her skirt until he could reach her panties. He peeled them down, past knees, past high heels.

He nudged himself between her legs, clasped her hips, and with one strong thrust buried himself inside her.

When it was over, they laughed shakily and self-consciously.

Finally she lifted her head from his shoulder. Awkwardly they separated. He noticed how flushed her face and chest were as she clumsily tried to match buttons to buttonholes.

He tucked in his shirttail, zipped up, and buckled his belt while she pulled on her jacket. She reached for her underwear, which he'd flung aside in haste, but she didn't put them on. He helped her to stand and then to smooth down her skirt. There was barely room for them to stand face-to-face.

He stroked her cheek. It felt feverish. Her lips looked swollen. He thought about kissing her again. He wanted to.

But before he could, she said, "You go first. I need to . . . tidy up."

"Okay."

"For propriety's sake I should return to my assigned seat."

That was disappointing. He'd hoped they would finish the flight sitting together, holding hands while they made small talk, savoring this delicious, guilty secret, looking at each other and shaking their heads and laughing over the absurdity of it.

He gave her his most engaging grin. "Can I change your mind about that?"

"No. It's best."

"Are you okay?"

"Yes." She said it a bit too quickly, and must have realized it, because she nodded, repeating, "Yes."

"Do you regret it?"

For the first time since they'd finished, she looked directly into his face. "Not in the least."

"Good," he whispered, smiling. "See you on the ground."

"See you on the ground."

He opened the door a crack, and when he saw that the coast was clear, he slipped out. He heard her lock the door behind him. None of the other passengers seemed to have stirred. The galley curtain was still drawn. Their glasses were still on the armrest. He collapsed into his seat, sated.

Feeling bloody fabulous, actually.

It was several minutes before she passed him on the way to her assigned seat. As she went by, she gave him a meaningful look but didn't say anything. He watched her get settled, then picked up his book, switched on his task light, and tried to read. But the words wouldn't register. He had a good vodka buzz going, and that was making him drowsy. And—who was he kidding?—he wanted to relive those few minutes in the lavatory.

What a reckless thing to do.

What fantastic fucking.

What an incredible woman.

As he drifted into sleep, he was aware of the sappy smile on his lips.

He woke up to the rattle of the drinks trolley being pushed up the aisle by the flight attendant, who looked as fresh as when they had boarded. He wondered how they managed that. His clothes were wrinkled and his eyes were gritty. His head was muzzy from the vodka, and he badly wanted to brush his teeth.

He yawned, stretched his limbs, and craned his neck to look behind him. Seat 5C was empty. He glanced toward the lavatories and saw that both were occupied.

"Coffee, Mr. Mitchell?"

"Bless you, my child."

The flight attendant smiled and reached across him to raise his window shade. He looked out and saw terra firma several miles below. He never failed to get a maudlin lump in his throat when he caught his first glimpse of the USA after returning from overseas.

He was ravenous and scarfed down the ham and cheese croissant. He drank a cup of black coffee. "We're about forty-five minutes out," the attendant told him as she poured him a refill. "Don't forget to fill out your customs form."

"Sure thing."

When one of the lavatories became available, he got up and took the provided toiletry kit with him. He used the toilet, washed his face and hands, brushed his teeth, and swished with mouthwash. Before he left, he gave the enclosure a glance and shook his head, chuckling to himself, still disbelieving that he'd had incredible sex in such an unaesthetic place.

He noted as he returned to his seat that 5C was still empty. He imagined—

Christ! What was her name?

His mind did a rapid rewind, then replayed everything they'd said. No, he was certain she'd never told him her name. No wonder she'd been reluctant to continue the flight sitting beside him. She must think him a prize jerk.

He stared out the window for several minutes, castigating himself for behaving like a heel over the name issue. When he looked forward again, he noticed both lavatories were unoccupied. He whipped his head around. She was in her seat.

He had missed her passing down the aisle! How had he done that? He'd had his head turned away. He hoped she didn't think that had been intentional and he was trying to avoid her. He tried to get her attention, but she had her head on the headrest, her eyes closed.

He was considering getting up and going to talk to her, but the announcement was made that they were on their final approach into Atlanta, that all passengers were to remain in their seats with their seat belts fastened for the remainder of the flight.

He looked back at her, ignoring the people in the seats behind his, who had to be wondering what in hell he was looking at. He willed her to open her eyes, but she didn't.

The pilots executed a textbook landing. Impatiently Derek endured the long taxi to the terminal. As soon as they were allowed to stand, he shot from his seat and moved into the aisle. But those passengers between him and 5C had crowded into the aisle, too. They were retrieving their possessions from the overhead compartments and heading toward the exit doors between cabins. In the crush, he lost sight of her.

Outside the Jetway, the flow of passengers had become a stampede toward the reentry gates. He couldn't see her ahead of him and guessed that she'd had to be swept along or get trampled.

He was pointed into a passport check line by a government official who didn't want an argument. He continued to scan the throng of passengers from his flight, as well as those from several other overseas flights that had arrived at virtually the same time.

Finally he spotted her three lines over and well ahead of him. He waved, but she didn't see him. He decided it would be more convenient to rendezvous in baggage claim than to try to make his way to her now.

It seemed to take forever, but he finally got through the passport check. In the baggage claim area, he rushed to the designated carousel and saw her on the far side of it, wrangling a suitcase off the conveyor.

Dodging passengers made short-tempered by weariness, he made his way toward her. She stopped when she saw him threading his way through the crowd.

He didn't stop until only inches separated them. He smiled down at her. "I'm an idiot, and a first-class jerk. I don't even know how to say hello, because I failed to get your name."

"But I have yours."

He was taken aback, not so much by what she said as by the way she said it. He was trying to get a handle on that cool tone of voice when he realized that her entire demeanor had changed. She didn't appear as vulnerable, as engaging, and certainly not as available. All her buttons were done up. In fact, the signal she was sending him now was *Don't even think about it.*

Her voice was cold. Her eyes, as languid and inviting as a tidal pool last night, were brittle and unfriendly. When she smiled, she did so with the self-satisfaction of a cardsharp playing his ace.

"You've been had, Mr. Mitchell."

CHAPTER

4

"YOU LOOK LIKE HELL."

Derek stashed his luggage in a corner of the reception area of his law office, then turned and frowned at his assistant. After being away for twelve days, he'd have appreciated a more cordial, less candid welcome.

"Why thank you, Marlene, I'm glad to be back. My trip was wonderful, thank you for asking. The weather couldn't have been better. All my flights were on time. Mom liked her gift. Dad was—"

"Okay, okay. I was just saying."

"I've been on an airplane for ten hours," he grumbled. "What did you expect?"

"I expected you to shower and shave before coming to the office."

"If I'd gone home to clean up, I probably would have stayed. The temptation to crawl into bed would have been too great. I knew things would be backed up here, so here I am, unshaven and unwashed and unhappy about it all."

"You haven't seen Maggie yet?"

"I've been away this long, a few more hours won't matter."

Marlene gave him a don't-say-I-didn't-warn-you look. Then, "Coffee?"

"That's the first nice thing you've said."

Subordinates called out greetings as he walked past their open office doors, but he acknowledged them with waves and kept going, not stopping for small talk. Making it to his own office without being waylaid, he closed the door behind him to discourage anyone hoping to butter up the boss by welcoming him back.

The roomy corner office was on the twentieth floor of one of Atlanta's modern glass skyscrapers, so he had an unrestricted view through the walls. Today the sunlight was a little too cheery and bright to suit his mood, so he used the remote control to partially close the blinds sandwiched between the panes of glass.

The decorator he'd hired to do the place had fed him ideas, but he'd made all the final decisions—the handwoven Turkish rug, the wood stain on the bookcases, the fabrics for the upholstered pieces, the leather for his desk chair.

He'd also insisted on incorporating personal belongings that held special meaning for him, even if they didn't particularly fit the decor. Sharing the bookshelves with volumes on law were the biplane model that he and his dad had made together the summer he turned nine, the baseball glove with which he'd helped his high school team win the state championship, and a beer stein with his fraternity letters engraved into the pewter.

The office was furnished with every modern convenience, but sprinkled with these dashes of nostalgia, it fit him like a comfortable pair of expensive sneakers.

He shrugged off his wrinkled jacket and hung it in the concealed closet, sat down in his desk chair, and dug into his burning eye sockets with his fingertips, saying under his breath, "You've been had, Mr. Mitchell."

What did that mean?

Hell if he knew. Hell if he'd ever know, because having said that, she'd turned and marched into the ladies' restroom, pulling her wheeled suitcase behind her. He'd have looked like a pervert if he staked out the restroom until she reappeared. Besides, the lady— whatever her name was—had made it abundantly clear that she wanted nothing more from him than a couple of Bloody Marys and a hot and nasty quickie in the airplane lavatory.

So he'd split, thinking *To hell with you* but wishing that the memorable interlude had ended on a sweeter note. He'd also nursed a nagging uneasiness over her parting words.

Whatever her game, he'd fallen for it. The come-hither eyes. That business with the top button of her blouse. The legs. Oh yeah, the legs. Jergens had never looked so good, felt so good on a pair of thighs. All that timid lip biting. Letting down her hair, for godsake. Just about every woman on the planet knew these drills.

But she had perfected them.

She'd taken him by his dick and led him into the restroom of an airplane full of people, where they could have been caught, exposed, made a laughingstock. He didn't know if sexual congress on a commercial aircraft was illegal—he'd have one of his clerks look it up—but it sure as hell wasn't *smart*.

What if they'd been bagged by a little old lady? Or a child? Imagine the hue and cry that would have been raised had little Suzie walked in on them. No one would have slept for the rest of the flight. All two hundred plus passengers would have wanted to take a gander at the pair who couldn't control their libidos, to catch a glimpse of the fornicators.

He imagined having his picture plastered on the front page of the *Journal,* being escorted out of the Jetway by an air marshal wearing a disapproving, even disgusted frown. The DA's office would probably have made a poster of it and circulated copies throughout the Fulton County Justice Center. He'd have never lived it down.

He didn't like losing, and would do whatever it took to win. But he could lose with dignity if he knew he'd done his absolute best, if there had been virtually no chance of winning to start with but he'd given his all to try to beat the odds. He could lose like that. He didn't like to, but he could.

But to be mocked, hoodwinked, made a complete and utter fool of, as this chick had done, that was untenable.

And *why?* Besides screwing her blind, what had he ever done to her?

Ah well. It would remain one of life's little mysteries.

He lowered his hands, stretching his stubbled cheeks before letting his hands drop onto the stack of mail, messages, and paperwork that had collected during his twelve-day absence.

Marlene came in carrying her notepad and a steaming cup of coffee.

"Thanks." He scalded his tongue on the first sip, but it was his preferred blend and tasted good.

She took her customary place in the chair on the other side of his desk. "So. How was Paris?"

"French."

"That bad?"

He smiled. "It's a beautiful city. Flowers in bloom. The food was outstanding. Good wine."

"You don't like wine."

"I managed to quaff a few glasses just to be sociable."

"The Seine?"

"We had Mom's party on a dinner boat."

"Notre-Dame?"

"Still there, but I didn't see the hunchback."

"Pretty women?"

"Everywhere."

Marlene sniffed with disdain. "They all smoke. That's how they stay thin."

Derek gave her a look, and her eyes narrowed on him. "Don't you dare say it. But it is the one diet I haven't tried."

He laughed. They'd been together so long, they could tease each other without offending. Marlene Sullivan had followed him when he'd boldly stormed out the door of a large and respected firm after a heated quarrel with the senior partner.

She'd helped him hang out his own shingle, and since then had been his right hand, guardian at the gate, social secretary, errand runner, and sounding board. She had a keen legal mind, frequently opening up another avenue of thought when a case proved tough and the direction in which he was taking it would lead nowhere except to conviction. He couldn't run his practice or his life without her, a fact of which she reminded him often.

He trusted her implicitly. She would carry to the grave anything he told her in confidence. Now, as he regarded her affable, matronly face, he considered telling her about his experience on the plane. *Brace yourself, Marlene. You're not going to believe what your boss did on his transatlantic flight.*

But no. He couldn't divulge that, not even to his loyal assistant, who'd seen him at his best but also at his absolute worst. Last night's sexual escapade would remain his secret.

He sincerely hoped.

"Anything new from the DA's office on Jason Connor?" he asked. The sixteen-year-old stood accused of killing in cold blood his mother and stepfather. Because of the brutality of the crime, he was being tried as an adult.

"I called over there, asked again for the discovery file. Got the usual runaround."

"They're stonewalling. Call and tell them I'm back, and I want the damn file." The trial date was fast approaching, and his young client faced execution if found guilty. "Has anyone talked to Jason recently?"

"Yesterday." She told him that one of his assistants on the case had gone to the jail. "He *saw* him. They didn't *talk*. The boy remained mute."

"Was he told that I can't help him if he doesn't help himself?"

"He was."

Derek made a mental note to go see the boy as soon as his schedule permitted, and to impress upon him that he was in dire straits. He picked up the stack of pink memos representing calls he needed to return. On the first one Marlene had printed in bold, red letters: *Ask me.*

He picked it up and waved it at her. "I'm asking."

"While you were gone, you missed some excitement. Paul Wheeler—"

"Who's that?"

"Wheeler Enterprises."

He cocked an eyebrow. "That Wheeler?"

"That Wheeler. Money out the wazoo. He was shot and killed in the Hotel Moultrie. Lots of media. Large funeral. Unidentified culprit is still at large."

He whistled and referred to the memo. "So who's Doug?"

"Brother and business partner of the deceased."

"The plot thickens."

"He's called three times over the last two days. Says it's urgent he meet with you immediately upon your return."

"How come?"

"Wouldn't say."

He was bone tired, he suspected he smelled none too fresh, and he was in a sour mood. But he liked the sound of this. Already his juices were bubbling. "Can he be here in an hour?"

Doug Wheeler looked the part of exactly what he was, a successful businessman. He was fiftyish and well maintained, although as he entered Derek's office he looked like a man with a lot on his mind. His handshake, however, was dry and firm.

"I understand you've just returned from a trip abroad."

"Paris. I came here straight from the airport. Which accounts for my rumpled appearance. I apologize." Derek felt particularly disheveled in contrast to Wheeler, who was immaculately dressed and groomed.

"No apology necessary, Mr. Mitchell. I'm just happy you agreed to see me today."

Derek motioned him into a chair. In the center of the furniture grouping was a coffee table, on which Marlene had set a tray with an ice bucket, two glasses, and bottles of water. He preferred meeting with clients in the seating area rather than from behind his desk.

"Help yourself, Mr. Wheeler."

Wheeler shook his head.

"My assistant, Ms. Sullivan, told me about your brother," Derek said as he poured himself a Perrier. "I'm very sorry."

"Thank you. It was ghastly."

"It was. She provided me a thumbnail sketch of what happened, but I didn't have time to read all the newspaper stories. Do you feel like talking about it?"

Derek listened for the next five minutes while Doug Wheeler related what he knew about the fatal shooting. Derek noted that it had occurred on the day he left for France.

Wheeler ended with "That's my knowledge of it, based on what Julie and the others who were in the elevator told the police."

"Julie's the woman who was with your brother when it happened?"

"Yes." Wheeler reached for one of the bottles of water, uncapped it, and took a drink.

Marlene had referred to Julie Rutledge as Wheeler's mistress. Derek wondered if her relationship with Paul Wheeler had caused the family any embarrassment. He assumed by Doug Wheeler's obvious reluctance to elaborate on it that it had.

"The culprit hasn't been identified?"

Wheeler shook his head.

"Ms. Sullivan told me that the police don't seem to have any real leads."

"As of this morning, no."

"Who's heading the investigation?"

"A detective name Homer Sanford."

"I know him. He's a good investigator."

"I suppose," Wheeler said, shrugging. "So far he hasn't come through on this case. He had nothing new to report to me earlier today."

Derek knew the former all-star football player to be a methodical and dogged detective. He was well thought of by his comrades. He was tough only on criminals. If he'd failed to produce, it wasn't for lack of trying.

"As I understand it," he said to Wheeler, "all Sanford had to go on was the bullet, and that the ballistics test turned up nothing."

"That's right. According to all the databases, the pistol hadn't been used in a previous crime."

Derek purposefully let the silence stretch out, waiting to see what Wheeler would say next. Up to this point, he didn't know why the man had called this urgent meeting. Finally he spoke aloud what had been on his mind since hearing about the shooting. "Seems an odd place for a robbery, doesn't it? The eighth floor of a hotel."

Wheeler's gaze locked on his. "Yes." Then his eyes skittered away. "It does."

"Has Detective Sanford mentioned the oddity of it?"

"Not to me."

"Huh."

Derek's jet lag was catching up with him. He didn't look at his watch, but he could tell by the placement of the sun that it was getting close to quitting time, and his body ached with fatigue. It was time to cut to the chase. "Mr. Wheeler, why did you ask for this meeting?"

"Because I know your reputation as a defense attorney. You're said to be excellent."

"Thank you."

"I want to retain you to represent my family during all this."

" 'All this' meaning—"

"The police interviews."

"They've questioned you regarding your brother's killing?"

He nodded. "Which is routine. Pro forma, I'm told."

Bullshit. Derek didn't believe anything the police did was pro forma, and apparently Wheeler didn't think so, either.

"During these interviews, have you had counsel present?"

"Yes." Wheeler made a dismissive gesture. "He's a capable man when it comes to petty lawsuits and traffic tickets. But we felt we needed someone with bigger balls. If you'll excuse the expression."

"I do, especially since the referred-to balls are mine." They shared a grin. "Who's 'we'?"

Derek's follow-up question caught the other man off guard. "I'm sorry?"

"You keep saying 'we.' You and who else?"

"My family. My wife and son."

"I see." Derek waited for Wheeler to elaborate. He didn't until he'd taken another gulp from the water bottle.

"Suspicion is automatically cast onto anyone who would benefit from Paul's death," he said.

"You?"

"Not specifically. I'm not Paul's heir. Although I will become CEO of the company, there's no monetary gain."

"Your wife?"

"Sharon. As the saying goes, I married well. Sharon's great-grandfather bought tens of thousands of shares of Coca-Cola stock when the company was young."

"Congratulations."

Wheeler smiled wanly. "She isn't after Paul's money. Besides, she was at home when he was killed."

"That leaves your son."

"Creighton." He paused, then added, "He's Paul's heir."

Derek leaned back in his chair and gazed at the man for a moment, then said, "If I was a cop, he's the first person I'd look at, Mr. Wheeler. No offense. I'm being brutally honest with you. The police always follow the money."

"I understand that. They're right to do so."

"How old is Creighton?"

"Twenty-eight."

Derek had hoped for younger, a minor with less independence and more supervision. "The police aren't holding him, are they?"

"No, nothing like that. The interviews have been very civil, and took place at our home, not at the police station."

"That's good. Counsel was always present?"

"I made sure of that. And, fortunately, Creighton has an iron-clad alibi. He was at our house on the tennis court taking a lesson from his private coach at the time of the robbery and shooting. I'd gone home to change for a golf game and saw them on the court when I arrived, which was only minutes before Julie called to tell me that Paul was dead. Our housekeeper, who wouldn't lie if her life depended on it, said they'd been playing there for at least an hour."

"Then what's the problem?"

"No problem, really. Retaining you is a precautionary measure. I don't want my son browbeaten because the detectives have nowhere else to look and nothing else to do."

"Why would they do that?"

Wheeler hesitated, then said, "Paul and Creighton had their differences."

"Over?"

"Just about everything," Wheeler replied with a snuffled laugh. "Basically Creighton doesn't apply himself to the business as Paul thought he should. Paul was a workaholic. So am I for that matter, but not to the extent my brother was. He didn't understand people who don't thrive on work. Creighton has other interests."

Derek raised his eyebrows in query. "Tennis?"

"He plays nearly every day. He likes cars. Clothes. But his real passion is film."

"You mean movies?"

"I think he's seen every movie ever made. They're more than entertainment to him. They're an avocation. One that consumes much more of his time than Wheeler Enterprises. He thinks . . . artistically." Wheeler sighed. "Paul couldn't understand or accept Creighton's disinterest in commerce and pressured him about it, even more than I did. *Do*. It was a real bone of contention between them."

"Was this antagonism between them well known?"

"To those well acquainted with the family, yes." He frowned. "Julie's mentioned it to the detectives."

"Hmm. The family discord was exposed to the police by the woman who was with your brother when he died. In a hotel. In the middle of the day."

Taking the hint, Doug said, "My brother and Julie . . . Paul never referred to her as his girlfriend per se. But everyone who knew him knew about their affair, even though they kept it under the radar."

"Why was that?"

"I suppose out of respect for Mary, Paul's late wife, whom he had loved body and soul. They were a prominent society couple. Inseparable. Totally devoted to each other."

"Children?"

"No. Apparently Mary couldn't conceive. But she and Paul made up for it with their philanthropic work. When Mary died, he was devastated. I didn't think he would ever look at another woman. But then Julie came along, and he fell head over heels."

"How long ago?"

"Going on two years. Something like that."

"Did they live together?"

He shook his head. "They were together all the time, though. Several times a week, at least, and for a nooner every Tuesday afternoon at the hotel. He told me once that it was their special time, and that nothing would interfere if he could help it. He worked his schedule around it."

"The hotel staff can confirm that standing reservation?"

"They already have. They provided records to the police." He set his empty water bottle on the table between them. "Can I count on you for legal counsel, Mr. Mitchell? Will you be our official spokesperson to the media? I hope we won't need your services at all. But if we do, I'd feel better knowing you're on standby."

"I'll have to do some homework. Catch up on the case and the ongoing investigation. I also want to meet your family, especially Creighton."

"Of course. He welcomes the idea of having you in our corner should the need arise. Naturally, we'll provide you a healthy retainer."

Smiling, Derek stood up and extended his hand. "You certainly will."

Wheeler laughed. "I'll have a check delivered by courier tomorrow."

"You can get the details from Ms. Sullivan on your way out," Derek said. Then his expression turned appropriately somber. "I'm terribly sorry for the reason behind this meeting. My sympathies to you and your family."

"Thank you."

Wheeler turned to go and had almost reached the door when Derek said, "Are the police looking at her? At the girlfriend?"

Wheeler looked confused by the question, then said, "For involvement, you mean? Like an accomplice?"

Derek shrugged.

Wheeler shook his head. "If they are, they're wrong. Paul adored Julie, and vice versa."

Derek kept his opinion of reciprocated adoration to himself. When a fortune like the Wheelers' was at stake, adoration often took a backseat.

CHAPTER

5

SHARON WHEELER WAS ADDRESSING THE LAST SEVERAL DOZEN acknowledgment cards being sent to people in thanks for flowers and other kindnesses extended to the family following her brother-in-law's death. It had been a time-consuming chore. Having been working on it for several days, she was glad to see the end of it.

When Creighton barged into the bedroom suite without even knocking, she actually welcomed the interruption. Until she saw that he was in a huff.

"Mother!"

"Here, darling."

Seeing her at the desk, he glared. He was holding something in his hand, which he waggled as he came toward her.

"What is that, sweetheart? A DVD?"

"Yes, Mother," he repeated, enunciating the words. "A DVD. A DVD that belongs to me."

"You'd left it here. I watched it last night. I didn't think—"

"No, you didn't *think*. You just used it without asking me first."

"Creighton, for heaven's sake, calm down. I didn't damage it, did I?"

"You left it out of the box. It was in the kitchen, just lying there on the counter. I happened to spot it as I passed through."

"Ruby probably—"

"If you're going to be careless, be careless with your own DVDs, or better still watch pay-per-view so you're not responsible for touching anything."

If he hadn't wanted anyone else touching his DVD, it had been careless of him to leave it behind. But she didn't point that out. Why vex him more than he already was? When he was in a temper, it was better just to let him vent it.

"I should have called and asked you before I watched it," she said. "I apologize."

He sailed the DVD onto her desk. "It's ruined now, and I really don't give a fuck for your apology."

"Don't use that kind of language with your mother."

They turned to see Doug standing in the open doorway. He walked in and tossed his suit jacket onto the bed. "Apologize to her."

"Like hell. She shouldn't have used—"

"Enough!" Doug barked.

Creighton lapsed into a sulky silence. Doug looked ready to strike him. Sharon felt miserable for having caused the row, because Creighton had reason to be upset. Being careless with one of his precious DVDs was an unforgivable offense.

"I'll buy you another DVD to replace this one," she offered quietly. Then she laughed lightly. "All this brouhaha, and the movie isn't even that good."

"That's not the point, Mother." Creighton sighed, probably over her stupidity for not seeing the point. "I'm outta here. 'Hasta la vista, baby.' Arnold Schwarzenegger. *Terminator 2: Judgment Day*." He turned to go.

"Stay where you are," Doug said. "I need to talk to you."

"What about?"

"Apologize to your mother first."

"Jesus, what am I, eight?"

Sharon hated conflict because she'd grown up in a continual state of contention. Her parents' marriage had been loveless and turbulent, the mansion in which they lived a war zone. Too much money was involved for divorce to be a workable solution, so they'd committed themselves to making each other miserable, with Sharon acting as the hapless arbitrator.

Consequently she avoided strife whenever possible, and the role of mediator came naturally to her. "It's all right, Doug. He didn't mean anything, did you, darling? He—"

"Don't excuse him, Sharon. I could hear him all the way downstairs. He owes you an apology. I insist."

She watched the two men in her life try to stare each other down, and for once it was Creighton who relented. He turned to her, bent at the waist, took her hand, and kissed it. "Please forgive me, Mother. I apologize for saying 'fuck.' "

Then he straightened and addressed Doug. "Which, by the way, was repeated sixty-seven times in this particular film. It has a running length of ninety-four minutes. So last night while watching it, she heard *fuck*, or a derivative thereof, spoken every one and a half minutes, give or take a few seconds. But if my saying *fuck* offended her, then I'm fucking sorry."

Sharon couldn't contain her giggle, but Doug wasn't amused.

Trying to defuse the situation, she said, "Look, I just finished addressing the acknowledgment cards. They can be mailed tomorrow. Everyone was so nice, but it's been an ordeal to write all these thank-yous."

"I appreciate your doing that," Doug said. Then he turned to Creighton. "I've just come from a meeting with Derek Mitchell."

Creighton shrugged, dropped down into an armchair, and rested his head against the back of it, apparently uninterested.

"Refresh my memory, Doug," Sharon said.

"He's the defense attorney. Remember we talked about retaining him."

"Oh, right." There had been some discussion over dinner a couple of nights ago, but her mind had wandered.

"He wants to meet with you," Doug said to Creighton.

"I'm getting sick of this. I really am. First those detectives and that limp dick lawyer of yours, hanging on to my every word, making notes." Creighton mimicked frantic scribbling. "Now this guy. What makes him so special, anyway? And why do I need him?"

Doug didn't address the questions. "His assistant made an appointment for you tomorrow."

"I can't tomorrow. You've got me taking those brick and stone people to lunch, remember?"

"Three o'clock."

"My car is being serviced at three o'clock, and I stay with it. I don't trust that cretin mechanic."

"Here's his address."

Doug extended him a business card. Creighton shot each of them a hateful look, then in one uninterrupted motion, he snatched the card, came out of the chair, and stalked from the room, slamming the door behind him.

Neither Sharon nor Doug moved or said anything for several seconds, then he went to the bed and picked up his discarded jacket. She followed him into the closet, which doubled as a dressing room they shared. He whipped off his necktie and began unbuttoning his shirt.

"It was my fault," she said. "I shouldn't have watched his DVD without asking."

"Don't do that, Sharon. It is *not* your fault. You're excusing him again. He's never going to grow up and assume responsibility if you undercut me every time I try and instill in him—"

"You sound like Paul."

She regretted the words the instant they left her mouth. They pained him, she could tell. He removed his shirt and tossed it along with his suit jacket into the hamper. She moved behind him and put her arms around his waist, leaning her cheek against his shoulder. "I'm sorry."

He gave a soft laugh. "I did sound like Paul." He turned to face her and pecked a kiss on her lips. "But he was right, Sharon. Creighton is spoiled and we're to blame."

"Chiefly me."

"No."

"Yes."

"You didn't want him to feel alone and unloved the way your parents made you feel."

She tilted her head up and looked at him. "You're a psychologist now?"

"You don't need therapy to figure that out. But we're both to blame for spoiling Creighton. I indulged him, too, because it was easier."

She laughed softly. "I don't recall him ever being easy."

"Neither do I, really." His grin was rueful.

"I just loved him so much, Doug. I wanted him to know it. I didn't want him ever to be mad at me." She hesitated, then said, "Maybe if we'd had more children . . ."

After Creighton, she'd miscarried twice before her doctor recommended a hysterectomy. Doug had never blamed her for not giving him more children, but Mary had once sadly joked that the Wheeler boys hadn't done so well in the progeny department. They hadn't married good breeders.

Doug rubbed his hands up and down her arms. "None of that." He kissed her forehead as he released her. "Just, from now on, when I crack the whip, back me up."

She nodded, but she didn't make a promise she might be unable to keep.

He sat down on a padded bench to remove his shoes. "I hope this lawyer puts the fear of God into him."

"What's he like?"

"I liked him. Shoots from the hip. Supposed to be hell on wheels in the courtroom. Prosecutors dread to see him coming. Doesn't like to lose and goes to the mat only when absolutely forced."

"Creighton asked why we need him. I wonder that myself." She had opened one of her jewelry drawers under the pretense of looking for something, but the fact was, this talk of lawyers made her nervous, so she was acting busy to hide it.

"The past five minutes demonstrate how recalcitrant Creighton can be. During the course of an interview, I'm afraid he'll fly off the handle and say something to those detectives that will rub them the wrong way."

"If he gets short with them, it's their own fault," Sharon said. "He's getting impatient with their questions, and frankly I don't blame him. He couldn't have been involved in that robbery and shooting. He was here. Why don't they start looking for the real culprit and leave Creighton alone?"

"Hopefully they will. But if not, at least we'll have Derek Mitchell talking to the police for us and keeping a muzzle on Creighton."

She gave the drawer a shove, and it closed with a clap. "That still doesn't explain why they're fixated on Creighton when he's got such a solid alibi."

Doug stood and removed his belt, carefully hanging it on a rack. "I'm sure that's the first thing Derek Mitchell will demand to know."

"Do you think Julie is responsible?"

"For the detectives' interest in Creighton?"

Sharon shrugged.

"No," Doug replied, shaking his head adamantly. He pulled off his trousers.

"It's possible, isn't it?"

"Why would she point the finger at Creighton?"

"Because Paul might have poisoned her mind against him."

"Paul wouldn't have done that. He wouldn't have spoken ill of anyone in the family to Julie."

Sharon made a scornful sound. "They shared a bed. Paul hated Creighton. He—"

"Paul did not hate Creighton," Doug said sharply. "They had their disagreements, and Paul didn't always approve of Creighton's behavior. But he didn't hate him. Please don't ever say that within anyone's hearing again, Sharon. They could get the wrong idea entirely." He headed for the bathroom. "I'm going to take a shower."

There was a Post-it note stuck to Derek's back door.

Warning! She's in a sulk. Good luck, buddy.

It was signed by Derek's next-door neighbor who looked after his house while he was away. In addition to collecting the mail, gathering newspapers, and watering the plants, he'd had to deal with Maggie and her shifting moods. After twelve days of it, Derek would be lucky if the guy ever spoke to him again.

He let himself in with his key. "Mags?"

No response. He hauled in his suitcase and roll-aboard, then shut the back door, loudly enough to be heard throughout the house, even upstairs. "Maggie?" Leaving his bags to be unpacked later, he went through the kitchen and past the dining room, checked the living room and his home office, both of which were empty, and then climbed the stairs, removing articles of clothing as he went. He'd been up for almost thirty hours with only that nap on the airplane to sustain him. He hoped Maggie would be merciful and not demand more of him than he had the energy to deliver.

When he left the airport, he'd intended to drop into the office only to check the mail and handle whatever was absolutely necessary. He hadn't counted on the meeting with Doug Wheeler, and hadn't regretted making the appointment on short notice.

Until now.

As he trudged upstairs, he felt like he'd been whipped with a chain. He was eager to do his research and learn more about Paul Wheeler's slaying. He'd even carried home the bundle of newspapers Marlene had collected for him, thinking he might give them a glance at least. But the details of the robbery that had turned to homicide would have to keep until he slept. His brain was almost as tired as his body.

He pushed open his bedroom door. Before leaving for Paris, he'd closed the shutters, and they were still closed. The room was dark except for the floor lamp beside his leather reading chair. The lamp had been dimmed to provide only a dull glow on that side of the room. The housekeeper, who'd come even during his absence, had left everything spotless, ready for his return.

Maggie was stretched out on the bed.

She didn't even lift her head from the pillow when he appeared, but her eyes were brimming with reproach. Even before crossing the threshold into the room, he said, "Look, first of all, I know you're still pissed because I didn't take you with me. But you and Mom have never got along, and this trip was about her."

Bravely entering the room, he laid his jacket on the chair and finished unbuttoning his shirt as he toed off his shoes. "And I know you expected me to come home as soon as I landed, but there were pressing matters that needed my immediate attention."

He approached the bed and sat down on the edge of it. Maggie rolled onto her back. "Mags." He sighed, turned away, stared into near space for a moment. He never asked a client whether or not they'd done the deed for which they were charged. He didn't need to know because it wasn't his job to pass judgment. His job was to see that the accused received the best possible defense.

But experience had taught him that most people who were guilty of a malfeasance were just itching to confess it. Like he was now. "Mags, something happened on the return flight that you should know. I met somebody. A woman." He glanced down. "Don't look at me like that. I'm not in the habit of picking up women on airplanes. It was the shortest fling I've ever had. Besides, she shut me down. It was over before it started." He turned to her, scratched her tummy. "So I'm still all yours."

The chocolate Lab whined, then sat up and enthusiastically licked the side of his face.

"Thanks for understanding."

The dog nuzzled his neck while he scratched her behind the ears. "Come on," he said, patting her rump as he stood up. "Keep me company while I take a shower." He noticed she took her time coming off the bed. "Is your arthritis acting up? I'll call the vet tomorrow. And by the way, you're not supposed to be on the bed."

While Maggie dozed on the bathroom rug, he took a long, hot shower, letting the water pulse against his shoulders until his skin was stinging. When he got out, he toweled off and gave his hair sixty seconds with the dryer, then wrapped the towel around his middle and returned to his bedroom, where he set the alarm clock on his nightstand. "Do you need to go out?"

Rather than head for the door, Maggie circled her mat at the end of his bed, then lay down, settling her head on her front paws. "Okay, but it's a long time till morning. Remember I asked."

He removed the towel and peeled back the covers on his bed. Sighing gratefully, he slid between the cool sheets and picked up the TV remote. He scrolled through his TiVo list and highlighted the local evening news. It was set to record every day because he often didn't get home in time to watch it live. He probably wouldn't make it till the first commercial tonight.

But he bunched his pillow beneath his head and brought up the picture on the flat screen mounted on the wall opposite his bed. The lead story was a major wreck involving a school bus. Bleeding kids, distraught parents, two small yellow body bags on the ground.

He fast-forwarded through that story and the one that followed, about patient mistreatment in a nursing home. He stopped when a picture of a Doug Wheeler look-alike flashed onto his screen. The name superimposed beneath it was Paul Wheeler. He caught the anchorwoman in midsentence, giving a recap of the crime.

There was a sound bite from Homer Sanford, who was lamenting the scarcity of solid leads but emphasizing the department's determination to capture the culprit. "Mr. Wheeler's assailant will be brought to justice," the detective pledged while his partner, Roberta Kimball, stood at his side. The top of her head didn't even reach Sanford's shoulder, but her demeanor was equally resolute.

The two halves of the partnership were comically mismatched, but together they made a formidable pair. It flitted through Derek's exhausted mind that, if he was a criminal on the lam, he wouldn't want these two on his tail.

Back to the anchorwoman. "Julie Rutledge, a close personal friend of Mr. Wheeler who was with him when he was fatally shot, met with investigators again this afternoon. Following that meeting, she had this to say."

Cut to the exterior of the police department, where a woman exiting the building was swarmed by reporters, all poking microphones and hurling questions as the camera zoomed in for a close-up.

Derek came off the bed so suddenly that Maggie leaped to her feet and gave two sharp barks.

He paused the picture, then dropped the remote. It landed hard and painfully on his big toe. Naked, hands on hips, he gaped at the frozen image on his TV screen. Then he ran his fingers through his hair, made three tight circles in the center of his bedroom floor, and slammed his fist into his opposite palm.

"Son of a *bitch*!"

CHAPTER

6

JULIE TURNED OFF THE FAUCETS AND SQUEEZED THE WATER FROM her hair, then stepped from the shower and reached for a towel. The mirror above the sink was foggy, but she could still see a ghostly reflection of herself. Her eyes, however, seemed sharp-focused with reproach.

To escape that self-incrimination, she buried her face in the towel. But the attempt to hide her shame, even from herself, was futile. Would she ever be able to look at herself in the mirror again?

Yes, she would. She must. It was too late for second-guessing.

She dried quickly and put on a pair of pajamas. In the kitchen she poured herself a glass of orange juice and carried it into her bedroom. Settling onto her bed, she picked up the phone and called the gallery.

"Chez Jean. How can I help you?"

"Are you trying to impress me by working late?"

"Hey, you're back! How was your trip? Was Paris fabulous?"

To their clients, she was Katherine Fields. To Julie she was Kate. When she answered the gallery telephone, the caller would swear she was French. Her pronunciation of the gallery name—a holdover from the previous owner, from whom Julie had bought the business—was perfect. But when in conversation with Julie, Kate lapsed into her native Georgian accent. She had a natural exuberance that bubbled out of her lanky frame like foam from a bottle of champagne.

At twenty-five, almost a decade younger than Julie, Kate held dual degrees in French and art history. The clientele adored her, not only for her sense of style and natural charm but also because she was knowledgeable beyond her years. They trusted her opinion, as they should.

"Yes, I'm back," Julie said. "Why are you open late?"

"I'm not. The door is locked. I was straightening up the back room, about to leave. But tell me about your trip. How was Paris?"

"Lovely as always, although I didn't see much of it."

"I told you you weren't staying long enough."

"I accomplished what I went for."

"You bought the painting?"

That had been the pretext of her sudden trip. "I did. And two others by the same artist. We're the first gallery in the States to feature his work, and he came by my hotel to thank me personally. He covered my hands with kisses. Very effusive. Very French."

"Cute?"

"In that effete, Euro-male sort of way."

"Hmm. Not my type," Kate said with regret.

"The paintings are being shipped. We should receive them next week."

"I'll get on the phone tomorrow and put out the word."

"Good idea. I'll be there in the morning."

"Sleep in," Kate said. "Your turnaround was so quick, you must have jet lag. Did you sleep at all on the flight back?"

Julie's cheeks grew warm at the memory of what she'd done on the flight back. "Not long and not well. But I'm going to bed now, so I'll be right as rain tomorrow."

After a slight hesitation, Kate asked, "How are you doing?"

"Fine."

"I mean about Paul."

"I know what you meant." Julie took a deep breath and let it out slowly. "I'm coping. What choice do I have?"

"You should get some grief counseling."

"I'll think about it."

"As if losing Paul wasn't enough, the guy who killed him is still free."

"I met with the detectives this afternoon, even before I came home. They made no headway while I was in Paris."

"It's never this hard to solve a mystery on TV."

Julie smiled in spite of the grim subject. "I'll see you tomorrow."

"Rest well."

Julie set her cell phone on the bedside table and picked up the TV remote. She was just in time to catch herself on the news, being ambushed by reporters as she left the unproductive meeting with Detectives Sanford and Kimball, who'd seemed more upset over her sudden departure from the country than by their failure to apprehend Paul's killer.

"Don't leave like that again," Sanford had told her sternly. "We didn't know you were gone until it was too late."

"Too late for what?"

"Too late to stop you from leaving."

"Was I supposed to ask permission?"

"You must admit it didn't look good," Kimball had said.

"To whom?"

The detectives hadn't answered that. Instead Sanford had asked, "What was so important in Paris that it couldn't keep?"

She'd told them about the artist who was all the rage. "Granted, the timing was inconvenient. Ordinarily I wouldn't have chosen to go during this period of mourning, but a narrow window of opportunity opened up, and I needed to get the jump on my competition, which is every other art gallery in the country."

It was a valid excuse for the sudden trip, and they'd accepted it without argument, never guessing that the real reason for the trip had been the flight home.

She'd had plenty of questions for them, but they all boiled down to one: Has there been a breakthrough? And their roundabout answers amounted to one succinct reply: No.

"However," Kimball had said, "we've got experts looking at the security videos from cameras in the hotel lobby. They record a frame every four seconds."

"Like in a bank."

Yes, they'd said.

"But what good will they do? We don't know what he looks like."

"No, we don't," Sanford had said. "So it's a long, tedious process of elimination."

"I'm afraid I'm still not following."

Sanford had explained. "We've come up dry with hotel guests and employees. We're still interviewing, but so far, nothing's sparked. We feel almost certain our boy walked in, did the deed, walked out."

Julie had looked at them in turn.

"It's mere speculation at this point, but that's what we're going on," Kimball had said.

Sanford had picked up. "We figure that, after he shot Mr. Wheeler, he ran into the stairwell where he'd left his shoes, along with a bag of some kind. Suitcase, duffel, something that wouldn't attract attention in a hotel.

"He whipped off the mask, the glasses, and the tracksuit. He had on clothes underneath so that all he had to do was put on his shoes. He stashed his disguise in his suitcase or whatever, ran down the stairs to the lobby, and walked out of the hotel before anyone realized what had happened and security put a clamp on anyone leaving."

Julie didn't remember the elevator's descent to the lobby, but she remembered those several minutes of sheer havoc after the doors opened and the people waiting for the elevator were exposed to the horror inside. Her bending over Paul, the blood forming a lake on the marble floor, and the distress of the other three passengers. That grisly scene had created pandemonium. The man responsible for it could easily have walked out unnoticed.

Unnoticed at the time, but caught on the security cameras.

"We're looking specifically at the time frame just before and just after your elevator reached the lobby and all hell broke loose, to see if the camera got someone leaving the hotel who can't be identified as an employee, guest, friend of a guest, someone attending a meeting or conference. Someone who didn't retrieve a car from the valet or request a taxi."

"That's hundreds of people," she'd said. "How long will that take?"

The two detectives had admitted that it was a labor-intensive task.

"Nothing else?"

They'd told her they hadn't found the mask, the glasses, or the tracksuit. His socks had left fibers on the carpet in the corridor, but they matched those of a popular name brand sold in nearly every retail outlet that carried men's socks. He hadn't touched anything with his skin, hadn't left a strand of hair, none they'd found, and even if they had scraped up some of his DNA, they still had to identify him before they could even try for a match that would place him at the scene.

"Cars in the parking garage?"

"We're checking each one," Sanford had told her. "There's a security camera at the exit. No one drove out within ten minutes of the shooting, and by that time, no one was allowed to. That's why we think he walked away. He'd probably left a car parked a few blocks from the hotel."

Julie's jet lag had compounded her pessimism and despondency. She'd decided on the spot to throw caution to the wind. "You have the lobby video for that day?"

"We've already viewed it several times," Sanford had replied.

"Did Creighton Wheeler appear on it?"

"No."

Kimball's reply had come so quickly, Julie knew with certainty that they'd specifically looked for him.

Following that, she had thanked them for their diligence and left. She hadn't expected to be pounced upon by reporters outside the building. "I don't have anything to tell you," she'd said as she tried to push her way through them.

"Do they have any leads, Ms. Rutledge?"

"You'll have to ask them."

"Are they any closer to finding the man who shot Mr. Wheeler?"

"Not to my knowledge."

"Do you think the robber acted alone?"

That question had halted her because it was the first time anyone had asked it of her. Now, as she watched the replay of that scene on her TV screen, she saw the conviction in her own face when she leaned into the microphone and said, "No, and I don't think it was a robbery, either."

The video ended there, and the anchorwoman reappeared. "Although our own Chris de la Cruz asked Ms. Rutledge to expand on that statement, she declined."

Julie clicked off the TV and turned out her lamp.

She probably would catch hell from the detectives for making that statement, but she didn't care. The crime was almost two weeks old. By now, they were probably working on a dozen other homicides in addition to Paul's. Each time she called or met with them, they reiterated their determination to see the case solved and the perpetrator brought to justice, but she wasn't naïve. Soon the demands of their job would place this case on the back burner in favor of a new one.

Maybe her statement to the reporters would keep things stirred up for another day or two at least. Anything was possible. A lot could happen within a day or two.

Within a day or two, you could do something at 37,000 feet that you would never have believed yourself capable of doing.

Creighton touched an icon on the video monitor that served as his remote, increasing the volume on the giant TV in his home theater.

The woman raised her head from his lap and with some pique asked, "Am I boring you?"

"If you were, you'd know."

He planted his hand on the back of her head and pushed it down. She returned to what she'd been doing. Actually, she was very good at it. Since he was a regular client, the agency knew what he liked and sent over only the best girls. As soon as she'd arrived, he'd said, "In the theater." Once he was settled in his chair, she went to work. Her blond hair was straight and fine. Idly he sifted his fingers through it as he watched the beginning of the newscast.

His elaborate theater system made even the mundane look good. He never watched television anywhere else. As for films, he preferred watching them in his private theater rather than in a movie house,

most of which were in tacky shopping malls, where there were mo-
rons gorging on popcorn, whispering, kicking the back of his seat,
and even—what was the world coming to?—sending and receiving
text messages on their cell phones.

He treated his collection of DVDs as though it was a national
treasure. The temperature and humidity in the theater were carefully
monitored and kept constant to preserve canisters of old film and
videotape. Each one of his films, videos, and DVDs was cataloged
and cross-referenced in computer documents that he updated almost
daily. White-glove treatment was given to all the electronics. Dust
was anathema, but his maid had been instructed never to even enter
this room. He did the cleaning himself.

The resolution of the picture on his screen was so high that he
could see the pores on the news anchorwoman's nose when they
came out of a depressing story about drooling, shitting old people in
a nursing home. Jesus, why didn't their complaining relatives just let
them die?

He wouldn't waste time watching the news except that he was
interested to learn if there was anything to report on his uncle Paul's
fatal shooting. It had been a week since the detectives had come
around yet again, this time asking him if he remembered a recent
quarrel between them that had taken place in Paul's office.

Figuring that a busybody at Wheeler Enterprises, probably his
uncle's prune-faced assistant, had snitched on him, he knew he'd do
better to admit it than to be caught in a lie. "Sure, I remember. He
chewed me out."

Over what, they'd wanted to know.

"Over my being worthless." He'd grinned at the black guy, then
at the woman with the wide ass and wretched taste in clothes.
"Which isn't at all accurate. I pointed out to Uncle Paul that I'm far
from worthless, that my trust fund from my maternal grandparents
has swelled to over seventy million dollars, which by anyone's calcu-
lations is a nice piece of change. I thought it was a rather funny
comeback, but Uncle Paul didn't see the humor in it."

The two detectives had seemed deflated that he'd owned up to
the quarrel. Had they been hoping to spring something on him? If so,
they were completely disarmed. His dad had hired a fancy defense

lawyer to be his mouthpiece from now on, but he wasn't going to be necessary. The case was cooling. Soon it would be cold. Just like poor Uncle Paul.

The girl tongued a sensitive spot, and his penis responded. He was close. In anticipation, he leaned his head back and shut his eyes. But they came open almost instantly when a familiar voice reached him from each surround-sound speaker. "I don't have anything to tell you."

There was Julie Rutledge, filling his screen. He was pleased to note that she looked tired and disheveled and a bit exasperated when asked if the PD was any closer to catching Paul's killer. "Not to my knowledge," she replied.

How cool was this? Getting a damn good blow job while watching his late uncle's ladylove on TV. He wished she knew. Maybe he'd call her later, say, "Julie, saw you on the news. I was looking straight at you when I came."

That delightful train of thought derailed when the whore raised her head again. "Hey, you're pulling my hair."

He relaxed his hold, but his complacent smile remained in place. Julie didn't like him, no doubt because of all the trash Paul had talked about him. Whatever Paul had told Julie had made her cold and distant toward him. For his own amusement, Creighton enjoyed and exploited her evident discomfort.

Straight into the camera she said, "And I don't think it was a robbery, either."

Creighton climaxed.

The whore looked up at him and petulantly asked, "What was so funny?"

Apparently she wasn't accustomed to johns laughing out loud when they came. "Nothing." He zipped up, then took her by the arm and hauled her up off her knees. "Time to go."

"What's your rush?" She trailed her hand up the front of his shirt, cooing, "I could stay awhile."

He pushed her away. "Out."

Sensing he meant it, she grabbed her handbag and sauntered from the room. He followed her through the apartment to make certain she didn't help herself to anything on her way out. She pulled the front door open and shot him a venomous look over her shoulder. "The other girls were right. You're rude."

"You're breaking my heart."

"Ask me, I also think you're weird as shit."

He could think of a dozen comebacks with zing, but good dialogue would be wasted on her. Without a word, he pushed her through the door and soundly closed it.

Retracing his steps to the theater, he paused to enjoy a view of Atlanta's glittering skyline from the living room windows of his penthouse. He trailed his hand along the back of the buttery soft leather sofa as he walked past and admired the pair of art deco doors that he'd salvaged from a razed theater to serve as portals into his own cinematic domain.

Once back in the cushy, custom-made theater seat that he had designed himself, he replayed Julie's appearance on the news. However, this second viewing left him not so amused as vexed. Just when the detectives were growing discouraged and probably on the brink of relegating his uncle's murder to the back burner, Julie had advanced a fresh perspective. Now Sanford and Kimball would be duty bound to explore the angle that the incident had been more than a mere robbery.

Since his uncle's slaying, Creighton had remained in the tall shadow of his father, letting him speak for the family while he himself avoided the media spotlight. He adored spectacle, but only on film. In reality, the limelight called attention to one's beauty and strength, perhaps, and he certainly wasn't modest about his. But while basking in the limelight, one sacrificed privacy. Anonymity had distinct advantages. Keeping to the background afforded one much more maneuverability and, thereby, power.

But now that Julie had shot off her mouth, the detectives' interest in him might be renewed and he would need that fancy lawyer, Derek Mitchell, after all.

It was all such a bother.

CHAPTER
7

JULIE LOVED THE LOOK OF HER GALLERY. IT HAD A DISCREET AND classy curb appeal that fit this stretch of Peachtree Street, where all the boutiques, antiques shops, clothiers, and eateries were as upmarket as their Buckhead clientele.

The potted orange trees on either side of the glossy black door and the fringed canopy extending across the sidewalk were touches that made the gallery inviting to novice art aficionados, who might be intimidated by austerity, while maintaining the high-toned ambience that serious buyers expected.

She turned in to the alley and followed it around to the rear of the building, where she parked and entered through the back door. She dumped her handbag and an armload of catalogs she'd brought from France on her desk. It remained cluttered no matter how hard she tried to keep up with paperwork. After her having been gone for several days, bills and other mail had piled up. Kate had placed a few telephone messages where she would be certain to see them. She sorted through them, but none was urgent.

Separating the office and storeroom in back from the main room of the gallery in front was a wide hallway thirty feet in length. It was here that she exhibited paintings of lesser quality and smaller price tags. As she walked along the hall now, she made a mental note to move some of them. She was a believer in frequently rotating the stock. A painting or objet d'art that had gone unnoticed could, in a new location, suddenly become a piece of interest to a browser.

The thick carpet and the Beethoven being piped through invisible speakers muffled her footsteps, so Kate didn't know she had arrived until she entered the main room. Brightly her assistant said, "Oh, here she is now."

The man with whom Kate had been speaking turned around. Julie drew up short, and for a moment her breath stopped.

Derek Mitchell, wearing a self-congratulatory smile for having jerked the rug out from under her, said pleasantly, "Good morning."

She found enough voice to return the greeting.

"Mr. Mitchell was already here when I arrived to open," Kate said. "I told him you probably wouldn't be in until ten-thirty or so, but he was happy to wait until you got here. We had an espresso."

Behind his back, Kate was grinning and bobbing her eyebrows. Julie could practically hear her saying *What a hottie!*

He was wearing a three-piece summer-weight suit, monochromatic shirt and tie, understated cuff links. Dressier than his traveling clothes had been. Excellent quality and fit. He oozed confidence and a rugged maleness that was vaguely out of keeping with the man-about-town clothing, as though the wardrobe had been carefully chosen for its deceptiveness.

Julie dragged her eyes off him and looked down at the dog lying at his feet.

"That's Maggie," he said.

"I know we don't usually allow pets in the gallery," Kate rushed to say, "but Mr. Mitchell assured me that Maggie is housebroken, and actually more human than dog. Isn't she beautiful?"

As though realizing that she'd been introduced, the dog raised her head and looked at Julie, yawned hugely, then plopped her head back down beside her master's Italian shoes.

Julie watched the shoes moving toward her. When they reached her, she raised her head and looked into Derek Mitchell's face. "Ms. Rutledge." He extended his right hand. Knowing she had to play out this charade for Kate's sake, she shook hands with him. "Mr. Mitchell. Welcome to Chez Jean. How did you know about us?"

"I did my homework." He held her hand a second too long before releasing it.

"He's in the market for something special," Kate said.

"Like what?" Julie asked, addressing the question to him.

"I don't know yet."

"For home or office?"

"His bedroom," Kate said. Again she bobbed her eyebrows, which Julie pretended not to see.

He said, "From what I know of you already, you have quite a reputation for providing customer satisfaction."

Julie's cheeks burned. For Kate's benefit, she said, "I try."

"Oh, I'm certain you do more than try. You go all out." He paused for several beats. Then, "I've driven past the gallery thousands of times and always admired the works displayed in the windows. But I haven't had reason to stop."

"And now you did?"

"Now I did."

She drew herself up. "Well, I'm sure Katherine will find the perfect piece for you. She's very knowledgeable."

"He came to see you."

"That's right, Ms. Rutledge. Not that Ms. Fields isn't perfectly charming and, I'm sure, knowledgeable." He shot Kate a smile over his shoulder, which she returned before he came back around to Julie. "But I'm placing myself in your very capable hands."

To her the double entendre was about as subtle as a freight train. A kaleidoscope of remembered sensations flashed through her mind. Her throat seized up with embarrassment, and it took every ounce of willpower not to show it. To make it worse, he knew exactly what she was remembering.

He'd effectively ambushed her. The smile, the dog, the disarming deportment—he'd completely snowed Kate. What possible explanation could she give her assistant if she shoved him and his well-behaved Lab out the door and locked it behind them.

Her mouth, dry as dust, could barely form a question. "Do you have something particular in mind, Mr. Mitchell?"

"I'm open to anything."

Okay, enough with the sexual innuendos. Curtly she said, "I need some direction. Otherwise I'll waste your time." *And mine* was implied.

"I don't know what I want until I see it, but when I see, I act quickly." He waited a beat, then said, "Maybe you should show me some things."

Trying to be helpful, Kate said, "There are some pieces in the parlor. I'll mind the store. Including Maggie." She knelt and stroked the dog's back. "We'll be fine, won't we, Maggie?"

Derek Mitchell smiled. "I don't hear her complaining. Lead on, Ms. Rutledge."

It having been decided for her, Julie turned and led him down the hallway to the small room off the left side of it, which she called the parlor. It was a room where discriminating collectors could study sculptures or paintings in the best light. They were given time to consider a piece from every angle, in comfort, serenity, and absolute privacy. It was where Julie usually closed the sale, so the chamber was intimate by design.

As she passed through the door, she touched a switch plate and the subtle lighting came on. Derek Mitchell followed her in. She closed the door and spun around to face him.

"What are you doing here?"

"Why'd you do it?"

Squared off across a narrow space, they spoke in unison, glaring at each other.

He was standing in a combative pose, with his hands on his hips, his suit jacket spread open. It was the posture he might take with a witness he was cross-examining, and Julie resented it.

"How dare you come here?" she said.

"How *dare* I? How *dare* I? This coming from the mile-high pickup artist."

She turned her back to him. "I won't talk about that."

"Hell you won't." He stepped round her so they were facing again. "There's a preponderance of evidence that our meeting wasn't by chance."

"Of course it wasn't. Do you think I would entice a total stranger into a public restroom if I didn't have a compelling reason?"

"More compelling than wanting to fuck?"

At first she was too shocked to speak, then when she did, her voice shook with indignation. "I want you out of here."

"Uh-uh, not yet." He blocked her path when she tried to go around him. "You sure as hell weren't acting bereaved over your dead lover when you went for my zipper."

"I refuse to listen to this." She sidestepped; he bodychecked her.

"If picking up men on airplanes isn't your thing—"

"It isn't."

"Then back to my original question. Why? You sucker punched me. I want to know why. Obvious to me now is that it had to do with Paul Wheeler. But what? When I boarded that plane in Paris, I didn't know anything about him. Why did you want me 'had' before I'd even heard of him?"

"You're smart, Mr. Mitchell. You'll figure it out."

"Save me the trouble. Tell me."

She shook her head and once again tried to move past him. This time, he caught her arm. "Would you rather I ask Doug Wheeler why his late brother's mistress seduced me on an airplane?"

Jerking her arm free, she said, "I don't care if you ask him."

He smiled as a jackal might. "You're bluffing. You care."

She glared up at him.

"Save us all the embarrassment, Ms. Rutledge. Why'd you compromise me?"

He was bluffing, too. He wouldn't tell Doug about the airplane episode because he wouldn't want anyone to know he'd been made a fool of. But he was accustomed to bluffing, and according to everything she'd read about him, it usually worked, on even the toughest prosecutors. Besides, she had accomplished what she'd set out to do. What was the harm in his knowing why?

"I did it so you couldn't represent Creighton."

"The nephew. What's he got to do with it?"

"Everything."

"His uncle's death?"

She nodded.

"He has an alibi."

"Nevertheless, I know he was responsible, Mr. Mitchell. Sooner or later, the police will know it, too. He'll be charged and tried. But you won't be there to see it. You can't defend him. Not after . . . after—"

"Ah. You can do it, but you can't say the word."

He was the first to back down from the long, antagonistic stare they exchanged. She caught a whispered swearword as he turned away from her and moved to the other side of the small room. For several ponderous moments he gazed at the painting on the wall. It was lighted to make visible each brushstroke.

Quietly, she said, "Now that you know, you can leave."

Ignoring that, he asked, "How did you know that Doug would retain me?"

"At the reception following Paul's funeral, I overheard him complaining to some friends that the police were still questioning him, the whole family, even though they had solid alibis. Someone said that was ridiculous, that it smacked of police harassment, and that maybe it was time Doug brought in a pit bull—that's a quote—to put a stop to it.

"Doug said he'd already considered that. He dropped your name. I did a little research. Read about your successes in some celebrated trials. You don't lose often. I was afraid that, with you as Creighton's advocate, he would get away with killing Paul."

A long silence ensued while he kept his back to her, still studying the painting. Finally he said, "Would anyone in their right mind pay good money for this?"

She had to smile. "You'd be surprised."

"What's the sticker price?"

"Fifteen thousand."

"You're kidding."

"No."

"Fifteen thousand dollars for a painting of a naked fat man?" He turned abruptly. "How did you know I would be on that flight?"

"What?" The switch of subjects had thrown her off, which she thought was calculated.

"Only my assistant had my itinerary, and she would never give it to anybody without my knowledge and approval."

"Sharon, Doug's wife. One day last week, I called to check on them, see how they were getting on."

"You're close to the family?"

"Friendly. Our common bond being Paul."

"Doug told me that Paul adored you. And vice versa."

"That's true."

"Huh." He subjected her to a slow, and skeptical, once-over, then returned to the original subject. "Sharon Wheeler wouldn't have had my flight number."

"Have you met her?"

"Not yet."

"She's . . . I don't mean this as unkindly as it's going to sound. She's not very bright and is easily manipulated. I let on as though Doug had told me that he planned to retain you and asked what had come of that. She said you were in Paris and weren't expected to return until the eighteenth, when Doug hoped to see you."

"You decided, just like that, to ambush me in Paris?"

"It seemed like a good strategy."

He snuffled a laugh. "Compared to what? A beach assault?"

"It was a drastic move, yes. But I had to catch you before you met with Doug. Sharon said you were on a family trip, which I saw as an advantage. You'd be relaxed. You'd have your guard down. You wouldn't be expecting—"

"To get screwed. In every sense of the word."

She let that pass. "Delta has four flights a day from de Gaulle to Atlanta. If Doug was trying to get an appointment with you on the afternoon of your return, it was reasonable to assume you'd be on the earliest flight."

"What if I hadn't been?"

"I would have been out the cost of a first-class ticket."

"And missed your opportunity."

"If that hadn't worked, I would have picked another time and place."

"To have sexual congress?"

She shifted her gaze away from his. "Not necessarily. The truth is, I didn't know what I was going to do. Plead, perhaps. Try to reason with you. Appeal to your common decency or to your sense of justice. But . . ." She raised her shoulder.

"You don't think I possess those."

She admitted it. "Based on what I'd read about you, I was afraid that tactic wouldn't work." She regarded him for a moment, then out of genuine curiosity, asked, "Do you ever have misgivings when you win an acquittal for someone you know is guilty of a heinous crime?"

"Do you believe in the rights granted by the Constitution?"

"Of course."

"Then there's your answer. You've changed the subject. Why'd you go the seduction route?"

"It seemed the most expedient and effective means of compromising you."

"As every woman since Eve has known."

"An airplane gives one a sense of disconnection from everything on the ground. Rules seem not to apply."

"What happens in the air stays in the air?"

"Something like that."

"So you got me tight on vodka while you were drinking Virgin Marys. Yeah, that much I figured out. You asked the flight attendant to pour you mix only while I got smashed."

"I didn't funnel the drinks down your throat."

"No, but you saw to it that I had a good time, didn't you? Tight skirt. High heels. Poor you. The injured party with the bruised ego. The story about the cheating husband, fact or fiction?"

"Fact. Just not on this trip."

"Huh. That's why you divorced him?" She gave him a look, and he said, "I did a little research of my own."

She volunteered nothing else about her failed marriage. He held her gaze a moment longer, then made a slow circuit of the room, looking at the paintings on display. He stopped at one of them, placed his hands on his hips again, and looked at the painting for such a long time, Julie feared his concentration would bore a hole in the canvas. Finally she asked, "When did you find out?"

"Who you were? Last night. I caught the news. Imagine my surprise. There you were, my mystery woman, in high def. You had a name, and I was glad of that. Julie Rutledge. But hold on. Ms. Rutledge is up to her neck in a high-profile criminal case that—too coincidentally to be a coincidence—has just been dropped in my lap.

"Her oblique parting statement, 'You've been had,' suddenly begins to make sense. A kind of sense, anyway." He turned to face her, apparently expecting her to respond. When she didn't, he asked, "What did you mean by your last statement to the reporter?"

"Exactly what I said. It wasn't a robbery."

"A masked man holds a group of people at gunpoint, demands they hand over their valuables, and it's not a robbery?"

"It was a murder, Mr. Mitchell. An assassination. Paul was meant to die. The robbery was to disguise that it was premeditated and planned."

"Planned by Creighton Wheeler, I presume."

"That's no presumption."

"You sound certain that he was behind it."

"I am."

"Well, apparently the police don't share your conviction, or he would already have been charged."

"They don't have any evidence."

"Do you?"

She remained silent. Even if she had a smoking gun connecting Creighton to the murder, Derek Mitchell was the last person on earth with whom she would share it. But that point was moot because she didn't have any evidence. She said, "The detectives are still questioning Creighton even though he provided an alibi. Doesn't that strike you as odd?"

"Not really. Cops do odd things all the time."

"I've had several meetings with Sanford and Kimball. Both strike me as extremely competent."

His chagrined expression led her to believe he agreed but was too stubborn to admit it. "I've never met Roberta Kimball," he said.

"Sanford?"

"I know him in passing and by reputation."

"Does that reputation include his propensity to do odd things?"

"Make your point," he said with irritation.

"My point is, why would Sanford and Kimball keep returning to

Creighton unless they suspected him of involvement, at least on some level? I *know* he's involved. And Doug fears it. If he didn't, he wouldn't have retained you before a pit bull of a lawyer was even needed. By hiring you, he was laying his groundwork."

"As you laid yours. So to speak."

The play on words was deliberate, and again, her cheeks flamed, but she didn't avert her eyes from his. "That's right. I made a preemptive strike."

"There are a lot of excellent trial lawyers out there, Ms. Rutledge. And the Wheelers can afford the best. Do you plan to fuck all of them?"

She marched to the door and yanked it open. But in an equally decisive motion, he reached over her shoulder and pushed it shut with the flat of his hand, then kept it there. She turned in the tight space he allowed her.

"You went to great lengths to disqualify me, Ms. Rutledge."

"You have no idea."

"I guess I should be flattered that you were so scared of me."

"You're noted for being ruthless. You and Creighton would have made a good team."

"What does that mean?"

"I think you get my gist."

"In fact I don't, because I don't know Creighton Wheeler. Furthermore, I didn't know you before that Delta flight. What happened on that airplane took place before I'd met Doug Wheeler or even knew that his brother had been shot and killed. Technically, I'm blameless. Off the hook. I can handle the case if I bloody well want to."

"Not even you, Mr. Mitchell, as arrogant as you are, would dare go to trial representing Creighton knowing that I would be testifying for the prosecution. And even if you were willing to flirt with disbarment, I'd make certain it never happened."

"You couldn't, not without admitting your own culpability."

"Which I would do. Don't doubt it for a moment."

"You'd go public with what we did in that lavatory?"

"Believe it."

"Your lover's body was barely cold. For all its nouveau sophistication, this is still the South. The old guard, who are Paul Wheeler's friends and associates, would be horrified." His eyes made a quick survey of the room. "Your fancy clientele would never darken the door of this place again. They'd never spend another cent of their old money with you. They might forgive you for what you did on that airplane, but they'd never forgive you for flaunting it and dragging Paul Wheeler's name, and that of his sainted wife, Mary, through the muck. You trash your reputation, you trash his."

"It's for him I did it." Speaking with vehemence, she pushed him aside so she would no longer be sandwiched between him and the door. "Paul's nephew had him killed. Paul would want me to expose Creighton's crime. He would expect me to go to great lengths, as you put it, to see Creighton punished."

His eyes were hazel, flecked with chocolate-colored spots. They held her gaze for what became an uncomfortably long time. "You did it for Paul Wheeler?"

She drew herself up to her full height and bobbed her head.

"That's the only reason?"

"Yes."

"For him?"

"*Yes.*"

He looked her over, his eyes lighting on spots he knew by touch. He smiled as he would when he knew he'd riddled an eyewitness's account. "Fool yourself, Julie. Or try. But you don't fool me."

CHAPTER
8

KATE POKED HER HEAD AROUND THE OFFICE DOOR AND looked at Julie expectantly. "Well?"

Julie pretended to be assessing the long-distance charges on the telephone bill. She hadn't escorted Derek Mitchell out. Treating her to that arrogant smile, he'd reached behind him and turned the doorknob, then left. She'd waited a full sixty seconds after his departure before leaving the parlor.

She'd slipped into the tiny bathroom reserved for her and Kate, where she swallowed two aspirin tablets to help stave off an oncoming headache, washed her hands, and wished they would stop shaking. Bracing them on the small sink, she took a series of deep breaths. *Get a grip, Julie.*

She retreated into the office and attacked the pile of mail. But she should have known that Kate's curiosity and sense of drama would be demanding details.

She kept her eyes on the phone bill. "Well, what?"

"What did you think of him?"

"Mr. Mitchell?" She feigned indifference. "He dresses with good taste. Whether or not that translates to artwork remains to be seen. I bounced some ideas off him, which will help me in the selection process."

"But what did you think of *him*? I thought he was perfectly dreamy."

Julie frowned. "Isn't he a little old for you?"

"About the same age difference as between you and Paul."

"That was different."

"How so?"

"I was older when I met Paul, so the gap didn't seem that wide. You're still years away from thirty."

Kate was irrepressible. "While y'all were in the parlor, I did a Google search. He's a hotshot lawyer. Criminal defense. He's done very well, and best of all, he's single."

Julie dropped the phone bill onto the stack of others and rubbed her forehead where the headache was defying the analgesics. "Kate, I've got a mound of work here to attend to."

Finally some of the younger woman's effervescence fizzled. "Okay. But I thought he was yummy. With the dog and all."

The phone rang. Kate reached across her to answer it. "Chez Jean. How can I help you?" She listened, then asked the caller to hold on and handed the phone to Julie. "Detective Sanford."

"Thank you for coming so quickly, Ms. Rutledge." Sanford motioned her into a chair in his cubicle, which unfortunately, had become familiar territory to her.

"You said it was important."

"We hope so." Roberta Kimball had been waiting with him when Julie arrived. "We've isolated a guy on the lobby security video."

Sanford sat down in his desk chair and got straight to the point. "He was definitely in the hotel during the time of the robbery, but he's not on the garage security videos, and he didn't use a valet."

"He didn't want a car traced, is what we guess," Kimball said. "We have him entering at twelve-forty-two and walking out at three-fifteen and change, which is approximately the same time the elevator reached the lobby and chaos ensued."

"Between the eighth floor and the lobby, the elevator didn't stop. Does the timing work?" Julie asked.

Kimball nodded. "He was relying on everyone's shock. While our young man from California was gathering his wits enough to close the door and push the Down button, our culprit would have had time to duck into the stairwell, take off the tracksuit, slip into shoes, and run down the eight flights. He'd have hustled, but we had a couple of officers, including Sanford here, run it. It can be done."

"He's not an employee," Sanford said. "Management doesn't believe he was a guest, either. None of the reception desk personnel remember checking him in, and they're trained to remember faces and names. Part of the service the Moultrie is famous for is addressing guests by name as soon as they arrive. The doorman is certain he saw him, but he doesn't remember handling luggage for him or passing him on to a bellman or check-in personnel."

"No one remembers anyone speaking in a voice like that which you and the others in the elevator described," Kimball said.

Before her trip to France, Julie had spent several hours listening to recordings of distinctive voices, but it had been a waste of time. "The other victims?" she asked now. "When they listened to the recordings—"

"They said the same as you. None exactly matched his, so that's a dead end."

After a pause, Sanford continued. "We're polling groups that were holding meetings in the hotel that day. Still waiting to see if one can claim him. One hotel housekeeper thinks she remembers seeing him that day on one of the guest room floors, but she can't be sure."

"She's not sure the sky is blue," Kimball said drily. "She can't be sure of which floor she saw him on, even if it is the same guy, and she's wishy-washy on that. We're not counting on her. Personally, I think she ID'd him because she wanted the attention."

"We're circulating this photo to guests of the hotel," Sanford went on. "But that's a hell of a chore. It's been almost two weeks. People are scattered all over. A few are overseas. So it's a time-consuming process, and eventually someone may identify him as a harmless visitor who was there to see them during their stay, in which case we'll be back to square one.

"Beat officers are showing the photo around to paid snitches. Nothing so far. Which doesn't mean they don't recognize him. Just means they're not disposed to identifying him. Same with pawn-shops. If he's fenced the stuff he stole, nobody's telling.

"We've also got cops looking through mug shots, but even if he's been booked for armed robbery or any other crime, appearances can change, and this isn't the best-quality photo because it's a freeze-frame taken off the video."

"A jerky video," Kimball added. "Poor lighting. Bad angle. He's not much more than a blob, but it's a start."

Sanford concluded with "We thought you should have a look."

He removed an eight-by-ten photograph from a manila enve-lope. Julie's heart was thudding as she reached for it. She glanced at it, then looked up at the detectives, and she knew her reaction must be apparent. *Are you kidding?* "This is it?"

"I warned you it was lousy. In fact, in light of this, the Moultrie has replaced their security cameras with newer models and updated their entire system."

Julie studied the photo but shook her head with dismay. "This could be anybody."

"You don't recognize him?" Kimball pressed.

"Not even vaguely."

"The photograph has been enlarged," Sanford said, "so it's even grainier than the video. Look again. Try to piece together the pixels."

Julie did as asked, but it was hopeless. The face was a smear of light and shadow, obviously male, but beyond that indistinguish-able. She passed the picture back to Sanford. "I wish I could give you a name, believe me."

"Well, it was worth a try." Sanford slid the photo back into the envelope.

"Have you shown it to anyone else? The other victims of the robbery?"

"We've both faxed and e-mailed it," Kimball said. "The ladies in Nashville got back to us immediately with a negative. We're waiting to hear from the Californian. It's still early out there."

"What about Doug? Creighton?"

Sanford nodded. "It occurred to us that the shooter could be an ex-employee of Wheeler Enterprises who had a grudge against his boss. We asked Doug Wheeler to come in, take a look. He referred us to his lawyer. As of yesterday, he has a new one."

Kimball snorted with obvious distaste. "Derek Mitchell. A scourge."

Julie tried to keep her expression impassive. "Why?"

"He wins."

"No, I mean why did they retain a new lawyer?"

Neither of the detectives ventured an opinion, but Julie detected that her seemingly innocent question had resonated with them. "It sounds as though they're nervous, doesn't it?"

Kimball and Sanford exchanged a look. As though taking a cue, Sanford stood up and excused himself to make a call. "You ladies are free to use my space here as long as you need to. Excuse me."

Once he was out of earshot, Julie smiled at Roberta Kimball. "You two communicate without language. I've noticed it on more than one occasion."

"We've been working together for a couple of years, but it seems like much longer. When we were assigned to each other, we clicked instantly. Our investigative methods are compatible, and so are our personalities."

"Yet you're so different."

"Can't argue that," she said affably. "Black, white. Male, female. Married, single. Tall and thin. Short and stout. Maybe the differences are why the partnership works."

Julie assessed the detective for a moment, then asked, "So which are you?"

"I'm the short and stout one."

Julie smiled. "Are you the good cop, or the bad cop?"

Kimball, not in the least abashed, smiled back. "Where do you shop?"

"Pardon me?"

"Where do you buy your clothes? You always look so . . . right."

"Thank you."

"Of course if I tried to wear a little black dress like that, it would be a fashion fiasco." Kimball's smile was good-natured and self-deprecating. She picked up a bronze paperweight that was shaped like the bulldog mascot of the University of Georgia and fiddled with it absently, all the time watching Julie. Finally she said, "We're both the good cop."

Julie drew in a long breath, let it out. "I suppose that depends on one's point of view."

"Yeah, I suppose it does."

"What's the next step with the security videos, the photograph?"

"We continue showing the still around, hoping somebody can ID the guy and either clear him or incriminate him. In the meantime, we're looking at the videos recorded three days prior to the shooting. The hotel keeps them for only four days before recording over them, so that's as far back as we can go.

"We've got techies looking at them frame by frame to see if they can spot this guy again. And if they do, he'll go to the head of the list as a viable suspect. Because in order to pull this off, he had to know where he was going, how long it would take him to do all that in the stairwell and get out before the shutdown."

"He would have cased the joint."

Kimball laughed at Julie's deliberate use of jargon, so Julie was caught a bit off guard when the detective asked abruptly, "What do you think of Creighton Wheeler?"

"I believe I've made plain my low opinion of him."

"You've dropped hints that you think he's behind this robbery and shooting."

Julie said nothing.

"Actually, your hints have been as obvious as an F-five tornado. Sanford and I would have to be really stupid not to have picked up on them."

"I don't believe you're stupid."

The detective returned the paperweight to the desk and folded her arms across her bulge, regarding Julie shrewdly. "Do you know Creighton well?"

"I base my opinion largely on what Paul had told me about him. But my personal dealings with him have borne out everything Paul said."

"What personal dealings?"

"As few as possible, I assure you. But Paul was a very social animal. Get-togethers with his family were unavoidable. Holidays. Birthday dinners. Like that."

"Do you think Creighton is capable of committing murder?"

Julie felt he was, but she couldn't say so with certainty, because she had no basis for her opinion except an intense distrust and dislike of him. Paul had alluded to a darker side of his nephew, which his golden good looks concealed. Her intuition about his true character was strong, but also subjective and therefore fallible. Hedging, she flipped the question. "What do *you* think, Ms. Kimball?"

"Honestly? I think everyone's capable of committing murder. But regarding Creighton Wheeler in particular, I think he's a smart-alecky, condescending, rich snot who needs an ass whuppin' about as bad as anybody ever did." Kimball frowned. "But it seems a little too obvious that he had his uncle bumped off when, upon said uncle's death, he's due to inherit a shitload of money."

"You'd have to know Creighton. He enjoys inside jokes."

"Inside jokes?"

"He likes being one up on everyone else."

"Example?"

"Hmm. Let's see. Okay, a perfect example. A few months ago I hosted a private showing for a new artist. Champagne and caviar. Distinguished guest list. You know the scene."

"The men in silk turtlenecks, everyone wearing black."

Julie smiled at the detective's accuracy. "During the course of the event, I noticed that Creighton and several of the guests were grouped around a particular painting. I went over to see what had drawn them to it."

Julie's blood still boiled when she recalled the incident and Creighton's smugness. "He had sneaked in a canvas and hung it on the wall. It was an awful still life he'd picked up at a flea market. He'd forged my featured artist's signature on it. He was mocking the artist, my reputation, and my clients, making them out to be gullible art snobs."

"What did you do?"

"I maneuvered them away from him. Removed the painting. No real harm was done. The artist never knew. But that's the kind of cruel trick Creighton likes to play. He likes to make a fool of a person, and anyone is fair game."

"He pricks with people. That's an annoying characteristic, but hardly a crime."

Not to have her theory so blithely dismissed, Julie said, "He knows you would think him too glaringly obvious to be a prime suspect. You see? That's his inside joke, and I promise you, he's laughing up his sleeve."

Kimball stared at Julie thoughtfully, then picked up the manila envelope containing the photograph of the unidentified man and tapped it against her palm. "I think that's it for now. We appreciate you coming in."

Dodge Hanley plopped down in one of the chairs facing Derek's desk and slid a folder across to him. "That's what I've got so far."

Derek opened the folder, scanned several sheets of printed material. "In a nutshell?"

Dodge exuded the odor of stale cigarette smoke. Despite all the warnings about the life-threatening effects of tobacco use, he hadn't even tried to break the habit and harbored a resentment bordering on scorn toward all smokers who did, calling them cowards. His nicotine-stained fingers drummed the arms of the chair, and he shifted in search of a more comfortable position, which was in vain, because he was never entirely comfortable unless a cigarette was in his hand.

"In a nutshell, she's clean. No arrests, not even a misdemeanor."

"Childhood?"

"Grew up in Aiken. Mom and Dad worked for the public school system. He was a teacher, she worked in the administration building. Churchgoing, tax-paying, solid citizens. No brothers or sisters. Parents now deceased."

Before going on, he took a wheezing breath. "Your girl there is smart. Got a full academic scholarship to Vanderbilt, and then four years later was awarded a fellowship to further her art studies in France. Met and married some Frog artist. Can't remember his name, but it's in there."

Derek didn't tell Dodge he already knew about her marriage and divorce. "What about him?"

"Nothing about him. No fame, no fortune, apparently no talent. He and she divorced after three years, but by that time Paul Wheeler had entered her life. Lucky break for her."

Derek raised his head and looked across his desk at Dodge, whose face, seamed and jaundiced from years of smoking, remained impassive despite his editorial comment. He was unflappable, cynical, and nothing much surprised him, because in the forty-plus years he'd been tracking down villains, he claimed to have seen it all. He ranked most human beings lower than animals.

He'd been a detective for the sheriff's department when he came up against Derek in the courtroom. Dodge was testifying for the prosecution, but his total recall and attention to detail made an impression on Derek during cross-examination. Following the trial, which Derek had won, he'd sought out the curmudgeonly Dodge and asked if he'd be interested in working full-time for his firm.

Dodge had scoffed. "And go over to the dark side? No thank you, Counselor."

"I'll double your salary."

"When do I start?"

Actually, Dodge had been happy to leave the sheriff's department, where stringent rules of investigation and interrogation were enforced. As he and Derek sealed their deal over beers, Dodge had asked, "Are you persnickety about how I obtain information?"

"No. But if you're caught doing something unethical or illegal, you're on your own."

"No problem." Dodge had slurped his beer. "I won't get caught."

Which didn't exactly assure Derek that his methods were aboveboard, but he never asked how or where or through whom Dodge secured his information, feeling he was better off not knowing.

Because of the smoking ban in public buildings, and Marlene's ill-concealed dislike for his ashtray bouquet, Dodge worked out of his home—wherever that was. Derek had no idea. Dodge had given him a cell telephone number and a post office box, to which Derek sent his paychecks. Otherwise, Dodge didn't advertise his whereabouts or what he did between assignments. But he responded quickly whenever Derek issued a request.

Last night, after seeing Julie Rutledge on the evening news, Derek had glanced through the files Marlene had sent home with him, specifically looking for references to Paul Wheeler's "companion." She was mentioned frequently, but there wasn't much personal information about her, and his home computer had yielded little that wasn't in relation to the gallery. He'd called Dodge and asked him to get the lowdown.

"When do you need it?"

"Yesterday."

"You got it."

As usual, Dodge had come through. He'd been waiting for him at the firm when Derek arrived after his volatile encounter at Chez Jean. He asked now, "How'd this lucky break for Julie Rutledge come about? How'd she and Wheeler hook up?"

Dodge patted his shirt pocket as though looking for a rogue cigarette. "That I don't know. He was a rich American with good connections in Paris. She worked in a highfalutin gallery and was supporting herself and her sorry husband, so what I'm guessing is—"

"Wait. 'Sorry husband'?"

"No reported income. Two arrests for drunk and disorderly. Or the French equivalent."

"Okay."

"Where was I?"

"So what you're guessing."

"What I'm guessing is that Wheeler met her through mutual acquaintances in the art world. But that's purely speculation, you understand."

Derek nodded.

"However it came about, she's soon shed of the deadbeat husband, and she and Wheeler are a pair. He brought her back to the U.S. and set her up in business here in Atlanta."

"Gee. Wonder how she returned that favor?"

Dodge's laugh sounded like loose gravel in a tin cup. "You think he was her sugar daddy?"

"Don't you?"

"Well, maybe he was to start. But Julie's a savvy gal. Wheeler didn't give her the money to buy the gallery, he loaned it. Actually, the bank loaned it, Wheeler just cosigned the note. The gallery didn't turn a profit the first year, but she's been in the black and making money since. Loan was paid back. She bought her house in Garden Hills herself, pays her own bills and credit card debts. She's financially independent of Wheeler. At least that's how it looks on paper."

Derek rolled back his desk chair and stood up. He stepped over Maggie, who was sprawled on the floor, snoring, and moved to the wall of glass. Minutes passed while he stared vacantly at the view and thought about what he knew of Julie Rutledge, past and present.

Well, shit.

On the one hand, Dodge's report was a letdown. Her background wasn't as sordid as he had expected. Dodge hadn't uncovered an ah-ha factor—like a long list of "benefactors"—with which Derek could condemn her. On the other hand, he was glad something criminal or iniquitous hadn't been excavated.

She was precisely what she appeared on the surface to be, an intelligent, cultured, and educated woman, successful in her own right, who'd had the good fortune to fall in love with a very wealthy man, and to have her love reciprocated.

She'd been kneeling beside the love of her life when the back of his head was blown off. She wanted his killer captured and punished to the fullest extent of the law. To that end, she'd shanghaied the man she thought might prevent that. She'd resorted to the oldest trick in the book, which also happened to be, as she'd emphasized to him, the most expeditious and effective.

Maybe it was as simple as that, and he was only trying to make it more complicated.

He was so lost in thought, he'd almost forgot Dodge was there until the investigator said, "Want to tell me how come you're so interested in her?"

"I've been retained by the family to represent them during the investigation into Wheeler's shooting."

"Niiiice," Dodge drawled. "Beaucoup bucks coming our way. But she's not a Wheeler. She hire you, too?"

"No, but she is—was—a fundamental aspect of Wheeler's life the last couple years. I wanted some background."

"Have you met her?"

"I saw her on TV." Which wasn't the whole truth, but it definitely wasn't a lie.

"You think she was involved?"

"I don't know what to think," Derek muttered, meaning it. He came back around. Dodge was already standing, preparing to leave. He could go only so long without taking a hit of nicotine. "What did you dig up on Creighton Wheeler?"

"Spends a lot of money, plays a lot of tennis, drives flashy cars. He's received a handful of speeding tickets, all of which a judge made go bye-bye. Didn't find anything that relates to his late uncle Paul."

"Could he have done it?"

"He has an alibi."

"Could he have done it?" Derek repeated in a quieter voice.

Dodge exhaled a breath fraught with noxious fumes. "Anything's possible."

"Gut feeling?"

"I wouldn't want my daughter to date this guy."

"You don't have a daughter."

"If I did."

"Why not?"

"He likes whores. Two, three a week. Not hookers. The agency girls. Not that there's anything wrong with that, but . . ."

"But you wouldn't want your daughter involved with him."

"Neither would you." Dodge ran his hand over his mouth, stretching out the lower lip before letting it spring back. "But to kill for millions when he's already got millions? What would be the point? Why not just wait the uncle out, let him die of natural causes, and then cash in?"

"I tend to agree," Derek said. "Besides, two good detectives have questioned him extensively since it happened, and they've got nothing on him. In fact, if you believe their press releases, they've got nothing, period."

"They've got something now." Dodge pointed at the folders he'd brought in. "It's in there, bottom of the stack."

"Give me a hint."

"And spoil the surprise? Suffice it to say, it's the latest, hot-off-the-presses goods from the hallowed halls of the PD."

Derek shook his head in wonderment. "Someday before I die, or before you do, promise you'll tell me who your moles are."

"I'll dance at your funeral, and my secrets will die with me." Dodge grinned and headed for the door. "By the way, your poker face could use some work, Counselor."

"What do you mean?"

Dodge turned. Tongue in cheek, he said, "I saw her on TV, too."

CHAPTER

9

"M R. MITCHELL, MR. WHEELER IS HERE."

Marlene stood aside, and Creighton Wheeler strolled into Derek's office.

Derek stood up and met the young man halfway. "Derek Mitchell."

"Creighton Wheeler."

Derek extended his hand, but Creighton was taking in the view beyond the wall of windows and didn't notice. Marlene said to buzz her if they needed anything and slipped out. Derek motioned Creighton toward the same grouping of chairs where he'd met with his father the day before. "Make yourself comfortable."

"I always do," Creighton said as he lowered himself into one of the chairs.

Maggie whined and ambled over to sniff him. "That's Maggie," Derek said.

Most people reached out to pat her on the head. Women clucked and cooed over her. Men asked if she was a trained hunting dog. Creighton Wheeler, however, showed a marked lack of interest, except to say, "Pleased to make your acquaintance, Maggie."

The office held much more interest for him. He continued his slow survey of it, but whether with appreciation or disapproval,

Derek had no idea. His expression was mildly curious, but otherwise it gave away nothing of what he was thinking.

Derek sat down across from him. "Help yourself." On the low table between them, Marlene had placed the ice bucket, drinking glasses, and bottled water.

"No thank you."

He was more handsome than most movie stars of his age. Of any age. Derek thought his blond hair might have been artificially high-lighted, but if so, it had been expertly done. His clear blue eyes were so guileless Derek automatically suspected him of guile. He gave off an air of boredom, condescension, and private amusement.

Derek decided instantly that he didn't like him. "You're half an hour late."

The blue eyes stopped their scan of the office and fixed on Derek. "Am I? Sorry. I was babysitting my Porsche. You can bill me for the minutes I missed."

"I will." Derek's smile was no more sincere than Creighton's apology. "My condolences over the loss of your uncle."

"Thanks, but it's not like I'm all torn up about it."

Derek wasn't surprised by his candor. A person with Creighton's arrogance usually didn't mince words. "Your father mentioned to me that the two of you had your differences."

" 'What we've got here is . . . failure to communicate.' "

Derek frowned. "I'm sorry?"

"Cool Hand Luke. Strother Martin as the prison warden. Great character actor. He was in Butch Cassidy and the Sundance Kid, too."

"Another Paul Newman movie."

Creighton gave Derek his first genuine smile. "I'm impressed. You know some cinema history. Remember the film where Newman played the burned-out lawyer?"

Derek realized he was being gigged, but he kept his expression pleasant and went along. "Remind me."

"The Verdict. 'This is the case, this is the case, this is the case.' Newman chants it. Very convincingly. He should have won his Oscar for that film instead of The Color of Money. When he died, we lost one of the greats."

"Your father told me that you were an ardent movie fan."

Creighton seemed to take exception to the term. "More than that. I studied film at UCLA."

"You wanted to be a moviemaker?"

He winced. "God no. Too much hard work. Lousy hours. Having to answer to assholes and put up with temper tantrums from strung-out prima donnas and has-beens? Not for me, Mr. Mitchell. I'd rather watch the movies other people make."

"As a critic?"

"No, only for entertainment. I had no ambition for the industry itself. Or for any other industry, for that matter. Which was just one of the issues my dearly departed uncle and I disagreed on. He thought I should have majored in business, gone to Harvard, gotten an MBA, gotten hard-ons over P and L statements and spreadsheets. I don't think so," he added drolly.

"But you do work in the family business."

"I have an office at corporate headquarters. I don't work."

He flashed Derek a perfect grin, which Derek felt an urge to damage with his fist. Curbing the impulse, he placed his hand on Maggie's head and rubbed it the way she liked. "Your father thinks you need the services of a criminal lawyer."

"He's a worrier."

Watching him closely to gauge his reaction, Derek asked, "Has he got cause to worry?"

"If you mean because those detectives are harassing me, then yes. If you mean because I'm guilty of something, no. I was playing tennis when my uncle was killed."

"So I've heard."

"Besides, if I had killed my uncle Paul, it wouldn't have been during a fucked-up robbery."

Derek poured himself a glass of water and took a drink. "Sure you won't have some?"

"No thanks."

"On the news last night, your uncle's companion told reporters she didn't think it was a robbery."

"Companion?" Creighton repeated with a sneer. "Synonymous with *whore*?"

"Is that what you think of Julie Rutledge?"

"I had a prostitute at my place last night," he said with a negligent gesture. "I'm not a moralist. I don't care that old Uncle Paul still got his rocks off. In fact, good for him. Just don't window-dress it. He made Julie out to be something special, when actually she would screw a dog if she thought it would benefit her."

Derek returned his glass of water to the table, wiped the condensation off his hands, and when that didn't work to stop the rush of resentment and anger coursing through him, he got up and walked to his desk.

"Why do you think the investigators keep coming back around to you?"

"Hell if I know," Creighton replied casually. "To give themselves something to do, I suppose. They've got to look busy to their superiors. They've got to justify their paychecks. Of course, Julie's sly little remarks don't help."

"Sly little remarks?"

"Every chance she gets, she nudges them in my direction."

"Why would she do that?"

"Because there's no love lost between us."

"How come? What happened?"

He chuckled. "Nothing. That's the problem."

Derek returned to his chair and sat down. "Sounds to me like there's a story."

Creighton smiled, seemed to consider whether or not to tell the story, then said, "Out of the blue, my uncle brought her back with him from Paris and made no secret of being besotted. Which surprised everyone because he'd thought my aunt Mary hung the moon. But my father said Uncle Paul was lonely, and wasn't it great that he'd met this woman he could care for. He said we should be nice to her, make her feel welcome, if for no other reason, for Uncle Paul's sake. So," he said with an indolent shrug, "we made nice.

"One Sunday night my mom asked them over for a cookout. We were all hanging out on the terrace. I went into the pool house to grab a Coke from the fridge. Julie followed me in, and in seconds she was all over me. I'm talking Kathleen Turner in *Body Heat*. So I thought what the hell, and played William Hurt for a minute or two. A conversation was taking place between my parents and Uncle Paul not twenty feet away, while his girlfriend's mouth is wrapped around my dick. I think the danger of being caught was a real turn-on for her."

Creighton was laughing at the memory. "It was crazy and kinky, and with any other woman it would have been fun. But screwing Julie wasn't worth the hullabaloo it would've caused if Uncle Paul had walked in on us, so I pushed her away, told her I wasn't taking my uncle's leftovers, and left her in the pool house while I rejoined the party.

"When she came out several minutes behind me, she was so pissed, she wouldn't even look in my direction. She told Uncle Paul she had developed a headache and wanted to go home. Like a good puppy—no offense to your dog there—he left with her. She's hated me ever since."

Derek could feel his pulse in every vein. His body was feverish. He had to clear his throat before he could speak. "You think she's implicating you out of spite?"

Creighton made a face. "Who knows why a woman does anything?"

Indeed, Derek thought. "It won't matter how hard she nudges the investigation toward you if the police can find no evidence against you."

"There isn't any. They haven't got anything."

"That was yesterday. Today they do."

Creighton's face remained perfectly calm. Derek had been watching, and the young man's demeanor didn't change one iota. His eyes didn't flicker. His mouth didn't tense. He didn't flinch. Nothing.

"They have video surveillance in the hotel lobby," Derek said.

"One would expect that."

"The police have isolated a guy who left the hotel within minutes of the robbery."

"Him and how many others?"

"Point taken. But they can put names to the others. Not this guy. Not so far anyway. He wasn't a guest. He didn't park in the garage, eat in the restaurant, or drink in the bar."

"My God! Monstrous! If that isn't criminal behavior, I don't know what is."

Derek gave him a look, then pulled a photograph from the folder he'd carried over from his desk and laid it on the table. Creighton leaned forward and looked at it, then laughed.

"This is the big crime-solving breakthrough? Jesus. Our tax dollars at work." Still chuckling, he said, "The only thing obvious is that it isn't a picture of me. I wouldn't be caught dead in that shirt."

"No recognition?"

He took another look at the photo. "You know, now that you mention it, he looks a little like the Elephant Man. Which is one reason I avoid being photographed. I hate being at the mercy of the camera as well as the photographer."

Derek returned the picture to the folder, made a point of lining up the edges of it with the other contents, then got up and returned the folder to his desk. As he turned back to Creighton, he announced what he'd decided the moment he laid eyes on the young man. "I'm not going to take you on as a client, Mr. Wheeler."

That elicited a reaction. "Excuse me?"

"I'm not going to—"

"I heard you," Creighton said testily. "Why not?"

Because you're a despicable smart-ass.

That was the basic, underlying reason. During the last several minutes, Derek had decided that he could never provide Creighton Wheeler with an impartial defense because he absolutely could not stand the cocky bastard. He had represented some of the slimiest miscreants in Georgia, and he'd never let a disagreeable personality be the determining factor for saying no. But his aversion to this man was so intense, Derek could not be his advocate on any level.

His reasons for declining to represent Creighton Wheeler had nothing to do with Julie Rutledge, really. Even if he'd never met her, his decision would have been the same.

Realizing he couldn't be that blunt with the young millionaire, he smiled at him as he returned to his chair and sat down. "I'm turning you down primarily because you don't need me, and I won't take your money, or your father's, for doing nothing. Sore losers have accused me of being unscrupulous. I'll own up to pulling some clever courtroom tricks. But I've never fleeced a client.

"You had two excellent motives for wanting Paul Wheeler dead. Your relationship with him was antagonistic, and you're heir to his estate. The police would have pounced on either one of those. Combined, it's a pretty incriminating package.

"But, they can't get beyond the fact that you lacked opportunity. You have an alibi, substantiated by several people. You couldn't have been in that hotel at the time of the shooting. Of course you could have hired someone to kill him—"

"It wouldn't have been that guy," Creighton said with derision, gesturing to the photographs. "What a moron."

"Exactly," Derek said. "You could afford the best hit man in the world. Someone with a much more subtle technique." He paused for a moment, then continued. "Paul Wheeler was worth a fortune. He was only fifty-two and in good health, so he might have lived another thirty or forty years. For the sake of argument, let's say you got impatient to inherit his millions. Would you actually risk the promise of his legacy, as well as the sizable trust fund you have now, by committing murder and losing everything?"

"That would be completely irrational."

"It would, yes."

Creighton plucked at the crease of his linen trousers. "I think the detectives are smart enough to see that. But what about Julie's bad-mouthing?"

"They haven't credited it. I surmise that Sanford and Kimball have taken her insinuations against you for what they are. Sour grapes. Reprisal. Jealousy. Whatever. They haven't acted on them, so we can assume, safely I believe, that they've dismissed them."

Creighton grinned. "I like the way you think, Mr. Mitchell. I want you as my lawyer."

Derek shook his head. "Sorry."

"My father has already paid you a retainer."

"Which he'll get back. I'll bill him for yesterday's meeting and for today, but the retainer check will be returned."

"Do you want to up your fee?"

"It's not a matter of money."

"Everything is a matter of money."

"Not this."

"Since when can you fire a client?"

"Since now."

Creighton held his stare for several moments, then again flashed the cocky grin that set Derek's teeth on edge. "What's the real problem here?"

Derek stood up, indicating the conclusion of the meeting. "The problem is that your father wanted me to be at your beck and call. I don't work that way. I've checked my caseload and trial schedule, and done some soul-searching."

"A lawyer with a soul?"

Derek gave him a token smile. "My soul, conscience, whatever you want to call it, won't let me take on a new client at the expense of those I'm already committed to. I've got my hands full preparing for Jason Connor's trial."

"The kid who slaughtered his parents?"

Derek didn't acknowledge that. "He's only sixteen, and his life is at stake. In order to accommodate you, I'd have to use some of the time allocated to his case. I'd be stretched very thin, and that wouldn't be fair to anyone. Bottom line, I won't do it."

"Father won't like it. And neither do I."

Derek went to the door and pulled it open. "I can refer you to someone equally good."

"There is no one equally good. Why do you think we came to you?"

"I'm flattered by the confidence you placed in me. I'm sorry I can't help you."

Creighton stared at him for a count of ten, then walked through the door with all the hauteur of the boy who was taking his ball and going home because he hadn't been chosen captain.

He walked past Marlene's desk without so much as a nod and continued down the hallway to the reception area, where a wall of glass separated the law office from the corridor. When he reached it, he put his back to the door, and holding Derek's stare down the length of the hall, pushed it open. He backed out and strode off in the direction of the elevator.

Marlene harrumphed. "He's pretty to look at, but his manners could use some improvement. He didn't even have the courtesy to say good-bye."

"He's a spoiled brat." Derek watched Creighton shoot his cuffs as he waited for the elevator. "Have you deposited Doug Wheeler's check?"

"Not yet."

"Good. We're sending it back."

She looked at him with surprise. "Really? Why? Because his kid is a brat?"

Derek slid his hands into his pants pockets and stared thoughtfully at Creighton as he stepped aboard the elevator. "Because 'What we've got here is . . . failure to communicate.' "

CHAPTER

10

CREIGHTON WAS GOOD AND PISSED AT DEREK MITCHELL, which was all the more reason not to let the F. Lee Bailey wannabe spoil his plans for the evening. He had talked himself into a buoyant mood by the time he entered the trendy club that evening. Christy's was a noisy, happening place, thronged with the after-dinner crowd not quite ready to call it a night.

The drinks were outrageously overpriced, and for the most part pastel. The club didn't attract drinkers who liked their beer from a bottle and their liquor neat. Instead it drew crowds of people wanting to impress and to be impressed.

The men were Atlanta's up-and-coming, and the women beautiful enough never to have to buy their own drinks. It was a well-dressed, well-heeled assemblage devoted to the pursuit of wealth, power, and the perfect tan. As Creighton walked in, he did so knowing that he possessed what they all strove for.

As he wended his way to the bar, he drew the attention of several women who telegraphed their availability. He looked them over and considered the prospects of each. But he passed them by. Tonight, he was in search of someone in particular. He would know her when he saw her.

Standing at the bar, he ordered a club soda and lime. The music pulsed. Conversation was frequently punctuated by shrieks of laughter. On any other night, the carnival midway atmosphere would have annoyed him, but tonight he could tolerate it, perhaps even enjoy it. Derek Mitchell notwithstanding.

Who did that smooth-talking asshole think he was, refusing him as a client? He had too many other clients? He was too busy? *Please.* He was nothing but a glorified ambulance chaser.

From the law office Creighton had gone to the country club for a hard tennis match with his coach, then went home and ordered in Thai for dinner. He ate off a tray while watching the DVD his mother had replaced after ruining his first copy. Her opinion of the movie was spot-on—it was awful. An inane vehicle for an equally inane starlet with a butterfly tattooed on her ass. Of the two, the butterfly was the one with talent.

He'd got only halfway through before switching it for an old Brian De Palma thriller in which the girl in peril gets drilled. Literally. With an electric drill. Very bloody and a little heavy on the deflowering symbolism, but the scene had respectable impact that had earned it a cult following all over the world. Two thumbs up for grisliness.

Then he'd showered and dressed to go out. So here he was, wearing his new Brioni suit, looking good, and with studied nonchalance, waiting for his leading lady of the evening to make her appearance.

It didn't take long. He was only halfway through his club soda when he noticed her at the far end of the bar, where she was trying to snag the attention of one of the busy bartenders.

She was slight in build and had straight blond hair, not unlike the whore who had gone down on him last night. Her hair shimmered in the subdued lighting as she shook her head in exasperation when a bartender failed to notice her and took someone else's order instead.

Creighton willed her to look in his direction. He liked the idea of her seeking him out before he approached her. As though she was responding to a summons, her gaze trailed down until she spied Creighton, leaning negligently and elegantly against the bar, staring at her as though he was captivated by a vision.

Little did she know that it was the other way around.

He raised his glass and arched one eyebrow in silent query. She hesitated, then nodded. Deliberately, slowly, never breaking eye contact, he made his way toward her. When he reached her, he said nothing at first, letting his eyes do the talking for him. He looked into her face as though visually eating it up. Women loved that.

Then he leaned toward her to make himself heard. " 'Of all the gin joints, in all the towns, in all the world, she walks into mine.' "

She blinked several times, looking apprehensive and confused. "Excuse me?"

Not a Bogie fan. Too bad. "What would you like?"

"Apple martini?"

She put a question mark at the end of it, as though fearful that he might have wanted her to order something else. From this he instantly drew two conclusions. One, she was playing out of her league. And, two, she knew it. Excellent.

As the bartender whizzed past, Creighton loudly snapped his fingers. "An apple martini for the lady."

"Got it," the bartender shouted over his shoulder as he hustled off.

Creighton then turned his full attention back to her.

"So that's how it's done." She snapped her fingers.

"That's one way."

"It wouldn't work with me. I don't have that air of authority that you do."

He looked her over from head to foot, then, with the perfect amount of insolence, drawled, "You don't need it."

She blushed prettily and modestly. She was wearing a slim black skirt, the kind of basic article that would come with a business suit from a moderately priced store where young professional women on a budget would shop.

She probably had removed the matching jacket when she got off work. The red satin tank top underneath had been discreet enough for the office but looked foxier now worn sans jacket and bra, no doubt taken off in the ladies' room and stuffed into her knockoff designer bag.

Office worker by day, by night she morphed into a hunter on the prowl for Prince Charming. She probably scrimped on lunch in order to finance the accoutrements with which to bait her trap—hair tints, makeup, stiletto heels, costume jewelry. In Creighton's opinion, what she did was practice an acceptable form of prostitution. But, fortunately for him, she was looking as though the man of her dreams had just stepped into her snare. Beneath the tacky blouse, her little nipples were tight with excitement.

"What's your name?" he asked.

"Ariel."

"Ariel. Beautiful."

"Thank you."

Leaning closer, he whispered, "The name, too."

She blushed. "What's your name?"

He told her, and she laughed. "I never heard that name before."

"Family name. You can cut it short and call me Tony."

"Hello, Tony," she said cheekily.

Her drink was delivered. He passed it to her, and she took a sip. "Is it all right?" he asked.

"Delicious, thanks."

"You're welcome."

"Aren't you ordering anything?"

He raised the glass he'd carried over with him.

"Vodka and tonic?"

"Club soda."

"You don't drink?"

"No."

"Never?"

He shook his head.

"Religious reasons?"

He flashed a wide grin. "Hardly."

"Then how come?"

"I don't like suppressants."

Looking up at him through her eyelashes, she asked, "What about stimulants?"

"I don't need them."

The verbal foreplay was almost too easy. Before he grew entirely bored, he asked her where she worked.

Even after she'd chatted about it for five minutes, he still didn't know precisely what she did at a company that sounded positively depressing. He tuned her out while he took in the details of her appearance. Upon closer inspection, he noticed a slight overbite, but it was fetching in its way. Her nose and cheekbones were sprinkled with freckles, which she tried to cover with powder. Her eyes were a nice shade of brown. Sherry-colored.

She drained her glass, and he signaled for another. She asked, "What about you, Tony? Where do you work?"

He laughed softly and leaned into her, letting his thigh brush against hers. "Nowhere."

"No, seriously."

"I don't work anywhere."

She took in his clothes, his wristwatch. "You seem to be doing all right."

"In truth, I'm filthy rich. Along with the ungodly family name comes an ungodly amount of family money. I consider it a fair swap."

She giggled. But when he didn't join her laughter, and she realized that he was stating a fact, her jaw dropped. "Seriously?"

"Seriously" again. Okay, so she was no genius. Even better.

The second martini arrived. She appraised him over the rim of the glass as she sipped from it.

He smiled. "Like me better now that you know I'm rich?"

"I liked you before."

He could tell she was plotting her strategy. Her curiosity was running rampant, but she wasn't going to let it get the better of her, so she moved the conversation away from his financial status as though it was of no importance.

"Since you don't work, what do you do?"

"I play a lot of tennis, but movies are my passion. Films, directors, writers, actors."

"Oh, God. I love all that stuff, too!"

"You do?"

"I think *Us Weekly* covers the red carpet events best. But I like *People,* too, especially when they do their best and worst Oscar gowns issue. What's your favorite movie? Mine's *Sex and the City* or maybe *Bride Wars.*"

Good God. "Seriously?"

It took her fifteen minutes to finish the second martini, during which she engaged him in meaningless dialogue while becoming more familiar physically. Her method was well practiced but detectable. She touched his hand each time she made a point. She spoke softly, forcing him to move nearer in order to hear her, until they were so close that one of those pert nipples periodically grazed his biceps.

It was time to move events along.

"Another?"

She shook back her hair, exposing her neck and chest. "Better not. Tomorrow is a workday." Playfully she nudged his leg with her knee. "For most of us."

"That's too bad. I was about to ask if you'd like to go somewhere else. Someplace where we don't have to shout to be heard."

Her eyes flickered with uncertainty. "Hmm, I . . ."

"No?"

"Well . . ."

"No need to explain." He touched her arm with understanding. "You don't know me."

Her eyes skittered away, then came back. "Where? I mean, where would you want to go?"

"You say. I don't care. I just want to prolong the evening." He clasped her hand. "Look, we can go in separate cars. I'll take my Porsche and you—"

"You have a Porsche?"

"Which I promise to take you for a ride in sometime soon. Just not tonight." Locking gazes, he said, "I don't want you to be afraid, although I completely understand why you would be. You hear things on the news."

"It's not that so much. It's . . . I'm a little jumpy because there's this guy. He calls my house a lot. Sorta creeps me out."

"Does he say obscene things?"

"No. Just holds on until I hang up."

"The police can trace those calls, find out who it is."

"Oh, I know who it is," she said quickly. "It's a guy I used to know. He caused some trouble." She made a motion with her hand, trying to belittle the importance of the trouble. "He's history."

Leaning in and squeezing her hand tighter, he snarled, "Want me to beat him up for you?"

She laughed. "No. He's not worth the bother, believe me."

"Well, you're right to be cautious." He dropped her hand. "Don't worry about it. We'll do it another time. If you come here often, we're sure to bump into one another again." He turned to signal the waiter for his tab.

She took the bait as he'd known she would. Quickly she laid her hand on his arm as though afraid he would vanish and her chance would be lost forever. "There's a café near my house. It's a greasy spoon, but it's open late. We could meet there for one cup of coffee."

He graced her with his best smile. "Sounds perfect."

"I need to go to the ladies' room first."

"I'll be right here."

Now that she'd made up her mind, she was eager and anxious to please. She squirmed through the crowd, making her way toward the restrooms. Just before disappearing into the hallway where they were located, she turned back and gave him a little wave.

Raising his chin in acknowledgment, he smothered a chuckle. She couldn't believe her good fortune. She was probably pinching herself, cautioning herself not to blow it, critically checking her reflection in the mirror and making adjustments, using breath spray.

Five minutes passed, and she still wasn't back.

To help pass the time, he faced the bar so he could gaze at his reflection in the tinted mirror behind it. The suit was a knockout. The time on the tennis court that afternoon had added a glow to his complexion and highlighted the blond streaks in his hair. No wonder her nipples had been so reactive.

He gave himself a complacent smile.

Which collapsed the instant he spotted Julie Rutledge.

There were several yards of bar between them, and numerous people, but her eyes were fixed on his in the mirror. Having caught him admiring his reflection, she smirked and turned away, heading for the exit.

"*Fuck!*" He turned from the bar, rudely pushed aside a yuppie, an anorexic girl, and a couple who were so into each other they were practically mating. He was mindful of nothing but Julie, who was making her way through the crowd more nimbly than he.

She was handing the parking valet her claim ticket when Creighton caught up to her. "Excuse us," he said to the valet. Wrapping his hand around her arm, he pulled her aside and backed her into the ivy-covered exterior wall.

His manhandling made her spitting mad. "Let go of me."

He did, but in a voice kept under control, he said, "Go ahead, Julie, make a scene. Yell for the police, why don't you? When they get here I can tell them that you're stalking me."

"Don't bully me, Creighton. You don't want the police hearing what I have to tell them about you."

"Which is?"

"How much you hated Paul."

"Sorry to disappoint you, but they already know. I told them myself."

"I know you were behind his murder."

He laughed. "You have a real flair for fiction. Have you ever considered writing scripts? Was it that fertile imagination of yours that held my dear uncle so in thrall? Or was it the way you tongued his balls?"

Seething, she held his stare as she slowly backed away from him. "Paul wasn't fooled."

"Fooled?"

"He knew your true character."

"Is that right?"

"And so do I."

"I hate to dispute you, Julie, when you're showing such admirable spunk. But in the words of Jeremy Irons as Claus von Bülow in *Reversal of Fortune,* 'You have *no* idea.' "

Maggie stood up and growled. Seconds later Derek's doorbell rang. He looked at the clock on his desk. "Who the hell?"

He'd come home, bringing a carryout dinner with him. He ate it while catching the first few innings of the Braves' game on TV, then went into his home office, where he'd been working for the rest of the evening. It would take him several days to bring himself up to speed on everything that had transpired while he was away, and he got more done at home after hours than he did in the office when his attention was in high demand.

Barefoot, wearing only gym shorts and an old T-shirt, he went through the house, turning on lights. He wasn't expecting company, and certainly wasn't expecting the person he saw through the peephole of his front door.

He undid the lock and opened the door. "What the hell are you doing here?"

Creighton Wheeler brushed past him and strode in. "I want you to get her off my back. I don't care how much it costs, or what strings you have to pull, or what hoops you have to jump through. Do whatever you have to, just get her to leave me the fuck alone."

"Come in," Derek said caustically as he swung shut his front door.

"She's gone beyond finger-pointing and name-calling."

"First of all, who is 'she'? Roberta Kimball?"

"Julie Rutledge," Creighton said, enunciating. "At first it was just insulting remarks dropped here and there. She's moved past that—" He broke off and warily regarded Maggie, who was still growling. "She won't bite, will she?"

Derek ordered his dog to sit. She'd responded to the anger in his voice, but it was his unexpected guest, not Maggie, who'd made him mad as hell. "Where do you get off, coming to my house at this time of night, storming in here? You've got your gall."

"And a lot of money."

Derek closed the distance between them and jabbed his finger toward Creighton's face. "Which entitles you to *nothing*. Certainly not the right to barge in on me at home. I will not represent you. I don't know how to make it any clearer."

Creighton assumed that arrogant stance that had caused Derek to despise him on sight. Derek didn't quail, and eventually something in his angry demeanor must have penetrated. Gradually, Creighton took several steps backward. He patted the space between them with both hands. "All right, all right. I'm sorry I didn't call ahead of time. That was rude. But it was imperative that I speak with you."

"Then you should have called my office and made an appointment during business hours."

"Would you have seen me?"

"No."

Creighton made a gesture that said, *Exactly*.

"I said everything I had to say to you this afternoon."

"When we met this afternoon, Julie Rutledge wasn't stalking me."

"*Stalking* you?"

"That's right. She's lost her reason. She must be suffering from post-traumatic stress caused by the shooting. Something. I don't know. I wouldn't care except that she's focused her craziness on me. She's accusing me of taking some part in that cock-up robbery when my uncle got shot. Yes, she actually said, 'I know you were behind his murder.' "

Julie had deceived Derek, but he didn't believe her to be unreasonable, suffering from PTSD, or crazy. In fact, quite the opposite. But he wasn't supposed to know her personally. He said, "She didn't appear to be deranged when I saw her on television."

Creighton seemed not to hear that. "I'm going to get a restraining order against her. Or rather, you are."

"I beg your pardon?"

"Tomorrow. I want you to go to a judge, or whatever it is you do to get a restraining order. In the frame of mind she's in, God knows what she's likely to do. I don't want her anywhere near me. Get a restraining order, so she can be arrested if she invades my privacy."

"It's not that easy, Creighton."

"The harder it is, the more money you'll make, so what are you worried about?"

Derek was worried that he might yet knock this rich son of a bitch on his ass for thinking that anything—including Derek Mitchell—was attainable if you threw enough money at it. But slugging him wouldn't accomplish anything except possibly getting himself sued, so he exercised amazing self-control and asked, "What set you off? What happened? What gave you the impression that Ms. Rutledge is a danger to your person?"

To demonstrate that he was prepared to listen, Derek backed

into a chair and sat down. Maggie parked herself at his feet and kept a suspicious eye on the man in the impeccably tailored cream-colored suit as he paced the entryway and told Derek about an encounter with Julie Rutledge at a nightclub called Christy's.

When he finished, Derek asked, "What was she doing there?"

"Haven't you been listening? She was stalking me."

"Was she with anyone?"

"I don't know. I don't believe so." Creighton's fingers were flexing and extending at his sides, revealing his impatience. "What the fuck difference does it make whether she was alone or not? I caught her staring at me in the mirror. I won't have her trailing me. You've got to do something about it."

"Wrong. I don't." Calmly Derek folded his arms over his chest. "You and Julie Rutledge happened to see each other in a popular bar. A chance encounter—"

"Chance, my ass."

"A chance meeting in a public place does not stalking make."

"She followed me there."

Derek raised one shoulder. "Possibly."

"Definitely."

"Do you have proof of that?"

"Of course not, I just know."

"She's followed you before?"

"I haven't seen her, but that doesn't mean she wasn't hiding in the background."

It was all Derek could do to keep a straight face. "Hiding in the background? Like behind the shrubbery? Why would she want to spy on you, Creighton?"

"Because she's delusional."

"Have you seen her lurking around your place? Your Porsche? Your tennis locker?" Derek saw that Creighton didn't like his intentional gibes.

"You think this is funny?" he asked tightly.

Derek dropped the nonsense and came to his feet. "If Julie Rutledge starts calling you in the middle of the night issuing death threats, or begins sending you dire messages through the mail, or boils a bunny in your spaghetti pot . . ." He paused, waiting for

Creighton to comment. When he didn't, he said, "That was a movie reference."

"I got it," Creighton said in that taut voice that barely moved his lips.

"If she starts doing things like that, *then* would be the time to apply for a restraining order."

"You would handle it?"

With reluctance, and only because he was tired and wanted Creighton Wheeler out of his house, Derek said, "I would consider it."

Creighton didn't look happy, but he appeared mollified, certainly calmer. "All right then. Good. I'll be in touch."

Derek went to the front door and opened it. As Creighton walked past him, Derek caught his shoulder and turned the younger man to face him. "I don't care how much money you've got, don't ever, *ever,* come to my house again."

Creighton snuffled a laugh. "Or what?"

"Or I'll hurt you."

Creighton flashed his most handsome smile. "Promise?" Then he blew Derek an air kiss and sauntered toward his Porsche parked at the curb.

CHAPTER
11

A DOYENNE OF ATLANTA SOCIETY PASSED JULIE AN ENVELOPE. "Here's your tax receipt. You can fill in the amount of the market value of the painting. What should be the floor of the bidding?"

Chez Jean had donated a painting to be auctioned that night at a charity event to raise money for a new children's cancer hospital. "One of her earlier works sold last week in Sausalito for seventy-two hundred."

"Let's make the floor five thousand."

"I hope it'll bring a lot more."

"I'm sure it will." The older woman assessed the painting with a discerning eye. "I intend to bid on it myself."

Julie smiled. "Good luck." She went on to explain how she planned to get the painting to the venue. Kate was discussing the merits of a work with another customer, an elderly gentleman who frequently stopped in but had never actually purchased anything. Julie suspected that he made his rounds of local shops in search of company rather than merchandise, but she and Kate enjoyed his visits. He never outstayed his welcome.

When the chime above the gallery door announced a new arrival, Julie turned, ready to greet a customer. Instead, Detectives Kimball and Sanford came in, and if they'd been outfitted in riot gear they couldn't have looked more like police officers. Their bearing was official. Everyone fell silent and stared.

"Good morning," Julie said pleasantly.

The two responded appropriately.

"I'll be right with you."

"Take your time," said Kimball, who seemed more at ease than Sanford, although Julie suspected that the female detective's nonchalance was a pose. Roberta Kimball didn't strike her as someone who frequented art galleries.

Julie turned back to the society matron. "I'll stay after the event and crate the painting for the new buyer to ensure it won't be damaged in transit."

"That would be lovely." Her wrinkled face took on a sad aspect as she patted Julie's hand. "I know this is a terrible time for you, dear." She cast a glance at the two detectives, who were studying the artworks—or pretending to. "Paul was a wonderful person. I still can't believe he died in such a horrible manner."

With that, the woman left. The elderly gentleman kissed Kate on the cheek and made his departure.

"Looks like we've cleared the room," Kimball said. "Sorry about that."

"You didn't cost us a sale. What brings you?"

The two detectives looked toward Kate, who was standing nearby, seeming uncertain of what she should do. Julie made introductions, which were followed by an awkward silence.

Kate asked, "Would anyone like an espresso?"

"I would, thanks," Kimball said. Sanford declined.

"We'll be in the parlor," Julie told Kate, who excused herself to get the refreshment.

Julie showed them the way. At this same time yesterday, she'd been sharing the parlor with Derek Mitchell. She wondered if she would ever go into the room again without thinking of him. Doubtful. He seemed to have left his essence, which assailed her as the three of them filed in.

The detectives sat down on the short sofa. Julie took a chair facing them. Sanford began by holding up a manila envelope. "We have more pictures."

"Of the same man?"

Kimball nodded. "We've got him passing through the lobby the two days prior to the crime. One of the pictures is a pretty good shot."

"May I see?"

Sanford opened the envelope, withdrew several eight-by-ten glossies, and passed them to Julie. "The top one is the best."

Kate came in bearing a small tray with a demitasse cup of espresso for Kimball. She served it while Julie studied the photograph. It was superior to the one she'd seen the day before, but not by much. It was grainy and out of focus. She flipped through the others, but as Sanford had said, the top one was the best of the lot.

"It's definitely the same man in all of them," she said.

Kimball sipped her espresso and gave Kate a nod of thanks.

"Unmistakably the same man," Julie continued. "But I've never seen him before."

Sanford's disappointment showed. "You're certain?"

"Positive. I don't know him."

Sanford sat back, stretched his arms out along the back of the sofa. He looked at Kate. "I'd take a glass of water if you've got it."

Kate, who was looking over Julie's shoulder at the photograph, jumped to obey. "Certainly. Julie?"

"No thank you."

The young woman went out, leaving Julie alone with the two detectives, who were studying her with a concentration similar to that with which Derek Mitchell had studied the painting of the naked fat man.

"What is it?" she asked.

"Walk us through it again," Sanford said.

"The holdup?"

"The whole thing. From the time you and Paul Wheeler left the suite."

She looked at Kimball, whose expression remained implacable. She'd finished her espresso and was sitting forward with her elbows on her knees. Sanford was still leaning back against the cushion. Both looked on full alert.

Julie patiently repeated her account. When she reached the point where she first saw the robber, she stopped. "Maybe if you'd tell me what you're particularly interested in, I could—"

"We don't want you to skip anything," Kimball said. "Keep going, please."

Julie waited while Kate came in and served Sanford his water, then picked up at her stopping point and talked them through the entirety of it, ending with the arrival of the paramedics. "Until they got there, no one was able to pull me away from Paul. I held him until I was forced to let go."

No one said anything for several moments. Sanford took a drink from his glass of water, then placed it on the table beside Kimball's empty demitasse cup. Kimball was the first to break the uncomfortable silence.

"We sent these new photos to the others. All have come back negative on an ID, same as you."

"The robber had on the mask, the sunglasses, the gloves. It would be impossible to match him to the man in these photographs."

"Right," Kimball said. "We didn't count on getting that lucky. But, while we had them on the phone, we had each of them talk through it again, just as we did you. And something the ladies said— both of them, independently—struck us. Something we either hadn't caught before or hadn't paid attention to."

Julie shifted her gaze to Sanford, but his liquid eyes gave nothing away. In the true spirit of their partnership, she suspected they had decided earlier that Kimball should take the lead this time round.

Looking back at her, Julie asked, "Well, what was it?"

"You didn't kneel. When the robber demanded that everybody drop to their knees, you remained standing."

"I knelt."

"But not right away. Why?" Kimball pressed. "Here's a masked man aiming a gun at you, yelling for you to drop. One of the women from Nashville admits to being so scared, she wet herself. She dropped to the floor immediately, afraid that if she didn't he would shoot her. Her friend did the same."

"The man from California—" Julie began.

Kimball cut her off. "Says he was too frozen with fear to move.

Then the robber poked the pistol at him and told him to get down, and he did. You didn't. They all say you defied him. You argued with him, told him that Wheeler had arthritic knees. It was ultimately he, Wheeler, who pulled you down beside him."

Sanford, finally becoming engaged, lowered his arms and sat forward, matching the posture of his partner. "Are you extraordinarily brave, Ms. Rutledge?"

"I've never considered myself to be, but my courage has never been tested to that extent. People react differently to mortal fear. I don't think we know how we'll react until we're placed in that kind of situation. I don't remember feeling particularly brave."

"What were you feeling?" Kimball asked.

She hesitated, then replied, "Resignation."

There was a short pause, then Sanford said, "You thought he'd kill you no matter what you did?"

She met the detective's incisive gaze, then looked at Kimball, who was watching her just as intently. "I knew he would. I knew the instant I saw him that the robbery was bogus. He was there to kill Paul and, I was sure, to kill me, too.

"If I didn't kneel down as soon as he ordered it, I think it was because I knew it wouldn't change the outcome. I was staring into the lenses of his sunglasses trying to see through them."

"In the hope of persuading him not to kill you?"

"No. To identify his eyes."

"Did you?"

She lowered her head, shaking it. "I was looking for Creighton."

"It wasn't him, Ms. Rutledge."

"I know that now."

The gallery phone rang. Julie heard Kate's muted French accent through the walls, "Chez Jean. I'm sorry, she's in a meeting just now."

She's being interrogated by the police. That would have been a more accurate statement. This interview had taken on the tone of an interrogation, and it was making her distinctly uneasy.

"Why is this important now? What difference does it make at what point I knelt?"

Sanford spoke in a low voice. "You say that, whether you had knelt or not, it wouldn't have changed the outcome."

"And it didn't."

"Paul Wheeler is dead, but you're still here."

"Stating the obvious," Julie said.

"Well, yeah, see that's why this could be significant," Sanford said.

Julie looked at them in turn. "Forgive me, Detectives. I'm still missing your point."

"Here's the point, Ms. Rutledge," Kimball said. "The case could be made that you didn't kneel when the robber ordered you to . . . because you knew you weren't in any danger from him."

Ariel Williams let herself into her house, glad that this day was almost over. She bolted the door behind her, locking out the world, happy for the sanctuary of home, where she was free to indulge her depression. Although she missed her roommate, Carol, who'd gone away for the remainder of the summer, she welcomed having the place to herself tonight.

She was office manager of an electrical products company that sold, installed, and serviced high-end lighting and security systems for commercial and residential clients. Everything coming into or out of the company crossed her desk first. It was her responsibility to route it to the proper department. She hadn't been in the job long, but already her competence had earned her the praise of her boss and the respect of her co-workers.

Ordinarily she loved the job. But today, each hour had been long and tedious, each task irritating. She'd counted the minutes until she could return home and get into bed with a carton of chocolate chip cookie dough ice cream. Last's night rejection deserved a whole gallon.

What a sap she'd been actually to believe that a gorgeous, rich guy like that would come on to her, the queen of self-doubt. He could have had his choice of any woman in that bar. How could she have thought he would choose *her* over all the sophisticated women in that place?

What a dimwit!

Yet when she'd left the ladies' room, she had fully expected him to be waiting at the bar for her where he'd said he would be. Even when she didn't immediately spot him, it didn't occur to her that she'd been abandoned. She figured he'd gone into the men's room. When after several minutes he still hadn't appeared, she went outside and described him to the parking valet, who was distracted and busy.

"Light-colored suit? Yeah, he was . . . Thank you, sir. Drive safely. Uh, he was here a minute ago."

"Did he retrieve his Porsche?"

"Porsche? We haven't had a Porsche tonight." He held up his hand to forestall her next question and emitted an earsplitting whistle to one of the other valets. "Hey, Greg, can you help these folks, please? He'll be right with you, ma'am. Sorry for the wait." Then back to Ariel. "He walked off with some chick."

He might as well have slapped her. "A woman? He was with a woman? Who?"

"You want your car, or what?"

She'd retrieved her car and driven home, feeling like the most gullible person ever to draw breath. As she passed the café where she had suggested they meet for coffee, she'd flushed with embarrassment. A man like him wouldn't have considered going to a dump like that.

She'd been an utter fool. How long had it taken him to split after she'd given him that jaunty little wave? Ten seconds? Five? It was humiliating to imagine how glad he must have been when she excused herself to go to the ladies' room, leaving him free to cut and run.

Now she dropped her handbag onto the floor and stepped over it as she headed for her bedroom, where she exchanged her work suit for her oldest, most comfortable pj's and swapped her high-heeled pumps for terry-cloth scruffs. She would not be going out tonight, and probably not tomorrow night, not even if friends called and invited her to a girls' night out. She just didn't have it in her to dress up, walk into a club, and make small talk. Her self-esteem, never all that robust, had been demolished.

In the kitchen, she removed a carton of ice cream from the

freezer, a spoon from the drawer, and carried them with her into her living room, where she curled up in the corner of the sofa and used the remote to turn on the TV.

She was so ashamed of her gullibility that she hadn't even shared last night's mishap with Carol, and they shared everything. She contemplated calling her now. A long talk with a best girlfriend over a half gallon of ice cream was the first step toward curing the blues.

But even as she reached for the telephone, it rang. She checked the caller ID. Although it said "Restricted" where the number should be, she knew who was calling. "Asshole."

Rather than answering the phone, she scooped up a big bite of ice cream and shoved it into her mouth. The phone stopped ringing. But only for several seconds. Then it started again. "Restricted."

It happened three more times before she snatched up the receiver. "Damn you! *Stop calling!*"

She'd thought he was gone for good. A bad memory best blocked.

The first time he'd called, she couldn't believe his nerve. As soon as he'd identified himself, she'd let him have it with both barrels, telling it like it was: He was a liar, a cheat, a criminal, and no woman in her right mind would let him near her. She'd told him to get lost and stay lost, and unless he wanted her to sic the police on him, he had better never call back.

But he had, and continued to.

He never threatened her. After the first few times, he never said anything at all. But his resentment reverberated in the silence, and the threat it implied was unnerving, especially now that she was alone in the house.

She wished she could afford her own company's security, but her budget wouldn't stand the strain of their most basic, no-frills system. However, to give her greater peace of mind while Carol was temporarily away, she'd had the door locks changed. Carol understood her caution and, saying it was better to be safe than sorry, had also agreed to split the cost of having special locks installed on all the windows. But tonight, that additional security didn't allay Ariel's nerves, which were already shot because of being dumped by the blond charmer. She didn't need this crap to upset her further.

Now that she'd opened up the floodgates of her frustration, she couldn't hold back. "You are truly pathetic, you know that? This is a chickenshit thing to do. Kids' stuff. You think of yourself as a ladies' man, but no real man would resort to heavy-breathing phone calls. Go back where you came from. Or go to hell. Just stop calling!" She slammed the phone down, feeling worlds better for having told him off.

Digging into the ice cream again, she reached a conclusion she thought was profound: Universally, whether a lowlife with a phone fetish or a smooth-talking rich guy, men were shits.

CHAPTER

12

JUST WHEN JULIE THOUGHT THIS DAY COULDN'T GET ANY WORSE, it did.

The main room of the community center where the charity function was being held had been decorated to resemble a sultan's tent. Bolts of brightly colored silk had been draped beneath the ceiling and gathered into the center, where a mirrored ball shone like a jewel. Waiters were dressed like Aladdin, their female counterparts like veiled belly dancers. Instead of flowers, centerpieces for the cocktail tables scattered about the room were made of peacock feathers.

Julie barely had time to appreciate the effect because, as she entered, the first person she recognized among the crowd was Derek Mitchell.

On his arm was a beautiful redhead in an emerald beaded gown. They made a striking pair. They were standing in a group of people, sipping from champagne flutes and chatting, when Derek caught Julie looking at them.

His smile settled. For several seconds they looked at each other. Was he wondering, as she was, why their paths were crossing now, when they never had before? Or maybe they had, and they just hadn't noticed each other. Although Julie thought that highly unlikely. If she had seen him before that morning at the boarding gate in de Gaulle Airport, she would have remembered.

The redhead said something to him, and he returned his attention to her.

Knowing that he was in the room was going to make what promised to be a long evening seem even longer. Unfortunately, Julie had committed herself to staying through to the bitter end, and beyond.

At least there wasn't a seated dinner to be endured, only a short program presented midway through the allotted time period when an architectural model for the new children's cancer hospital would be revealed, followed by a heart-wrenching video to emphasize the need and to appeal to those in attendance to donate generously. The painting Julie had donated to the silent auction was one of forty items, including lavish vacation packages, a luxury SUV, and a ten-carat diamond pendant.

"Hello, Julie."

Addressed from behind, she turned to see Doug and Sharon Wheeler. Doug gave her a quick hug. She and Sharon exchanged air kisses aimed at their cheeks. Sharon was in red chiffon, with canary diamonds at her throat and ears. "You look beautiful tonight," Julie said truthfully.

"Thank you. My feet already hurt." Sharon stuck her foot out from beneath her floor-length gown to show Julie her jeweled shoes.

"The shoes are worth the pain."

Sharon smiled, pleased. "I thought so, but ask me again after I've been standing in them for hours."

"I didn't expect to see you tonight," Doug said.

Paul had accepted the invitation for both of them just days before he died, but Julie refrained from telling them that. "I donated a painting to the auction." She nodded toward the area in the center of the room where the items were displayed in an oasis created by faux sand dunes and live palms.

"I hope you're not upset," Sharon said.

"About what?"

"The funeral." Her pretty face wrinkled with distress. "I hope you didn't take it as a snub. It just wasn't appropriate for you to sit with the family, Julie. Mary's sisters were there. Paul's nieces and nephews. It would have been awkward for everybody." She reached out and touched Julie's hand. "But I couldn't bear it if your feelings were hurt. Please say you understand."

"I understand you perfectly, Sharon."

The vacuous Sharon grinned with relief, but Doug had caught the meaning underlying Julie's words. He stared at the patterned carpet between his patent shoes, looking embarrassed by both the snub at the funeral and his wife's inability to recognize what an affront it had been.

Without Paul acting as the pivotal center of the group, they had no tether. Julie wondered what her relationship with them would be like in the future, or if she would continue to have any relationship at all.

"Is Creighton with you?" She posed the question casually even though it nearly choked her to speak his name.

"He begged off," Sharon said. "He'd made plans with friends."

To Julie's knowledge Creighton didn't have any friends. He had paid companions—a masseur, his tennis coach, a golf pro with whom he played. Paul had told her that he sometimes picked up women for one-night stands, but that he'd never had a girlfriend in the traditional sense. He was a recurring customer of notable madams, Paul had told her.

His movie characters count for friends, I suppose, Paul had said with annoyance during one of their conversations about Creighton. *They're always with him. They live inside his head. I think he carries on conversations with them.*

Creighton had people who were hired to keep him amused. He had his fantasy world. But he couldn't boast of having friends.

That was just another of Sharon's self-delusions. It had become clear to Julie soon after she'd met them that either Sharon was unaware of her son's true personality or she suffered from a dire case of denial.

"Have you talked to Sanford and Kimball recently?" Doug asked.

"Doug, this is a social occasion," Sharon complained in a whining voice. "Our first since . . . you know. Can't we go one night without talking about it?"

"Forgive me, Sharon," Julie said. Then to Doug, "I spoke with them as recently as this morning. They came to the gallery with the latest set of photographs of this man they're calling a person of interest."

"Ever seen him before?"

"No."

"Same here. The detectives came to my office. I told them I didn't know him from Adam. They asked me to take the pictures home and show them to Sharon."

"He was a stranger to me," she said.

"Creighton?" Julie asked.

"He hasn't seen them yet. Not to my knowledge." Doug sipped his highball, a bit nervously Julie thought.

She said, "They're going on TV with the clearest of the photos."

"So they told me. Starting with the evening news tonight, I believe." Doug consulted his wristwatch. "We'll miss it."

"The police hope someone will recognize the man and come forward with a name," Julie said.

"I have little doubt someone will. Probably a guest of the hotel. 'Oh, that's my cousin so-and-so. He dropped by every day I was in Atlanta.' " Doug took another swallow of his drink.

"And then what?" Julie asked rhetorically.

"Your guess is as good as mine. Beyond that fuzzy photograph, they've got no leads."

Sharon, who'd been busily scanning the crowd and only half-following their conversation, threaded her arm through Doug's. "I think that diamond pendant has my name on it."

"Uh-oh."

"Don't you want to help kids with cancer?"

"Julie, if I'm not back in fifteen minutes, please come rescue me and my credit card." Doug said it with a smile, but Julie knew he was grateful for a reason to end their discussion about the police investigation.

"Stay after him to get you that diamond, Sharon. The cause needs the money."

"I'll do my part," Sharon said gaily.

They left Julie standing alone, but she wasn't without company for long. Over the next hour, friends and acquaintances approached her, some seemingly determined not to mention Paul's name, others talking of nothing else. With some she had a brief exchange before they politely excused themselves, looking relieved that an unpleasant duty had been accomplished.

Others acted as though they wanted to take her on as a pet project and make certain that she didn't sit at home alone just because she no longer had an escort. They talked of future lunches and dinners, wine tastings, even a bicycling tour of Tuscany. She pretended an interest in all, but made a commitment to none.

If she hadn't promised to oversee the sale of the painting, Julie would have left. She hated being an object of curiosity or pity. She was weary of people watching her to see how well or how badly she was handling the sudden loss of Paul. Given the circumstances, she could have begged off and skipped the event entirely. No one would have blamed her.

But as she moved through the crowd toward the area where the painting was displayed, she knew her decision to come had been the right one. Following her meeting with the detectives this morning, she mustn't alter her routine, curb her activities, or do anything that would make it appear she had something to hide.

Kimball's implication had left her momentarily speechless. Then she'd stammered, "Are you . . . are you implying that I . . . I knew the robber? That I knew what was going to happen? That I had something to do with it?"

"Don't get excited," Kimball had said in a patronizing tone that was infuriating. "The idea has been advanced, that's all."

"Who advanced it?"

"Another detective, someone not as close to the case as we are. He doesn't really know you. Anyway, Sanford and I dismissed his theory, but it's our job to explore every possibility, no matter how far-fetched."

Not for a moment had Julie bought the blasé explanation. She'd told them straightaway that she wouldn't say anything more without an attorney present and asked them to leave.

How could they even consider that she would want Paul dead? It was a preposterous notion. Also a frustrating one. Because each minute they spent exploring this false theory was one not spent on pursuing the culprit. While they had a magnifying glass on her, Creighton was living his life with impunity, getting away with murder.

"What's the current bid?"

The familiar voice yanked her away from her dark thoughts, and she turned quickly. Derek Mitchell was standing directly in front of her, ostensibly looking at the painting when actually his eyes were on her. He was alone.

"Eight thousand."

He whistled softly. "Getting up there."

"Are you interested?"

"I have a bare spot in my bedroom."

There were a dozen implications in that statement, and none of them escaped Julie. Looking beyond his shoulder, she could see the redhead in animated conversation with several other people. Derek followed her gaze, then came back around. Julie said, "Maybe you should consult her before you place a bid. What if she doesn't like it?"

"Mine is the only opinion that counts. But I welcome yours."

Julie, unable to maintain eye contact, stared into the black enamel studs of his tuxedo shirt. "It's a nice painting by a promising young artist."

"May I?" He placed his hand on her waist and gently moved her aside so he could get to the table in order to write down his bid. Even after he'd removed his hand, she felt the heat of his touch. She picked up a pen and handed it to him. He bent over the table to write down his bid.

"Hi." It was the redhead. "You're Julie Rutledge."

"That's right."

The woman was even more resplendent up close. She introduced herself, although later Julie couldn't recall her name because at the time she was too aware of Derek Mitchell's closeness and the imprint of his hand on her waist. She was discomfited by it, and hated him for having that effect on her. She hated herself more.

"I knew Paul Wheeler," the redhead was saying. "We served on a committee together a couple years ago. He was a real gentleman."

"Yes, he was."

"My condolences." The woman smiled at her kindly.

"Thank you."

Derek passed the pen back to Julie. She clutched it. It was warm from his grasp. "Don't give the pen to anybody else," he said, smiling down at her. "I'd really like to have that painting."

"You can always raise your bid."

"I'll be monitoring it closely throughout the evening." He and the redhead excused themselves and moved along.

Julie had barely caught her breath when Doug sidled up to her. "When did you meet Derek Mitchell?"

She played dumb. "Who?"

"The man you were talking to. The lawyer."

Julie glanced toward Derek and the redhead. "That's Derek Mitchell? I didn't exactly meet him."

"You looked friendly."

"He bid on the painting."

Doug leaned past her to read what Derek had bid. "Jesus. I guess he could afford to turn us down."

Julie also read his bid and gasped when she saw that he'd tripled the amount of the standing one. She turned in time to see his wide shoulders disappearing into the crowd. Continuing the dumb act, she said, "What do you mean he turned you down?"

"After careful consideration—or so he said—he decided he couldn't represent us."

"Did he say why?"

"He said he was too busy."

"Oh."

"But he was lying."

No one topped Derek Mitchell's bid for the painting. When the winning bidders for all the items were announced at the end of the evening, the crowd applauded him, which he acknowledged with a modest wave. The redhead went up on tiptoe and kissed his cheek.

Soon after those announcements were made, there was a stampede for the doors. Julie moved in the opposite direction. An employee of the facility helped her carry the painting to a utility room, where she replaced it in the crate designed for transporting it safely.

Fortunately, a courier had been hired to deliver all the auction items that couldn't be carried out by their new owners, relieving Julie of having to deliver the painting personally to Derek Mitchell.

By the time she passed through the main room, the only people left were the cleanup crew, who were busily disassembling the make-believe setting. No one remained in the large reception area of the building, or in the corridor that took her past empty meeting rooms toward the elevator bank that served the parking garage, where upon arrival she'd parked herself in lieu of waiting in the long line for a valet.

She got a case of butterflies as she approached the elevator and punched the Up button. When the empty elevator arrived, she hesitated before stepping into it. But she did so, telling herself she was being silly. She couldn't go the rest of her life avoiding elevators.

Nevertheless, her heart was thudding when the elevator reached the level of the garage where she'd left her car and the double doors slid open. There was no one there. Certainly no one in dark glasses and a ski mask with a shark woven into it.

She stepped out and headed for the ramp. The ceiling was low, the lights dim; there was no one else about, so her footsteps sounded extraordinarily loud.

Then she heard a metallic click. She stopped and turned in the direction from which the sound had come. That corner of the garage was completely dark and partially concealed by a concrete pillar, large enough for a man to hide behind.

Large enough to hide the man who flicked the cigarette lighter on, briefly letting the flame burn before flipping down the lid and extinguishing it.

Julie instantly realized that she'd been cast in the role of damsel in distress. "Isn't this scene a bit cliché, even for you, Creighton?" Her voice echoed in the vast, empty space. "It's been in too many movies to count. A victim alone in a dark and deserted parking garage? Come on," she scoffed. "It's unworthy of you."

The lighter flicked on again, burned for several seconds, went off with a snick of metal against metal.

It was an ordinary action, yet the setup lent it a creepiness that was effective. She didn't believe that Creighton would leap out of the darkness and attack her. He was only trying to frighten her, paying her back for showing up at the bar last night, punishing her for catching him admiring his reflection in the mirror. He was merely staging a scary scene to rattle her.

Or was he?

Thus far, he'd got away with having Paul killed. That might have made him feel invincible. Creighton was already confident that rules didn't apply to him; the success of Paul's murder might have made him reckless, willing, even eager to do his own killing rather than to have someone do it for him.

And, he had every reason to want her dead.

Suddenly she was very afraid. She unlocked her car with the keyless remote and got in quickly, locking the driver's door as soon as she'd closed it. The roar of her car's engine reverberated against the concrete surfaces. Her tires squealed as she backed out and headed for the exit. She drove past the dark corner without even deigning to look in that direction, but out of the corner of her eye, she saw the small blue and yellow flame flashing on, off, on, off in a taunting sequence.

She took the spiraling lane down to the street level with such speed she was dizzy when she stopped to pay the attendant. As she pulled onto the boulevard, she watched her rearview mirror. No one followed.

Her hands were cold but sweaty as she clutched the steering wheel. Her shoulders burned with tension. Creighton would enjoy knowing he'd rattled her. But he didn't know, did he? She hadn't played his silly game. She'd mocked him, then left. Hastily, yes, but, she believed, without giving an outward appearance of being afraid. He couldn't have known how much he'd unnerved her, and there was satisfaction to be found in that.

But when she got home, she discovered that the joke was on her after all.

Her first indication that something was wrong was when her garage door opener failed to work. She left her car in the driveway and used her key to go in through the front door. When she flipped on the light switch, nothing happened. But the power outage was restricted to her house; lights were on in her neighbors' homes.

She felt her way to the hall table, where she kept a small flashlight in the drawer. The battery was still good, but the beam was weak and she didn't see the bench before she bumped into it, causing her to stumble.

Usually the bench was positioned lengthwise against the wall opposite the table. Now it stood crosswise in the center of the foyer.

The electricity being off was one thing. Having a piece of furniture out of place was another. She was absolutely certain she hadn't moved it there.

Had the house been burglarized? Worse, was the thief still inside? Her instinct was to turn and run out through the front door while calling 911 on her cell phone.

But she ordered herself to remain calm. Before jumping to conclusions or giving way to hysterics, she stood stock-still and listened for any sound. She heard nothing other than the cottony thud of her pulse against her eardrums.

Nudging the bench aside with her knee and moving forward cautiously, she shone the flashlight into the living room and then into the dining room, but nothing appeared to have been disturbed in either of those rooms. Everything seemed to be in place. They certainly hadn't been ransacked.

Aiming the light down at the floor, she noted that the fringe at each end of the runner beneath her feet lay straight, untouched since her maid had raked it. The likelihood of an intruder leaving the rug fringe undisturbed was highly remote.

"Damn you." The whispered curse was meant for Creighton. He'd done this to her. He'd made her afraid in her own house. He'd made her scared of an ordinary bench, when it was almost certain that her housekeeper had moved it while she swept the hall today and simply forgotten to return it to its proper place.

Using the beam of the flashlight to guide her, she made her way to her bedroom. On the threshold, she hesitated and swept the light across the room. Seeing nothing amiss, she went in and was moving toward the closet when she heard a sound from the front of the house.

All the reassurances she'd given herself were banished by a resurgence of fear.

She switched off the flashlight and dropped to the floor. In total darkness she crawled to the side of the bed and blindly groped beneath it for the pistol that Paul had secured to the underside of the box springs with duct tape.

She found it and tugged until the gun came free. Feeling blindly, she ripped off the stubborn tape. The revolver felt heavy and cold in her hand, foreign, deadly. *It's loaded, but as a safety precaution, I've left two chambers empty,* Paul had told her. She could hear him stressing to her that she would have to pull the trigger three times before the pistol would fire a bullet.

Her skin broke out in a cold sweat. She breathed in insufficient pants. The fear she'd experienced in the parking garage was compounded a thousand times, now that she realized her home had been breached. She understood just how vulnerable she was.

Pressing her lips together, she forced herself to breathe through her nose so her raspy breaths couldn't be heard. Her heart was hammering as she scooted across the floor on her bottom until she had backed into the corner. Holding the pistol with both hands, she aimed it at the doorway just as a silhouette appeared in the opening, a darker shadow against dimmer ones.

"Stay where you are!"

Unmindful of her shouted warning, the figure stepped into the room.

She pulled the trigger.

CHAPTER

13

THE EMPTY CHAMBER CLICKED LOUDLY.

"Julie?"

"I mean it!"

He took a step forward. She pulled the trigger again. Another portentous click.

"The next time, you'll die!"

"Julie, it's me."

She gulped a sob of relief. Shakily, she lowered the pistol to the floor and released her grip on it, then drew her knees to her chest and lay her head on them.

"Are you all right?" Derek followed the sound of her gasping breaths to the corner and hunkered down beside her. He touched the back of her head. "Are you hurt?"

"No."

"Your front door was standing open. Why are all the lights out? What happened?"

She burbled a near hysterical laugh. "I nearly shot you."

"Why are you in the dark?"

"No electricity."

"Where's your fuse box?"

"In the closet. Behind you, on the right. I dropped a flashlight on the floor somewhere near the door."

Unfamiliar with the room, he bumped his way across it. He found the flashlight. Its beam danced crazily around the room as he moved toward the closet. She heard the rattle of clothes hangers, the creak of the metal door on the fuse box. Moments later, the lights came on. The sudden brightness stabbed her eyes, and it took a moment for them to adjust. By the time they had, Derek was kneeling beside her again.

"The breaker switch had flipped. Probably a power surge."

"I guess."

He saw the pistol. "You really did almost shoot me."

"I really did."

"Are you hurt?" he asked again.

She answered by shaking her head.

"Want to tell me what's going on?"

"I came home. The lights were out. I . . . I freaked out." She told him about the bench in the foyer. "I thought I might have walked in on a burglar and he was still here."

"Why didn't you leave and call the police?"

"I'm glad I didn't. I feel foolish enough as it is."

She tried to stand, but her knees were still too weak. He cupped her elbows and helped her to her feet. "Thank you." Feeling ridiculous, she brushed past him. "Excuse me. I need some water."

In the bathroom, she filled a glass with water from the tap. As she was drinking from it, something caught her eye in the mirror. Slowly, she lowered the glass, then turned and stared at the lacy teddy hanging on the hook on the back of the door. She didn't recall the last time she'd worn it, but it hadn't been recently. Certainly not so recently that it would be hanging on the bathroom door instead of lying folded in a bureau drawer.

"Everything all right?" Derek stuck his head around the door. One look at her face, and his expression changed. "What's the matter?"

"That shouldn't be there." She motioned toward the teddy as she moved him aside so she could get through the door. As she stood in the center of her bedroom, her eyes frantically scanned the room.

"What do you mean it shouldn't be there?"

"Just what I said." She looked for anything, even the smallest thing, out of kilter.

"It doesn't belong to you?"

"Yes, but I haven't worn it in . . . I don't remember the last time I had it on."

Swiftly she left the room and went down the hall into the guest bedroom. She switched on the light and took only a quick glance but didn't see anything out of place.

In the living room, however, she saw something that had escaped her notice earlier, when she'd had only the flashlight for illumination. On the end table, a book was lying opened, facedown. Her bookmark was beside it, not between pages, where it belonged.

Derek moved up behind her. "What?"

"I never leave a book lying opened facedown like that. It ruins the spine. My dad loved books. He was very strict about how they were handled. He taught me never to . . ." She turned her face up to Derek's. "I always use a bookmark."

Without waiting for him to respond, she hurried into her kitchen and saw immediately that several items on the countertop had been moved. The cookbook on the easel had been closed; it was always left open because she liked the photograph. A bottle of wine had been uncorked but otherwise left untouched.

Most telling was the decorative wrought-iron rack where she kept three bar towels. She and Paul had bought them at a Paris flea market soon after they met. She wasn't fussy about the way they hung on the rack. In fact, she liked them to look as though they were used frequently, which they were. Now they were perfectly folded over the rack, their hems aligned.

"He's been here."

She didn't even realize she'd spoken the words out loud until Derek took her by the shoulders and asked gently, "Julie, what are you talking about?"

Flinging her arm in the direction of the towel rack, she cried, "Don't you see? It's like in that movie."

Derek turned her around and looked at her with perplexity. "What is? What movie?"

She worked herself out of his grasp and stepped past him. "You need to leave now." Returning to the bedroom, she opened a bureau drawer and began gathering up articles of clothing. Then she took a duffel bag from her closet and tossed the things into it.

"What are you doing?" Derek was standing in the open doorway, watching her, mystified.

"I'm not staying here tonight. I can't be sure the electricity won't go off again. Until I can have the power company come and check it, I don't want to be here." It sounded like a plausible excuse for clearing out, when actually her reason for going was twofold. Fear, primarily. And the untenable knowledge that Creighton had violated her home. "You can feel how hot it's become with the AC off. So I'll just—"

Derek hooked her arm and brought her around to face him again. "What's really going on?"

"I told you. I—"

"Julie."

She was breathing rapidly through her parted lips and knew that if her expression gave away half the apprehension she was feeling, it was useless to lie. "He was here."

"Who?"

"Creighton."

He assimilated that. "What makes you think so?"

She glanced around, looking for obvious evidence of an intrusion but realizing that no one would notice the subtle signs except herself. "The bench. He moved it. And the other things. The teddy on the bathroom door." She hugged herself, rubbing her arms, loathing the thought of his hands rifling through her lingerie. "I didn't open that bottle of wine. The book in the living room. I never would have left it like that. The bar towels."

"Your maid—"

She shook her head. "It was Creighton. There was a movie. I can't remember the title. Julia Roberts faked her death to escape an abusive husband. But he caught on to her, and when he found her, he . . . he . . . lined up the towels. He had this thing, this control-freak thing. When she saw the towels she knew—"

She stopped, realizing how deranged she sounded. She took a deep breath and got control of her quavering voice. "I asked you to leave. Why are you still here? What are you doing here in the first place?"

He ignored the questions. "You're certain someone broke in?"

"Absolutely certain."

He watched her for a moment, then said calmly, "You should call the police."

She shook her head.

"If you're not up to it, I'll call them."

As he reached for his cell phone, she grabbed his sleeve. "Don't call the police."

"But if you suspect your house was broken into—"

"I don't suspect it. I *know*."

"Can you tell if anything was taken?"

"He didn't break in to steal. He broke in to show me he could."

"Creighton?"

Reading the doubt in his eyes, she spun away from him and went into the bathroom.

Derek followed her as far as the door. "I advise you not to touch anything until the police have had a chance to investigate."

"Didn't you hear me, Mr. Mitchell? I have no intention of reporting this. You don't believe me. Why would they?"

"I didn't say I didn't believe you."

"You didn't have to. In any case, I'm not calling the police. There's no evidence of a break-in. They would think I was crazy."

"If you've had an intruder, it should be reported."

"Then you report it," she snapped. She began yanking the pins from her hair and dropping them onto her bathroom dressing table. "You spend the rest of the night at the police station, answering questions, telling and retelling your story. I did all that the day Paul was shot. And almost every day since. It got me nowhere. I'm not doing it again." She shook loose the coil of hair at the nape of her neck and in an undertone added, "I won't give him the satisfaction."

She collected some grooming necessities, then carried them into the bedroom and dumped them into the duffel. She zipped it, picked it up, and motioned Derek toward the door. "I'll see you out."

"Where will you go?"

"To a hotel."

"Do you want to change first?"

They were both still in evening clothes, although the collar button of his shirt had been undone and his bow tie was untied, hanging flat against his chest. She was indifferent to her own appearance. "No, I'll go like this."

"I'll drive you."

"Why would you?"

"You're in no condition to drive."

"I'm fine."

"You're shaking."

She realized that she was. Her fear, now overlaid with anger, was causing her to tremble.

Derek stepped around her and picked the pistol off the floor. "Do you have a permit to carry this?"

She took it from him and pushed it between the mattress and box springs of her bed.

"That's a no-nonsense weapon," he remarked.

"Paul gave it to me and insisted I keep it handy. His wealth made him a target for kidnapping. He was paranoid about it, afraid someone would try to get to him by harming me."

"How many chambers were left empty?"

"Two."

"Lucky me."

"And me. If I'd shot you, I'd have had no choice but to spend the rest of the night at the police station."

It seemed ludicrous to lock her house, but she did so. Derek's car was parked at the curb. "I'm calmer now," she said. "Perfectly capable of driving."

He shook his head.

"You could follow me just to make sure I arrived safely at my destination."

"I'll drive." To squelch further argument, he took her duffel from her.

"I'll call Kate in the morning and have her bring me home."

"Sounds like a plan."

He put her in the passenger seat, tossed her duffel into the backseat, then went around the hood of his car and got in. They covered several blocks in silence, then she repeated her earlier question. "What were you doing at my house?"

"I needed to talk to you."

"About what?"

"Did you confront Creighton at a club last night?"

"Oh."

He looked across at her. "That's a yes?"

"I'm admitting nothing."

"Very judicious of you."

She gave him a sharp look. "Doug told me tonight that you'd refused to represent them."

"I did."

"He said the reason you gave was that you were too busy to take any new clients. But he doubted that."

"Doubted and didn't accept. I know this because he deposited the amount of my retainer into the firm's account this afternoon. He did it by electronic wire transfer, leaving a paper trail a mile wide."

"So until you can return his money—"

"I'm the attorney of record. At least the firm is. The effect is the same." He stopped at an intersection and looked at her. "Which means, we've still got a conflict."

Their stare held for several moments, then he pulled away from the stop sign.

"That being the case," she said, "why did you come to my house?"

"I didn't want to call."

"Because of phone records?"

He shrugged. "Doesn't hurt to be careful. Just in case. Anyway, after your run-in with Creighton at the nightclub, he came to my house, uninvited. Made me mad as hell, and I told him so. He was frothing at the mouth. Accused you of stalking him, said you were suffering from post-traumatic stress disorder, that you could pose a danger to him."

"That's absurd."

"*Did* you follow him?"

"No."

"You just happened to show up at that particular bar, on that particular night, at that particular time, and what do you know? There's Creighton, your nemesis."

She looked out the passenger window. "I know he goes to Christy's and places like it. I went to several before I found him there."

"Why did you want to see him?"

"To rattle him."

"Well, you succeeded. He wanted me to get a restraining order against you. I came to your house tonight to issue a warning."

She turned her head back to him. "A threat, you mean."

"No, a warning, Julie. This talk of a restraining order is lunacy, but there are other lawyers who would pursue it just to separate Creighton from some of his money."

"I could just as easily get a restraining order against him," she said. "He was waiting for me in the parking garage when I left the function tonight."

"What?"

"Oh, yes. All very spooky." She told him what had happened, adding bitterly, "I guess invading my house to play his sick mind games wasn't payback enough."

"Did you see him?"

"In the garage? No. But I know it was him. He copied a scene from another movie. He has this thing with movies."

"Yeah, I know. He's laid a few quotes on me. Seems like a walking encyclopedia of films."

"He's obsessed. The garage scene could have come from several, but because of the cigarette lighter, I'm guessing *All the President's Men*."

"Deep Throat."

"You know the movie?"

"American history class."

"My father used it as a lesson on the Nixon administration. He was a teacher."

"Eleventh-grade history."

She looked at him with surprise, then her eyes narrowed. "How do you know that?"

He brought the car to a stop across the street from a small boutique hotel two blocks off Peachtree, cut the motor, and turned to face her. "Let's wait here for a minute before you go in, see if anyone's following you."

"No one's following me," she said angrily. "Answer my question. How do you know what my father did for a living?"

"I had the firm's investigator run a background check."

She went hot with rage. "On me? Why? Afraid I was carrying an STD? You could simply have asked."

"Julie—"

"What else did you learn through this background check?"

"That you did postgrad studies in Paris. Later married an unsuccessful artist."

"Who beat me up." Seeing his expression shift, she laughed. "Oh, did your investigator miss that? What a shame. That's the juiciest part."

"Want to tell me?"

His eyes were steady on her face, his voice quiet, his entire demeanor inviting confidentiality. "Why not?" she said flippantly. "You'll only send your bloodhound to do some more sniffing, and he might miss something really tasty. Wouldn't want that to happen."

Fat raindrops had begun to spatter the windshield. They struck the glass like clear paint balls. "I'd been in Paris almost a year when I met Henri. He was a struggling artist, penniless and tortured with self-doubt. I would be his muse, he said. Over picnics of wine and bread, he waxed poetic about how the beauty and purity of my soul would inspire him to paint masterpieces." She smiled wryly. "Even tripe sounds melodious when spoken in French. It was all very romantic, bohemian, and passionate.

"We married. I worked in a gallery while he painted. Eventually he began to drink more than he painted. He brought home equally drunken friends. They soothed his tortured soul and helped stave off his self-doubt. I had much less lofty opinions of them than he did.

"The blush soon faded from our romance. Our lifestyle began to be less bohemian than downright seedy. And his passion turned from painting to abusing me. Only verbally, but our quarrels were ferocious. They left me feeling as weak and bruised as if they'd been physical."

Whenever Julie thought back on those days, she couldn't place herself in that situation. Her memory could reset the stage, but she couldn't feature herself as a player in the tawdry scenes. It was so alien to her life now, it seemed like a terrible nightmare that someone else had dreamed.

"*Sleeping with the Enemy,*" she said softly. "That was the title of the movie I couldn't recall." More raindrops splatted on the windshield. Larger. Louder. Wetter. "One day I came home from work and caught Henri in bed with a woman, one of those unwashed, drunken ones that he kept around to boost his flagging self-confidence. She was a more sympathetic muse, it seems.

"But, of course, he insisted that he was the wronged party. If I'd been more supportive, not so demanding, not so critical . . ." She stopped, making a helpless gesture. "You get the drift. I was to blame for his being an alcoholic, adulterer, and failure. When I argued that point, he hit me."

Out of the corner of her eye, Julie saw Derek's hand form a fist.

"Only once," she said, "but that was enough. I called the police and he was arrested. I later dropped the charges, but I filed for divorce. He refused to accept that I would leave him. Filled with remorse, he pleaded with me to take him back. He would work, he would be faithful, he would stop drinking." She took a breath. "I won't bore you with the details, Mr. Mitchell. If you want them, you can order your investigator to dig deeper. To summarize, I was in a mess and was having trouble extricating myself from it."

"Paul Wheeler to the rescue."

"Yes." She turned to him. "He pulled me from the mire my life was in and set me on a new path. Anything else you want to know?" She expected more questions about her marriage, or Paul. He surprised her.

"Why do you hate Creighton so intensely?"

"You've met him and you have to ask? Do *you* like him?"

"Irrelevant."

"Not from my viewpoint."

"Why are you so sure he broke into your house tonight?"

"Why are you so sure he didn't?"

"I'm not. I don't know. But you seem convinced. Why?"

She folded her arms, leaned back against the car door, and appraised him. "I thought lawyers never asked a question they didn't already know the answer to."

"In cross-examination."

"That's what this feels like."

"Does it?"

"Yes."

He didn't relent. "Did you dislike Creighton from the time you met him?"

"Yes, but Paul had told me things about him, so I was prepared not to like him. He lived up to my low expectations."

"There wasn't a particular episode or event that turned you against him?"

She tilted her head. "Which kind of question is this, Mr. Mitchell? One you know the answer to? Or one you don't?"

"This is curiosity."

"I don't believe you."

"You don't? Shucks." He grinned and said in a wheedling tone, "I've got such an honest face."

"I hate to disillusion you, but your grin is anything but honest. It's the smile of a card sharp with four aces up his sleeve."

He chuckled. "I've been the target of worse insults." He waited a beat or two, then said, "Just one more question. Do you wear black because you're in mourning?"

The sudden shift in subject took her aback. Which he saw and took advantage of. "Every time I've seen you, you've been wearing black. On the plane, black suit. Except for the blouse. Ivory. With pearl buttons. Small, round pearl buttons."

Remembering the haste with which he'd undone them, she felt a rush of blood to her face.

"In your gallery, a black dress. And again tonight." His eyes moved from her low V-neckline to her hem and back up. "Slinky and sexy, but still black. Is that because of Wheeler?"

"It's because I like wearing black."

"You wear it well. You were a standout tonight amid so much color."

"Like emerald green." She hesitated, then said, "The lady is lovely, by the way."

"Yes, she is."

"Did she know that you were coming to my house after dropping her off?"

"No."

Moments ticked by, and the mood inside the car changed. There was a shift in the air. Or rather, no shift at all. At once, it seemed stifling and still.

"I should go in." But even though she reached for the door handle, she didn't open it. It was raining in earnest now. Across the street, the hotel doorman had stepped into the lobby for shelter. "I've heard of this place, but I've never been inside."

The logo on the canopy was the letters CH, entwined and written in gold script. Coulter House had been the original name of the estate built in the last century. Several years ago investors had converted it into an exclusive luxury hotel that catered to people with platinum cards.

"It's nice," Derek said. "Small but elegant. Exceptional service." Catching her inquisitive look, he added, "I put out-of-town clients up here."

Jagged forks of lightning were followed instantly by crashes of thunder. They watched the storm track across the sky and listened to the rain pelt the roof of the car, but neither moved or said anything for several minutes. The windows began to fog. After a time, he asked, "Did you recognize the man in the photograph?"

"The man in the lobby of the Moultrie? No. Not even when I saw the latest set of pictures."

"There's a set?" he said. "I've only seen one."

"He appeared on the security videos from days leading up to the robbery." She told him about Kimball and Sanford bringing the photographs to the gallery that morning. "One of the pictures is fairly clear, but I still don't know the man. Neither Doug nor Sharon recognized him."

"Creighton didn't, either."

"You believe that?"

"I showed him the picture myself, Julie. I was watching his face for a reaction, and I'm good at reading reactions. He didn't have one."

"Of course he didn't! He would know you were looking for one. Don't you see? He plays roles. He—"

She checked herself. For the present, he was Creighton's attorney. Already he was wondering if her allegations against Paul's nephew arose from nothing more than an intense dislike, or else why had he asked her about it?

She said, "The TV stations were going to show the man's photo on the news tonight."

"Maybe that'll shake something loose."

"Maybe. In the meantime, the detectives have gone off on another tangent."

"What's that?"

"That I was the one who set Paul up to die in that elevator." When he didn't say anything, she asked, "Cat got your tongue?"

"Yeah. I'm speechless. I didn't see that coming."

"Neither did I."

"What in hell gave them that idea?"

She told him about defying the robber. "Apparently since I didn't drop to my knees immediately, I'm high on the list of suspects."

"Why didn't you kneel?"

"I was looking for Creighton behind the sunglasses and mask."

"It wasn't him."

"How many times have I heard that?"

Another silence stretched between them, which only emphasized the ferocity of the storm. Finally he said, "When do I get my painting?"

"It'll be delivered tomorrow. It's not worth anywhere near what you paid, you know."

"It's an investment."

"You may have to wait years for a return."

He remained indifferent. "The money went to a good cause. Besides, I wanted the painting."

"Whether your lady friend approved it or not."

"She is my friend," he said quietly.

"It's none of my business."

"Then why do you keep bringing her up?"

She had no response to that.

"Lindsay and I met when she and my best buddy from law school got engaged," he said. "I was best man in their wedding, and I'm godfather to their son, Jackson. Soon after Jackson was christened, my friend was killed. Just like that. Car wreck during morning rush hour on Eighty-five. She and I helped each other get through it, and we continue to rely on each other's friendship.

"Sometimes, like tonight, she needs a safe, hassle-free escort to an event. And the reason she doesn't know I'm here with you is that, as close as we are, I don't know what she looks like naked and never will."

Julie took a deep breath and let it out slowly. "Well, you've certainly succeeded in making me feel rotten. That was what you were trying to do, right?"

He closed his eyes and, frowning severely, pinched the bridge of his nose. "Yeah, that's what I was trying to do."

"Why?"

He dropped his hand and looked at her. "Because not once, not ever, have you addressed me by my first name, and I'd really like it if you would. Because as of right now, I'm the Wheelers' attorney of record. Because you've accused one of them of several felonies, which places us on opposite sides of a legal issue. Because it's inappropriate and unethical for us to be alone. Because I invented a reason to come to your house tonight just so we *could* be alone. Because I'm having the devil of a time keeping my hands off you, and all I can think about is how you feel under that dress."

Moving like a spring had been released, he reached across the console and curved his hand around the back of her neck beneath her hair, drawing her toward him. "Why'd you come on to me on that airplane?"

"You know why."

"I know what you *said.*"

"That's why."

"No other reason?"

"No."

"You're lying."

His mouth stamped hers, then his lips rubbed hers apart, his tongue moved against hers, and her bones seemed to melt.

The kiss was thorough and deep and sexual, not a conclusion in any sense whatsoever, but a prelude, a foretelling of what would happen unless she stopped it. Breaking free, she murmured, "Please don't do this to me. Please don't." But at the same time she whispered the plea, her lips were moving against his, wanting more.

They kissed again, their mouths hotly fusing. He brushed her neck with his fingertips, then his hand dropped to her breast and caressed her through the fabric of her dress. She whimpered a protest, broke the kiss, and turned her head aside. "Don't."

His thumb stroked her, eliciting the expected response, which she felt from her nipple to her womb, and it shocked her into pushing him away. "No, Derek!"

He released her immediately and sat back in his seat, staring at her with incomprehension, breathing hard. "Well, at least that got you to say my name."

She grappled for the door handle and tugged hard. She scrambled out, her legs getting tangled in her long gown. The driving rain felt like a thousand needles pricking her exposed skin. Instantly her hair and dress became drenched. She opened the rear door and reached in to grab the duffel.

"Thank you for the ride."

Derek watched her run across the street, stumbling on her gown until she gathered it up in her hand and raised it to her knees. The doorman saw her coming and rushed out to meet her with an open umbrella. Together they entered the lobby through the revolving door.

Derek let fly a spate of obscenities. He wanted to gun his car's engine, peel out fast enough to make the tires smoke, show her just how angry he was.

It would be an adolescent thing to do, but he felt as callow as an adolescent. Necking in the front seat of his car and fogging up the windows. Copping a feel across the console. That was suave. That was mature.

That was bullshit was what that was.

He couldn't believe he'd resorted to it. But when he gave that pathetic summation of his frustrations over their situation, he could have sworn she looked as unhappy about it as he, as hungry for another taste, another touch.

So he'd gone with his instincts, and tasted and touched, and goddammit if he didn't believe that she'd wanted him to. He couldn't be wrong about that. Not twice. On the plane and tonight, she'd been into him as much as he'd been into her. Dead lover or not, she had wanted him.

Or he was a prize chump, and she was the schemer that Creighton had said she was? She took every opportunity to disparage Paul's nephew, even going so far as to accuse him of being behind the murder. Indisputably Creighton was a condescending and arrogant son of a bitch, but he'd been conditioned to be. You couldn't grow up being that rich without assuming a strong sense of entitlement.

But was he a criminal? A man who would frighten a woman in a parking garage and break into her house just to mess with her head? Was he capable of conspiring to have his uncle executed?

One thing bothered Derek a lot. So far, Creighton's behavior had been obnoxious, but Derek had no reason to believe that he was blameworthy of a crime. Whereas Julie . . . He knew firsthand how capable she was of duplicity. Was it as Creighton had said? Was she a woman scorned who saw an opportunity to get vengeance, in spades, on the man who'd rejected her in the pool house of his parents' mansion?

The argument could be made that if she had come on to Paul Wheeler's nephew while Wheeler was within earshot, she wouldn't have had any compunction against fucking a stranger in an airplane lavatory less than two weeks after his coffin had been sealed.

Inside Derek's head, Creighton's words echoed. *She would screw a dog if she thought it would benefit her.*

Ariel Williams called the hotline number three times and hung up three times. She rested her forehead on the perforated metal mounting of the pay telephone and wiped her damp palms on the legs of her jeans.

She didn't want to do this. She *did not* want to become involved. Even though she'd gone out in the middle of a stormy night to find a pay telephone, so the call couldn't be traced to her phone, she was afraid that some freakishly high-tech system using satellites or something would lead the police straight to her door.

She didn't need another shock tonight. She'd suffered a huge one when, mere hours after Billy's heavy-breathing call, his picture had popped up on her TV screen. She'd dropped the spoon into her bowl of chocolate chip cookie dough ice cream, at first thinking that her eyes were playing tricks on her. Was he so inescapable that she was imagining him in every shadow and behind every tree?

The photo was blurry and the angle wasn't great. He'd done something weird to his hair. His flashy clothes had been replaced with very ordinary ones. But there was absolutely no doubt in her mind that it was Billy Duke. The police were looking for him in connection with a robbery and fatal shooting, asking anyone with information to notify them immediately.

She had called Carol and shared her alarm. Carol had urged her not to do anything, at least not before she'd slept on it and considered the consequences of becoming involved. "He's somebody else's problem now."

She'd reminded Ariel of the additional locks on the house, which had allayed her panic somewhat. But not her conscience. It ate at her until she could stand it no longer. Carol's advice notwithstanding, Ariel knew what she must do.

So here she was.

Nervously, she glanced over her shoulder through the grimy glass of the telephone booth, one of the few remaining in the whole city. The rain was torrential, the lightning menacing. Each time it flashed, she cringed. Few cars were on the streets. It wasn't a night to be out for any reason, no matter how important.

Even once she'd resolved to do what her conscience dictated, she'd tried to talk herself into waiting until morning to call the hotline number. By then, someone else might already have identified Billy. Maybe she would hear on the morning news that he'd been apprehended and was in police custody, relieving her of all responsibility.

But what if no one else recognized him? If he was involved in the killing of Paul Wheeler, it was her civic duty to report what she knew, and to do so immediately. Wheeler had been a notable citizen, a generous benefactor of numerous charities. She hadn't known him, of course, but according to all she'd read and heard about him, he'd been a decent and well-respected man. But no matter who he was, or how much money he had, he hadn't deserved to be killed like that.

She'd seen that lady on TV, the one who'd been with Paul Wheeler when he got shot, and it had broken Ariel's heart to see how torn up she'd been to lose the man she loved in such a violent way.

Civic duty aside, Ariel was doing this for that poor lady.

She willed herself to redial the hotline number.

After only two rings it was answered by a policewoman who identified herself by name but otherwise sounded bored. Since the news story had aired, there was no telling how many complete fruitcakes had called in. She probably expected Ariel to be one, too.

"Are you the person I talk to about the man in the picture? The one they showed on TV tonight?"

"Yes, I am. Your name, please?"

"You don't need my name."

"It will be kept anonymous."

"You don't need my name," Ariel argued reasonably. "But if you want his, I can give it to you."

CHAPTER
14

DODGE WAS LEANING AGAINST THE WALL IN THE CORRIDOR outside the courtroom when Derek emerged. He looked antsy and in desperate need of nicotine. "What took so freaking long?"

"I had to convince my client to take the deal the DA was offering."

"Time served?"

"Plus two years." They got into the elevator and suspended conversation until they had exited the superior court building and Dodge was lighting up. "The guy in the security camera picture, his name's Billy Duke."

"Says who?"

"Anonymous caller. Woman. Sounded young and nervous. Call came in a little after midnight and was traced to a pay phone. No one saw her, 'cause all the shops around there were closed at that hour."

"Was she a lonesome lady wanting conversation, or was she for real?"

"Most lonely hearts call from home. They think she was legit." Dodge hawked up a wad of phlegm and spat it into the narrow band of landscaping against the building, then took another long pull on his cigarette.

"What's the 'but'?"

"But Georgia DMV doesn't have a driver's license on any Billy or William Duke that fits. One William Wayne Duke here in Atlanta turned out to be a nineteen-year-old black guy. William S. Duke is white. He's also eighty-four. It ain't either of them in that photo. Another—"

"Okay," Derek said, interrupting, knowing that Dodge's information would be comprehensive and long in the telling. "So where are the police in terms of locating him?"

"Still looking. He's not on county or state tax rolls. They're running him through national databases, looking for tax returns, arrests, driver's licenses. In the meantime, Sanford and Kimball are on their way to see the Wheelers and Julie Rutledge to ask if they recognize the name, or ever heard the deceased mention it."

"Doubtful, since they didn't recognize his face."

Dodge shrugged. He flicked his cigarette butt into the street and lit another.

"That's littering."

"Sue me." He inhaled, exhaled, looked at his boss. "So, Counselor, what are you thinking?"

"I don't know. I thought this would be a complete bust, that the guy in those pictures would turn out to be a shoe salesman from Cleveland, a solid citizen who may have fudged on his income taxes but wouldn't kill a fly, much less shoot a man in the head at point-blank range. I had a whole profile for him."

Derek ran his hand around the back of his neck, then propped his hands on his hips, as he tended to do when frustrated. "Now I don't know. Could be that, the shoe salesman scenario. Could be the lonely woman syndrome, a spinster hoping some strapping young cop would trace the call to her and turn out to be the love of her life."

"Could."

"Or this Billy Duke could be the shooter."

"You took the words right out of my mouth."

Derek reached for his cell phone and checked for messages, then dialed his office. While it was ringing, Dodge asked what he wanted him to do. "Stay on it. Let me know as soon as you know something. Hey, Marlene." Derek waved Dodge off and started down the sidewalk in the opposite direction, toward the parking lot where he'd left his car. "He got two years. No, it goes in the win column. It could've been a lot stiffer. Listen, call the Wheelers, please. . . . Yeah, both of them. The wife, too. Arrange a meeting in my office. . . . When? ASAP."

Julie placed a call to Kate early that morning, asking that she come and drive her home from the Coulter House, promising to explain when she arrived. Kate was astonished to see her carrying the formal dress she'd worn to the charity event. "It's not what it looks like," Julie said as she slid into the front seat of Kate's car. "I promise."

She told her assistant only that her electricity had gone out and that, although it had been briefly restored, she hadn't trusted it to stay on throughout the night. "It may be a damaged transformer in the neighborhood."

Kate didn't press for more information, but she wanted to know why Julie hadn't driven herself to the hotel. "Not that I mind in the least picking you up."

"My car was making a funny noise. I didn't want to chance it breaking down during the rainstorm. I called a cab."

Kate looked at her askance. "Your electricity and your car? You've got some bad karma working."

Julie forced a laugh. "I must."

She got out at the curb and told Kate that she had some things to do before coming to the gallery, but that, if she was needed, she was reachable by phone. Once inside her house, she phoned her maid, who was scheduled only twice a week, and asked if it was possible for her to come that day, and to bring her husband to help her move heavy pieces of furniture.

"I want the house thoroughly cleaned from the inside out. Every surface sanitized."

The couple arrived within half an hour. Julie sat by the front door, waiting for them. She was uncomfortable being in the house alone, feeling Creighton's presence like a damp, fetid fog.

While the maid and her husband were dividing the labor and or-ganizing their supplies, Julie went through each room, looking for irregularities that might have escaped her notice last night. In the dining room, the paintings on the walls had been switched. The armchairs in the living room had been reversed. She discovered several subtle changes like that which only the individual who lived in the house would notice.

Creighton had been very clever that way.

His most overt prank was to leave an anatomically correct dildo, along with an unopened package of batteries and an illustrated instruction booklet, in the drawer of her bedside table. It disgusted her, but she was glad she'd responded to her intuition to check all her drawers before turning the cleaning project over to her maid.

Julie assigned herself the job of laundering every article of clothing and collecting what couldn't be laundered to be sent to the dry cleaners. She was just finishing that chore when Kate called.

"I just got off the phone with Detective Kimball. She and Sanford need to see you."

"When?"

"As soon as possible, she said. I promised to notify you immediately."

"What's it about?"

"She didn't share that. She suggested they come here. Is that okay? I'm supposed to call her back."

"Ask them to give me an hour."

The detectives were already at Chez Jean when Julie arrived, and so was her attorney, whom she'd called as soon as she hung up from Kate. Fortunately he'd been free.

Julie said, "Have you been introduced?"

The detectives mumbled disgruntled hellos as they shook hands with Ned Fulton, who'd been recommended to her by Paul's corporate lawyer.

Kimball said to the attorney, "This isn't an interrogation, Mr. Fulton. You're superfluous."

"My client doesn't think so," he returned blandly. "Not after the sly allegation you made yesterday."

Kimball looked miffed but didn't say anything more.

Sanford got straight to the point. "The hotline received a call late last night," he told them. "The man in the photo was identified as Billy Duke."

Both detectives, Kate, and Ned Fulton turned to Julie.

Her reaction was to raise her shoulders. "That name means nothing to me."

"You sure?" Kimball asked.

"You don't have to answer," Fulton said.

"I'm happy to answer. I don't know anyone by that name."

"Did Paul Wheeler?" Kimball asked.

"If he did, he never mentioned him to me. I've never heard the name."

"A derivative maybe? Bill or William, either first or last name?"

"I'm sorry, no," Julie said. "Who called to identify him?"

"We don't know." Sanford looked unhappy over having to admit that. "The caller refused to identify herself."

"*Her*self. A woman?"

Kimball nodded. "Basically she said she'd seen the picture on TV and knew the guy. Left his name with the policewoman and hung up. We traced the call to a pay phone, and immediately a squad car was dispatched, but by the time it got there, she'd split. No one was around. The street was deserted."

Julie thought about it for a moment. "Could it have been a crank call?"

"Possible," Sanford said. "But it felt right to the policewoman, who'd been answering crank calls since the telecast. She said the woman sounded young, a little scared. Short-winded, you know. Like she was nervous. We've been doing follow-up since dawn."

"And?" Ned Fulton prompted.

"And nothing so far," Sanford said.

Kimball went on to give them a rundown of the efforts being made to find Billy Duke, none of which had been successful. "We'll throw out a wider net, see what turns up. Even if we find him, doesn't mean he's our perp."

Ned Fulton stepped forward. "Ms. Rutledge has said she doesn't recognize this man's name or face. Is there anything else?"

The detectives silently consulted each other. Sanford said, "I guess that's it for now." Looking at Julie, he added, "Of course, if you should remember anything . . ."

"I want to find this killer more than even you, Detective. If I had anything to contribute, believe me, I would."

As they made to leave, Kimball, showing her more human side, asked about the outcome of the charity event. "Was it successful? Did the rain keep people away?"

"Luckily, it didn't start raining until it was over."

"Good turnout then?"

"Very good, yes."

"Did the painting bring as much as you'd hoped?"

Quietly Julie said, "Much more actually."

Kimball got into the passenger seat of their unmarked car. Sanford drove. She asked, "Well, what do you think?"

"I think this case is fucked up."

"That's your professional assessment? That's what you're going to say to the chief when we're called on the carpet to give an update of our progress?"

"Why'd she hire an attorney?"

"You sound cranky."

"I'm hot."

"Turn up the air conditioner." He did. She adjusted the vents to blow on him. "Better now?"

"Why'd she hire an attorney?" he repeated, but in his more customary mellow tone.

"It's the smart thing to do," Kimball replied. "Wouldn't you?"

He rolled his shoulders, more or less conceding that he would.

"She's being cautious. Doesn't mean she's guilty."

"Doesn't mean she's innocent, either."

"True." She sighed. "But we're reaching, Homer. It's a stretch for me to think she actually set Wheeler up to get shot. A, I believe she was nuts for the guy. B, she just doesn't seem the type."

"What type's that?"

"The type who would arrange a shooting like that."

"You only think that because she's cultured and well dressed."

"And we're giving the prospect credulity only because we don't have anything better."

"We've got this Billy Duke. Well, we don't *have* him. Hell, you know what I mean."

"Yeah." She sighed again. "I know what you mean."

Sanford drove another block in thoughtful silence. Braking at a traffic light, he asked, "Why'd she get all squirmy when you asked her about that shindig last night?"

She laughed. "Squirmy? That's a new one."

"Her voice lowered, her eyes shifted. She acted squirmy. How come, I wonder."

"You think she's lying? Why would she lie about a charity auction, a painting?"

"Not lying, specifically, just—"

He was interrupted by Kimball's ringing cell phone. "Hold the thought." She unhooked the phone from her belt and flipped it open. "Kimball." Her eyes cut immediately to Sanford. "Hello, Miss Fields. Kate."

Sanford looked over at her so fast, his neck popped. His eyebrows were raised in surprise and inquiry.

Kimball listened, said, "Um-huh. Um-huh." Listened some more, then, "Sure. When would you like to come in? Okay. We'll be there." She snapped her phone closed. "Well, well."

"Julie Rutledge's assistant? That Kate Fields?"

"The very one. She needs to talk to us about something important."

"Did she say what?"

"Yeah. You were right. Her boss is squirmy."

"He's adorable!"

"She," Derek corrected. "Maggie."

"Hi, Maggie." Sharon Wheeler leaned down and scratched Maggie behind the ears. "I've never had a dog, but they always seem to like me."

She and Doug Wheeler had arrived at Derek's office minutes earlier, and she had taken an instant liking to Maggie. Doug had introduced Sharon and Derek at the charity event. She was beautiful in a well-bred, well-packaged, Southern-belle way. But there was no substance to support the pretty exterior. Derek sensed she laughed even when she didn't quite get the joke. He imagined she moved through life feeling a bit lost but had become adept at covering her uncertainty with practiced charm.

Derek also surmised that Doug was well aware of his wife's vacuousness but loved her in spite of it. Smiling fondly, he watched her petting Maggie. "Why don't we get a dog?"

She beamed at him. "I'd love that."

"Ah, the gang's all here." Creighton breezed through the door Marlene held open for him. "Hello, Mother, Father. Mr. Mitchell." He clicked his heels and saluted Derek crisply. "Reporting as ordered, sir."

Derek wanted to slam-dunk him straight through the floor and all the way to China. "Did you break into Julie Rutledge's house last night?"

Exclamations erupted from both his parents, but Derek tuned them out. His focus was on Creighton. The younger man stared at him for several seconds, then turned his head to look behind him. Coming back around and perfectly mimicking De Niro, he said, " 'You talkin' to me? You talkin' to *me*?' "

"Answer the question."

Creighton snuffled a laugh. "Oh, you're *serious*. I thought for sure you were joking."

"What's this about, Mr. Mitchell?" Doug demanded.

Derek held Creighton's placid stare for several seconds more, then turned to Doug. "Never mind. Private joke. The reason I called you here was to give you a final piece of advice. Free advice, because I'm returning all your money." He paused, then said, "If any of you know this guy in the photo who's been identified as a Billy Duke, you should tell the police now."

"I've already told them I don't know him. Not by face or name," Doug said querulously. "I could have told you that over the phone." He seemed perturbed by having been called away from work unnecessarily.

"I no longer trust our telephone conversations, Mr. Wheeler,"

Derek said. "I wanted to see you in person, so there could be no mis-understanding of my meaning. Despite the large sum of money you deposited into my account, I will not act as your attorney. Collectively or individually."

Sharon looked confused. Doug looked affronted. Creighton remained passive.

"That's the piece of free advice?" Doug asked.

"Sooner or later the police will track down this Billy Duke, whether or not that's his real name. It may turn out that he's perfectly harmless, a model citizen. Or, he could have a connection to your brother's death. If he does, if he had any dealings with Paul or Wheeler Enterprises, and you know about it, you'd be much better served to let the police in on it now, rather than having to own up to it after they've made the connection."

Doug looked at his wife, who blinked up at him vacantly, then at Creighton, who said, "I told the two detectives—who interrupted my massage, by the way—that I never saw the guy, never heard of any Billy Duke." He grimaced. "That redneck name alone . . . I mean, *please*. And is Duke a middle name or last name? Is it Billy Duke Smith? Or Billy Joe Duke?"

Sharon giggled.

Doug looked at his watch. "I've got a meeting. Is that all, Mr. Mitchell?"

Derek stepped forward and offered him his hand. "Again, I'm sorry about what happened to your brother. I hope they catch the culprit soon. Good luck to you."

Doug shook his hand brusquely, then nudged Sharon toward the door. Creighton fell into step behind them.

"I need a private word with you, Creighton."

Turning back, the young Wheeler looked like he was going to tell Derek to drop dead. Then he smiled pleasantly. "All right."

Doug couldn't conceal his worry. "Private word about what?"

Creighton replied, "A small matter I mentioned to Mr. Mitchell a couple days ago." He kissed his mother on the cheek. "Are you going to be at home the rest of the afternoon? If so, I'll stop by."

"Oh, good. See you soon, darling."

They left. Creighton turned to Derek and fluttered his eyelashes. "I'm all yours."

Derek advanced on him until they were standing close. He kept his voice low but distinct. "You're an asshole. You're a prick. Furthermore, you're a prick made stupid by his own arrogance."

" 'You talkin' to *me*?' "

Derek ignored that, knowing that to respond would be to give the jerk precisely what he wanted. "Another piece of free advice."

"Gee. I'm honored."

"I would forget about that restraining order bullshit if I were you. It could backfire, especially with you playing Deep Throat in parking garages."

Creighton shook his head slightly. "Am I supposed to know what you're talking about?"

"Julie Rutledge has accused you of frightening her in the parking garage last night when she left the community center. Then she gets to her house and feels certain that someone has been there, shifting things around, playing a practical joke that isn't funny."

"And you would know this . . . how?"

"I bought the painting she contributed to the auction. She called this morning to thank me." Derek prided himself on being able to lie with the best of them. "It wasn't the warmest, most gracious thank-you I've ever received. Rather obligatory. Last night I was pointed out to her as your family's attorney. Seems she has no higher opinion of you than you do of her."

"I told you why that was."

"Yeah, you did. But she's got nothing good to say about you, either, so who's a guy to believe? You? Her? Neither of you?"

"Let me ask you a question, Mr. Mitchell. Did you witness the alleged incident in the garage? Did she file a complaint with the police about the alleged break-in at her house?"

Derek said nothing.

Creighton smirked. "Ten to one says she didn't. Why? Because no such break-in occurred. As for me hanging out in a parking garage, that doesn't even warrant discussion. Don't you get it? She's telling wild stories, planting seeds of doubt about me in your mind, the same way she's done with that pair of detectives. She hates me. She has since the pool house episode." He laughed shortly. "In hindsight, it would have been better if I'd just let her suck me off."

The fury that surged through Derek was almost stronger than he could control. "The more you say, the more I wonder if Ms. Rutledge's stories about you are that wild."

Creighton gave Derek the smug smile that he was beginning to find really irksome. "Julie is lying. She's lying to support her accusation that I had something to do with the shooting of Uncle Paul. Which is preposterous, for reasons we've already discussed and which, frankly, are beginning to bore me. Now, since you've severed our professional relationship, I don't need your permission to leave, do I?"

Derek held his stare for several seconds, then raised his hands at his sides as though in surrender and took several steps back. Creighton shook his head and gave a short laugh, then left through the open door.

"First off, I want you to know that I feel just terrible about this." Kate Fields twisted the tissue in her damp hands. She looked at Roberta Kimball and Homer Sanford in turn, receiving from each a nod of sympathetic understanding.

"I love Julie," she said. "She's been so good to me. Giving me this job straight out of college. Placing such trust in me, not just as an employee but as a friend. I wouldn't do or say anything to hurt her."

"We don't question your loyalty to Ms. Rutledge," Kimball said. "However, you have an obligation to us as officers of the law, as well as to yourself, to tell the truth."

"Of course, I know that." Kate sniffed into the tissue. "I've been hoping for a miracle, praying that something would happen to prevent me from having to tell you."

"Tell us what?" Sanford leaned forward. "You suggested to Detective Kimball that Ms. Rutledge hadn't been entirely truthful with us."

"I don't know that for certain." She cut her eyes between them. "But she . . . she may know more than she's telling you."

"More about what?" Kimball pressed. "The shooting?"

Kate shook her head. She swallowed. She asked herself for the thousandth time if she must do this, and arrived at the heartrending conclusion that yes, she must. Her conscience wouldn't permit otherwise. "The truth about this man Billy Duke."

The two detectives exchanged a look that immediately made her regret her decision to share with them what she knew. "Oh, please don't suspect her of conspiracy or something. She couldn't have had anything to do with Mr. Wheeler's death. She absolutely could *not*. She loved him. You don't know, you can't imagine, how it was between them. They were wholly, totally devoted to each other." Tears she'd been trying to hold back spilled from her eyes.

Kimball passed her a box of Kleenex. "Kate, we know this is painful for you, but it's vitally important that you tell us what you know about Ms. Rutledge and Billy Duke."

Kate yanked a fresh tissue from the box. After several starts and stops, she brought her sobs under control. "I recognized him from his picture the first time you showed it to Julie. I was serving you espresso, remember? We were in the parlor, and—"

"I know when you mean," Kimball said. "How did you recognize him?"

"He came to the gallery."

"When?"

"I can't be certain of the date."

"After Mr. Wheeler was shot?"

"No. A few weeks before. I'm positive about that."

"Did he come to see Ms. Rutledge?"

"Yes."

Kimball cut her eyes over to Sanford, but then they came right back to Kate. Again, that silent communication between them seemed significant and made her feel even more miserable for betraying the woman she admired above all others.

"But Julie didn't see him."

"She refused?"

Kate shook her head. "No, she wasn't there. He came in. Asked for her. I told him she was consulting clients in their home, and that I didn't expect her back for the rest of the day. I offered to help him.

He said no, his business was with Julie, and that he would catch her later."

Now that what she'd been holding back was finally out, she exhaled with relief. At the very least she could swear that she'd never seen Julie and this Billy Duke person together, in conversation.

"Did they ever make contact?" Sanford asked.

"Not to my knowledge."

"Did he return to the gallery?"

"Never. Not while I was there, anyway. And he didn't seem like someone who'd be into art. He didn't look at any of the paintings, not like he'd discussed a particular piece with Julie and had come back to reconsider it. I didn't get the impression that he was a potential client. He didn't show any interest in our inventory at all."

"Only in Julie."

Reluctantly, Kate nodded at Kimball. "Only in Julie."

"Did she ever mention him to you?"

"No, but I didn't know his name until this morning, when you told us."

"But he acted as though he knew her?"

Kate hesitated. This had been the question she most dreaded. "Well, yes. He referred to her by her first name, giving me the impression that he was someone she'd met or had had some prior dealings with. And the way he said he would catch her later, in those words, sounded casual, like something an acquaintance would say. Doesn't it?"

The detectives murmured agreement that it did. "Did you ever tell her about his visit?" Kimball asked.

Kate told them she had. "He didn't leave his name or a business card, or a phone number, so all I could tell her was that a man had come in asking for her and had left saying he would get in touch. Since there was no point of reference, she dismissed it, and so did I. I didn't think any more about him until you showed the picture from the security camera. I recognized him instantly, but when Julie told you very matter-of-factly that she didn't recognize him, I . . . I . . . ."

"You kept quiet," Sanford said with a trace of chastisement.

"I didn't want to get her into trouble."

Sanford asked, "What about now?"

"What do you mean?"

Kimball leaned toward her. "Kate, are you withholding other information that could mean trouble for her?"

"No." When they regarded her doubtfully, she added, "I swear I'm not! Actually, it's a relief to get it off my chest. Although . . ." Her lower lip began to tremble, and she felt the pressure of unshed tears. "Julie has been through hell since the day Mr. Wheeler died. I hope that by telling you this I haven't made things more difficult for her. Especially after what happened last night."

The detectives looked at each other with puzzlement, then back at Kate. Sanford asked, "What happened last night?"

CHAPTER

15

"H ERE YOU GO, MAGS." DEREK'S CELL PHONE STARTED RINGING as he set Maggie's food bowl on the kitchen floor. "Eat up." He looked at the caller ID and flipped open his phone. "Hey, Dodge."

"Is this a bad time?"

Not that Dodge ever cared if he was catching his boss at a bad time. When he had news to impart, he didn't wait for a convenient time to impart it. "Just got home. Feeding Maggie. What's up?" Derek took a beer from his fridge and twisted off the cap.

"Just heard something interesting off the PD grapevine."

"Sanford and Kimball located Billy Duke?"

"Nope, but they might've got a lead."

"I'm listening."

"Appears there's a link between the mystery man and Julie Rutledge."

Derek lowered the beer bottle from his mouth and carefully set it on his kitchen counter. "Come again?"

"Yeah. She's got this young woman who works for her."

Derek envisioned the pretty and pert Kate.

"She went behind Julie Rutledge's back to have a closed-door meeting with the two detectives."

Dodge's methods of obtaining information might be murky,

but the information itself never was. It was always one hundred percent reliable. Which was why Derek suddenly felt sick to his stomach.

Dodge was saying, "She cried her heart out for having to rat on her boss. Divided loyalties, you see. The woman she idolizes versus conscience, with some civic duty thrown in. They practically had to wring the information from her." Dodge paused. "Are you still there?"

"Yeah, I . . . Maggie was whining to go out, and I had to open the door. Go on."

"Well, what was eating at her, she recognized Billy Duke from his picture. A few weeks before Wheeler was hit, he came to that fancy gallery Ms. Rutledge owns. She wasn't there, but he asked for her by name, and the girl says it seemed to her like he was acquainted with her boss. Familiarly acquainted. Didn't state his business, just said he would catch Julie Rutledge later, and left."

Impatiently Derek pulled at the stubborn knot of his necktie. Sweat was trickling down his ribs. "He could have been a customer."

"The girl didn't think so. Besides, that would be one hell of a co-incidence, don't you think?"

Yes, he did. Derek had staked defense arguments on coinci-dences just that remarkable, but juries would stretch reasonable doubt only so far. "How did Kimball and Sanford react to this news?"

"They treated her with kid gloves, commended her for doing the right thing, like that. But you can bet they pounced on it and are looking at Wheeler's lady friend through a high-powered magnifier. Oh, something else."

Jesus. There was *more*?

"Small thing, but you never know. This girl told the detectives that the electricity had gone off in Julie's house last night, and that she hadn't been quite right since."

"What did she mean by 'not quite right'?"

"Acting strange. Doing weird shit. She stayed home this morn-ing. Kate called her house about a routine matter at the gallery. The maid asked if whatever she'd called about could keep. Said Julie was on a tear to have the house cleaned top to bottom. Told Kate she was discarding stuff right and left, even a set of bar towels. Antiques from France that she was partial to on account of Paul Wheeler had bought them for her.

"Now, if these towels were a gift from him, you'd think she'd want to keep them, wouldn't you? This Kate did. She told the detectives that maybe it's just grief setting in, or a delayed reaction to Wheeler's getting popped, something like that, but bottom line, Julie isn't herself these days." It was a long speech for Dodge. He paused to gasp a breath. "What's your take, Counselor?"

Derek was blotting up streams of sweat with his shirt. "My take doesn't matter. I'm no longer involved. I told the Wheelers today that they needed to obtain other counsel."

"You're shittin' me."

"No."

"How come?"

"Unless one or all of them are charged, they don't need me."

"And if one or all of them *are* charged?"

"The firm doesn't have time in its schedule for a trial of that magnitude."

"Huh," Dodge said with evident regret. "It's a juicy case, Counselor. All that loot. All that sex. More salacious details to come. Kind of a shame we'll be outside observers."

"Yeah. But even though we're out of it, I'd like you to tell me any scuttlebutt you hear regarding Billy Duke and his relationship to Julie Rutledge. Keep me posted."

"I'm on it." Then, after a telling pause, Dodge asked, "Want to tell me why?"

Derek forced out a dry laugh. "As you said, more salacious details to come."

The investigator snickered and hung up.

Derek reached for his beer, but discovered he no longer had a taste for it and poured it down the sink. He stared into near space, so lost in his thoughts that Maggie had to practically scratch the paint off the back door before he realized she was there, asking to come in.

"Sorry, girl." He bent down and scratched her behind the ears.

"Talk me out of what I'm about to do, Maggie. Please, I'm begging you."

Panting with contentment, she plopped down on the cool tiles of the floor.

"Thanks for nothing." He retrieved his cell phone from the countertop and punched in a number he'd looked up earlier and committed to memory.

"Hello?"

"It's me."

Julie didn't say anything for several beats, then, dubiously, "Okay."

"Can you meet me?"

"Now?"

"In Athens. There's an Italian restaurant on Clayton, just off the corner with Jackson."

"Where—"

"Near campus. You'll find it."

"Athens is an hour drive."

"At this time of day an hour and a half."

He hung up before she could refuse.

The restaurant was redolent with the aromas of oregano and garlic, the yeasty smells of beer and fresh-baked bread, the fruity bouquet of inexpensive wine. It was crowded with UGA summer school students, which was why Derek had chosen it. There was little likelihood they would be recognized here.

He was no longer representing the Wheelers, so technically this meeting with Julie wasn't unethical. But it felt covert for reasons he couldn't specify. Perhaps because of the way he and she had started. Everything since that Paris-to-Atlanta flight had felt illicit.

Sometimes deliciously so.

He arrived first and, with the help of a ten-dollar bill, managed to jump the line for tables, which was long even during summer. He secured a booth and was watching the door when Julie came in.

She was dressed in jeans faded almost to white and a snug red pullover. In that getup, and with her hair hanging loose, she didn't look much older than the coeds. A group of frat boys, conditioning themselves for upcoming rush week with pitchers of beer, vocally appreciated her ass as she walked along the bar on her way to the booth.

Ignoring their remarks, she slid in across from him, her eyes inquiring.

He said, "I ordered red. Is that okay?"

"Red's fine."

"The spaghetti is cheap, and so's the wine, but both are good. I came here a lot when I was a student."

"You went to Harvard Law."

"But I got my BA here."

A waiter brought a carafe of red wine and two glasses. He asked if they'd had time to look at the menu. Derek told him they'd let him know when they were ready to order. "In the meantime," he said, "I'd like to rent the table and buy some privacy." He slipped the guy another ten.

After the waiter left them, Derek filled both their glasses and raised his. "In vino veritas."

Julie clinked her glass against his, then took a sip.

"Do you mean it?" he asked.

"What?"

"That in the wine there will be truth."

"You sound doubtful."

"Because you and bald honesty rarely go hand in hand."

Her eyes flashed with annoyance. "That's why you had me come all this way, so you could tell me that you doubt my veracity?"

He sipped his wine, set down his glass, then let her have it. "Kate Fields went to see Kimball and Sanford this afternoon and told them that she recognized Billy Duke from his picture because he had come to the gallery asking for you a few weeks before Paul Wheeler was killed."

She pressed herself back against the seat as though she'd just learned that he had a highly contagious disease. "That's impossible."

"Which aspect of it is impossible, Julie?"

"All aspects of it."

"Think, Derek. I didn't know you were coming to my house. I wasn't huddled there in the dark, on the outside chance that you would walk in so I could stage an emotional meltdown."

He leaned forward and thumped the table with his fist. "If you were so certain you'd had an intruder, why didn't you let me call the police? Why didn't *you*?"

"It would have been pointless," she exclaimed. "Creighton made sure that things looked perfectly normal to anyone else."

"Okay, but no one saw him in the parking garage, either."

She stared at him for a moment, then whispered, "You think I'm lying. About it all. About everything. Don't you?"

His suspicion seemed to have wounded her, diminished her. She looked very small against the tufted back of the booth. Her eyes had gone soft with bewilderment, looking at him the way Maggie did when he scolded her for pulling the stuffing out of one of her toys.

On the drive there, he'd given himself several stern admonishments to exercise extreme caution when in the presence of Julie Rutledge and her bottomless gray eyes. He'd ordered himself not to think about last night's kiss, the way her mouth had clung to his, the unmistakable way her body had reacted to his touch.

But in spite of those lectures, he had no immunity against her bruised expression. His chest, and lower, grew tight with the desire to reach across the table and touch her, to tell her he was sorry, to ask her to disregard his nasty suspicions and what he'd said.

Instead, he steeled himself to be ruthless. "Did you come on to him?"

She processed that, then laughed drily. "*Creighton?* Are you insane?"

"In the pool house at his parents' home. You tried to give him a blow job while Paul was less than twenty feet away. He said that the risk of getting caught was a turn-on for you."

She was utterly still and silent for a count of ten, then she flew into action, grabbing her handbag off the seat and slinging the strap of it onto her shoulder as she clambered out of the booth. She bumped into a waiter holding a tray of food and drink high above his head, nearly sending several orders of pasta and two carafes of wine to the floor, but she didn't stop to apologize or even slow down.

Hissing an expletive, Derek shot from the booth, dug a twenty-dollar bill from the pocket of his jeans, and shoved it into the hand of their startled waiter as he charged after Julie.

He fought his way through the crowd bottlenecked at the door and, when he exploded onto the sidewalk, looked frantically in both directions. Julie was already half a block away, walking rapidly, weaving between other pedestrians with the sinuousness of a water snake.

She darted across the street, causing a driver to brake hard and honk the squawking horn of his Volkswagen. Derek defied oncoming traffic in order to run after her, catching up with her after another two blocks when she reached the parking lot where she'd left her car. She was pawing through her handbag in search of her keys when he closed his hand around her biceps, turning her toward him.

"Julie."

She wrenched her arm free. "And the horse you rode in on."

"Listen to me—"

"Not anymore."

"I believe you."

"I don't give a damn whether you do or not."

He captured her hand. "I *want* to believe you."

"Right."

"Dammit, I do. And you know why."

She stopped trying to pull away and looked up at him warily, as though asking *What's the catch?*

He said, "Tell me everything you know about Creighton."

"What for?"

"Curiosity."

"Prurient interest?"

"Okay, call it that. Call it any damn thing you like. I just want you to tell me what you know." He glanced around and nodded toward the park benches in front of the Athens City Hall. Looking back at her, he said, "Please?"

After a momentary resistance, she let herself be led down the sidewalk. They sat on one of the benches of weathered wood. Two squirrels played chase on the grass in the small side yard of the building, eventually racing up the trunk of a tree and disappearing into the foliage. A couple strolled past, their arms around each other, talking and smiling. Otherwise, he and Julie had their immediate surroundings to themselves.

She began without prompting. "I can only tell you what Paul told me."

"That's what interests me."

"It's not much. Paul was very protective of his family."

"Families with that kind of wealth typically close ranks, especially if one gets into trouble."

"I suppose it was like that. Any time he talked about Creighton, he was very discreet. It was more what he didn't say than what he did."

"Making you believe there was much more to tell."

She gave him a wry smile. "You're leading the witness."

He smiled back. "I'm good at it."

"I'll bet."

Their shared smile lasted for several seconds, then her expression turned serious again. "Paul once made a reference to bailing Creighton out."

"Out of jail?"

"I don't know if he meant it literally or figuratively. I didn't ask for specifics. If he had wanted me to know them, he would have told me."

She became quiet, and Derek sensed the reason for her silence. "I don't want you to share a confidence if you don't feel comfortable about it."

She glanced at him, then lowered her head. "You read people very well."

"Part of my job."

"Talking about this, I feel like I'm being disloyal to Paul."

More disloyal than when you were making love to me? Derek didn't speak the thought aloud, of course. He waited.

Eventually she reached a decision and began to talk. "Paul never

said anything flattering about Creighton. He made clear his disapproval. But he really opened up to me about him only once. He was
very angry at him, more so than usual. He was venting over something Creighton had done or failed to do. He called him totally irre-
sponsible and lacking initiative."

"A typical complaint by the older generation of the younger."

"Yes, but he went on to say that he shouldn't be surprised that
Creighton was a dissolute adult because he had exhibited bizarre behavior even as a boy."

"How bizarre? Did he elaborate?"

"No. Except to say that sometimes Creighton was cruel to other
children, without provocation. Yet they yielded to him. He was a
masterful manipulator and could get others to bend to his will. He
was a leader, but not necessarily in a good way. Paul also said that
one of Creighton's schoolteachers had resigned at midterm, naming
him as the cause for her abrupt departure."

"Why? What had he done?"

"I don't know. Paul claimed not to know, either. He said the
teacher had declined to give them an explanation. She simply refused
to go back to the classroom, even though it was a private academy
and she was giving up a well-paying position."

Derek digested all that. "Did Creighton ever undergo counseling? Psychiatric treatment?"

"Sharon wouldn't hear of it. Doug was wishy-washy. Paul kept
after Doug until he gave in. Later, however, Paul realized that the
therapy was a waste of money. Creighton knew what to say, knew
how to manipulate the analysts."

"His mother seems blind to his flaws."

"He's very skillful at role playing. He can be the affectionate son,
the nephew falsely accused of involvement in his uncle's murder,
whatever suits him at the time." Turning toward him so that their
knees touched, she said, "He operates in a fantasy world, Derek."

She hesitated, realizing she'd used his given name again, but
went on before he could comment on it. "Creighton's life is a movie
script, and it's a work in progress. He's rewriting it constantly." For
emphasis, she placed her hand over his. "You're in his script whether
you want to be or not."

"Me?"

"You. Me. Everyone. He casts us in roles. I think Paul knew he was dangerous, or strongly suspected that he was. But he was reluctant to accuse his own nephew of being a psychopath. However, he did tell me to stay away from Creighton."

"He warned you against him?"

"Not in so many words. He said the less I had to do with him, the better."

While Derek was pondering that, he noticed her brushing a mosquito off her arm. "You're getting eaten alive."

Together they stood and started walking back toward her car. While they'd been talking, night had fallen. The public buildings were empty. Music, voices, and laughter wafted from the various bars and restaurants across the street, although the area wasn't as congested as it was during the fall and spring semesters. A jogger listening to her iPod ran past. A bearded professor type rode by on a rattling, rusty bicycle, which looked as old as he.

When they reached Julie's car, she unlocked it, opened the door, and tossed her handbag inside, then turned to face him. "You listened well, but I sense that you still don't believe me wholeheartedly." When he was about to speak, she said, "I know I'm right. Don't bother answering."

So he didn't. He placed his hands on her arms and rubbed them up and down. He lowered his head for a kiss, but she turned away. "Julie." He placed his hand in the small of her back and drew her forward until her lower body was pressed intimately against his. Nudging aside her hair, he sighed directly into her ear. "I think about it all the time. About us. Like this." She pushed against him, and he groaned with disappointment. "Don't pull away."

But she did. Her expression was hard, closed. "With one breath, you accuse me of lying. With the next, you whisper erotically and try to kiss me. It can't be like that, Derek. Not with me it can't."

"I don't think you're lying."

"You just don't think I'm telling the truth."

"There's a difference," he said.

"Maybe someday I'll figure out the distinction."

She tried again to pull away and get into the car, but he held her.

"The distinction is in the shading, Julie. The detectives sense it, too, or you would already have been dismissed as a possible suspect. You're telling us what you want us to know. What are you leaving out?"

"Nothing."

"Something." He placed his finger beneath her chin and forced her to look at him. "I don't believe for one minute that you came on to Creighton in that pool house."

"After what I did on the airplane, why should you find that hard to believe?" When he said nothing, she laughed, but it was a bitter sound. "Wait, I know. Having sex with Creighton might have been a turn-on, but greedy fortune hunter that I am, I wouldn't have jeopardized my setup with Paul by doing something so foolish."

He said nothing, which actually spoke volumes.

"Don't try and see me again." She pushed herself away from him and quickly got into the car.

"Julie—"

"I mean it." After a brief tug-of-war, she managed to loosen his hold on the car door and slam it closed. As soon as she got the car started, she drove away. He stood looking after her taillights until they disappeared around the nearest corner.

Cursing beneath his breath, he turned just as a form peeled away from the dark trunk of a nearby tree and took the shape of a man. "Next time, when you're having a tiff, I recommend you use the club-and-cave method. It worked well with the lady Neanderthals, or the species wouldn't have propagated and none of us would be here."

Creighton Wheeler, hands in his pants pockets, stepped out of the deep shadows beneath the tree and walked toward him with an ambling gait, as though out for a Sunday stroll. Tuneless whistling was all that was lacking.

Derek tried to cover his dismay and to sound as nonchalant as possible. "Somehow I don't think the caveman tactic would woo a woman like Julie."

Creighton broke a smile, his teeth looking brilliantly white even in the darkness. "You're probably right. Too bad you can't consult my late uncle on what woos her best. He should know. They were a couple for two years, so he must have been doing something right. Of course, there was the . . ." Leaning in, he whispered, "M-o-n-e-y. Maybe he tickled her clit with hundred-dollar bills. What do you think?"

Derek thought he might commit murder. His body was trembling with fury—at himself for having placed himself in this absurd situation, at this bastard for being so goddamn smug. "Who were you following, Julie or me?"

"Tonight? You."

Derek caught the qualifier, and Creighton saw that he'd caught it. He laughed and raised his hands in surrender. "I confess, this isn't the first time I've done some amateur sleuthing. Last night, wasn't that thunderstorm romantic? The lightning, the thunder, the pounding rain. Very primitive. Did it bring out the animal in her?"

"You son of a bitch. Today, when we talked, you were well aware I was with Julie last night."

"You were with her, all right." Creighton fanned his face. "I got turned on imagining what was going on behind those steamed-up car windows. A lot of heavy breathing, to say the least."

"Which of us were you following last night?"

Creighton shrugged indolently. "I never did buy that claptrap about you having too many clients, no time for us Wheelers. Don't you think I would have thoroughly checked you out? Well, I did, and what I gleaned from my research is that your talent is exceeded only by your ambition and greed. Which makes you the perfect defense lawyer.

"So why, I asked myself, would you decline to let us throw lots of money at you for doing virtually nothing except field a few questions from the media? And you adore the spotlight, Mr. Mitchell. See? For several reasons it just didn't make sense, and I hate holes in the plot, to say nothing of lame motivation for a lead character. I determined to find out the real reason you'd turned us down."

"You started following me."

"Nobody says no to a Wheeler, Mr. Mitchell. Especially not to this Wheeler. But I wasn't just pissed. I was intrigued. I sensed . . ." He waggled his fingers in the air. "Illicitness. Eroticism. Maybe you were emanating a primal mating musk."

"Isn't that taking the prehistoric analogies a little far?"

"Whatever." Creighton lowered his voice again. "Lo and be-hold, at whose house do you turn up last night? Imagine my aston-ishment. But suddenly all your dodging and weaving as to why you can't represent me makes sense. You, my defender, are fucking my accuser. Truthfully, I would never have guessed that. As a plot de-vice, it was worthy of Scorsese."

He glanced in the direction Julie had gone. "I'm sure she's filled your head with sordid tales about me and my misguided youth, passed along to her—and greatly exaggerated—by my late uncle Paul.

"Did she tell you that he insisted I get psychiatric counseling? Yes? Did she also tell you that, after months of treatment, it was de-cided that I was perfectly normal, while Uncle Paul, in his obsession over me and my shortcomings, was the one the doctor suspected of being mentally unstable and emotionally maladjusted?"

He laughed. "Sometime, you must tell me how you and Julie met. Was it before or since Uncle Paul met his tragic end?" Then he held up his hand, palm out. "You know what? I don't want to know. I'd rather make up my own naughty scenarios.

"The truth is, Mr. Mitchell— Can I call you Derek? The truth is, if you'd told me straight off why you had to decline my business, I'd have been amused. You and Uncle Paul's mistress. What a stitch."

Suddenly he dropped the pleasant pose and his entire aspect be-came menacing. "But you didn't tell me. So now, I'm telling you. If you've been double-crossing me, you're good and fucked, and I don't mean by the fair Julie. When I get through with you, you won't be able to look at a courtroom, much less go into one."

Derek had heard enough. He stepped up to Creighton and poked a finger into his chest, causing a dent in his starched oxford cloth shirt. "Don't threaten me. I'm not your lawyer. I told you that the first day you came to my office. I'll see whoever I want to, and you can't do a friggin' thing to stop me.

"And you couldn't know that I was at Julie's house last night unless you were there yourself. If I catch you near her or me again, I will go to the police and have them slap your pansy ass in jail and keep it there until they've run a thorough investigation of her house to see if someone did indeed make themselves at home there, moving stuff, handling her things. I'm talking complete fingerprinting, collecting DNA evidence, lab tests that take a good, long time.

"It may never result in an indictment, but in the meantime, you'll spend some uncomfortable weeks behind bars. I've got clients currently in jail whose destinies depend on how well I do for them in court. One visit from me and they'll see to it that you're made miserable. They can mess you up bad, in ways you can't even imagine." Derek came another step closer. "Do we understand each other?"

Creighton shivered, whispering, " 'Wow. I'm sexually aroused, Commander.' Tom Cruise. *A Few Good Men*." He grinned, winked. "No wonder Julie creams over you."

The hardest thing Derek ever had to do was walk away from him, leaving all his shiny teeth intact.

As soon as Julie returned home, she called Kate. The younger woman's voice was hoarse when she answered, as though she'd been crying for hours. No doubt, having seen Julie's number on her LED, she also sounded wary.

Julie relieved her immediately. "I know about your visit to the police station today, and it's okay."

"Oh my God." Kate sobbed and blubbered an explanation.

It was several minutes before Julie could work in a word. "I don't blame you, Kate. Not at all. You did what you had to do, and it took a lot of courage. I want to assure you that I'm not angry, but also assure you that I don't know that man. What he was doing in the gallery asking for me, I have no idea. But I swear to you, you don't need to feel conflicted about talking to the detectives. You didn't damage me by telling them about him, because I don't know him."

"Lord, Julie, you don't know how relieved I am. I was sure you would hate me."

"That could never happen."

"They made me feel even guiltier by asking me not to tell you that I'd talked to them. I've been worried sick, wondering how I was going to behave normally. I'm so glad it's out in the open."

Lest Kate be misled, Julie said, "The detectives didn't tell me."

"Then how'd you know?"

"I can't answer that without breaching a confidence."

"Then don't answer. But as long as you know about my conversation with them, I guess it's okay for you to know that they don't think this guy's coming to the gallery is a coincidence."

"I don't believe it's a coincidence, either."

"You think he was the one who shot Paul?"

"I don't know. Tonight, I'm too tired to think about anything. I'm going to bed. See you in the morning."

Before she could hang up, Kate rushed to say, "I didn't tell them about the hotel, about you spending the night out last night."

"Oh. Well, that has nothing to do with anything."

"I didn't think so, either. So I left that part out when I told them about your housecleaning binge."

Julie was about to ask how Kate knew about that, but the younger woman was gushing her gratitude for Julie's calling. "I'll be able to sleep now."

"Rest well," Julie told her. "We'll both feel better tomorrow."

Julie went to bed shortly after that call, but she was too restless to sleep. She was in turmoil, wondering what Kimball and Sanford were doing with this new information and how they were going about trying to link her to Billy Duke. She wondered if they had made any headway toward finding him.

And, despite her determination not to think about Derek, her thoughts revolved mostly around him, as they had done since the moment she'd sat down beside him on the airplane. Sabotaging him had been her goal, but something totally unexpected had happened: she'd started liking him.

He had appealed to her immediately, and more than just the way he looked. Beyond his engaging smile and arresting eyes, she liked his quick, self-deprecating wit and confident, easy manner. He wasn't nearly as conceited as she had thought he would be. Rather, he'd poked mild fun at himself. He hadn't dominated the conversation with stories of his celebrated cases and courtroom victories but was a good listener who seemed genuinely interested in everything she said.

She hadn't anticipated finding such an agreeable, likable man inside the handsome package. Nor could she ever have forecast being so sexually attracted. Within minutes of sitting down beside him, she had decided what she was going to do.

She could admit to herself now that the seduction hadn't been solely about compromising him. It had been about *her*. All the sadness, fear, frustration, and rage that had been simmering inside her since Paul's death had reached a boiling point when Derek joined her in the lavatory. The eruption of this emotional brew had been explosive.

With the first kiss she must have communicated that she wanted to be taken immediately, completely, and possessively, because his hands, strong and warm and commanding, had slid beneath her hips and rocked her forward to meet each thrust and then had secured her tightly against him when he gasped his release.

Once it was done, she'd wanted to forget it. Mission accomplished.

But she'd been a fool to think that she could be that objective, or that she could convince herself, even for one instant, that it wasn't about the sex. Tonight she'd rebuked him for telling her he thought about it constantly. But he wasn't alone in that preoccupation. Her mind wouldn't let it go, instead returned to it frequently. The episode was like a recording that had been looped to play over and over again inside her head. At odd times, some of them most inconvenient, she would join it in progress, catching a memory that was sharp and sweet and drenched with sensuality.

Worse, each time she was with him, those recollections came up full with surround sound and in Technicolor. Her reaction to being near him was shamefully and intensely physical. Even when she was angry with him, she couldn't deny the unique ache of longing. And of wishing that things could be different. Because anything coming of this mutual attraction was unthinkable, of course. The timing couldn't be worse. The circumstances were impossible. And yet—

Her telephone rang.

She groped for it in the darkness and flipped it open. "Hello?"

"Julie."

"Derek?"

"I believe you. Everything. All of it."

She threw off the covers. Something was wrong. She could tell by his voice. "What's the matter? What's happened?"

"The son of a bitch killed Maggie."

CHAPTER
16

BILLY DUKE STARED AT HIS REFLECTION IN THE CRACKED, MOT-tled mirror and wondered where in hell was the cocksure, good-looking, snappy-dressing, smooth-talking man he'd been just a few short weeks ago.

His hair had grown out some since he got the buzz cut. He missed his wavy mane, which had been unfashionable but one of his trademarks. He missed his smart clothes, replaced now by T-shirts and jeans that had seen better days.

"Lose the look," Creighton had said. "You can't stand out. You must become, for all intents and purposes, invisible."

So he'd lost his "look," but it was the man himself who seemed the most changed and unfamiliar. Where was his swagger? The guy in the mirror looked nervous and anxious, disheveled and desperate. He barely recognized himself.

Billy Duke wondered what had happened to him.

Creighton Wheeler, that's what.

He bent over the stained sink and splashed cold water onto his face. The water smelled faintly of sewage. The towel was thin to the point of being see-through. The place was a dump, but the accommodations were the least of his problems.

Creighton had paid an unexpected visit to the motel this morning. Billy had spent each of the hours since then reviewing everything that had been said, everything that had passed between them.

The first thing he remembered was waking up with a powerful thirst. To delay having to get up, he remembered trying to work up enough spit to swallow, but his mouth had been arid. Reluctantly, he'd pried his eyes open.

His heart had nearly burst with fright. "Fuck!"

A hand had clamped down on his windpipe, trapping the screamed expletive. " 'How bad you want to survive?' "

Billy couldn't have told him. He couldn't have uttered anything except inarticulate choking sounds. He'd thrashed his legs and bowed his back, he'd tried to dislodge the hand around his throat, but Creighton Wheeler had had all of his one hundred and seventy-something pounds bearing down on it, and it didn't budge. He'd pressed down so hard, Billy had feared his Adam's apple would pop like a Ping-Pong ball.

" 'You want to survive bad enough to stop me, pussy? Or are you relying on my generosity, my love of humanity, to stop me from killing you?' "

Billy's eyeballs had begun to bulge. His face had become distorted and congested with blood. Inside his head yellow skyrockets had begun to explode against an expanding field of inky black. His extremities had started to tingle. His brain had begun shutting down. Synapses had ceased to connect.

However, a small part of his brain had still been capable of reasoning, and with it he'd been thinking how remarkably calm Creighton was despite his evident fury. If Creighton had been yelling, he wouldn't have been nearly as frightening. It was that malevolent whisper, that cold control that had convinced Billy that the guy might actually kill him, that these might be his last few seconds on earth, and that he would die staring into Creighton's handsome, composed face as he slowly but inexorably squeezed the life out of him.

But just as suddenly as he had attacked, Creighton had released him. He'd removed his hand from around Billy's throat as though throwing him off. Billy, on his back, had clutched his neck, gasping and coughing. When he'd been able to push air past his swollen lar-ynx, he'd wheezed, "What the fuck? You scared the shit out of me."

"Is that what I smell?" Unruffled, Creighton had sat down in a chair and calmly wiped his hand with a pocket handkerchief, as though touching Billy had left it dirty. Replacing the handkerchief in the breast pocket of his linen sport jacket, he'd said, "Louis Gossett, Jr., won an Oscar for those lines in *An Officer and a Gentleman*. He was choking David Caruso."

"Fuck you and Louis whoever." Billy liked movies okay, but this guy's obsession with them had begun to get on his nerves. "I've got to pee."

In the bathroom, he'd done his business, drunk a glass of water, and inspected his neck for bruises. He'd thought then what a bastard Creighton was. But as he was to learn, Creighton Wheeler was only getting started.

He'd dressed and gone back into the main room, a combination living and sleeping area separated from the kitchenette by an el-shaped bar of chipped, rose-colored Formica. In the center of the ugly room, looking like a magnolia blossom atop a heap of dung, had sat the golden boy, who looked so fucking perfect, it had made Billy resent even more the motel room in which he'd been se-questered.

"They have your picture."

Billy's heart had given a little bump at the tone in Creighton's voice. Or rather, the lack of tone. To cover his concern, he'd sat down on the edge of the bed to put on his shoes.

"They have your picture," Creighton had repeated. "It was on TV last night."

"I saw. So what?" Shoes on, he'd got up and sauntered into the kitchenette.

"I came here this morning to assure myself that you had left. But here you are, two weeks after the . . . event. You should have left At-lanta that afternoon, Billy. That was the plan."

"You think I like it here?" He'd looked around the motel room with disgust, making his guest aware of its deficiencies. "I would have split according to *plan*. I would've been long gone. Except for

the matter of the money. Which was also part of the *plan*. Every day
I use my laptop to check the balance of that Cayman bank account.
So far, zilch. Has it slipped your mind to make the deposit? Have you
conveniently forgotten that part of the *plan*?"

"No," Creighton had replied calmly. "But your memory of the
terms is fuzzy. The terms were that when you had left Atlanta, without anyone hot on your trail, the money would be deposited. I had to
wait a reasonable amount of time to guarantee that you weren't
being sought as a suspect. When I'm satisfied of that, you'll be paid."

Billy had snorted. "I wasn't born yesterday."

"You don't trust me to keep my word once you're gone?"
Creighton had tipped his head down coyly. "That's not cool. Not
after what I did for you."

The reminder had been subtle but effective. Billy hadn't taken it
further. "Coffee?"

"No."

Billy had set about brewing a pot for himself. "That photo
they've got of me is a joke. Useless."

"It was clear enough for me to recognize you."

"Because you're the only person in Atlanta who knows me."

"Your former girlfriend knows you."

The reference to her came like a bolt from the blue. Billy had
hoped Creighton had forgotten she lived in Atlanta. "Emphasis on
'former,' " he'd said, making a dismissive gesture. "Besides, she has
no idea I'm here. I've completely changed my appearance. Hair.
Clothes. She wouldn't recognize me from that blurry picture as the
Billy Duke she knew. And even if she did, the last thing she'd do is get
involved in another police matter. Not after what happened the last
time she did."

"You could be wrong about her."

"I'm not. I know her. She wouldn't. You can relax."

Creighton had looked relaxed, sitting there idly tapping the air
with his tasseled loafer. Relaxed in the way of a reptile just before it
struck.

"Didn't I warn you about security cameras?" he'd asked.

"You did. But how was I supposed to get into the hotel without
getting my picture taken? There are cameras at every entrance. At

least that older hotel had an outdated security system. The newer ones have cameras in the elevators, on each floor, all over the damn place. If your uncle Paul had been banging his girlfriend in the Buckhead Ritz . . . By the way, why were they in that hotel? Why not someplace newer and fancier?"

"It's one of the few privately owned hotels in the city. The owner was an old friend of Uncle Paul's. He died a few years ago. Uncle Paul had a sentimental streak."

"Hmm. Well, it worked to our advantage. If they'd been somewhere more newfangled and busier, I'd have had to come up with another plan."

"In hindsight you should have."

Billy had dismissed that with a shake of his head. "His Tuesday lunches with her were infallible. I knew he'd be there. I knew the time frame. That information allowed me to plan. And, you wanted her there when I popped him. You were very specific about that." When enough coffee had dripped into the carafe, he'd taken it off the burner long enough to fill half a cup, glad that he had a prop, something to hold on to. "Are you sure you don't want some?"

"No thank you."

Creighton's stare had been disconcerting. Billy, not to be outdone, had stared back through a cloud of steam as he blew on his coffee to cool it. He'd decided it was time he went on the offensive.

"I'm surprised you came here, Creighton, even if you didn't expect to see me. We agreed that we absolutely, positively, could never have contact. After weeks of being alone, I'm grateful for the company, but frankly, I'm pissed that you broke the agreement."

"Your TV debut last night changed that. I had to take the risk. I had to know that you'd gone. But since that's not the case, it gives me an opportunity to tell you that you've overstayed your welcome, and to ask you what the fuck you were thinking."

His tone had been as sharp as a needle. Billy had reacted as though he'd been jabbed. "About what?"

"The robbery. That ridiculous mask."

"You said to be creative. You said it couldn't look like a hit."

"You didn't fool anybody."

Billy had noted then that, even though Creighton hadn't moved, he'd seemed to be vibrating inside, as though his temper was being held in check only by his skin. Who the hell was *he* to get upset with *him*? Billy had resented him acting like he was the boss. He might have more money than God, but he wasn't *that* special.

"I told you, you can relax. I'm not Billy Duke for nothing, you know. They won't catch me. I was completely covered, head to toe. I disguised my voice. I burned the clothes I was wearing, including the mask. I broke up the sunglasses and tossed them into a Dumpster.

"The pistol is in pieces, scattered in storm drains all over the city. Even if the police found all the parts and pieced them back together—the chances of which are slim to none—the gun's untrace- able. I filed off the serial number, and the first shot ever fired from it was at your dear ol' uncle's skull." Creighton had remained unim- pressed. Irked, Billy had added, "Look, they can't link me to the crime. All right?"

"They can place you in the hotel."

"Along with hundreds of other people. If I'm ever identified and questioned, I have a perfect explanation. I went in to use the tele- phone."

"To use the phone?"

"The pay phones off the lobby. I was looking for a job, answer- ing want ads in the newspaper." Reaching behind him, he'd picked up a stack of folded newspaper pages from the bar and held them where Creighton could see them. "Ads, circled in red ink. Ads with asterisks beside them. Contact names jotted down. I was concentrat- ing on jobs in the area of the hotel. Because my cell phone was on the fritz, the hotel was a convenient, air-conditioned, quiet place from which to make calls. I used it as an office for several days leading up to and including the day Paul Wheeler was shot.

"If the police check those phones off the lobby, they'll see that I placed several calls to local businesses on each of those four days, numbers listed in these marked ads, inquiring about the jobs they were advertising.

"I even went to two of them and picked up applications, al- though I never filled one out. So, see, I have a reason for being there, and it can be backed up by irrefutable phone records and the office people I talked to.

"And, on the day of the so-called robbery, I made an appoint-ment with one of the prospective employers for three-forty-five. You'd told me your uncle and the woman were usually out of there by three. She must've given him seconds that day, because they didn't leave the suite until three-ten. Seemed like forever I was waiting in that stairwell, watching the door to their suite. Soon as I saw them leave, I put on the mask and glasses, and bolted down one flight to the eighth floor to stop the elevator. Wasn't easy. But it worked, didn't it?"

Creighton had been smiling now. "It did."

"Did you ever doubt it?"

Creighton had shrugged, leaving Billy to think that maybe he hadn't had complete confidence in Billy's abilities to pull it off.

Billy didn't like Creighton Wheeler, but he wanted his approval. "I waltzed out of the lobby seconds before all hell broke loose. Made it to my appointment with time to spare."

"You actually went?"

"I was interviewed by the human resources gal. She liked me. Said my credentials were impressive. I think if I'd had all the paper-work filled out, she'd have offered me the fucking job."

They'd shared a laugh, then Creighton had said, "Give me the stuff."

Billy's laughter had faltered. "What stuff?"

"The jewelry you took off the people in the elevator. It wouldn't do if you were caught with my uncle's wristwatch."

"Hell, Creighton, I didn't know you wanted it. I threw it all away. Tough call, too. That watch alone was probably worth twenty grand."

"Fifty."

"Fifty? Jesus. Well, it's not worth shit now. I threw it into the back of a garbage truck while the trash men weren't looking. I watched them compact it. The other things were dropped into trash bins all over the city. I suppose there's a chance a homeless person might find a ring, or a watch, but even if they turned it in to the po-lice—oh, that'll happen—it could never be traced back to me."

Creighton had still been looking at him with eyes that seemed never to blink. Billy remembered now wanting to make a dent in the millionaire's mask. So he wouldn't feel inferior, like he was the subordinate in their partnership, he'd wanted to awe and dazzle Creighton. He'd asked, "When the police were questioning you, were you shown photos of the murder scene?"

"Why?"

"Just wondering," he'd said, making it sound casual.

"No, I wasn't. I believe they were shown to my father."

"I think you would've enjoyed seeing what that elevator looked like." Billy had got excited while describing to Creighton the exhilaration he'd experienced when he pulled the trigger. "I thought I knew what to expect. I watch movies, too, you know." He'd grinned. "But, man! It was louder, more . . ." He'd used his hands to indicate an explosion. "Made a hell of a mess of that elevator, let me tell you."

The son of a bitch hadn't even commented on the gory scene Billy had created. "When do you plan to leave, Billy?"

"I told you when."

"When the funds are deposited into the Cayman account?"

"Cover that last detail, and I'm *adios*. We never see each other again."

"Perfect."

"Just like we planned."

Creighton had come slowly to his feet. "Except that I have one last detail of my own." He had smiled, but in a way that made Billy's heart hitch.

"What detail?"

"I'm not as *relaxed* as you are. Especially about your ex-lover."

The hitch in his heart had become a hammer. "She doesn't even know I'm in Georgia."

Creighton's smile had turned sad. "Billy, you really shouldn't lie to your partner."

"I'm not lying."

Creighton had leaned in and whispered, "I've talked to Ariel."

Billy'd almost thrown up his coffee. "You did? When? Where?"

"I know about the phone calls."

Still trying to brazen it out, he'd stammered, "Ph-phone calls? I don't know what you're talking about. What phone calls?"

"Don't try that bluster on me, Billy. You know what phone calls I'm talking about."

"I swear I don't." He'd denied it with all the passion he could muster. He was ashamed now of how desperate he must have appeared to the rich bastard. "Look, I don't know what Ariel told you, but there's no way she could know I'm within a thousand miles of here. We agreed to keep it that way, right? We're partners, you and I."

"As such, we shouldn't have secrets. Which is why I'm telling you now that I've decided to make sure your former girlfriend doesn't come back to haunt us."

"How do you plan to do that?"

"Leave it to me."

"I'm telling you, we don't have to worry about her."

"Well . . ." Creighton had winked. "Just to be on the safe side."

Billy had rounded the bar so quickly, he'd rapped his hip bone against the corner. He'd raised his hands, palms out, and given Creighton that sheepish, boyish grin that had never failed him before. "Okay, I'm caught. I did phone her house a couple of times. Like a prank, you know. Just for shits and giggles. What's the big deal?"

Creighton had checked his watch and turned toward the door. "My masseur will be waiting on me."

"Wait, what are you going to do?"

"Get a massage," he'd replied with the innocence of an altar boy. "Oh, you mean about your former sweetheart?" He'd pursed his lips as though thinking about it, and Billy had wanted to hit him. "Well, after what she did to you, after the level of her betrayal, I believe her punishment should be severe, don't you? She showed you no mercy, right?"

"She's just a kid," Billy had said, trying to keep his inflection indifferent. "And I wasn't exactly fair to her, either."

"Trust me, Billy. We'll both feel much more confident of success if we don't leave this one loose end." Billy had been on his heels as Creighton had walked to the door. He'd reached for the doorknob, but Billy, acting on impulse rather than common sense, had grabbed it ahead of him.

"You're not going anywhere, Creighton. Not until we've talked about this. Until we're clear."

Creighton had looked surprised and offended. "That sounds like a threat."

"No threat. I just want to make sure there's no misunderstanding about this."

"I think we understand each other perfectly." With that, Creighton had shot a pointed look down at Billy's hand around the doorknob. Billy had turned the knob and opened the door.

Creighton had been almost through it when he stopped and snapped his fingers. "I almost forgot. I left you a present. Over there by the TV. Enjoy."

The so-called present had been a movie on DVD.

He hadn't watched it because he'd wanted badly to take a long, hot shower. Though he'd never seen Creighton less than immaculately groomed and dressed, the guy gave off an unaccountable air of foulness. It would be hard to make this room worse than it was, but somehow Creighton Wheeler's presence had polluted it.

The shower had helped, some. But a nagging worry had stayed with him throughout the day. He tried putting a positive spin on everything Creighton had said and the way he'd said it, but sinister implications seemed glaringly apparent. Foreboding clung to Billy's skin like the sour sweat that had defied even his shower. He began to wish he'd never met Creighton Wheeler.

He had seemed like a guardian angel when he first approached Billy. He'd appeared when least expected. He'd insinuated his way into Billy's life, and Billy had allowed it. Indeed, he'd welcomed it. Because Creighton had saved a complete stranger's—his, Billy Duke's—butt. There was never any question that Billy would show his gratitude by repaying the favor. Besides, Creighton had been very persuasive.

And things had gone just as Creighton had said they would. Paul Wheeler was dead, and all credit went to Billy Duke. For days following the shooting, each time he watched a news story about it on TV, he could barely contain his pride. With one bold act, he'd gone from playing in the minor leagues to hitting a grand slam at the World Series.

While he'd been staying cooped up in this dump of a place, the days had grown long and tiresome, but he'd consoled himself with visions of his future. When the agreed-upon hundred grand was deposited into the bank account set up for him in the Caymans, he'd be outta here. His conscience was clear because nobody had been snuffed except a stingy old man, a despot who had made his nephew's life miserable. Billy Duke would live out his days a rich man. He and Creighton would get off scot-free, just as they'd planned.

But Creighton's behavior this morning had been high on the creep scale. Things he had said, the way he'd acted, had left Billy with the unsettling doubt that their partnership might not end as rosily as projected. Creighton's mention of Ariel might have been a bluff just to gauge how Billy would react. Creighton had said they had an understanding about that, but did they? He'd said he would deposit the money into the account, but would he?

Billy had spent the day wrestling the fear that his alliance with Creighton had been a colossal mistake.

But now, as he gazed at himself in the mirror, he asked where that jerk got off, nearly choking him to death? And why had he let him get by with it?

Suddenly, in a blinding moment of clarity, Billy cursed himself for being such a limp dick. It occurred to him that he was playing right into Creighton Wheeler's hands. This was Creighton's MO. He was trying to psyche Billy out, and Billy had almost let him!

He laughed at himself for being so damn gullible and susceptible to the other man's mind-fucking. This was what rich men like Creighton Wheeler did. They instilled fear by dropping subtle warnings. That's how they wielded power over other people. Creighton had played a mind game with him, and it had almost worked just as it had before.

"Screw that!"

Billy stalked into the main room and gave the finger to the chair in which Creighton had sat that morning, looking so goddamn perfect and untouchable. Who'd the guy think he was, to second-guess the way Billy had carried out his uncle's execution? He had his nerve. His ass hadn't been put on the line, had it? So how dare he criticize.

Billy reminded himself that he was a wolf, wily and witty, surviv-
ing on instinct and cunning. He was a lean, mean machine. Grinning
with renewed confidence, he knelt and retrieved the black velvet bag
from the bottom drawer of the bureau. "I wasn't born yesterday."

He chuckled, remembering that he'd said those very words to
Creighton. He had gazed at Billy in that smarmy way of his that
made Billy want to deck him, which he should have done.

Creighton Wheeler wasn't nearly as smart as he thought he was.
Did he really think Billy Duke would fail to leave himself an escape
hatch? There was more than one way to skin a cat, and Billy always
had options in place just in case the original plan got fucked up.

He opened the drawstring on the bag and shook the contents
onto the bed. Most of the pieces were inexpensive and disposable,
although a pair of diamond ear studs belonging to one of the scared
old ladies might be worth a coupla thou.

But Wheeler's watch, now that was a huge bargaining chip.

And, now that he thought about it, so was Julie Rutledge.

From the start Billy had sensed that the broad bugged Creighton
almost as much as his uncle did. He'd been emphatic that Wheeler
die in her presence, preferably in her arms. He'd drummed that into
Billy's head until Billy had got sick of hearing it and had told him
so. He hadn't mentioned his uncle's mistress since, not even this
morning.

But, having a knack for seizing or making an opportunity where
one could be found, Billy had checked out every aspect of Julie Rutledge's life as soon as he arrived in Atlanta. He'd done this covert
surveillance thinking that she might make a better partner for him
than Creighton. He'd thought he might pull the ol' switcheroo, the
double-cross.

For instance, he could go to her, tell her of Creighton's plan, and
see if she could think of an alternate scheme that would spare her
lover's life—*and* be more lucrative to Billy.

Win-win. See?

But in the end, he'd decided against it. For one thing, although
she had a swank gallery and looked like a classy piece of ass, she
didn't have the *major* bucks that Creighton Wheeler did. Her home
was nice, but nothing compared with the high rise where Creighton

lived—yeah, against Creighton's explicit instructions, Billy had checked out the building. In the long run, he'd decided his best bet was not to approach Julie Rutledge but to stick with Creighton and his plan.

Once, Billy had even considered going to Paul Wheeler and telling him what his nephew had in store for him. But, based on Creighton's description of him as a real hard-ass, Billy was afraid that Wheeler would call the cops on him, and that would be that. He would go to prison, and Creighton would go on living the life of a prince.

Because no one would believe that a rich guy like Creighton Wheeler was in cahoots with a hustler like Billy Duke. And that's what really nagged at Billy. As things stood now, if he was caught, he'd go down alone.

He picked up Paul Wheeler's wristwatch and rubbed his thumb across the smooth face. Damn! It had been a brilliant move to hang on to it. Not because it was worth fifty grand but because, as long as he had it, he had some leverage with Creighton Wheeler.

But how to put it to best use? He needed to extricate himself from Creighton as gracefully and as profitably as possible. Without getting caught, of course.

He must devise a way.

But his mind needed a break. One could think on a problem so hard that the logical solution became more stubbornly jammed.

So, while he was mulling it over, he put the DVD that Creighton had left him into the player and settled back to enjoy the movie.

CHAPTER
17

JULIE HAD TO RING THE DOORBELL THREE TIMES BEFORE HE answered.

He was dressed as he'd been when they separated, in a pair of jeans and a white shirt with the cuffs rolled to his elbows, but now he looked unkempt. His shirttail was out, and his hair looked as though it had withstood a hurricane-force gale. His eyes were bloodshot and wet. A man in heartache.

He had no reaction to seeing her, not surprise, gladness, or annoyance. His features were drawn with acute sorrow.

She said his name, just that, softly and with compassion.

Saying nothing in return, he left the door standing open and retreated down an entry hall. She stepped inside, closed the front door, followed him around a corner and into a compact room. Two of its walls had built-in bookshelves. They were neat but functional, not for show. Louvered shutters were closed over a single tall window.

The room was minimally furnished. A desk with a computer, stacks of newspapers, unopened mail. An armchair. And a tobacco-colored leather love seat on which Derek was sprawled, his head resting on the padded armrest, his forearm covering his eyes.

Now she was here, Julie wasn't sure what to do. He'd hung up directly after telling her his beloved Maggie had been killed. Acting impulsively, she'd got up, dressed, and within minutes of answering her phone was speeding toward his home.

When her plan to prevent him from representing Creighton was still unformed, she'd looked up his address. Habersham was one of the most prestigious streets in the city, and like most of the homes on its winding trail through Buckhead, Derek's was situated on a deep, tree-shaded lot. It was an older home to which renovations had been made without any sacrifice of its original character. At any other time, she would have enjoyed taking in all the details.

But tonight she was more interested in the owner than in the well-appointed house. In her haste to get here, she hadn't paused to question what was compelling her to come. Now, she questioned the advisability of intruding on his grief.

Gingerly she lowered herself onto the seat of the armchair. "Can I get you anything?"

He shook his head.

The house was as silent as a stone. Not even a ticking clock, or the creak of settling lumber, disturbed the profound silence that pressed against her eardrums like water pressure at fifty meters. She thought of leaving, just going, without disturbing him further. She could slip out and he probably wouldn't even notice or remember later that she'd been there. But something kept her perched tensely on the edge of the chair.

Finally he lowered his arm and looked at her, just looked, said nothing.

"Do you want me to leave?"

"Why did you come?"

"Because . . ." She stopped. She'd been about to say, *Because I know how much Maggie meant to you* or *Because I know how wrenching a loss like this can be.* But suddenly she realized the reason she was here, and it made her ill. She had raced here in order to apologize.

"If it weren't for me," she said thickly, "Maggie would be alive. I'm sorry. I'm so sorry."

She shot to her feet and rushed for the door, but Derek called her back. "You didn't kill Maggie." He sat up. "*He* did. That sick fuck. He killed her."

He placed his elbows on his knees, dropping his head into his hands and plowing his fingers through his hair. His abject despair touched Julie to her core. She went to the love seat, sat down beside him, and placed her hand between his shoulder blades. "How long had you had her?"

He glanced at the rug beside his desk chair, where Maggie must have napped while he worked. "Ten years."

"She was mentioned in most of the articles I read about you. She was described as your constant companion. She was as much a celebrity as you."

He gave a soft laugh and wiped his eyes with the heels of his hands. "She knew it, too. I swear she posed for pictures."

"Think of that. Think of how well she was loved, how much she loved you. Focus on the good times you had together."

He raised his head and looked toward the open office door. "That'll be hard. For a while anyway."

She followed the direction of his gaze, then returned to his profile, which had gone rigid. "You found her when you got home from Athens?"

"I took my time getting back. Stopped to get something to eat." Again, he planted his elbows on his thighs and dug into his eye sockets with his thumbs. "You know the scene in *The Godfather*? The racehorse. In the bed."

She exhaled a thread of breath through parted lips, murmuring, "Oh my God, Derek."

He lowered his hands from his eyes and looked at her. "Yeah. It unmanned me. I screamed. He wanted to hurt me, he wanted to get to me, make the worst possible impact. He did."

The doorbell rang, and Julie jumped, looking at him with alarm.

"That'll probably be the police. I thought you were them when you rang the bell."

"They took their sweet time."

"I told them there was no rush, that the damage was done. Excuse me."

He left her to answer the door. She followed. The uniformed patrol officers looked awfully young and terribly rigid, as though they'd just graduated from the academy and had to overcompensate for their inexperience by being stiff-lipped and terse.

They exchanged very stilted introductions with Derek, who then motioned them upstairs. "First door on your left."

As he and Julie watched them go up, she said quietly, "They're like machines. The shock of what they'll see might render them more human."

"Don't count on it. They know me by reputation. They'll go through the motions of investigating, but the Atlanta PD isn't going to go all-out to track down my dog's killer. I don't expect these two to do much more than file the report. The only reason I called them was because I wanted it on the record."

The doorbell chimed again. "That'll be the vet," he said. "I called him to help me with . . . with Maggie."

He went to the door and admitted a man about his age. It appeared he'd dressed swiftly, in threadbare jeans and a faded Falcons T-shirt. Maybe he'd chosen the old articles of clothing because he knew that, after doing the chore he'd been called to handle, he would probably have to throw the clothes away.

He and Derek hugged each other awkwardly, in the way of men finding themselves in an emotional situation. When Derek stepped back, he indicated Julie and made a low-key introduction, to which she and the doctor responded in monotones.

Then Derek said to the vet, "This way." As they passed her, he said, "Don't come upstairs."

Julie found her way to the kitchen. The appliances and countertops were sleek and spotless, those of someone who didn't cook often. The coffeemaker was so newfangled it took her a while to figure out how to start it once she'd filled the water tank and scooped grounds into the wire mesh filter.

Seeing Maggie's food and water dish near the back door, she moved them inside the pantry. They would be painful reminders.

The two police officers entered the kitchen, looking no less stern than they had before going upstairs. Each gave her a once-over but said nothing as they passed through the room and used the exterior door to go outside.

From the window in the breakfast nook, she watched their flashlight beams dance along the ground and sweep across the shrubbery. One officer shone his up into the branches of a tree, as though the culprit might be hiding there. But neither did any real investigating, and within a couple of minutes of going out, they came back in. One tapped his flashlight against the control box of the security system, and the other nodded.

"Do you think he tinkered with the alarm system?" Julie asked. "Are you going to fingerprint that doorknob? Did you see footprints outside?"

Ignoring her questions, one asked, "What's your name?"

She told him.

"Common spelling?"

"Yes."

"Were you here?"

"When?"

"When he found the dog."

She shook her head. "I arrived only a few minutes before you."

Asking nothing else, they filed out of the kitchen, moving as one unit.

Derek had predicted correctly. They were going through the motions, but just barely. She followed them to the foot of the staircase, where they reunited with Derek. She hung back while they conferred with him in muted voices. One took notes. Derek asked them several questions, to which he received perfunctory answers.

Then the officer taking notes closed his notebook. She heard the other tell Derek that they would be in touch. He showed them to the door, where one touched the brim of his hat. "Sorry about your dog, Mr. Mitchell."

Derek closed the door on them without replying. He shot Julie a look as he passed through the hall but said nothing as he started up the staircase.

She returned to the kitchen. The coffee was ready. She'd just located mugs and spoons when she heard noises and went back to the front of the house. Between them, Derek and the vet were carrying a black plastic bag down the stairs. Derek's eyes were leaking tears.

She went ahead of them, opened the front door, and stood aside. They carried the bag from the house to the curb, where the vet had left his pickup. Julie watched from the open doorway as they gently laid the bag on the ground, lowered the tailgate, then lifted the bag into the bed of the truck.

The vet stepped away, leaving Derek alone. He stood there for what seemed to Julie a long time, but the moments were fraught with such emotion that perhaps it wasn't nearly as long as it seemed. Finally Derek placed his hand on the bag, said something, then raised the tailgate and closed it.

The vet, with remarkable sensitivity, Julie thought, didn't say anything more, just climbed into the cab of his truck and drove away. Derek's knees seemed to give way. He sat down on the curb, facing the street, and stayed there for a time. Julie saw his shoulders shaking. She stayed where she was in the open doorway, knowing that he needed this time.

Eventually, he stood up and walked slowly back to the house. His white shirt was white no more. His jeans were dark with blood. When he got to the door, he said, "I'm going to shower," and once again climbed the stairs.

When he hadn't reappeared after fifteen minutes, she filled a mug with coffee and carried it up. She located his bedroom because it was the only room with the light on. The door to the adjacent bathroom was closed. Behind it, water was running. His bed had been stripped. In the center of the mattress was a dark, wet stain, larger than a man, as repugnant as anything Julie had ever seen.

Another bag, like the one in which Maggie's body had been placed, had been sealed and put in a corner. Derek's bedding and clothing, she thought. On the floor, propped against the wall opposite the bed, was the painting from the auction, still in the crate in which she'd secured it. Just the night before, but it seemed a lifetime ago.

The water shut off, and a couple minutes later he stepped from the bathroom with a towel wrapped around his waist. She extended the mug toward him. "I'm afraid it's gone cold."

"Thanks anyway." He took the mug from her, but he stared into the coffee without tasting it. "I'd rather have a drink."

"My house." She spoke decisively, even though the idea only just then had occurred to her. "Get dressed."

Creighton entered his condo building through the lobby and stopped to pick up his mail. Wedged into the narrow slot on the front of his brass mailbox was a folded sheet of paper. He spread it open, read the message quickly, then cursed as he headed for the elevator.

Billy wanted to see him. Immediately. Underlined and printed in capital letters.

He formed a fist, crumpling the note. The idiot had actually come into his building, stuck a note in his mailbox, when how many times had Creighton told him not to contact him under any circumstances?

Of course Creighton had broken that covenant this morning when he'd gone to the motel, but Billy wasn't allowed the same privileges.

He took the elevator up to his condo and went straight to his bathroom, where all the walls were mirrored. He stripped and turned on the shower. That fucking mutt of Mitchell's had made a mess.

Killing it had been in the back of his mind for a couple of days. An Ace hardware store had equipped him, complete with painters' overalls, just in case he decided to reenact the scene from *The Godfather*.

The rude manner in which Mitchell had treated him today in his office had doomed his dog. Creighton had got some payback for that by catching Mitchell in Athens with Julie, groping her like a horny teenager. Then the guy had had the nerve to dress him down. When Mitchell had stopped at a restaurant on his way back to Atlanta, it had seemed providential that Creighton go ahead and do the dog.

A man who defended thieves for a living really should know better than to leave his house without setting the alarm. That had been Creighton's only concern. That and the dog barking. But the drivethrough at Burger King had solved that problem. She'd growled and barked a couple of times, then he'd tossed her the burger and she'd almost choked herself gobbling it down.

It didn't take any time at all.

Then, in the shelter of shrubbery in Mitchell's backyard, he'd removed the ugly jumpsuit, boots, and gloves he'd worn over his clothes, stuffed them into a garbage bag, then tossed the bag into a Dumpster behind a supermarket on his way home. He'd stopped at a car wash with a high-powered hand wand and used it to blast the gore off the knife with which he'd severed the jugular and the hacksaw that had finished the job.

But he could smell stale blood on himself. He liked the odor only when it was fresh.

As he scrubbed himself now, he thought about Billy, who apparently couldn't take instruction. He sensed edginess in the note he'd left, a mounting desperation that could prove troublesome.

Creighton could relate to having an urge so strong it made your skin itch from the inside. Of course, he knew how to govern his impulses, but he mistrusted Billy's ability to do so. He reasoned that, despite the risk involved, he must heed the man's frantic summons.

By the time he'd lathered and rinsed twice, his plan was in place. He dried off and slicked his hair back with gel, which made it appear shades darker. He dressed in black jeans and a black T-shirt.

Then he raided his kitchen, packing the items he took from the pantry and fridge in a foil-lined tote bag provided by the gourmet market where he shopped.

A half hour after entering his building, he left through the same door. Tonight he was driving something less conspicuous than the Porsche. The SUV was navy blue with tan trim. The interior was tricked out with every available option, but from the outside, it looked like any one of a thousand such vehicles on the streets of Atlanta and her suburbs. Which was why he had driven it today. It hadn't attracted attention in either Athens or Derek Mitchell's neighborhood.

And, just as a precaution, he'd switched the license plates on it twice this week.

He wasn't happy to be again climbing behind the wheel. He'd already covered a lot of ground this evening. Driving to Athens, then speeding back ahead of Mitchell. Dealing with the dog—although the cheeseburger had made them friends, he'd had a hell of a time getting her onto the bed, which Mitchell had apparently made off-limits.

He'd had a full day already. He would much rather have been settling in to enjoy the cool, dark serenity of his home theater with an unlimited selection of films to watch.

But "A man's gotta do what a man's gotta do." Colin Firth. *Love Actually.*

To avoid his car being seen at the motel, he parked in the shadow of a discount carpet store that was already closed for the day, then took the tote bag and walked across the full parking lot of a seedy-looking lounge next to the motel.

How convenient, he thought. He actually detected a path worn into the blacktop between the door of the lounge and that of the motel office.

Billy's room was the last on the ground floor of the wing that extended behind the building, away from the busy street. As Creighton approached the room, he glanced over his shoulder, but as far as he could tell, just like this morning, his arrival had gone unnoticed. This wasn't the kind of place that catered to people who wanted to be seen.

He tapped the door once. Billy opened it almost immediately and sagged with relief upon seeing him. "Thank Jesus. I was afraid you wouldn't come."

Creighton nudged open the door with the toe of his shoe and stepped into the room. The air inside was warm and humid, and reeked of Billy's anxiety. "I sensed an emergency." He carried the tote bag into the kitchenette and set it on the bar. "But what were you thinking to come into my building?"

"Nobody saw me."

"You're sure of that?"

"Positive. Do you think I'm an idiot? I don't want to get caught any more than you do."

Billy was trying his best to maintain his swagger, but Creighton detected fissures in his cocky façade. Which validated Creighton's decision to act quickly, before the man shattered completely and ruined everything.

He took a bottle of beer from the tote bag. "I think you have a touch of cabin fever. How about a beer?"

"Thanks."

"Bottle opener?"

"Behind you. Top drawer."

Creighton found a rusty church key and used it to open the beer. It foamed over the lip of the bottle and onto the countertop. Some dripped onto the floor. Creighton ripped off a paper towel and knelt to wipe it up. Billy seemed not to notice the mess or the time Creighton was taking to clean it up. He was pacing like an animal in a cage.

Once he'd tidied up, Creighton turned around and passed the bottle to Billy, who snatched it and sucked from it greedily. "Thanks."

"You're welcome."

"Aren't you having one?"

"I don't drink."

"Right. I forgot." Billy looked at the tote bag as though noticing it for the first time but showed little curiosity in it. He rolled his shoulders and assumed an aggressive stance. "Listen, Creighton . . ."

"I'm listening."

"I don't want you to do it."

Creighton began removing food and utensils from the tote bag. He knew exactly what Billy was talking about, but he pretended bewilderment. "Do what?"

Billy drank from the bottle of beer. "Nobody else gets hurt, okay?"

"Oh. You're referring back to our conversation of this morning. Why are you obsessing over that?" He smiled as he unwrapped a package of deli sliced ham. "It's not your concern, it's mine. And I'm not worried in the least. You shouldn't be, either. I trust you like ham."

"She wasn't part of our deal."

"Not initially. But I'm flexible. Another beer?"

Billy looked vexed, but he said ham was fine and agreed to another beer.

Creighton turned his back to open the second bottle, but he saw out of the corner of his eye the nervous movements that Billy didn't want him to see. Billy wiped his hands on the seat of his jeans. He ran one hand around the back of his neck. His teeth pulled at a loose piece of skin at the corner of his lip.

Creighton swapped bottles with him, the empty for the full one. "Ready for a sandwich?"

"Sure. Okay. I haven't eaten much today. There's mayo in the fridge."

"I brought deli mustard."

"Great."

Creighton nodded toward one of the barstools. "Sit down, Billy. You're making me nervous." Billy took a seat, but he was far from relaxed. He propped his foot on the lower rung of the stool and jiggled his knee. By contrast, Creighton's motions were slow and methodical as he prepared two sandwiches, spreading slices of bread with mustard, stacking the ham just so. "Swiss or provolone?"

"Doesn't matter." Watching him, Billy said, "You don't have to do it."

Intentionally misunderstanding, Creighton said, "I don't mind. Really. For weeks, you've been eating out of cans. I thought you'd welcome the change of cuisine."

"Cut the bullshit, Creighton. You know what I'm talking about, and it's not the goddamn sandwich. You don't have to kill her."

Creighton continued stacking cheese and ham onto the slices of bread.

Billy propped his forearm on the bar and leaned across it. "She doesn't know anything about Paul Wheeler. It would never cross her mind that I was involved in that."

"It might."

"It won't. How could it?"

"Things have a way, Billy. The smallest thing can trip you up. You're my partner. I have an obligation to protect you."

"No you don't. The main reason I wanted to see you tonight was to tell you that we're square. I'm gonna split. Tomorrow. You were right. I should have left Atlanta right after killing Wheeler. Did you see that black detective on the six o'clock news this evening?"

"No, I missed that."

"Well, one of the people I got cute with, a secretary at one of the businesses where I picked up a job application, she recognized me from the security camera photo and called the police."

"She didn't have any information on you, did she? Not even your real name?"

"No."

"Or an address. Phone number?"

"No."

"Then I don't see the problem." Creighton had brought along the well-sharpened knife, clean and sanitized now, that he'd used on Mitchell's dog. He took it from the tote bag and used it to halve the sandwiches, then laid it on the counter and slid a paper plate toward Billy. "Eat."

"Thanks."

"My pleasure." Creighton took a bite of his sandwich. "Hmm. Delicious if I do say so. I love that black pepper crust on the ham, don't you?"

Billy bit into his sandwich, chewed, washed the bite down with beer. "So, you're good?"

"Good?"

"With leaving things alone. I skip town. We never see each other again. We don't have any further contact. Nobody else dies."

Creighton held his gaze as he took another bite of sandwich and chewed it thoughtfully. "You surprise me, Billy. When we met, you couldn't say enough bad about this girl."

"I know what I said. That's how I felt then, but now . . ." He swallowed a gulp of beer, reached for his sandwich, but changed his mind, returned it to the plate, and rubbed his forehead instead.

"What's on your mind, Billy?"

"I'll tell you what's on my mind. That fucking movie."

Creighton blotted his mouth with a napkin. "Which movie?"

"The one you left this morning."

"You watched it?"

"Yeah."

"Brilliant, isn't it?"

"It's sick. That guy, the killer, he's sick. That scene where he—"

"I can guess the one you mean. It's the signature scene. The brutality is so graphic, the effect is—"

"Whatever," Billy said with agitation. "I can't get it out of my mind."

Creighton whispered, "Did it turn you on?"

Billy's jaw dropped. "Hell no."

Creighton winked. "Just a little?"

"Jesus, Creighton. No."

Creighton wanted to laugh. He was enjoying the hell out of this. Poor Billy, not so much. Creighton almost felt sorry for him.

"Look, Creighton, I was pissed off at her. At one time I might have said something like 'I could kill her.' But I didn't mean it. It was just talk." He gestured toward the TV. "I wouldn't want anything like that happening to her."

"Billy, you hypocrite. You vaporized my uncle's brain. It was sprayed all over that elevator. You boasted of it this morning, and unless I'm wrong you were disappointed that I hadn't seen pictures of your handiwork."

"That was different."

Still amused, Creighton said, "Really? Enlighten me."

"I didn't know him. I didn't have any feelings for him. It was quick. He never knew what hit him."

"I see." Creighton pushed his plate aside and brushed bread crumbs from his hands. He'd eaten all of his sandwich. "You don't mind me murdering the lover who betrayed you, so long as it's benevolent."

"No. Yes. I mean . . ." He came off the stool like it had suddenly become hot. "I mean I don't want you to do it at all."

"It's only fair, Billy." Creighton calmly wrapped the leftover ham and cheese. He replaced the cap on the mustard. He picked up the knife and used the razor-sharp tip to point at Billy's plate. "Are you finished?"

"Yeah, thanks. What's only fair?"

Creighton dumped the scraps, including the paper products, into a gallon-size plastic bag, sealed it, then put everything, even the empty beer bottle, back into the tote bag. "Hershey's Kiss?"

"No thanks. What's only fair?"

Creighton removed the foil wrapper from the candy and popped it into his mouth, then dropped the foil into the tote bag. "She's a loose thread for me, too. By rights, you should be the one to eliminate her. She's your baggage, after all. But"—he smiled—"I can see how difficult that would be for you. I understand how you'd have conflicting emotions over it. So, I'll relieve you of the distress it would cost you."

Billy looked like he was having trouble keeping down the beer and sandwich. "You can keep—"

"My uncle Paul's watch?"

"What? No. I told you. I threw away all the stuff I took in the robbery."

Creighton held his gaze for a moment, then gave the squalid room a slow, detailed survey. "Honest Injun? If I searched this place, do you cross your heart and hope to die that I wouldn't find a bag of jewelry?"

"I swear."

"Your cell phone."

"Huh?"

"Your cell phone. You're too smart to have been making phone calls from this room."

"It's one of those disposable ones. I bought it before the robbery."

"Ariel told me—"

"I never said anything. I told you. I just called a few times and hung up. If she told you it was me calling, she's guessing, that's all."

Creighton held out his hand, palm up.

Billy worried that loose piece of skin on his lip, then went to a bureau drawer, took a cell phone from it, and gave it to Creighton, who slipped it into his pants pocket.

"Makes no fucking difference," Billy muttered. "No calls can be traced to me."

Creighton smiled. "I feel so much better now." He hesitated, then said, "It goes without saying that if you've e-mailed—"

"There's my laptop." It was on the nightstand. "Check it out. Of course I haven't e-mailed. All I've used my computer for is to check on that bank account using the password you gave me."

"When did you last check it?"

"Yesterday."

"I made the deposit late this morning, just after I left here. You don't have to take my word for it. You can check it now."

Abruptly, Billy said, "I don't want the money."

"What?"

"You can keep the hundred grand."

Creighton laughed softly. "Well, thanks for your generosity, but that's the best hundred grand I've ever spent. I'm free of my narrow-minded, penurious Uncle Paul."

"Keep your money. Just don't kill . . . don't kill . . ."

"Ah. Just don't kill your former sweetheart." Creighton looked at him sadly and shook his head. "But I want to, Billy. I want to do it for you. The cunt betrayed you. Not once, but twice."

"Twice?"

"Somebody called and identified you to the police, don't forget."

Billy wiped his sweating forehead. He glanced toward the television set again, and Creighton could have sworn he paled another shade. "Are you . . . How are you . . ."

Unh-unh-unh." Creighton wagged his index finger. "I didn't tell you how to kill Uncle Paul. It's only fair I get to decide my method. Let it be a surprise. When they find her, it's sure to be on the news."

"When are you going to do it?"

"Do you know what a smash cut is?"

"A smash . . . No I don't know. What?"

"It's an abrupt edit. A sudden shift of scene. Used to shock the audience. Very effective. Lots of impact. Packs a wallop. It'll be like that. No one will see it coming. Especially her." He shook the second beer bottle to make sure it was empty, then placed it in the tote bag.

"However, I do think it's a good idea for you to leave Atlanta. We shouldn't see each other again. You could definitely stand a change of scenery." Creighton gave the quarters a scornful glance. "This place is a dump. No wonder you're not acting yourself tonight."

He dampened a paper towel and used it to wash the church key before replacing it in the drawer, then he wiped the bar with the towel and placed it in the tote. He checked to see that he hadn't forgot anything, then picked up the bag, using both arms to hold it against his chest. "Can you get the door for me, please?"

Billy had stopped whining and now seemed eager to get rid of him. He moved quickly to the door and opened it. "So long, Creighton. Been nice knowing you."

"We won't see each other again."

"Right. Have a good life."

"When you vacate, just be sure not to leave anything behind that could lead them to you. Or to me, Billy. Especially to me."

"Like I said before, I don't want to be caught, either."

"I'd rather be dead." Creighton waited a beat, then added, "Wouldn't you?"

CHAPTER
18

JULIE HAD EXPECTED A TOKEN ARGUMENT, OR A QUESTION AT the very least. But a few minutes after she'd announced to Derek that they were going to her house, he came downstairs dressed in a fresh pair of jeans, polo shirt, sneakers.

Together they left his house, got into her car, and made the ten-minute drive in silence. He followed her inside, entering through the garage directly into the kitchen. She set her handbag on the table and moved to a cabinet. "I haven't restocked since Paul died, but I have bourbon and vodka. There's a bottle of white wine in the fridge." Not the one she'd found opened last night. That had been thrown out.

"Bourbon."

"Water?"

"Just ice."

When the drink was ready, she carried it to him where he was standing in the center of the kitchen. He looked at the wrought-iron towel rack, now empty.

She said, "They were a keepsake, but he ruined them for me. I threw them away today."

Sipping from his glass, Derek took in the pots hanging above the range, the corked bottles of flavored oils and vinegars, the shelves of cookbooks, the array of utensils at the ready, so different from his near sterile kitchen.

"You cook." It wasn't a question.

"I learned while I lived in France."

His eyes met hers. "Did you cook for Wheeler?"

"Often."

He took another sip of bourbon.

"Would you like something?"

"No."

It was an abrupt and decisive response, so she didn't force the issue. "I want to show you something. It'll take a while, so if you're sleepy, it can wait till tomorrow."

He looked down into his glass, swirling the liquor around the ice cubes. "I don't think I'll sleep tonight."

She nodded sympathetically, then motioned for him to follow her. She led him into her living room. "Make yourself comfortable." He sat down on the sofa. She moved to the wall unit that served as a media center.

While she was setting things up, Derek asked, "When do you think Creighton was here?"

"My maid left at noon, so he had all afternoon. I'd taken my formal dress to the gallery yesterday morning so I could change there and go straight from work to the event."

"How'd he get past your alarm?"

"A faulty interior motion detector had caused several false alarms. I hadn't had time to replace it and had stopped setting the alarm to avoid fines from the city. How'd he get past yours?"

"I rushed out to meet you in Athens. Didn't think to set it."

While they were talking, she'd removed a DVD from its case and inserted it into the player.

"We're going to watch a movie?"

Using the remote, she went through the menu on the screen to play the movie, then joined him on the sofa, passing him the DVD case. "Hitchcock."

He read the title. "*Strangers on a Train.* I've never seen it."

"It's old. Some consider it a classic. Creighton does."

Derek turned his attention to the screen, and within minutes, he was engrossed, as audiences had been for decades, by Robert Walker's eerie portrayal of the millionaire murderer. An hour into the film, Derek took the remote from Julie's hand and hit Pause. "Creighton and Billy Duke swapped murders."

"Creighton and someone." Julie looked into the close-up of the actor's face frozen on the screen. His benign manner and soft voice concealed the mind and soul of a ruthless killer. "I believe Creighton got the idea from this film. Once, over dinner at Doug and Susan's, he talked endlessly about the brilliance of Hitchcock, this film in particular. He can quote the script, chapter and verse. Hitchcock made films that are better known than this one. *Psycho, The Birds, Rear Window.* This was Creighton's standout favorite, I think because the millionaire so reminds him of himself. If nothing else, he's a narcissistic egomaniac."

"He avoids cameras because he doesn't feel they do him justice."

"Maybe that's part of it. Anyway, after it was hammered into me time and again that Creighton couldn't have been the masked robber who shot Paul, I remembered his talking about this movie. I ordered the DVD and watched it." She smiled without mirth. "I don't think it was a coincidence that Creighton was playing tennis when Paul was killed."

Derek looked toward the screen. "The other main character is a tennis pro."

"Creighton's little inside joke."

Derek leaned forward and set his glass on the coffee table. The ice cubes had melted, and the liquid inside had diluted to the color of herbal tea. He'd become so captivated by the film and what it portended that he'd forgot his bourbon.

He got up, made a slow circuit of the room, pausing occasionally to look at something: a framed photograph of her and Paul, a trio of antique French books, a vase of dried green hydrangea. He stopped with his back to her and stared at a painting on the wall, his hands propped on his hips, the stance with which he'd studied the painting in the parlor of her gallery.

"Do you like that one better than the fat man?"

He came around to her and gave a crooked grin. "Much."

They looked at each other for a long moment. Maybe he was remembering, as she was, the harsh words they'd exchanged that day, and why. Finally she asked, "What do you think of my hypothesis? Am I crazy?"

"No."

"Am I reading too much into a movie script? Adapted from a book, by the way. Do you think I'm making the plot fit because I want it to?"

He sat down on an ottoman, bringing him closer to the TV screen, and stared into the frozen black-and-white image. "This guy wants his father killed so he can get his inheritance sooner rather than later."

"In Creighton's case, it was his uncle Paul. But like in the movie, the relationship was contentious."

"The millionaire meets the tennis player on the train and, over lunch in the dining car, casually offers to kill his wife."

"Because she is a slut. She's carrying a baby the tennis player feels certain isn't his. Furthermore, he's deeply in love with another woman. He's desperate for a divorce his wife won't grant. But, being the hero of the film, he doesn't wish her dead."

"The millionaire forces the issue. Without the authority of the tennis player, he kills the wife."

"The audience witnesses her murder reflected in the lenses of her eyeglasses."

"Genius filmmaking."

"Because it's so unsettling to watch."

Derek picked up the thread of the plot. "Now that the millionaire has done his part and killed the troublesome wife, it's the tennis player's turn to return the favor. The psycho expects him to kill his father. The tennis player balks."

"He didn't realize the psycho millionaire was serious when he proposed this deal to him on the train. The tennis pro thought he was talking in the abstract. Look, *I* want somebody dead, *you* want somebody dead. Why don't we swap murders? Strangers killing strangers. No links to each other. No one would suspect."

Derek frowned. "If this Billy Duke was the shooter, if he killed Paul for Creighton, are you assuming that Creighton has killed someone for him?"

"If he's following the plot, I think it's a fair assumption. Of course, I don't know for certain."

"For the sake of discussion, let's say you're right. Creighton got what he wanted. Paul is no more, and Creighton's in the clear. Except for . . ." He looked at Julie. "Billy Duke. If I were him, I'd be covering my back."

"Especially now that his picture has been shown on television."

"That's bound to have made Creighton nervous. If he disposes of Billy Duke before the police can run him down—"

"Then Creighton will have got away with conspiring to kill Paul," she concluded softly. "My fear is that Billy Duke is already dead and all possible links between the two destroyed. I'm afraid that Creighton has already got away with it."

Derek left the ottoman and this time paced the room from end to end before stopping to stand in front of her. "Have you shared this theory with Sanford and Kimball?"

"No."

"So why me? Why now?"

"I can answer both questions with one word. Maggie. You've experienced Creighton's unspeakable cruelty. I've been telling you for days that he was unconscionable. You don't have to take my word for it any longer."

He studied her for a moment. "I've had a lot of practice sifting the whole truth, and nothing but the truth, out of evasion and just plain bullshit. I'm generally good at it."

"You still are. I know you think I'm right."

"And yet . . ."

"I'm untrustworthy, and I hate Creighton."

He waited her out, his incisive gaze cutting to the bone.

Finally she relented. "All right, there *was* an incident at Doug and Susan's house. We were having a cookout on their terrace. Mosquitoes loved Paul, and they were attacking that evening, so I went into the pool house to get some insect repellent.

"While I was in there, Creighton ambushed me. What he described to you happened, except he was the aggressor, not I. He unzipped his pants and forced my hand around his erection. He said if I didn't do what he wanted, he'd raise a hue and cry, Paul would come running, and what would Paul think of his ladylove then, standing there groping his more handsome and much younger nephew?

"I managed to get away from him. He didn't raise a hue and cry, and I realize now that was an empty threat. He only wanted to humiliate me. I tried to go on with the evening, but I couldn't bear to be near him. Each time I looked at him, he would wink, or make some other insinuating gesture. He sickened me. So I told Paul I had a headache, and we left."

"Did you ever tell Paul about it?"

"No."

"Why?"

"The antipathy between him and Creighton created friction with Doug and Susan. His family, especially Doug, was vitally important to Paul. I didn't want to be the cause of a rift between the brothers." She raised her hands, palms up. "There you have it. The whole truth, nothing but the truth."

"Why didn't you tell me your side of it before?"

She held his gaze for several beats. "Because, on the plane, I . . ." She lowered her head. "That's why."

He turned away and paced the same path one and a half times before she asked, "Should I advance my theory to Sanford and Kimball?"

"After talking to Kate, they're operating under the belief that you and Billy Duke are in cahoots."

"I can disabuse them of that."

"Just like that? If you go to them with this far-fetched idea—"

"You think it's far-fetched?"

He stopped pacing. "Julie, I tell my clients this all the time. It doesn't matter what I think. It's what the jury thinks that matters, and at this point, the jury is composed of Sanford and Kimball. Can you disprove you know this Billy Duke character?"

"No."

"No. So as far as the detectives on the case are concerned, you're implicated."

"Than what do I do? Sit on my hands, do nothing, let Creighton get away with murder?"

Taking umbrage at her tone, he leaned over her, tapping himself in the chest with his index finger. "I want him, too, Julie. I want him ground to mincemeat. What he did to Maggie is a felony, but I have no hope whatsoever of the police pursuing it, or of a prosecutor proving that Creighton did it, or of me ever getting a shred of satisfaction in a court of law." He straightened up, turned his back to her, gave himself several moments to calm down, then came around. "He's proven himself to be incredibly smart. We've got to play it smarter."

"By doing what?"

"Let me put Dodge on it."

"Who's Dodge?"

"My investigator."

"The one who investigated me? Handy man to have at your disposal."

Ignoring her caustic tone, he said, "Very handy. I've already told him to keep me posted on the manhunt for Billy Duke. But I'll have him start looking for the man himself. Hopefully he'll have better luck than the police have."

"If they can't find him, how can this Dodge person?"

"You don't want to know," Derek said under his breath. Switching subjects, he asked, "Did Wheeler ever mention if Creighton had been arrested? Have a juvie record?"

"He never said. Can your investigator find out?"

"Nigh on impossible, but we'll see."

"He's going to be busy. In the meantime, do I go about my business as though I haven't been elevated to the top of the suspect list?"

"Do you have an attorney?"

"Ned Fulton."

"I know him. Good man. Sharp attorney. Call him first thing in the morning and tell him about Kate's interview with the detectives. You won't have to tell him the implications of it. He'll realize what they are."

"What are you going to do?"

"I've got to be in court at nine." He consulted his wristwatch. "Seven hours from now."

"You're welcome to sleep in my guest room."

"Thanks, but I need—" He broke off. His head dropped forward, and he rubbed his forehead. "I was about to say I need to get home and let Maggie out." He lowered his hand and closed it into a tight fist, which he ground into his opposite palm. "That son of a bitch. I almost regret calling the police. Now that the shock has worn off, at least a bit, anger has moved in. What I'd really like to do is hunt down Creighton Wheeler and, when I find him, kill him with my bare hands. He's made this a personal fight. I'd love to respond on a very elemental and primitive level. An eye for an eye."

She gave him a soft smile. "Tempting, I grant you. But I recommend that you finish watching the movie instead."

He shook his head, weariness settling on him again. "I've seen enough. But I'll crash here if you don't mind and call a taxi in the morning. Tomorrow at some point I've got to buy a new mattress."

"The police may need to see it again."

"Fat chance."

"Do you think you can sleep?"

"Not a wink."

"You might surprise yourself," she said. "You're exhausted."

"Do I look that bad?"

She raised her hand, intending to touch his cheek, but pulled back before she did. "You look angry and bereaved."

"I'm experiencing alternate surges of both."

"I know exactly how that feels."

Moving efficiently, she turned off the television and the lamp, then motioned for him to follow her to the guest bedroom. It was an uncluttered room, decorated in a neutral palette of earth tones, punched up here and there with touches of red and animal prints.

"It's not a king-size bed."

Derek was looking at her, not into the room. He didn't even glance at the bed.

"The bathroom is through there," she said, gesturing toward a closed door across the room. "I think you'll find everything you need, but—"

"Julie." He waited until she had turned to him, and even then she stared at the Polo insignia on his shirt before reluctantly lifting her eyes to his. "I haven't thanked you for rushing over tonight."

"Don't thank me, Derek." Remorsefully she lowered her head, shaking it slowly. "Regardless of what you say, if it weren't for me, you'd still have Maggie."

He cupped her cheek in his palm and tilted her head up. "Creighton saw us together."

Speechlessly, she gaped at him.

"In Athens. But even before. He saw me here with you last night. Followed us to Coulter House. He remarked on the romantic storm, the foggy car windows. He doesn't know how we met, or when, but he lashed out at me for having sexual congress with 'his accuser.' In coarser language than that, but he knows the reason I wouldn't represent him, and it pissed him off. To get back at me for turning him down and for failing to tell him why, he cut off Maggie's head." He struggled with a tight throat before he was able to continue. "You were circumstantial."

"I dragged you into this mess."

"Dragged? I don't remember you dragging me up the aisle of that airplane." His eyes grew dark and fierce, and he took a step closer. "I remember everything else."

No doubt he would enjoy knowing how vividly she remembered, too. She'd been reliving the encounter earlier tonight in stunning detail. Standing this near him, feeling his body heat, having his fingertips lightly caressing her face, she felt her memory being reawakened. Dangerously. Especially when he leaned down and placed his lips against her neck.

She angled her head back, breaking the contact. "I hope you can rest. Good night."

He reached out and caught her hand. "Stay with me."

"No, Derek."

"Just lie beside me. That's all."

She gave him a knowing look, one he couldn't misinterpret, and pulled her hand free.

Swearing under his breath, he pushed his fingers through his hair. "Why not? The cat is out of the bag. Creighton knows. Soon Doug will. What's the harm now?"

"The harm now is—"

"Are you pregnant?"

"What? No!"

"If you're carrying Paul Wheeler's baby—"

"I'm not!"

He held her gaze, gnawing the inside of his cheek, his body taut with frustration. "You loved him."

"Yes."

"Him or what he did for you? He rescued you from an unhappy marriage, helped set you up in business, and treated you like a princess. You gave him frequent home-cooked meals and the all-important Tuesday afternoons."

She felt a flash of red-hot anger. "Is that what you think of me? If so, you're no better than Creighton. My relationship with Paul wasn't anything like you paint it to be."

"It was love," he said, his inflection snide.

"Yes, it was."

"For both of you?"

"Yes."

"For you as much as Wheeler?"

"Why do you keep coming back to that? Why do you doubt that?"

"Because you sought me out on that airplane."

"And you know why."

"I might buy that reason as the only reason, except that when I touched you, you were wet."

She opened her mouth to speak, but no words were there.

"And because you came, Julie," he said roughly. "You came."

Creighton Wheeler was a fucking lunatic.

No sooner had Billy closed the door behind him than he bent at the waist and, with his hands planted on his knees, took several deep, cleansing breaths.

There was something seriously wrong with the man, something

missing in him. He was empty and cold, like one of those holes in space that swallows light. Creepy like nobody Billy had ever run across.

He cursed the day Creighton had walked into his life. Damn him and his foolproof plan, which Billy should have recognized as too good to be true. But, actually, by the time Creighton had explained the "plot," as he'd called it, the first act had already been played, hadn't it? Billy had been suckered before he'd even been given a choice.

Although, in all honesty, he couldn't claim to be a victim.

No, he'd been willing enough to go along. Even glad to. He'd been seduced by Creighton's aristocratic charm, which came from having money. Creighton had been the embodiment of everything Billy Duke had always aspired to be. So Billy had latched on, hoping that some of the millionaire's polish would rub off on him.

And, stupidly, Billy had believed that Creighton had chosen him for his enormous potential, talent, and savvy.

But that was history, and it was too late to call back decisions already made. Now, he was in damage-control mode. He had to think of a way out of this whereby he could get away clean. And not only from criminal prosecution. He also must escape Creighton Wheeler. Of the two, that might be the trickier to pull off.

When you bargained with the devil, you had to watch your back for the rest of your life. He'd been a fool not to realize this sooner. Billy Duke was a thread Creighton wouldn't leave loose.

He had left himself extremely vulnerable. It occurred to him now that Creighton hadn't touched a thing in the room, not this morning, not tonight. Everything he'd touched, he'd taken away with him. You could be damn certain the DVD case had been wiped clean of his fingerprints.

There was nothing linking Billy Duke to Creighton Wheeler. If the cops busted through the door right now, Billy would be up shit creek all alone. In his possession were the items taken in the robbery. Keeping them no longer seemed a smart thing to have done. And how long would the hundred grand stay in that account if Billy was arrested? Only as long as it took Creighton to go online and, with a few keystrokes, empty it.

The only thing connecting them was Ariel. All day, in an attempt to warn her against Creighton, he'd been calling the number he knew, but apparently she was at work, and he had no idea what her job was now. If he got near her, she'd call the police, and they would arrest him on the spot for Wheeler's murder, and he couldn't protect anyone if he was in jail.

The thought of Creighton reenacting the scene in that movie with his ex made his stomach heave. Their affair had turned out badly, but while they were together, he had loved her. In his way, he truly had loved her.

So if you don't want her to die, think!

He had a good grasp on all the ways he was screwed.

Now, he must concentrate on what he had going for him.

He went to the bureau drawer, took out the bag of jewelry, and set it on the bed. He then took out another cell phone, one he'd bought as a backup. Just in case Creighton somehow got wise to him. "I wasn't born yesterday," he mumbled.

These were his resources. Limited, yeah, but he had to make them work for him. He snapped open the new phone and speed-dialed the number he'd already programmed into it. It rang several times without an answer. He hung up. He considered redialing and leaving a message for Ariel, but he knew she wouldn't listen to it. The minute she heard his voice, she would delete it. He had to make her talk to him. Tonight. That was imperative.

At the same time he was saving the life of a young woman who would die solely because of her former association with him, he had to devise a way to protect himself. But how?

Starting with the day they'd met, Billy reviewed everything that had passed between him and Creighton, and the one thing that Creighton had been fanatical about was that his uncle's murder could not come back to him. "An equal swap. It's only fair," he kept saying. Tonight, as he'd left, he'd said it again. "Be sure not to leave anything behind that could lead them to you. Or to me, Billy. Especially to me."

So, wasn't that the key to the solution of Billy's problem?

The only way he could escape Creighton was to leave him free and clear of any suspicion. If Creighton was absolutely certain that he'd got away with conspiring to have his uncle killed, it would be pointless for him to kill anyone else. Right? Hopefully.

Thinking along that track, Billy stared at the velvet bag. At the phone. At the bag. And suddenly, he had two simultaneous recollections. One was Creighton's frequent refrain. The other was something that had been said to him years ago, at a time when he'd been in a real jam. (At least it had seemed like a real jam. Compared with the jam he was in now, that had been kids' play.)

But when it was happening, the situation had looked grim. He was guilty as charged. Indefensible. But his lawyer wasn't that worried. He'd told Billy that when your defense didn't have legs to stand on, you left it alone and stacked a case against somebody else instead.

"Your defense boils down to one statement, Billy boy: 'Some other dude did it.'"

Billy remembered with perfect clarity the sly lawyer's words, and they caused him to laugh out loud. Hot damn, he wasn't without ideas or advantages, at all!

Creighton Wheeler thought he was so fucking scary, but not even he could outfox Billy Duke.

CHAPTER
19

H E ARRIVED AT COURT ON TIME.

As expected, Derek hadn't got a wink of sleep in Julie's guest room. At dawn, he'd called a taxi to pick him up. It had taken a half hour to arrive. He'd been sitting on the curb waiting when it finally pulled up.

Last night, Julie had stalked away from him and angrily slammed her bedroom door. It had remained shut all night. He'd left without seeing her.

His house had seemed incredibly empty and cold without Maggie there to greet him. Nausea had risen in his throat when he entered his bedroom and saw the obscene, dark, moist Rorschach form on his mattress. He'd showered and dressed in a hurry, and was in and out of the house in under fifteen minutes.

He'd driven to his office. Marlene, bless her, had already been there and the coffee was brewed. Handing him a steaming cup, she'd given him a critical once-over, noticing his bloodshot eyes. "Hard night?"

"Maggie's dead."

She'd listened in stunned silence as he told her what had happened, leaving out any mention of Julie and his spending the night at her house.

"You're sure Creighton Wheeler is responsible?"

"Yeah, I'm sure." For the time being, that was all he wanted to say on the subject. "Call a staff meeting for eleven o'clock. Unless someone's in court, I want him here. I need concise, and I emphasize that, updates on the cases each is working on."

Regardless of everything else that was happening, Derek still had a legal practice to run. Actually, he was glad to have the work and responsibility. He needed somewhere to channel his anger-fueled energy, so that he wouldn't hunt down Creighton Wheeler and kill him bare-handed. Work wouldn't provide him near the satisfaction, but of the two, it was the acceptable outlet for his wrath.

"If our meeting spills over into the lunch hour, have box lunches delivered. No one leaves. If anyone has lunch plans, they're to be canceled."

As he'd rattled off directives, Marlene had furiously scribbled notes in her pad. He'd finished his coffee in one gulp and checked the time. "Call my cleaning lady and warn her before she goes upstairs. Tell her to dispose of the bag in the corner. Call a mattress company. Ask them to—"

Marlene had interrupted. "All that will be taken care of, Derek. I'll see to it that you have a new bed when you get home this evening. I'm more worried about *you*. How are *you*?"

"I've been better." The sympathy in Marlene's eyes had caused his to sting with renewed emotion. "I'm going to be late for court." He'd headed for the door, saying over his shoulder, "And get in touch with Dodge. This hearing shouldn't take more than an hour. I'll meet him here after."

He was going to court to appeal for a postponement of the Jason Connor trial. The DA's office had finally delivered their discovery files, but not until yesterday afternoon, shortly after his meeting with the Wheelers.

Despite his volatile mood and gritty eyes, he walked confidently into the courtroom. He greeted his client, who was shackled and unresponsive. Derek wanted to smack him for the attitude but instead applied himself to the business at hand and argued persuasively, citing the delinquency of the DA's office to hand over discovery.

After twenty minutes of heated argument, the prosecutor said, "Your Honor, the file was delivered in good faith as soon as it was complete. If the demands on Mr. Mitchell's time didn't permit him to look through it, then he shouldn't have taken this case. Which he did only to get himself some headlines."

Derek could have kissed him. He'd let his mouth run away from him, and Derek knew, even before the judge pronounced it, that the matter would be ruled in his favor. He was granted another month in which to shake loose something from the recalcitrant teen before he went to trial.

He asked for a minute alone with his client, and the jail guards granted it. "Jason, I can't help you if you won't help me."

Except for his perpetual scowl, he was a good-looking boy. Compact build, dark hair, dark eyes, sullen lips. "Help you how?"

"By giving me something to work with. Something to build a defense around. I did look through the discovery file. They've got you, unless I can argue a reason for you taking that knife to your parents."

He waited. Got nothing. Jason shifted his legs, which caused his shackles to rattle, but otherwise, he didn't respond.

Derek said, "Know what I think? You're a punk and a jerk, and not nearly as tough as you want everyone to think."

The boy turned his head toward Derek then, his eyes ablaze. "What the fuck do you know about me?"

Having won his attention at last, Derek leaned in. "I know you're going to death row if you don't lose the attitude and give me something."

"I was mad. Okay?"

Derek slapped his palm on the table. " 'Mad' isn't going to hack it, Jason. Kids get mad at their parents all the time. They don't butcher them. Are you listening to me? I'm trying to save your life."

"Who asked you to?" He shot from his chair. The guards leaped forward. "Why don't you just leave me alone?" he screamed at Derek. He wrestled with the guards as they escorted him away.

Disheartened, Derek was packing up his briefcase when one of the bailiffs approached and handed him a standard letter envelope. "Guy asked me to give you this. Said you'd know what it was in reference to."

Dodge was standing in the shade of his office building, smoking, when Derek arrived. He looked Derek over with the same critical eye as Marlene had, but he didn't remark on his haggard appearance. He extinguished his cigarette in the soil of a potted plant as they entered the building. They were alone in the elevator.

Derek said, "Jason Connor is bound and determined to let the state execute him."

"Bummer."

"Creighton Wheeler killed Maggie last night."

Dodge looked at him sharply.

Derek didn't spare him the gruesome details, describing them as they entered the law firm and made their way toward his corner office.

"That motherfucking son of a bitch," Dodge muttered.

"I heard that," Marlene said.

"Sue me."

Sue me was Dodge's favorite expression—his favorite *clean* expression.

Marlene fanned her hand in front of her face, waving away his tobacco stench, as she handed Derek a handful of memos. "None of those is urgent. Attendance at the staff meeting will be one hundred percent, and I've warned them they'd better look sharp." Then, in a gentler tone, she added, "The vet called and wanted you to know that he's awaiting your instructions on the remains."

Derek nodded and went into his private office, Dodge trailing him. He asked, "What are you going to do?"

"Have her cremated."

"May wait a day or two on that," Dodge advised. "The police might want to examine the body again."

Derek made a scoffing sound. "I called the Zone Two headquarters before going to court. The rookies who came to the house are off duty this morning, but I talked to their supervisor. They filed the report. I was given a case number and was assured their investigation is ongoing, that they would be in touch if they had something to report."

"But you're not holding your breath."

"No."

"How do you know it was him?" Dodge lowered himself into one of the chairs facing Derek's desk.

From his jacket pocket, Derek took the envelope delivered to him in the courtroom and walked it over to his investigator, who looked at it curiously, then opened it, removed the single sheet, and read the two typed lines.

" 'How's that for wet work?' Michael Douglas. *A Perfect Murder.*" He looked up at Derek. "*Wet work* refers to getting your hands bloody. What's Michael Douglas got to do with it? Did I miss something?"

"Creighton Wheeler is a walking reference book on the movies. A historian. What he did to Maggie—"

"*The Godfather.*"

"Yeah."

"Jesus."

"Yeah."

Dodge put the paper back in the envelope and slid it across Derek's desk. "You gonna hand that over to the police as evidence?"

"For all the good it'll do."

"Especially now that we've handled it."

"They probably wouldn't have followed up anyway, but I'm going to request they send it downtown to CID."

Dodge grimaced. "Criminal's got its hands full with people killing people."

"I'm not hopeful anything will come of it."

"Why's this Wheeler son of a bitch got it in for you? Because you said no to representing him?"

Derek settled into his desk chair and swiveled it several times as he contemplated the scruffy investigator. He searched his mind, heart, and soul, and could find no reason why he shouldn't trust him. "Dodge, I'm going to tell you something."

"Judging by your tone, you're going to have to kill me after. Frankly, I'd just as soon not know."

Derek smiled grimly, then started at the beginning, with the return flight from France, and told Dodge everything, concluding with Julie's theory that Creighton had swapped murders with someone, presumably the man identified as Billy Duke.

When he finished, a lengthy silence ensued. Finally Dodge said, "I need a smoke."

"Well, you can't have one until you give me some advice."

"You're the brains here, Counselor. You're the one paid big bucks to get people out of trouble."

Derek took the older man's querulousness for what it was—a delaying tactic. He needed time to assimilate everything Derek had told him. Awarding him the time, Derek got up and went to the window. Looking out, he envied the people fighting traffic, rushing to make appointments, running errands, coping with everyday vexations, having a normal day.

Normal had deserted him the instant he'd looked into Julie Rutledge's face. She was right in that respect: He was in this mess because of her. If not for her, Maggie would be alive. On the other hand, if not for her, he would be defending Creighton Wheeler, and the prospect of being that sicko's advocate made Derek want to throw up. He would follow a punk like Jason Connor all the way to his execution. He wouldn't defend Creighton Wheeler against a ticket for jaywalking.

As though following his thoughts, Dodge spoke. "No matter what else, this Creighton Wheeler is an asshole who needs to be taken out. I know some guys. For a case of cold Bud and a C-note—"

"Dodge."

"I'm serious."

Derek chuckled. "I know you are. And it's tempting, believe me. But I'd rather ruin his life than end it."

"For Maggie only, or do you think the Rutledge broad is right, that Creighton was the mastermind behind Paul Wheeler's killing?"

Derek disregarded Dodge's referring to Julie as a broad. "I'm inclined to believe she's onto something. I watched a good portion of that Hitchcock film. The villain is eerily reminiscent of Creighton. He's charming. Handsome and glib. Wealthy."

"And a psychopath," Dodge said. "I saw that movie, too. Long time ago. My first wife—or maybe it was number two—kicked me out of the house. I had to stay in a motel a couple of nights till she cooled off. There was a Hitchcock film festival playing in one of those old theaters that do that sort of thing, and the TV in my room didn't have cable, so I went and saw all the features."

He paused and thoughtfully scratched his cheek. "I can see where the gal is going with this, him being such a movie nut, and all. If he did that to Maggie, he's pure-dee evil."

Derek turned away from the window, knowing that the older man's observations didn't stop there. "But what?"

"Nothing." Dodge patted his pockets in search of a phantom cigarette.

"Come on. What?"

He shrugged. "Somebody gets so pissed off at somebody else, they kill their dog. Happens all the time."

"Do you think that's all this is? Creighton was holding a grudge because I wouldn't be his lawyer, so he sneaked into my house and beheaded my dog? That's all this amounts to?"

"I don't know," Dodge replied, in as testy a voice as Derek's. "I'm just saying."

"Saying what, exactly?" Derek returned to his desk and sat down, and although Dodge tried to avoid looking at him straight on, Derek waited until he was. "Are you implying that Julie Rutledge manipulated me once, and she might be doing so again?"

"What I'm saying," Dodge wheezed, "is that the surest way for a woman to get what she wants is to use that which we poor slobs cannot do without. That also happens all the time."

"But she isn't using it. She hasn't let me touch her. Not since the airplane."

"But you want to."

Now Derek was the one to avoid eye contact.

"And she knows you want to."

Derek didn't respond.

"And the longer she holds out, the more you want it, and the more you want it, the blinder you get. There's a direct correlation, you know, between a stiff dick and blind stupidity."

Derek got up from his chair so quickly he sent it spinning. "Okay, say you're right. Like the police, you think she conspired to have Paul Wheeler killed and now is trying to lay the blame on Creighton." He braced himself on the back of a chair, leaning over it to make his point. "She loved the guy, Dodge. To what end would she want him dead?"

"Hell, I don't know. And I'm not saying that's the way it is. I just don't want you canceling out the possibility. You gotta admit there are some strikes against her. Sanford and Kimball aren't fools. On the contrary, each one's good in his own right. Together they're damn good. They wouldn't be looking at her if they didn't feel there was something out of joint.

"You your own self said you didn't see anything that had been disturbed inside her house. You're only taking her word for it that Creighton Wheeler broke in and messed with her stuff, that he was spooking her in the parking garage."

"She didn't kill Maggie. I was with her."

"You said you took your time getting home and that you parted with her practically spitting at you."

"She *did not* kill Maggie."

Dodge backed down. "Probably not. But the rest . . . ?" He paused to suck in another noisy breath. "Just consider that she might not be as lily-white as you want her to be. Look at her objectively before you get caught up in something that would ruin your career, your reputation, and your life. You're too smart to throw away everything over a piece of ass."

Derek glared at him.

"Puff up and get mad at me if you want to, doesn't change the truth of what I'm saying. Besides, you asked," Dodge added defensively. Then he clicked his tongue against his teeth and muttered something to himself. "I know whereof I speak, Counselor. Women will fuck you up worse and faster than anything, and I've got the track record with them to prove it. When one gets to you . . ." He looked at Derek and sadly shook his head.

Derek relaxed his hostile posture and returned to his desk. Never having felt so tired, he slumped in his chair. He knew Dodge was only giving it to him straight for his own good. Looking at him, he asked bleakly, "What's your advice?"

"Walk away from it."

Derek held his gaze for several moments.

"Right." Dodge sighed, patting his pockets again. "I didn't think so, but I dared to hope."

"Whether Julie has cooked up this whole elaborate thing, or Creighton conspired to have Paul Wheeler killed, the key to the mystery lies with the guy who actually did it."

"This Billy Duke?"

"He's the best lead so far. Can you find him, Dodge?"

In answer, the investigator stood up and headed for the door.

"Something else."

Dodge turned back.

"Can you find out if Creighton Wheeler has a juvie record?"

Dodge frowned. "You don't ask for much, do you?"

"Impossible?"

"Well, Moses parted the Dead Sea."

"The Red Sea. Will you try?"

Again Dodge turned toward the door, but Derek stopped him again. The older man groaned. "I really need a cigarette."

"About Julie. You raised some valid questions, Dodge. Thanks for the input."

The investigator looked mollified. "Hell. Wasn't my place to lecture you. And I may be way off base about her. I hope I am. But what I know for dead certain . . ."

"Yeah?"

"She's under your skin something bad."

Julie and Kate had a brief reconciliation that morning in the back room of the gallery when Julie arrived. Kate had been waiting for her. No sooner had she cleared the door than the younger woman began apologizing again.

"I told you last night that no apology or explanation is necessary," Julie told her. "You had to go to the police with what you knew. It was the right thing to do."

They hugged each other, then Kate went into the main room to watch the store while Julie attacked the paperwork she'd neglected for days. The first call came at eleven-thirty. Because Kate was busy with customers, Julie picked up the phone on the second ring.

"Chez Jean."

Nothing. She was almost certain the caller was still there, but when she got no response after saying hello twice, she hung up.

It happened again two hours later. Julie said hello only once before hanging up.

The third call came shortly before closing. Kate was signing a receipt for the UPS deliveryman, so Julie answered the phone. "Chez Jean." After only a few seconds of that expectant silence, she muttered, "Get a life," and angrily replaced the phone in the charger.

"Who was that?"

"A breather."

Kate set the package she'd signed for on Julie's desk. "He called twice this morning before you got here."

"You didn't say anything to me."

"The first time, I figured it was a wrong number. The second time, I just hung up and didn't think any more about it. Till now."

Julie tried to retrieve the number on the caller ID. "Private caller."

Apparently Kate didn't attach any significance to the calls other than that they were annoying. "He'll get discouraged and go away," she said and gathered up her things, preparing to leave. "Why don't you come out for a drink with me, Julie? Maybe grab an early supper somewhere."

"Thanks, but I want to finish up here before I go."

"Okay then, see you tomorrow." Kate touched her shoulder affectionately before leaving through the back door.

Julie glanced at the wall clock and switched on the small TV on her desk. The early edition of the news was coming on. She watched the entire half hour, but there was no mention of Paul's killing or the search for Billy Duke. She didn't know whether to be relieved or disappointed.

She had expected the detectives to show up today, confronting her with what Kate had disclosed to them yesterday about the man's visit to the gallery. She'd notified Ned Fulton to be on standby should she need him. But there had been no word from the police.

She hated to think of the hours they would waste trying to link her to this man she didn't know. But her hands were tied. The only way she could tell them to suspend their futile search for a connection that didn't exist was to betray Derek as the one who'd told her about it.

Derek.

She hadn't heard from him today. Which wasn't surprising, but she didn't know whether to be relieved or disappointed about that, either. As she went up front to check the bolt on the main door, she admitted that she was mostly disappointed.

Angry as she'd been with him last night for the embarrassing thing he'd said, it had been a letdown to get up this morning and find him gone, without a word, without a note. He'd even remade the guest room bed, making it appear that he'd never been there.

On her way back to the storeroom, she paused in the open doorway of the parlor, imagining that, if she inhaled deeply enough, she could still catch the scent of his shaving soap. It drew her into the room. Wistfully, she moved to the painting of the naked man that he had so disliked and smiled at the recollection of his asking if anyone in their right mind would pay good money for it.

He had discombobulated her completely by showing up at the gallery that day. He was the last person on earth she'd expected or wanted to see. And yet she'd been hungry for the sight of him again. She'd taken note of everything—his stance, the shape of his hands, the growth pattern of his hair, the barely discernible scar on his chin. She'd looked at so many photographs of him beforehand that all those physical characteristics had been familiar to her even before she met him on the airplane.

Can I buy you an after-lunch drink? He'd flashed a nearly wicked grin, which, thinking of it now, still made her tummy take a balloon bounce. Smiling ruefully, she whispered, "You had me at hello."

"Jerry Maguire."

Her heart lurched. Gasping in fright, she spun around. Creighton filled the open doorway. He was leaning negligently against the jamb, ankles crossed, his expression sardonic. "Are you turned on by this portly gentleman with the itty-bitty weenie?" Then, in a silkier tone, "Or have I caught you daydreaming about the stud-muffin attorney?"

Knowing she couldn't reveal either her fear or her revulsion, she made her voice sound demanding. "What do you want, Creighton?"

"Julie, Julie. I sense hostility. Since you were practically my auntie, I thought I'd stop by, see how you're faring."

"You could have asked me how I'm faring when you called today."

"Called?"

"It's rather silly and unworthy of you to play that phone game, Creighton. Severing the head of a helpless animal is more like you."

"I have no idea what you're talking about. Not the reference to the phone game, or decapitation." He tsked. "Honestly, Julie."

She was finding it difficult to breathe. Her loathing of him was suffocating her, and that gave her courage. "The gallery is closed. You're intruding. I'm asking you to leave. If you don't, I'm going to call the police."

He picked up the cordless phone off the cocktail table and extended it to her. "Do. That would make for an interesting scene. You, me, the two detectives who are already suspicious of you, getting cozy in your little parlor here. Me telling them that you'd invited me here, that now that my uncle Paul is out of the way, you wanted to pick up where you left off that evening in the pool house."

"They would never believe you. Derek didn't."

He arched one eyebrow. "Derek didn't?"

"I told him the truth about it."

"He raised the subject?"

She said nothing, causing a slow grin to spread across his face.

"The fact that he did leads me to believe he doubts your version. But don't despair. Maybe you'll have better luck with the detectives." He waggled the phone. "Want me to dial for you?"

She shoved him aside and passed through the door. "If you won't leave, I will."

She continued down the hallway in the direction of the storeroom, keeping her back straight, pretending that her heart wasn't in her throat, pounding with fear. After Maggie, there was no question about the violence he was capable of.

He hooked her elbow with his hand and slammed her against the wall, pining her there with his body, his fingers around her neck. "Maybe you liked fucking Uncle Paul. Stranger things have happened. I figure you enjoy fucking the daring and dashing Derek Mitchell more. But what I think you like best of all is fucking with me." He ground himself against her. She struggled to get free, but that only caused him to smile the triumphant smile that made her skin crawl.

"Let me go."

"You like messing with my life, don't you, Julie? Hmm? You think you can fuck me over by swaying the lawyer to your side? Think again."

"I'm warning you, Creighton."

"Of what? What are you going to do?" His fingers tightened around her neck. "You're way out of your league, sweetheart, and, sadly, too proud and foolish to realize it. You should back off while your sweet, soft skin is still intact."

He released her abruptly and grinned when she hugged herself protectively. "Not that I'm not tempted to drag my tongue over every inch of that delicious skin. 'I've always wanted to do that.' Robert Patrick, *The Faculty*. I've also longed to discover what about your snatch kept my uncle so bewitched. But, alas, Julie dearest, we'll have to save that salacious exploration for another time. Tonight I've got a date."

Having said that, he strolled to her back room. As he passed her desk, he paused and looked down at the package. "Don't forget to open your parcel."

He went through the back door and soundly closed it behind him. Julie remained huddled against the wall, her legs trembling so badly they could barely support her.

Eventually she made her way to the back room, still relying on the wall for support. She staggered to the door through which he'd passed and bolted it decisively, then spun around and leaned against it, breathing loudly through her mouth.

She stumbled to the desk and reached for the phone, but reconsidered and left it where it was. Creighton wouldn't have come here if he hadn't believed he could manipulate the situation, use it to his advantage and damage her. He probably hoped she would report the incident to the detectives so he could distort anything she told them, making her look ridiculous or guilty.

Her gaze dropped to the package on her desk.

From the shipping label, it wasn't readily apparent who had sent it. It appeared innocuous, but she mistrusted Creighton's nonchalant reference to it.

Her mind whirled with cinematic images of people finding horrifying things inside ordinary boxes.

There wasn't a sound in the gallery except for the pounding of her heart as she opened the lap drawer of her desk and picked up the box cutter. She slid the button that exposed the razor blade and applied it to the box's packing tape, making one long slash that reminded her of a scalpel slicing through skin. She quickly cut through the tape at the short ends of the box, then laid the opener aside.

Her fingers were so cold she could barely feel the pasteboard as she folded back first one side of the top, then the other. Inside were green foam chips. Standard packing material. Perfectly harmless.

She extended her hands, then quickly closed them into fists and yanked them back. She took several deep breaths and willed her heart to slow. Tamping down her anxiety, she stretched her hands toward the box again. After one agonizing second of sheer dread, she plunged them into the weightless material. Dozens of the green chips spilled over her arms, out of the box, onto her desk and the floor. Heedless of them, she groped.

She found the object secured in Bubble Wrap.

She grasped it with both hands and pulled it out.

Immediately recognizing what it was, she gave a soft cry. Her knees gave way, and she sank to the floor, her whole body trembling uncontrollably. A sob issued from her mouth.

It was the blown glass bowl she had special-ordered for a client. Nothing more.

As she sat there trying to recapture her breath, she looked at the door through which Creighton had passed.

She imagined hearing gloating laughter.

CHAPTER
20

DEREK'S FIRM WAS PRESENTLY HANDLING OVER A DOZEN active cases. Three times that many were pending. He was well versed on each and had hands-on involvement in the defenses being prepared even if other lawyers in the firm were representing the client in court.

After the lengthy staff meeting, his mind had even more data to store and process. But when he answered his cell phone and Dodge said, "I've got him," Derek's brain sharp-focused, and he didn't have to ask who his investigator was referring to.

"Where?"

"Sleazy motel out toward the airport."

"How'd you find him?"

"I've got a paid snitch who frequents the bar adjacent to it. He's got a thing for this Korean gal who runs the motel, so he was hanging out there and showed her Billy Duke's pictures. She started acting fidgety. He called me, so I went to see the lady myself. After I greased her palm, she admitted to recognizing Billy Duke when they showed his picture on TV. He's been renting the room for almost a month, but not under that name."

"Why didn't she report it?"

"She's illegal. I had to give her a coupla hundred to keep her from going completely apeshit, afraid she would get deported."

Dodge paused to inhale. "I think my snitch can forget a romance with her, but anyhow, I've got Billy Duke. Want me to knock on his door, say hi?"

"No. We've got to call Sanford and Kimball."

"Do we?" Dodge asked, suggesting that they didn't.

"What does Billy Duke drive?"

"The Korean claims not to know."

"If he leaves, follow him, but notify me immediately. Keep your eyes glued to the door of his room."

Derek clicked off and asked Marlene to get either Sanford or Kimball on the phone. "Tell whoever you talk to that it's urgent."

While he waited, he considered calling Julie, but Dodge's words of caution prevented him. If she was telling the truth, she would know soon enough that Billy Duke had been captured. If she was lying, and Duke was her accomplice, Derek would be breaking the law by telling her he was soon to be apprehended.

For the time being, his integrity was preserved.

When Julie got home, she was still trembling. Creighton's surprise visit to the gallery had completely unnerved her. Untenable but true: He had the ability to frighten her. He had played one of his sick mind games, and she'd fallen for it. He'd made her afraid to open an ordinary package.

Using her remote, she closed her garage door as soon as she'd driven her car inside. But being safe in her garage didn't relieve her fear. Remembering the pressure of Creighton's fingers against her throat, how he'd ground his body aggressively against hers, she folded her hands over her steering wheel and laid her forehead against them, breathing deeply.

Whenever she saw him now, outside the bar, in the gallery, he became more physically aggressive. Was this a sign of increasing psychosis?

The garage had retained all the heat of the day. It didn't take long for her skin to become clammy with perspiration, but still she shivered in fear of Creighton. Whatever he'd started when he plotted to kill Paul wasn't finished. She was almost certain of that. He felt threatened by her to some extent or he wouldn't be issuing threats, he wouldn't be warning her to back off. Something was brewing. But what? If she didn't even know what crime he planned, or who the victim might be, how could she prevent it?

Eventually the compressed heat forced her out of her car.

Since the break-in, she took special care to keep all the doors to her house locked, including the one connecting the garage and kitchen. She used her key now to unlock it.

Faulty motion detector notwithstanding, she'd also started setting her alarm system religiously, even when she was going to be away from the house for a short period of time. She kept it set when she was at home as well.

So when she pushed open the door into the kitchen, she expected to hear the warning beep. Its failure to go off was more startling than a shrill alarm, its silence portentous and terrifying.

Her heart began to beat wildly. The gloss of perspiration became sweat, bathing her instantly as adrenaline surged through her system. She could barely breathe. Her mind went into overdrive, but she forced herself to think rationally and not to panic. Not yet.

Could her maid have forgotten to set the alarm when she left?

No. Her maid hadn't come today. There'd been no need after the thorough cleaning the house had received yesterday.

Had she herself failed to set the alarm that morning? She racked her brain, trying to remember her actions, and she could swear that the last thing she'd done before locking the door was to set the alarm.

Soundlessly, she set her handbag on the kitchen table and slipped off her shoes. In bare feet, she tiptoed to the counter and slid a butcher knife from the wood block. It had a long, serrated blade, but she would have felt more confident with her handgun, which she'd replaced beneath the bed. She crept to the door leading out of the kitchen and stopped to listen.

The house was as silent as a tomb except for the drumming of her own heart.

After five minutes, when her muscles began to quiver with the strain of holding so still for so long, she forced them to relax. Was she yet again playing right into one of Creighton's mind games?

Had she set her alarm this morning? She'd been upset with Derek, first for saying what he had last night, *You came,* then for leaving without an apology or word of any kind. Maybe—apparently— she'd been so preoccupied with thoughts of him that the newly formed habit of setting her alarm had slipped her mind.

Nevertheless, she held the knife in front of her as she went through the house, checking for an intrusion. Nothing had been disturbed. Leaving the living area, she looked cautiously down the hallway that led to the bedrooms. Again, she paused to listen but heard nothing.

Still on tiptoe, she approached the guest bedroom. The bed was as Derek had left it. The door to the bathroom stood open. Before she could talk herself out of it, she crossed the room. The bathroom was as it always was—ready for a guest. She worked up enough nerve to check the closet and felt rather foolish when she theatrically flung open the door. It was empty except for extra hangers on the rod and a folded blanket on the shelf above. To top off her foolishness, she got down on all fours and checked beneath the bed.

Standing again, she shook her head and stepped back into the hall. The door to her bedroom was open.

She was steps away from it when he sprang into sight. He appeared like a monster in a spook house. Suddenly. Jarringly.

Julie had been expecting a scare. Nevertheless, she screamed.

When Derek arrived at the barbecue joint across the boulevard from the Pine View Motel, Dodge was seated at the counter facing the window where he had a full view of the motel and surrounding buildings. Derek sat down on the stool beside him and pushed away a plate of stripped bones and congealing sauce.

Dodge said, "The ribs aren't bad."

"No thanks."

The restaurant staff was serving up plates of barbecue and side dishes to a dozen or so diners, but neither the servers nor their customers were aware that a police stakeout was taking place.

Keeping his voice low, Derek said, "I spotted two squad cars at the end of the block."

"They've got one at the other end, too. Plus two on the street behind the motel. And them. Plainclothes."

Derek followed the direction of Dodge's nod. An unmemorable sedan was parked in front of the lounge. In the glow of a neon sign, Derek distinguished two silhouettes inside, a man behind the steering wheel, a woman in the passenger seat.

"She used to leak information to me," Dodge remarked offhandedly.

"Used to?"

"We had an arrangement."

"What kind of arrangement?"

"An arrangement. But it went south. If we talk to her, don't let on like you know."

"My lips are sealed."

The arrival of Sanford and Kimball suspended conversation. Derek and Dodge watched the two detectives park in front of the motel office. Kimball got out of their car and went inside. It was like looking into a goldfish bowl. She dinged the bell on the desk. The Korean woman parted the strings of beads acting as a curtain that separated a back room and approached Kimball, who flashed her badge.

Derek said to Dodge, "Part of the deal I made with Sanford. If she cooperates and gives Kimball the key, they won't report her to Homeland Security."

"You believe that?"

"Probably not."

Kimball left the office sixty seconds after going in, brandishing the room key. Sanford left their unmarked car where it was. Together he and Kimball walked along the row of rooms facing the street, turned the corner, and proceeded down the long leg of the el, appearing in the pools of yellow light cast by overhead fixtures, disappearing in the dark patches between.

When they were several yards away from the last room, they moved more cautiously until they were in position on either side of the door. Sanford tapped on it with the barrel of his service weapon. Nothing happened. He said something, then tapped the door again. When still there was no response, he bobbed his head toward Kimball, who leaned forward and fit the key into the lock. Then they moved with speed, swinging the door open and rushing inside.

The two plainclothes officers exploded from their car and ran toward the room, pistols drawn.

"Let's go." Derek burst through the door of the barbecue joint at a run. He sprinted across the boulevard and made it easily. Dodge was puffing by the time he got across. He was keeping up with Derek, but his labored breathing sounded like the exhaust of heavy machinery.

They had almost reached the room when the two plainclothes emerged from it. There was no sense of urgency about them now. Their guns were back in their concealed holsters.

Seeing Dodge, the woman pulled up short. "What the hell are *you* doing here?"

"I found him. Called it in."

"Congratulations. But you're too late. He isn't here."

"Shit!" Derek hissed.

Her partner looked at him. "What's it to you, Perry Mason?" Then to Dodge, "Are you still working for him?"

"He's got a good medical plan."

The cop spat on the pavement, then struck out along the breezeway. "I'll be in the office."

When he was out of earshot, Dodge asked the woman, "Can you get us into that room?"

"You asshole."

Dodge exhaled a long breath. "I had to go, Dora. I got a call."

"You stiffed me with the check."

"The counselor here needed me ASAP."

"That dinner cost me twenty-two bucks."

"I said I was sorry. Come on now. Don't be mad."

She glanced over her shoulder toward the open door of Billy Duke's room. "Soon as Sanford sees you, he's gonna shit."

"He'll feel better after."

"Don't tell him I saw you first."

"You're questioning the manager?" Derek asked.

She glared at him suspiciously. "Maybe I am."

"Ask her—"

"Don't be telling me my job, Mr. Mitchell."

Dodge stepped closer to her. "He wouldn't think of it, Dora. But if you learn anything interesting—"

"Forget it, Dodge. I don't want Kimball on my ass, either." She started walking away.

"Have you forgot that I let you be on top?"

She kept walking but gave Dodge the finger over her shoulder.

Dodge chuckled. "Feel the love."

He followed Derek toward the open door of the motel room. Hearing them, Sanford turned away from the closet where he was rummaging. He placed his gloved hands on his hips. "Thank you for the tip, Mr. Mitchell. But that doesn't entitle you to join the party."

"Everybody know everybody?" Dodge asked. No one responded.

Derek said, "Any sign of Billy Duke?"

"Billy Wood," Kimball said as she emerged from the bathroom. Like her partner, she was wearing latex gloves, but her hands were empty. "That's how he was registered. He paid for a month's rental in cash when he checked in, ten days before Wheeler was shot. The owner has seen him only once since then. She spotted him carrying a bag of trash to the Dumpster around back."

"You only talked to her for a few seconds," Dodge said.

The detective smiled. "I'm good."

"Then why couldn't you find him?"

Kimball gave him a drop-dead look. Sanford looked annoyed with all of them. "Why did you have your man looking for him, Mr. Mitchell?"

"I have a vested interest."

"I heard you are no longer representing the Wheelers."

"I'm not."

"Then why are you so hot to find this guy?"

"No comment."

"Has it got anything to do with your dog?"

Derek looked sharply at Kimball, who'd asked. She shrugged. "Word circulated today. I'm sorry. Truly."

Strangely, Derek believed her and was touched by her sincerity. "Thanks."

"Goes for me, too," Sanford said. "Horrible thing for someone to do."

Before any more could be said about Maggie, Dodge asked about the referenced Dumpster. "You got people searching it?"

Kimball slipped back into her detective persona. "We're not amateurs. Officers will sift through everything in it, but it may have been emptied since Billy Duke, or whatever his name is, took out his trash. The lady at the desk wasn't sure of the day she saw him. Before all is said and done, someone might pull landfill duty."

"What about a car?"

"Unknown," Sanford said.

"Our lady at the desk says she never saw him in a car," Kimball said. "He probably parked it somewhere within walking distance but came and went from the room on foot. We've got officers canvassing the area."

Dodge grunted his pessimistic outlook on that. "This neighborhood, you'll need informants. Be prepared to spend some money."

Apparently the detectives agreed, because neither disputed him.

Derek left the investigators to their shoptalk. He hadn't stepped over the threshold because, if there was evidence to be found, he didn't want to contaminate it. He was absorbing what the detectives and Dodge were saying, but he was also trying to get a feel for the room and the man who'd occupied it.

It was a sad quarters, with obvious patches in the plaster walls and water stains on the ceiling. The bed was unmade, and the sheets looked dingy, like they'd been slept on for weeks without being laundered. If Duke had been taking out his own trash, maid service must not have been included. Behind Kimball, through the open door of the bathroom, Derek could see towels lying on the floor as though they'd been negligently dropped or cast aside.

But in the whole of the space there wasn't a single personal belonging, nothing that wasn't a permanent fixture in the room.

"He's not just out, he's left," he stated despondently.

Sanford frowned. "Seems so. No clothes in the closet. Nothing in the bureau drawers."

"Nothing in the bathroom except a stench," Kimball said. "Apparently the plumbing isn't that efficient."

"Did you check the bathroom sink?" Dodge asked.

"Beads of water are still there," Kimball said. "So he couldn't have been gone that long."

"Is there a window in the bathroom?"

"Not large enough for an adult person to squeeze through."

"I've been watching the place since six-ten this evening," Dodge told them. "He didn't come out of that door since then. So he had to have been gone when I got here, but not so long that the sink had time to dry."

"Midafternoon?" Sanford ventured.

Dodge raised one shoulder in a laconic shrug.

"I'm less interested in what time he left than where he went," Derek said impatiently.

"We'd like to know that, too," Sanford said.

"But we still don't have anything tying him to that shooting. He might be just a guy on a business trip."

Derek didn't think Kimball really believed that any more than he did. "Who, on a business trip, pays by cash instead of a credit card?"

"And goes by two names," Dodge added. "Two that we know of."

With asperity, she said, "I get it, I get it."

Derek looked around the squalid room. "The vibe I'm getting from this place is that it was his den, a place to hide."

"I'm with you." Dodge indicated the metal trash can. "Empty."

"So's the one in the bathroom," Kimball told them.

"When he cleared out, he didn't leave anything behind," Derek said.

"Nothing visible." Sanford reached for his cell phone. "I'm going to have it dusted for prints. Maybe we'll get one we can send through databases. Anybody using an alias has probably been arrested and printed at some time in his life. At the very least, we'll get his real name."

Kimball had moved into the kitchenette, observing out loud, "He washed the dishes. And emptied the trash can. But he didn't mop the floor. It's sticky." She ducked down out of sight behind the bar. When she stood up several seconds later, Derek caught the significant look she shot her partner.

"Did you find something?" Derek asked.

She shook her head. "No. We might want to get an ID on what-ever this is he spilled, that's all." Then she frowned. "Why are you still here? You're not even a cop, and we told you to leave."

Dodge nudged Derek. "You seen enough?"

"I guess." But he made no move toward leaving.

"What is it?"

"Something doesn't jibe."

"What are you two whispering about?" Sanford asked.

Ignoring him, Derek took another slow visual tour of the room. His gaze slid past the television set, then sprang back. He realized what had bothered him. Everything else in the room was outmoded, but the television looked fairly new and had a built-in DVD player. "Check the DVD player."

Sanford regarded him curiously, but he searched for the remote and found it amid the tangled sheets on the bed. He used it to turn the set on, then went to it and punched the button to open the tray for the DVD. It slid out. Empty.

He looked at Derek expectantly.

Derek sighed with disappointment. "Just a hunch."

Ariel sprayed on perfume, checked herself in the mirror one last time, and grabbed her bag. After the ice cream binge three nights ago, she'd decided that she wasn't going to let one jerk make her fat. As her daddy used to say, the only way to get over being thrown is to get back on the horse.

She was going out, and she was going to have a good time.

And, by the way, *Up his!*

She was careful to lock the dead bolt behind her. As she was making her way to her car, her neighbor across the street called out to her. Inwardly she groaned, but she waved and called, "Hello, Mrs. Hamilton." The elderly lady lived alone and apparently was lonely. She often waylaid Ariel, usually when she was in a hurry. Or so it seemed.

"Ariel, hold up!"

Having been taught to respect her elders, Ariel tossed her purse into her car but waited while Mrs. Hamilton limped over.

"Your flowers look nice," Ariel said as she approached. Mrs. Hamilton had the best-looking yard on the street and boasted of doing all the work herself.

"Thanks, sweetie." She placed her age-spotted hand against her chest as though to help her catch her breath. "I'm worried for you."

"Why's that?"

Usually Mrs. Hamilton asked if she was eating right, chided her for staying out too late, urged her to use sunscreen. So she was taken aback when the old lady said, "A man came looking for you today, while you were at work."

"A man?"

"I think he was on drugs," she said in a whisper. "I didn't like the looks of him at all."

"What did he look like?"

Ariel's heart began to thud as her neighbor described Billy Duke to a tee. Not as she'd first known him, but as he'd looked in the hotel security camera photo.

"What did he want?"

"I saw him snooping around your house, peering in the windows, banging on the door. I yelled across at him, told him you weren't home and couldn't he see that?"

Any other time, the image that conjured would have been comical, but Ariel didn't feel like smiling.

"He came tearing across the street. I beat it inside and hooked the latch on my screen door, but he waved his hands and started shouting like a crazy man, 'Please, help me!' "

"Help him?"

"He said he was desperate to talk to you, that it was a matter of life or death, and did I know where you worked. He'd called your place of employment and they told him you didn't work there anymore."

"I've switched jobs recently." Thank God she had.

"He asked did I know your cell phone number, and I told him if I *did*, which I *didn't*, I wouldn't be giving it to him. I threatened to call the police if he didn't scram, then slammed the door in his face. I watched through the blinds, though. He got in his car and drove off." Mrs. Hamilton looked at her with concern. "It's none of my business, of course, but he didn't seem the sort you should be keeping company with, Ariel."

"Don't worry, Mrs. Hamilton. I'm not." She squeezed the older woman's hand. "If you see him again, call the police."

"I certainly will! Be careful."

Ariel assured her that she would, and the old lady returned to her yard. Ariel considered going back inside and calling the police herself to report Billy's unwelcome visit. But that would mean involvement, which she'd promised herself and Carol that she would avoid. She hoped Mrs. Hamilton's warning had scared him off.

She determined not to let Billy Duke spoil the evening she'd planned for herself, but when she entered the glitzy bar, she was still trying to shake off a vague uneasiness.

It got worse when she saw Tony, leaning against one of the cocktail tables in the back of the room, looking impossibly elegant and handsome.

CHAPTER
21

JULIE'S SCREAM ECHOED IN THE HALLWAY.

He took one step toward her, then placed his hands on either side of the doorjamb, bracing himself in the opening. His skin looked waxen, inhuman. His eyes were sunk deep into their dark sockets.

Julie turned and ran, but he lurched after her, caught her shoulder, spun her around, and fell against her, impaling himself on the knife. It sank into him up to the hilt. He opened his mouth to cry out, but what spewed from his maw was a sickening bile that splattered Julie's chest.

She screamed in horror.

She tried to push him off her, but he clung tenaciously, his arms draped over her shoulders. They did an odd dance while she struggled to get him away from her. He hung on.

Then he began to convulse. No longer able to maintain his hold, he dropped to the floor, landing on his back and shaking so violently that his shoulder bones and heels hammered noisily against her hardwood floor.

Julie leaped over him and staggered into her bedroom. She grabbed the cordless phone off her nightstand and frantically punched in 911. Nothing happened. She dropped the phone. It clattered to the floor. Her cell phone was in her handbag in the kitchen. She stumbled back into the hall.

The man's convulsions weren't as severe now. She tried not to look at the hilt of the knife sticking out of him as she knelt down beside him. "I'll call for help. But I've got to go get my phone. I'll be right back. Try to . . ."

His eyes were open, but they stared at the ceiling without acknowledging her. He seemed not to have heard her or to be aware of her presence. He seemed already to be in another place. He twitched.

Then he went completely still.

Derek and Dodge crossed the boulevard and had just reached the parking lot of the barbecue restaurant when Derek saw Kimball and Sanford blast out of Billy Duke's abandoned motel room like a demon was after them.

Running full-out, they headed toward the motel office. Sanford got in on the driver's side of their sedan and slapped a portable light onto the roof while Kimball stuck her head into the door of the office. She shouted something to Dora and her partner, who were questioning the Korean woman. Then Kimball joined Sanford in the car. He revved the engine, and they peeled out fast enough to make the air stink of smoking rubber.

Derek looked at Dodge, then, without saying a word to each other, they dashed for Derek's car. He scrambled behind the wheel while Dodge clambered into the passenger seat. He hadn't even got his door closed when Derek punched the accelerator hard.

"What do you think?" he asked as he wove through traffic, matching Sanford's speed but without the benefit of a flashing cherry on the roof of his car.

"Don't know, but it's hot."

"Billy Duke?"

"Maybe. Mind if I smoke?"

"What do you think?"

They rode in taut silence. After ten minutes, Dodge remarked, "They're heading toward your neck of the woods."

"More in the direction of Julie's." Derek grew queasy when he realized he was following the unmarked police car deep into her neighborhood. "Oh Jesus, no."

"What?" Dodge asked.

Derek didn't answer. As soon as he saw the emergency vehicles lighting up her block with flashing lights, he braked hard and shoved the gearshift into Park. Before Dodge's shout of caution even reached him, he was running down the sidewalk, shoving aside neighbors who'd congregated in small groups to speculate on the nature of the emergency.

Ignoring the crime scene tape already encircling her lawn, he ducked beneath it and ran toward her front door. A uniformed cop stepped into his path. "Hey! Hold it."

"What's happened?"

"You live here?"

"No."

"You family?"

"No."

"Then beat it."

"I'm Derek Mitchell, an officer of the court. *What happened?*"

The cop frowned, glanced around, said, "Fatal stabbing."

Derek's knees went to jelly. "Who . . ." His throat seized up before he could complete the question, which seemed to strike a compassionate chord with the cop.

"Wait here." He turned his back and started for the open door.

"Fuck that." Derek lunged past him and cleared the front door, nearly colliding with another officer, who blocked his path and then put both hands on his chest. "Who let you in?"

"Get out of my way!" Derek tried to throw off the officer's hands, but they didn't budge. The first officer grabbed his arms from behind. "Lay off me!"

"Come on, pal, calm down or we're gonna cuff you."

"Let go of me!"

Homer Sanford appeared in the archway of Julie's living room, wearing his most fearsome game face. "Mitchell? You again? What the hell?"

Wildly, Derek tried to read the detective's expression. "Julie?" he croaked.

Sanford stared at him for several beats, then hitched his head toward the room behind him. Derek took a step, or tried. The cops were still holding him. "Let him go," Sanford ordered. The uniformed men released him. He stumbled into the living room, pulling up short when he saw Julie, pale as death, but alive.

She was sitting on the sofa huddled inside a chenille throw, although the room felt like a greenhouse to Derek. Beneath the throw, her clothes were soiled. Blood and something else, vile-looking and smelly. Her complexion was the color of bread dough, making her eyes look dark and huge as they connected with his.

A tall, skinny black guy was standing near the fireplace with a small spiral notebook in his hand. He looked self-conscious. Another detective, a senior guy that Derek recognized—Graham? Grant? Something like that—was sitting on the ottoman Derek had sat on last night to get a closer view of the TV. He was facing Julie and Roberta Kimball where they sat side by side on the couch.

It was a strange tableau that held for several moments, then Graham/Grant said to Sanford, "Get him out of here."

"I'm Derek Mitchell."

"I know who you are. And *I* am Sergeant Graham, the detective conducting an investigation into a fatal stabbing. Now that we've got introductions out of the way, get the hell out of my crime scene."

"I'm Ms. Rutledge's attorney."

Julie's eyes widened marginally, but she didn't dispute him. Kimball looked like somebody had goosed her from beneath the sofa cushion. He thought Sanford muttered something, but he couldn't be sure.

Graham turned to Julie. "You've already called your lawyer?"

"I didn't . . . didn't call anyone but 911."

"He must've followed us here," Kimball explained. "He was at the motel where Billy Duke had been staying." Grudgingly, she added, "He's actually the one who ran him down. Rather, his PI did."

"How come you were looking for him, Mr. Mitchell?" Graham asked.

But before Derek could reply, the detective's gaze shifted to beyond his shoulder. Derek turned. A gurney with a body bag strapped to it was being rolled toward the front door by two EMTs under the guidance of an investigator from the Fulton County Medical Examiner's Center. Recognizing Derek from numerous trials in which he'd testified, he nodded an acknowledgment but didn't address him.

Instead, he said to Graham, "I'll let you know when the autopsy is scheduled, Sergeant."

"Can you tell me anything now?"

"He was dead when the paramedics arrived. Signs of struggle and trauma. He's got what appears to be a common kitchen knife protruding from his gut." He proceeded on his way without further comment.

Derek looked at Sanford. "Billy Duke?"

"We don't have a positive ID yet."

Graham came to his feet. "There's a lot we don't have. Ms. Rutledge, you'll need to come to the station with us, answer some questions."

"Now?"

"Right now."

"May I clean up first?"

Graham considered it, then said, "Detective Kimball stays with you." To the detective, he said, "Her clothes are evidence."

As Kimball escorted Julie past Derek, he reached for her hand. She looked lost, overwhelmed. He curbed the impulse to put his arms around her. It was a struggle to keep a professional demeanor. "I'll meet you there, Ms. Rutledge. Don't say anything to anyone unless I'm with you. Understand?"

She nodded and whispered a thank-you.

He gave her hand a reassuring squeeze before releasing it. Trailing the throw, she moved toward the hallway. As Kimball passed him, she gave him an arch look and said under her breath, "Curiouser and curiouser."

She was right about that.

An hour later, Julie recounted her story for Sergeant Graham and the young, black detective, who had yet to speak a word, at least in Julie's hearing. She figured he had recently earned detective status and was still being mentored by Graham. Sanford and Kimball, she knew, were in the adjoining room, watching her through the two-way mirror.

Derek was beside her, the epitome of professionalism. He'd been at the police station when she arrived with Graham and his junior partner. They hadn't exchanged a word on the drive from her house. She supposed the detective knew Derek by reputation, knew that he would raise hell if a client was urged to talk without his being present.

Now, the young detective made some adjustments to the video camera, then gave Graham a thumbs-up. Graham stated the date, time, and the names of those present and then politely asked her to tell them what had happened.

She did. She told them everything she could remember from the time she'd entered through her back door and noticed that the alarm didn't chirp to that horrible moment when Billy Duke had shuddered one last time, then gone perfectly still.

When she finished, there was silence in the room for several moments, then Graham said, "Thank you, Ms. Rutledge."

"My client wants to cooperate. Now, if that's all—"

"It isn't," Graham said to Derek. Back to her: "I couldn't help but notice that in your account you referred to the victim by name."

"I'd been told his name was Billy Duke."

"By whom?"

"By Detectives Sanford and Kimball."

Derek said, "And he was an intruder, not a *victim*."

"That's debatable, Mr. Mitchell. Ms. Rutledge had a butcher knife. Billy Duke was unarmed. He's the one in the morgue."

"He was unarmed?" she asked.

"Not even a pocketknife," the detective replied.

"I didn't know," she said weakly. "I assumed—"

"Did he threaten to harm you?"

"His presence alone was a threat to my client."

"Thank you, Mr. Mitchell," the detective said but kept his judgmental gaze on Julie. "When your alarm didn't beep, why didn't you leave the house? Why didn't you call the police right away? You said you thought someone was in the house."

"I said I 'feared' someone was in the house."

"What's the difference?"

"Fear can make you imagine things. I began to think I was being silly." She glanced down at her entwined fingers, which she was gripping so tightly they had gone as white as bone. "I experienced a traumatizing event a few weeks ago."

"I know you were with Paul Wheeler when he was shot."

"Ever since then, I've been . . . not myself. I get frightened easily. I thought this was one of those times."

"You thought you were imagining an intruder."

"Yes."

"But you kept the knife while you searched the house."

"In case I was wrong."

"In case you were wrong, you were prepared to mortally stab an intruder?"

"Don't respond to that," Derek said.

Graham left it alone. "When you first saw the man, did you recognize him?"

"He scared the living daylights out of me. I didn't immediately think: *Billy Duke.* I'd never seen him in person, only in those security camera photographs. Honestly, all that registered with me was that he looked like a zombie. He was deathly pale. His skin looked artificial."

She described him the best she could. "He came toward me, then sort of braced himself in the doorway. Like this." She imitated how Billy Duke had stood, sagging forward in the open doorway. "He was sick. Injured. Something. He wasn't well. Which I think explains why he fell against me. I don't think he was attacking me. I could be wrong, of course, but I don't think he was coming at me to hurt me. He was coming at me for help."

"Help."

"That's what she said," Derek said in a clipped tone. "The guy, who looked like the walking dead, lunged out of her bedroom toward her. Like any normal person would, she turned and ran. He spun her around, then threw himself onto her like he needed help standing. It's on the video."

"Thank you, Mr. Mitchell. I remember what she said."

"Then why do you keep badgering her? What part isn't clear to you?"

"I didn't stab him," Julie said. "He fell into the knife. Then he began to convulse."

"I remember you saying that, too," the detective said.

Julie met his skeptical gaze. "It's the truth."

"He vomited on you."

"You saw my clothes."

"He fell to the floor."

She nodded.

"He jerked spasmodically. Then he twitched a few times and died."

"That's what happened."

"Which could also happen if he got a knife in the gut."

She said nothing.

"You told the 911 operator that an intruder inside your house was dead."

"That's right. I tried to call on the house phone, but the call didn't go through. I was on my way to get my cell, but he died before I could."

"How did you know he was dead? Did you touch him, check him for a pulse?"

"No. But I knew. His eyes . . . I knew. I retrieved my cell phone from the kitchen, where I'd left my handbag. I called 911, then went outside and remained on the front porch until the ambulance arrived. The paramedics examined him and told me he was dead. The first policemen arrived almost immediately. They stayed with me until you got there."

"You know the rest," Derek said. "Anything else you want to ask my client before we leave?"

Graham looked at the younger detective, who still hadn't uttered a word. He shook his head. Graham glanced toward the two-way mirror. Seconds later, Sanford and Kimball walked in.

Julie looked at them in turn, but their expressions gave no hint as to why Graham had subtly invited them to join the group. Uneasily, Julie glanced at Derek. He didn't seem to like their inclusion, either. He came to his feet. "Y'all are putting in an awfully long day."

"So are you," Kimball said. "You're popping up all over the

place tonight. You still haven't explained why your hired help was looking for Billy Duke."

Derek said, "Do you have a question for my client?"

"When did you switch sides, Mr. Mitchell?"

"Oh, you have a question for *me*."

"Don't be a wiseass," Kimball said cantankerously.

"Kinda strange," Sanford said.

"What is?" Derek asked.

"First you're representing the Wheelers. Then you're not. Now you're representing Ms. Rutledge."

"Thank you for the history lesson." He placed his hand beneath Julie's elbow to signal her to stand and end this conversation.

But Kimball stepped forward. "Hold on." Looking down at Julie, she said, "You've stated before, and again just now, that you'd never met Billy Duke, never even seen him in the flesh before he died in your house."

"That's the truth."

"Have you ever been to the Pine View Motel?"

"Don't answer," Derek said.

"It's all right," Julie told him. "I've never heard of the Pine View Motel."

"You're sure?"

"Don't answer."

"Positive," she replied, heedless of Derek's advice.

"We found something in Billy Duke's room that didn't seem to belong in a scruffy place like that." Kimball took a small plastic bag from the pocket of her blazer. Balancing it on her palm, she extended it toward Julie. "Have you lost a button?"

Julie felt the floor drop out from beneath her.

Inside the bag was a round pearl button with a small chrome eye on the underside of it, a button that belonged on an ivory-colored charmeuse blouse, a button Derek would also recognize.

He was standing close. She could feel the heat of guilt and embarrassment coming off him as palpably as it was radiating from her. Nobody said anything for several moments, then Sanford prodded her. "Ms. Rutledge?"

"I—"

"It's a button, for godsake," Derek said. "You can buy them by the dozens. It could belong to anybody."

"Does it belong to you, Ms. Rutledge?"

Derek was undeterred. He took Julie by the arm and pulled her to her feet. "The man you've been searching for in connection with a brutal murder appeared in my client's house this evening. She feared for her life. He attacked her and was accidentally stabbed. Tragically he died, whether of the wound or of some unknown cause, which won't be revealed until the autopsy. You know how to reach me."

Before leaving Chez Jean, Creighton had told Julie that he had a date, but that was wishful thinking. He could get to Ariel any time he wanted, of course. He knew where she lived, where she worked. But he'd rather make this second contact appear as random as the first.

Hoping she would be a creature of habit, he'd returned to Christy's and stood at one of the tall cocktail tables along the wall. The position placed him in shadow but afforded him a view of the whole bar, and particularly the entrance. If she came in, he would see her.

Again, he'd left the Porsche at home in favor of the SUV, not wanting the valet to remember him. He'd dressed down, too, wearing designer jeans with a linen sport jacket, but neither as distinguishable as one of his suits.

Even should he catch someone's eye, it was doubtful they would know his name. To the vexation of his parents, he rarely accompanied them to charity events or social gatherings where photographers were likely to be clamoring for snapshots for the society pages of the newspaper. He didn't want his face and name out there, making him easily identifiable.

His mother, bless her ignorance, thought his camera shyness was endearing, believing it arose from a deep-seated shyness. He didn't know what his father thought about it. Probably he didn't think about it at all.

Creighton went to such great lengths to avoid being photographed, one would have thought he was ugly. As handsome as he was, it was difficult to make himself invisible, but he'd learned how not to stand out and had become quite adept at becoming part of the wallpaper instead of the centerpiece.

When he desired anonymity, he kept to the shadows and did nothing to draw attention to himself. Tonight it was vitally important that he not be remembered, so he didn't flirt with the cocktail waitress who took his order for a club soda, didn't make eye contact or conversation with anyone. It was still relatively early, and the place hadn't reached full capacity, so he was able to keep the table to himself without being asked to share it.

He'd been there almost an hour when Ariel arrived alone, and looking even more uncertain and self-conscious than she had on the previous occasion. In a vain attempt to conceal her insecurity, she'd applied eye makeup with a heavy hand. When she came in, she gave a toss of her blond hair, but the movement looked rehearsed, not natural.

Just inside the entrance, she paused to scan the crowd. When she spotted him, she tensed. The indecision in her expression was as plain as day. This was the guy who'd come on strong and with promise, then cruelly abandoned her and made her feel like a fool. Should she ignore him, or confront him and tell him what a bastard he was, or try again to make him like her?

She went with option one. Giving another haughty toss of her head, she walked to the bar and, with a show of bravado, snapped her fingers to get the bartender's attention.

Creighton waited until she'd been served the pastel green martini that looked positively nauseating, then moseyed over. She sipped her drink, not deigning to look at him.

" 'I'm sorry' doesn't begin to cover it."

She turned her head toward him as though just then noticing that he was there. She didn't say anything.

"I was called away unexpectedly. You were in the ladies' room. There was no way to let you know that I couldn't carry on with our plans."

She went back to her drink. She smiled at the bartender when he walked past and made certain that Creighton noticed she didn't give a damn about him and his apology.

"I had to leave, Ariel. I had no choice."

She set her martini down hard enough to slosh some of the sticky liquid onto the bar. "The parking valet told me you left with a woman."

"My assistant."

That deflated her. "Assistant?"

"My family had been frantically trying to reach me. I was out enjoying myself and didn't answer their calls to my cell phone. They asked my assistant to track me down."

"Why?"

"My niece." He looked down at the bar, rubbed at a puddle of condensation beneath his water glass. "She was raped."

"Raped? Oh my *God*!"

It was the perfect lie for this occasion and elicited the expected response. He exhaled a sigh. "By a guy she considered a friend."

Ariel's eyes were as round as saucers, full of concern, outrage, and empathy.

"He drove her to a remote place. Made her . . . use her mouth on him, then . . ." He stopped as though it was too difficult for him to continue.

She covered his hand with hers. "You don't have to tell me any more."

Actually he was enjoying describing how he'd lured sweet little Allison Perry to go for a ride with him. He had just obtained his driver's license. To commemorate the occasion and his sixteenth birthday, his parents had given him a BMW convertible.

Allison had been dazzled and told him she'd never ridden in a convertible before. But when things got interesting, he'd had to raise the top to muffle her screams. Ultimately, he'd had to knock her unconscious to silence her.

Later, it was his word against hers as to the tone of the encounter. Ultimately—not without some histrionics first—the Perrys declined to follow through with the police investigation and were persuaded that "the children" would be much better off if it were kept private. The amount of hush money paid to them had been dear, but it hadn't cost Creighton anything except a stern lecture.

Now, he said to the wide-eyed Ariel, "My assistant knows I

come here sometimes, so this was one of the places she looked. She found me while you were in the restroom. I . . ."

"It's okay. I understand." She pressed his hand.

"I didn't know your last name."

"Williams."

"I didn't know where you lived. Like an idiot, I hadn't got your number. You must have thought . . . God knows what you thought."

"I was pretty bummed."

He touched her cheek. "I'm sorry."

"How's your niece?"

"She'll live. She'll never get over the trauma, of course."

"Is the guy in jail?"

"Pending formal charges."

"I hope they lock him up and throw away the key."

"He'd better hope so, too."

"Why's that?"

"Because if I ever get my hands on him, he'll wish he was safe behind bars."

Her face glowed with admiration for his chivalry. He ordered her another martini and suggested they move away from the bar and find a more private spot. The place had grown more crowded. A group had claimed his table, but he steered Ariel to a corner where it was quieter and darker. By the time she'd finished the second martini, she was mellow and then some.

He looked at his wristwatch, swore softly.

"What?" she asked.

"My parents and I are visiting my niece in the hospital tonight."

"Oh."

"Do you want to stay, or can I walk you to your car?"

If he was leaving, she had no desire to stay. He was glad to learn she hadn't used the valet. "Too expensive," she told him as she led him around the building, across an alley, and into the employee parking lot behind an office building where everyone had left for the day. Hers was the only car in the lot. There was no one around.

"I appreciate your understanding more than you know, Ariel."

"Don't mention it. I just feel so bad for all of you. That poor girl. Her family."

They were quiet for a moment, then he placed his hands on the backs of her arms and rubbed them lightly. "You were disappointed?"

"When I came out of the ladies' room? Devastated. I probably shouldn't admit it, but I was."

"Let me make it up to you." He leaned into her and brushed his lips across her cheek. "Can I see you tomorrow night?"

"Hmm." She turned her head so that their lips came into contact.

The smell of apple liqueur was strong on her breath. It nearly gagged him. But when he groaned softly, he made it sound like he was aroused. "Can I come to your place? I want to be alone with you. Will that be a problem?"

"Not at all. My roommate is out of town."

He jerked his head back and scowled. "Roommate? Male or female?"

She giggled. "Female."

He smiled. "Ah. Good. We'll have the apartment to ourselves?"

"House, actually. And yes. All to ourselves."

He leaned into her again and nuzzled her ear. "I'm loving the sound of this. If I were to come over tomorrow night, any chance the roommate will come home unexpectedly?"

"No."

"How can you be sure?"

She told him about her roommate—Carol—having a teaching job lined up for the fall, but she was working as a waitress to tide her over till school started. Barely taking a breath, she went on ad nauseam about Carol and this cool sports bar in Athens where she worked and made oodles of tips because she was cute and well endowed. "And"—eye roll here—"you know how you men are about big boobs. Those college boys, especially."

Coyly, she continued on that track for several minutes until he thought for certain he was going to throttle her. Finally she ended with "To keep from driving back and forth each night, with all the drunk drivers on the road, she's staying at a house that belongs to one of the other girls who works at the bar. She's gone to Spain for the summer to study the language, so Carol is, like, subletting."

When she paused to take a breath, Creighton jumped in. "All that to say, we're in no danger of being interrupted at an . . . inopportune moment?" His fingertips brushed the sides of her breasts. He watched her eyes to make sure she'd noticed.

She had. Her breathing was light and rapid when she whispered, "No danger at all."

"Perfect." He kissed her again, pressing her against the car and forcing himself to push his tongue into her mouth. When he pulled back, he framed her face between his hands. "Tomorrow night then?"

Her head wobbled an agreement.

He asked for her address. He asked what time he should be there. She offered to cook dinner, and he asked if he could bring anything, and she said just himself. "Then it's a date." He gave her another hard, quick kiss, then released her and stepped back. "Get out of here before I forget how badly my niece needs my support."

"You must go to her," she said. She unlocked her car, got in and turned on the ignition, then lowered the window. "See you tomorrow night."

Playfully, he touched the tip of her nose. "You can't imagine how much I look forward to it."

CHAPTER
22

JULIE LOOKED ACROSS AT DEREK, WHO WAS BEHIND THE WHEEL OF his car, intent on his driving. "They didn't arrest me."

He hadn't told her where they were going. Strangely, she was apathetic about their destination, so long as it wasn't her house. Although she probably wouldn't have been allowed to stay there tonight even if she'd wanted to because it was a crime scene.

"They will," he said. "Tomorrow. Tonight if they get a warrant."

"They'll find the blouse. It's hanging in my closet. I just got it back from the dry cleaners. When I removed the plastic bag, I noticed the button was missing." She gave him a quick glance. "I thought I'd lost it on the airplane."

"How did a button off your blouse get in that squalid room at the Pine View Motel, Julie?"

"I don't know."

"I'm your attorney, not the police. If you were ever there, you can tell me."

"I can't believe you just said that."

He stopped at a red light and turned to her. "I'm trying to help you."

"By calling me a liar?"

The light turned green, and the driver behind them honked his horn. Swearing under his breath, Derek sped through the intersection. The air was charged with resentment. Finally he said, "What explanation do you have for your button—assuming it is yours—getting into that room?"

"Creighton. He took the button when he was in my house. He took something innocuous, something I wouldn't miss right away, planning to use it to link me to Billy Duke."

"Maybe Creighton wasn't your intruder. Maybe it was Billy Duke all along."

"No. I'm positive it was Creighton. It was so like one of his tongue-in-cheek, I'm-smarter-than-you pranks." She looked over at Derek. "I would have told the detectives about that if you hadn't hustled me out of there."

"They wouldn't have believed you."

"Like you don't."

"It's reasonable. As you say, it feels like Creighton."

"However?"

"You can't prove it, Julie."

"I thought the burden of proof was on the police."

"It is. But believe me, it helps if you can cancel their suspicions. As it stands, everything you've done looks peculiar. Yesterday you ordered your maid to thoroughly clean the house."

"Because Creighton was there, and I couldn't stand the thought—"

"I get it. But you can't prove he was there. Especially now that everything's been sanitized. Under oath, I'd have to testify that I didn't see any signs of an intrusion. This housecleaning resonated with Sanford and Kimball."

She looked at him inquisitively.

"It's part of the scuttlebutt, Julie. Dodge heard about it through the police grapevine. It could be alleged that you were destroying evidence. Now, I've got to ask, in case it comes up again, what possible excuse can you give for having your maid scour everything you own with disinfectant?"

"Creighton had gone through my things. The house felt unclean."

"I can relate to that," he said. "My house will never feel the same, either." Leaving the rest of it for the time being, he told her about the note he'd received from Creighton.

"As if what he did weren't bad enough, he taunted you about it."

"Because he wanted me to go after him. He probably expected me to immediately after I discovered the carnage. Since I didn't, he sent the note. It was a red cape and tough to ignore, believe me. I wanted to beat the shit out of him. But if I had, he'd have won. I'd rather beat him in a court of law, have him put away forever.

"I sent the note to the police," he continued. "But there's a problem with the chain of evidence. They'll contend, rightfully, that I could have typed it myself. Several people handled it. They won't consider it a smoking gun."

"Have they questioned Creighton about Maggie?"

"Not to my knowledge, although when they asked by rote if I had any known enemies, I named him first."

"He's a convincing liar. He denied knowing what I was talking about when I mentioned Maggie to him."

"What?" He shot her a look, but they were in traffic, so he had to return his attention to the road. "When was this?"

"He surprised me at the gallery just after closing. He probably watched until he saw Kate leave, and then slipped in through the back door."

"It wasn't bolted?"

"Since I was there when Kate left, she hadn't locked it behind her. Or Creighton might have a key. I wouldn't put it past him. All I know is that he appeared, and he frightened me." She recounted the incident.

"His casual comment on the UPS box made me afraid to open it for fear of what I'd find inside. That's why I was so jumpy when I got home. What I told the detectives was the truth. I was shaky and scared, but I thought I had let my fear get the best of me and that I was being foolish. That's why I didn't leave or call the police when my alarm failed to go off." Quietly she added, "I should have heeded my instinct."

Thinking about Billy Duke's final moments caused her to shudder. The details were vivid in her memory. The sight and smell of him. The feel of the knife as it punched through his skin. How hot and wet the gore was that plastered her shirt to her skin. How horrible the gurgling sounds were that he made as he tried to speak. The rapping of his bones against the floor.

The street scene beyond the hood of the car became blurred as tears filled her eyes. "I hope they discover that something else killed him. That it wasn't the knife. How could I live with myself?"

He reached across the console and took her hand. "You were in mortal danger, Julie."

"Maybe I wasn't."

"You didn't strike him with the knife. He fell against it."

"I swear he did. But still . . ."

"Try not to think about it. We're almost there."

"Where?"

A few minutes later they arrived at Coulter House. He parked in front and turned to look at her. "Both our houses have been corrupted. Is this okay?"

"Any place would do."

"But 'any place' wouldn't give us this service."

He got out and came around to open the door for her. The doorman greeted him by name. Derek asked, "Do you have a vacancy?"

"I'm sure we do for you, Mr. Mitchell."

A few minutes later, a bellman used an old-fashioned brass key to open the door of a suite on the top floor and ushered them in. A sitting room was separated from the bedroom by a pair of French doors with panels of sheer fabric stretched across the panes of glass. When he was assured that they didn't need anything for the moment, the bellman left them.

"They like their chintz," Derek remarked as he switched on a floor lamp.

She smiled. "They do. But it's charming. Actually, I'm impressed that you know what chintz is."

"My mom does amateur decorating for her friends."

"I'd like to hear about that."

"Food first."

"I can't eat, Derek."

"You'll eat."

He ordered up a supper of corn and crab chowder, accompanied by green salads and crusty rolls. She discovered that she could eat after all. He also ordered a bottle of white wine for her while he sipped a whiskey from the minibar. When they had finished eating, the room service waiter came and removed the table.

Julie carried her glass of wine to the sofa and sat in the corner of it, taking off her shoes and tucking her feet beneath her. "Why are we here?"

"I told you. Both our houses have been tainted by blood. Maggie's. Billy Duke's."

Technically what he said was correct, but she thought there was more to it. She continued to look at him until he gave her a guilty smile. "We're here because I don't want you to be found. Not yet anyway."

"By the detectives, you mean. You think they'll arrest me?"

"I don't know. I'm sure they'll search your house. It's a crime scene, but they'll cover their asses and obtain a search warrant, entitling them to turn it inside out."

"Like my life has been."

He said nothing to that.

"Are you afraid of what they'll find?" she asked.

"Yeah, I am. Not because I think you're lying to me. But because I think you're right about Creighton. If he was clever enough to take that button and plant it in Billy Duke's room, God knows what else he's done to make it look as though the two of you, you and Duke, were working together."

She stared down into her wine, circling the rim of the glass with her fingertip. "I'm afraid."

"I know."

"This afternoon at the gallery, I was truly afraid that he would hurt me. Physically. I revealed my fear to him. I didn't want to. I tried not to, but—"

"But you're human."

She smiled wanly, and he returned her smile. "Terribly so, it would seem." She sipped her wine, then set her glass on the end table, folded her hands in her lap, and took a deep, cleansing breath. "Talk to me, Derek. Talk to me about anything else. Tell me about your mom's home decorating."

He laughed. "It's a hobby, but she has a knack for it. Friends come to her for an opinion on what color to paint the walls, and she winds up redoing their whole house."

For the next half hour, he talked about his family, and his animation made it apparent how fond of them he was. His older brother, who was a CPA, lived in Augusta with his wife and two teenage daughters. "The oldest goes to college in the fall. I can't believe it. Seems like yesterday she was in pigtails, coming to me to kiss her bony, skinned knees."

His sister had quit her nursing career when she married an anesthesiologist from Houston. "He's a nice guy, but so boring he could put you to sleep without the juice. They've got three boys. Aged nine through four. Getting them through the Louvre without mishap was a challenge."

Julie laughed. "I'm sure."

"I was afraid they'd damage something, and that would create an international incident. 'American Hell-raisers Rampage Through Louvre.' 'U.S. Delinquents Destroy Priceless Antiquities.' "

It felt good to laugh.

"Actually, they're great kids." He was lounging in a club chair, his feet on the matching ottoman. He'd taken off his suit jacket, his necktie was loose, and his shirtsleeves were rolled back. He raised his arms and linked his fingers behind his head. "How come I've done all the talking? Tell me about you."

"You know about me, thanks to your Dodge."

"I'm sorry about that," he said, looking like he meant it. "I was acting in the best interest of my clients, who at the time were the Wheelers. Checking you out was part of my job."

"Actually, it's sort of a relief that you already know everything. All my skeletons have been exposed."

"Have they? I know the facts of your life, but not much else."

"Not true. You know that I'm passionate about art."

"You don't have a thing for that fat man, do you?"

She laughed. "No, but I have to keep an open mind for my clientele. Some of what I sell I wouldn't want in my house."

"What about the painting I bought? Could you live with it?"

"It I like. You've got good taste."

"Thanks."

"You know that I enjoy cooking."

"I don't know how good you are."

"Very good."

"Can I test that claim?"

"Maybe. Sometime."

This exchange didn't rule out a future between them. But it didn't promise one, either. Each realized that, and it caused an awkward silence.

Eventually he said, "Your parents. Did you have a good relationship with them?"

"We had a few bumps. Typical stuff. But on the whole, we had a very happy family life. My dad was devoted to my mother. She loved him. They loved me."

"Why do you sound surprised?"

"Not surprised. Grateful, maybe."

"Why grateful?"

After a thoughtful moment, she said, "Mom was very young when she had me. I'm sure it was a struggle for her to finish her education and launch her career when she also had a husband and child to care for. Dad wasn't a demanding husband. Not at all. I wasn't a difficult child. But . . . but she never got to explore other options. She never traveled or experimented to see if she liked something better than school administration. She was just settled very early on. I often wondered if she regretted the choice she'd made."

"Did you sense any resentment toward you or your dad?"

"None whatsoever. She treated me, both of us, with absolute love." She gave a small shrug. "That's what I marvel over. And why I'm grateful."

He shifted his position in the chair, then met her gaze and held it, as he would with a witness before asking the big, delineating question. "How did your folks feel about you and Paul Wheeler?"

"Dad was almost a decade older than Mom. He had died a few years before I met Paul. Because of my unhappy circumstances in France, Mom didn't tell me about her cancer until it was quite advanced. She knew about my meeting Paul, but she never saw us together.

"When I received word that she was declining fast, he paid for my airfare to come home. I arrived too late to say good-bye to her. Fortunately, Paul had come with me. I was so crushed by her death, by not being there with her, I don't know what I would have done if he hadn't been there. He was a tremendous help."

"From what I know of him, he would be."

Another silence stretched between them. Wanting to switch subjects, she said, "I read about your case in the newspaper."

"Which one?"

"Jason Connor."

He sighed. "Tough case."

"How can you defend what he did? He killed his parents in cold blood."

"He's *accused* of killing them."

"The newspaper said they were hacked to pieces."

"A 'crime of rage.' I've read the news coverage, too," he said drily. "I hope prospective jurors haven't."

"He's described as a chronic troublemaker."

"True. But skipping school, smoking pot, petty thefts, and a few fistfights are a far cry from double murder. He's also a rude smart-ass with a chip on his shoulder and a hatred for humankind. He's made it clear he doesn't appreciate me or my efforts on his behalf."

"Is it true that you waived your fee?"

"Yes."

"Why?"

"Because this rude smart-ass deserves a better defense than the mediocre one he'd get from a public defender who would just go through the motions because he secretly agrees with the state. And because this kid, who never has had much going for him, is going to be executed if I can't spare his life." She was about to say something, when he stopped her. "Julie?"

"What?"

"If we talk about the Connor case, we're going to argue."

She acknowledged that he was right. "I suppose we should be talking about *my* case. Now that you've appointed yourself my lawyer."

"Looked to me like you needed one."

"Thank you for that." She arched one eyebrow. "I don't suppose you'll waive your fee for me."

He grinned. "You, I'm charging double."

Though they'd tried to make light of it, their common problem permeated the comfortable room like a foul odor. "When you showed up at my house, Kimball told Graham that you'd followed them from the motel where Billy Duke had been staying."

"Right."

"What were you doing there?"

"Dodge had sniffed him out. He called me. I called Sanford. He and Kimball charged to the scene, and weren't at all happy to see us there. Even more frustrating to them, Duke's room had been cleared out. No trash, no trace of him."

"Or of Creighton."

He shook his head. "I suggested they check the DVD player. Empty."

"There's no link between him and Billy Duke."

"Doesn't look that way."

"But the police can link Billy Duke to me."

"You said you didn't want to talk about it." He lowered his feet from the ottoman and pulled himself out of the chair. "Why don't you try and get some sleep?" He nodded toward the bedroom. "I'll take the sofa."

"Do you want to use the bathroom?"

"Thanks."

He disappeared through the French doors.

Feeling at a loss, Julie moved to the window and opened the louvers of one of the wood shutters. The night sky was clear. There was a three-quarter moon. The street below was quiet and, as far as she could tell, empty of anyone who was curious about them.

Derek emerged from the bedroom. "All yours."

She closed the louvers and turned to him. "I was thinking about Creighton following us here the night of the storm. He could be out there now. I hate to think of him watching me, watching us. He's no longer simply a nuisance, Derek. He's gone from obnoxious to sinister."

"Had he ever laid a hand on you before today at the gallery?"

"Not like that. At Christy's, he squeezed my arm, backed me into the wall. Today was different. It wasn't just manhandling, it was aggression."

"During our encounter in Athens, he was snide and sarcastic. He issued some threats, talked big, but beheading Maggie was quite a leap. I asked Dodge to see if he could unearth juvenile records on him. He said he'd try but wasn't optimistic."

Julie had been sifting through what they did know about Creighton. "You know how they say serial killers accelerate? The more they kill, the more frequent the killings become?"

He nodded.

"Should we tell Sanford and Kimball about Creighton's visit to the gallery? Tell them what he said and how he behaved."

"They know about Maggie. They offered condolences but didn't mention Creighton in connection to it." He placed his finger beneath her chin and tipped her head back, turning it from one side to the other, looking at her neck. "There's no bruising."

"He didn't apply that much pressure to my neck. He was pressing me against the wall with his body."

"If we reported it, and the detectives questioned him, he would admit to being there but deny that anything untoward had taken place. Stalemate."

"But you believe me, don't you?"

He smiled. "I wish I had a nickel for every time a client has asked me that." He dropped his hand to his side. "Try and get some sleep."

She went into the bedroom and pulled the French doors closed behind her, well aware that he had avoided giving a direct answer to her question. That was his special gift.

Fortunately, it was also hers.

For half an hour Derek lay on his back, staring at the ceiling, trying to talk himself to sleep. It didn't work. The sofa was too short for him, but it wasn't the accommodations that were keeping him awake. It was sharing them with Julie.

He hadn't heard a sound from the bedroom for the past twenty minutes, and yet he sensed she wasn't sleeping, either. He saw no light or movement through the sheer fabric over the French doors, but somehow he knew that she was awake and as restless as he.

Cursing in whispers, he threw back the light blanket, swung his feet to the floor, and stood up. He reached for his shirt, then changed his mind and left it lying on the chair. In bare feet he walked to the French doors and eased them open. They made no sound, but immediately she turned away from the window, where she was standing, looking out as though on watch. She was swaddled in a white terrycloth robe provided for hotel guests. It covered her from earlobes to ankles.

For what seemed to him an eternity, they stood on opposite sides of the room, looking at each other. Later, he didn't remember walking toward her. He only remembered reaching her and fearing what she would say when he asked, "If I touch you, are you going to push me away?"

She took a quick breath and shook her head.

Slowly, expecting her to bolt at any second, he untied the belt of the robe and placed his hands inside. He brushed his knuckles over her bare tummy, and she shivered. "Are you afraid, Julie?"

"Very."

"Of?"

Her eyes closed briefly, then opened when she replied, "Mostly of this."

But she didn't object, didn't flinch, when he pushed the robe off her shoulders. It slid down her arms and onto the carpeted floor. Her bra was lacy, the same kind she'd been wearing on the airplane. Her breasts swelled above the cups. He drew his finger across the smooth slopes, then took her face between his hands. "Lie to me about anything else. Don't lie to me about this."

"I'm not. I won't."

Her voice was tremulous, and so were her lips as he lowered his to them. Unlike before, they started slowly and carefully, exchanging breaths, their lips glancing and pulling away, testing. But without either initiating it, the kiss became deep. Reservation and timidity deserted them. His memory had locked in how good she tasted. Often, since that return flight from France, he'd been bedeviled by sudden and ill-timed recollections of how sexily her mouth had responded to his kiss.

But as sharp as his memory had been, it didn't compare with the reality.

He reached around and unhooked her bra. It went the way of the hotel robe. He enfolded her, hugging her to him. Feeling her breasts full and soft against his chest, he groaned, lost to the sensations of being flesh to flesh with her.

For an endless time they kissed. Just that, but passionately, breathlessly, until they were finally forced to break away. While they caught their breath, she rested her forehead against his sternum and rolled it from side to side, brushing her damp lips against his chest. Then she reached up and threaded her fingers into his hair, drawing him down for more.

There wasn't much to the back of her panties. His hands felt hot against her skin as he tightly squeezed her ass, securing her lower body against his. She made a low sound that vibrated out of her throat, into her mouth, against his tongue, driving him mad.

He raised his head and locked gazes with her as he unbuttoned his trousers and slid down the zipper. She moved away from him, and by the time he was out of his clothes, she was on the bed, on her back, reaching for him.

He bent over her, slid the panties down her legs, then placed his hand between her thighs, cupping her sex in his palm. And for several seconds, their eyes communicated an intimacy more fervent than mere touch. The heel of his hand ground against her where she was most sensitive. Her breath caught, and the small of her back arched up.

Then he covered her. As he sank into her, his hands slid over hers where they lay supine on either side of her head. Their fingers interlocked, and moments later, when they came, he was uncertain if he was trying to hold on to her or on to his own soul as it was launched into a free fall.

"Are you going to sleep there?"

"I may die here," he mumbled. "Happily."

She laughed softly and sifted strands of his hair through her fingers. "I like the way you dress."

"Huh?"

"I like your clothes. You're one of the best-dressed men I've ever seen."

"We're sated from a fabulous bout of fucking, and that's what's on your mind? My *clothes*?"

Another laugh bubbled out of her. "I also like how you look without them."

"Oh yeah?"

"Yeah."

After a beat, he said, "I think I prefer you naked." He raised his head and surveyed the territory on which he was sprawled. "Yeah, definitely. Naked."

He pressed a kiss into the soft hair on which his cheek had been resting, then kissed his way up her belly. She sucked in her tummy when he rubbed it with his stubbled chin. "Sorry about that," he murmured.

"I'm not. I like the scratchiness."

"Even on . . . ?"

Her face filled with heat. "Especially on . . ."

"I was afraid it might be too abrasive for those tenderest spots."

"Not the way you did it."

Matching the huskiness of her voice, he said, "Good to know."

He kissed her breasts in turn, then remained focused on one and played his tongue over the tip. Julie watched him as he caressed her. She touched his face, ran her thumb across his well-defined cheekbone. Like a sail, her whole being seemed to billow with emotion. "Derek?"

"Hmm?"

"Derek?"

"Don't distract me. I could do this for a week."

"I can't wait a week."

He raised his head and looked into her face, and her need must have been apparent because he responded immediately. In one fluid motion, he levered himself above her and buried himself inside her again.

She splayed her hands over his butt. "Don't move. Not yet. I just want to feel you."

He did as she asked, except that he dipped his head and kissed her slowly and evocatively. When he finally angled his head back, he was startled to see tears streaking her cheeks. "Christ, Julie. Am I hurting you?"

"No. *No.*" She clutched him when he tried to withdraw.

"Then what?"

"I—"

"Wheeler?" His voice was filled with uncertainty and dread. "Are you crying because of him?"

"No," she whispered. "Because of *you.*"

"Me?"

"This was the last thing I thought would happen to me now. I didn't . . ." She paused to lick a tear from the corner of her mouth.

"What? You didn't what?"

"I didn't count on this." She smoothed her hands up his back and across his shoulders. She touched his hair, his eyebrows, finally his lips, where her fingertips stayed. In a voice barely audible, she said, "I didn't count on you."

When she woke up, the bathroom door was closed and she could hear the shower running. She stretched and yawned and wished she had the day in which to be lazy and reflect on what had happened last night, to relive each precious moment of it. She'd thought she was replete, but thinking about Derek's hands, his mouth, caused her body to tingle with erotic memories and renewed desire. Wanting him again made her feel rosy and sappy.

And terribly sad.

A cloud of steam followed him out of the bathroom. He was naked, and totally blasé about it, while her cheeks burned with sudden self-consciousness. She raised the sheet to cover her breasts, and her misplaced shyness caused him to grin.

"Too late. I already peeked."

That alone, and the inflection with which he said it, caused a fillip of sensation in her lower belly. "Good morning. How long have you been up?"

"About ten seconds."

His arousal evident, he walked to the bed, sat down on the edge of it, and peeled back the sheet. He slid one hand between her thighs and with the other guided hers to his penis. She stroked the swollen head. "Do we have time for this?"

"It'll have to be quick."

He applied his thumb to her, causing her breath to catch. "That won't be a problem."

When he came out of the bathroom after his second shower, he was wearing his boxers. She pulled the sheet over her and kept it there. "Is there any news?" she asked.

"You made the news."

She glanced beyond the French doors into the sitting room, where there was a TV.

Her eyes moved back to Derek. "I woke up an hour before you. I caught the newscasts." He came over to the bed, leaned down, and cradled her face between his hands. "News teams from all the local stations are parked outside your house, where, they're reporting, Paul Wheeler's suspected killer died mysteriously yesterday evening. Doug was ambushed by reporters as he left his house for work."

She moaned miserably.

"His statement to them was that he was astonished to learn that his brother's close personal friend, you, may have known his killer."

"This is a nightmare."

"It may get worse before it gets better, Julie."

"That's why I feel ill."

He dropped his hands from her face. "Wishing it away won't make it go away. Today will be an ordeal, I'm afraid. You'd better get up."

"I only have the clothes I arrived in." She looked around for them.

"I asked the valet service to press them for you." He kissed her briefly, then moved toward the French doors. "I'll order us some breakfast."

She couldn't possibly eat, but she didn't argue as she slipped from the bed and went into the bathroom. She took a shower, washed her hair with the hotel shampoo, and used the hair dryer. She didn't have any cosmetics beyond what she carried in her purse for touch-ups. She applied some powder to her nose, blusher to her cheeks, and lip gloss. It would have to do.

Since her clothes were still with the valet, she pulled on the robe she'd wrapped herself in last night and joined Derek in the sitting room. Room service had already delivered the order. He removed the silver lid from one of the dishes. "Their cheese blintzes are worth the calories."

"Derek, I can't eat."

"That's what you said last night."

He held out a chair for her. He poured coffee from a thermal carafe. And he was right, even her nervous stomach couldn't resist a few bites of the blintzes. "What's your plan?" she asked him while she sipped her second cup of coffee.

"Wait and see what happens. I don't want you exposed until I have a fair idea of what you'll be facing."

She looked toward the door. "Will the staff here squeal on me?"

He shook his head. "They don't ask about the people I put up here, and I don't tell. They boast of their discretion. Besides, I've spent a small fortune with them over the years. They owe me."

She picked at one of the blintzes with the tines of her fork. "Are they accustomed to you spending the night with your female clients?"

He set his cup in his saucer and waited until she met his eyes. "It's never happened before."

To cover her pleased embarrassment, she took a sip of coffee. He reached across the table for her other hand and studied it as he stroked her fingers. "I wonder what would have happened if we'd met before you went to France. Before you met Paul Wheeler."

"We might have despised each other on sight."

"I doubt that," he said softly.

"So do I," she whispered.

"We might have fallen in love, got married, had kids."

Her throat became too tight to speak.

He reached across the table and touched her cheek. "It could still happen, Julie. When all this is past, we could have a life together."

The moment was shattered by the ringing of the room phone. Each of them looked at it, then back at each other, warily. Derek got up and answered. He listened for a moment, his eyes never wavering from Julie's, then he said a brusque "Okay" and hung up. "That was Dodge. He's downstairs. He's coming up."

CHAPTER
23

ODGE KNOCKED. DEREK OPENED THE DOOR. THE INVES-
tigator stalked in. When he saw Julie, he bobbed his head. "I
figured."

Derek said, "Julie Rutledge, Dodge Hanley."

Without acknowledging the introduction, Dodge said, "The
snooty desk clerk with the bad rug and a cob up his butt said you
probably wouldn't welcome being disturbed this morning. He
hinted that you hadn't spent the night alone. But I didn't want to
think you could be this stupid."

"Would you like some coffee?"

The older man took in Derek's boxer shorts, then looked over at
Julie, where she sat swaddled in the robe.

"We only had one set of clothes," Derek explained. "They're out
being pressed."

Dodge grunted. "Convenient."

Derek crossed his arms over his bare chest, realizing as he did so
that he struck a ridiculous pose. "Did you come here to cast asper-
sions, cast stones, or tell us what's going on?"

"Nothing good," the investigator muttered. He walked over to
the table and looked down at Julie's plate. "Are you going to finish
that?"

"Help yourself."

He scooped up the leftover blintz and ate it like a burrito, licking the ricotta and strawberry sauce off his fingers when he was done. "Myself, I haven't had time for breakfast this morning. I've been fielding calls."

"From whom?" Derek asked.

"From everybody I bribed last night. My expenses on this case are going to be out your ass, and I can't say I'm sorry." He poured coffee from the carafe into Derek's cup and slurped it.

"What have you heard?"

"They searched her house, starting with the attic rafters and working down."

"Let me guess," Derek said. "They found a blouse with a button missing. We knew they would. Doesn't prove the button found in Duke's motel came off Julie's blouse. It's not one of a kind."

"We're not in court, and I'm not a juror," Dodge said. "Save your shots, Counselor." He glanced at Julie. "You're gonna need them."

"What else?"

Dodge sat down at the small table across from Julie and addressed himself to her. "They found a pistol under your mattress."

"Paul gave it to me for protection."

"Lucky for you it's not the caliber of the one used to shoot him."

Derek said, "If they lift prints from it, mine will be on there."

Dodge went whey-faced and looked up at his boss. "Swell."

"I told you about it. When I walked into her house, the lights were out, she had the weapon—"

"Okay, okay." Turning back to Julie, Dodge said, "Forget the firearm. That's the good news. Your friend Wheeler wore a fancy watch."

"A Patek Philippe. It was taken during the robbery."

"Um-huh. So imagine how tickled Sanford and Kimball were when it turned up at your house with all the other loot that was stolen that day."

Derek watched the blood literally drain from her face. "That's impossible."

" 'Fraid not, Ms. Rutledge. It was all in a little black velvet pouch as described by the victims of the robbery, yourself included.

Found in a shoe box in your closet, sitting right on top of a pair of black satin shoes. By the way, Detective Kimball remarked on what great shoes you've got."

Julie was staring into near space. Derek doubted she'd heard anything Dodge had said beyond the pouch being found. He had to speak her name twice before she came out of her daze. When she looked up at him, her eyes were wide with disbelief.

"He must have planted it there. Billy Duke. He was coming out of my bedroom. That must have been what he was doing in there. He kept the jewelry and came to my house to leave it to be found."

She divided a wild, desperate look between him and Dodge. He wasn't sure what his expression revealed, but Dodge's was patently skeptical.

She came out of her chair, a cornered animal making a defiant stand. "If I had masterminded that holdup and murder, do you think I'd be stupid enough to keep the jewelry? In a *shoe box*?"

Dodge said nothing. Derek ran his fingers through his hair. "Of course you wouldn't."

"But a double-crossing partner might want it to be found on your property."

Julie rested her small fists on the edge of the table as she leaned toward Dodge. "I didn't have a partner. I had never seen that man until he staggered out of my bedroom."

"And threw himself against an eight-inch serrated butcher knife you just happened to be holding at gut level."

"Okay, Dodge," Derek snapped. "What else can you tell us?"

Dodge released his stare at Julie and turned to Derek. "They lifted a print out of that rathole motel and sent it through all the databases. Had a positive ID in no time flat. William Randall Duke."

He pulled a small notebook from the breast pocket of his wrinkled sport jacket and flipped back the glossy blue cover. "Our boy had a couple of misdemeanors to his credit, but served no significant jail time. Graduated to felony when he was tried for extortion in Oregon three years ago. Had an affair with a woman who alleged he blackmailed her. He claimed he was paid—ten of thousands, by the way—for services rendered. All the evidence was circumstantial, basically his word against hers. He was acquitted.

"Popped up in Chicago a year later, charged with stalking. But, turns out the lady was lying to her husband about the nature of her relationship with Duke." He looked up, divided a glance between them. "He liked the ladies, apparently. And they seemed to like him. The charge in Chicago was dropped.

"Fast forward. A few months ago, he was tried in Nebraska on another extortion charge. This time he was accused of fleecing a middle-aged widow out of thousands in cash and goods. She and Duke were hot and heavy for several months, but he'd got on her fighting side, and she was having the book thrown at him. The night before she was to give testimony in court, which in the DA's opinion would have cooked Duke's goose, the widow turned up dead."

"Dead?"

"As a doornail, Counselor. Murdered on a supermarket parking lot. She went in for a gallon of milk. It and her body were discovered lying beside her car. The milk was cold, her body was warm. Killer got away clean as a whistle. Nobody saw nothing. 'It's like a freaking phantom strangled her.' That's a quote from the kid who found her body. Sack boy. Went out to gather up abandoned shopping carts."

"Duke killed her?"

Dodge smirked. "He had a rock solid alibi. He'd been denied bail because he was considered a flight risk. He was a guest of the county."

"He was in jail?" Julie asked.

"Locked up tighter than a— Locked up tight," he amended. "The DA pulled out all the stops, but his key witness was dead, and he didn't have much else. Jury was out less than two hours, including time to eat lunch. Duke was acquitted. The widow's murder remains unsolved."

Neither Derek nor Julie spoke while they assimilated this information. Then Derek said, "He came from Nebraska to here?"

"No one has been able to determine when he arrived in Atlanta. No record of employment. At least not with his authentic Social Security number. Between that business in Nebraska and three days before Wheeler was hit, when he appeared on the hotel security camera, he was under the radar." He closed the notebook and replaced it in his pocket. "So ends the life and times of William Randall Duke."

"Does he have family here?"

"That's being researched, but he doesn't appear to. He was born in Washington State to a single mom. She committed suicide when he was in eighth grade, and he went through the foster care system. No known family ties anywhere."

"He squeaked through two serious trials without being convicted."

Dodge said, "Which begs the question why a slick operator like him pulled a dumb stunt like breaking into Ms. Rutledge's house to plant stolen goods when he had thus far eluded capture."

Both men turned to Julie for an answer. She was hugging her elbows, her hands tucked into the wide sleeves of the robe. "He was afraid of being caught with it."

"Then why didn't he just toss it in the nearest ditch? Why was he hanging around Atlanta in the first place? Why hadn't he skipped town as soon as he popped Wheeler?"

They were logical questions to which she had no answers.

The knock sounded unnaturally loud. Derek opened the door. A housekeeping maid wished him a good morning and passed him their clothes, neatly pressed and on hangers. "Thanks." He took the hangers from her and automatically reached toward his pocket for a tip before he remembered he didn't have on any pants.

"I've got it." Dodge joined him at the door, gave the maid a five-dollar bill, then followed her out into the hallway.

"Where are you going?"

"To smoke. Get your pants on, for crissake. And call the desk downstairs. Tell that tight-ass I'm coming back up as soon as I've had a cigarette. I don't want to go through that rigamarole again." He lumbered off down the hall.

Derek closed the door. Julie took one of the hangers from him, then without a word headed for the bedroom.

"Julie?"

She looked back at him. "Your sidekick doesn't trust a word I say."

"He doesn't trust anybody."

"What about you?" She looked at him for a moment, then said, "You've never asked me, Derek."

"Asked what?"

"Whether or not I'm guilty of having Paul killed."

"I never ask."

"Ask me."

He hesitated, realizing that she was testing his trust in her. "Did you?"

"No."

When he didn't say anything in response, her expression became so remote it was difficult for him to believe that they'd experienced such rare and wonderful intimacy not an hour ago, when her face had gone soft with rapture even as her body strained to take more of him.

Her eyes, which last night had cried tears of passion, were now cool. And the lips still whisker-burned from his kisses were tinged with sarcasm and sadness. "I bet you wish you had a nickel for every client who's said that, too."

It took her longer than usual to dress because her hands were shaking and she couldn't concentrate on even the simplest task. By the time she returned to the sitting room, the room service table had been taken away, and Dodge was back. He was sitting on the sofa, notebook in hand.

Derek was pacing, taking occasional glances out the window where he'd opened the louvers of the shutters. The patterned carpet was striped with buttery sunlight. She realized that, to most people, it was a beautiful day.

Derek stopped pacing when she came in and got straight to the point. "They located an abandoned car a few blocks from your house. It had a duffel bag packed with clothes and toiletries, some magazines, personal stuff. They've lifted prints from the car, and should verify soon that it was the one used by Duke. He left it there and walked to your house. One of the windows in your bedroom had been jimmied. He came in that way."

"How did he avoid the alarm? Every window has a contact."

"The phone line had been cut."

"That's why the first 911 didn't go through. The phone was dead." Looking at Dodge, she said, "I've been meaning to upgrade my security system to a radio signal."

"I recommend it," he said caustically.

"What else?" she asked.

Derek motioned for Dodge to take it from there. "The lab guys will go over that car the same way they're going over the room at the motel."

"They won't find any evidence of me in either," Julie said.

The two men exchanged a look. Sensing the significance of it, Julie sank onto the arm of the chair that Derek had looked so comfortable sitting in the night before. "They already have, haven't they?"

Dodge said, "A strand of hair that looks like yours was found on the car's headrest, passenger side, caught in the nap of the upholstery. I say 'looks like yours' because it'll be sent to the lab for a match."

"I was never in any car driven by Billy Duke. Creighton must have taken a strand of hair from my brush. Something. I don't know! All I know, and know absolutely, is that he's responsible for this. All of it. We should check to see if he was in Nebraska at the time of Billy Duke's trial."

"I don't follow," Dodge said.

"He could have killed that widow for Billy."

"That train movie scenario?"

Dodge's tone suggested derision, which she ignored. "Exactly like that. He killed that woman to prevent her from testifying against Billy, which obligated Billy to kill Paul for him."

"How would a playboy in Atlanta learn about a case of extortion in Omaha?"

"I don't know."

"The widow and her larcenous lover might have been big news in Nebraska, but—"

"I don't know how he did it!" she shouted, cutting him off. "I just know he did." She turned, appealing to Derek, and said, "Don't you see? He's a genius. He's bold. He doesn't have any fear because he doesn't have a conscience. He's probably watched a hundred movies where someone is framed for murder. He would know what to do to make me look guilty. It would be a game to him. He would delight . . ." Realizing that she was beginning to sound desperate and hysterical, she rolled her lips inward to avoid saying anything more.

After a time, Dodge coughed, hawked, swallowed. "Derek told me that Creighton paid a visit to the gallery yesterday."

"He terrorized me. Although I'm sure you don't believe that, or you think I'm exaggerating."

"Look, Ms. Rutledge, what I think is that the world would be a better place without this guy in it. If he's the one who killed Maggie, he's a motherfucking sadist. But his picture's been shown to the Korean woman who runs the motel, to the other residents there, to the staff at the Moultrie, where you and Paul Wheeler were cozied up. Nobody recognized him. Or that fancy car of his, either, and it's bound to have attracted attention."

"He has another car. An SUV of some kind. I think he has several vehicles."

Dodge jotted that down and said, "I'll check it out," but Julie didn't think it was a top priority with him.

"He keeps his private life very private. What I mean is, you called him a playboy, but that's a misnomer. Playboys are seen with beautiful women. They host lavish parties. They have coteries of hangers-on. They crave and cultivate attention. Creighton does none of that. Conceited as he is, don't you think it's odd that he keeps so to himself and avoids the public eye?"

"Lots of rich people shun publicity."

"But Creighton's shunning it contradicts his personality. There must be a reason for it. Have you checked to see if he has a police record?"

"I've been kinda busy today," Dodge replied testily.

Derek, speaking for the first time in several minutes, said, "Tell her about the phone."

She glanced at him where he stood at the window, his back to the room. His back to her.

"Billy Duke had a cell phone on him when he died." Dodge reached into his breast pocket again and withdrew a sheet of paper.

"Lady friend of mine, policewoman, confiscated this for me in exchange for a fancy dinner at the restaurant of her choice. It's a record of all the calls made from that phone. First one was made night before last, indicating it was a new phone."

"None of Creighton's numbers are on there," Derek said.

"He would have insisted that Billy Duke not call him."

Dodge passed her the sheet. "On the other hand . . ."

Julie scanned the number that had been underlined each time it appeared on the list. "The gallery."

"Called five times yesterday."

"He did call. I mean, I guess it was him."

Derek came around and gave her a hard look.

"There was no reason to mention it," she said defensively. "I answered the gallery phone three times yesterday when the caller didn't speak. You don't have to take my word for it. You can ask Kate."

"She was on an extension?"

"No. But she said it had happened to her, too. Look how short these calls are. A minute or less."

"A lot can be said in sixty seconds."

She shook the paper at Dodge. "This only proves he placed the call. It doesn't prove anyone talked to him."

Derek looked at Dodge, who frowned and said, "Still doesn't look good. Especially since he went to the gallery that time asking for you."

"I never met the man."

"Then why would he come to see you, Ms. Rutledge?"

"I have no idea."

"You don't?"

"No."

"Huh." Dodge studied her for a moment, then looked aside and began patting his pockets.

Apparently it was a nervous habit that signified something to Derek. "What, Dodge?"

The older man stopped fidgeting. He looked at Derek, then at her. When he looked back at Derek, his expression was sympathetic. "One last thing they've dug up, and, Counselor, it's the mother lode."

"Tell us."

Dodge tilted his head toward Julie but didn't take his eyes off Derek. "She knows. Ask her."

Everything inside her began to crumble. Molecule by molecule she felt herself collapsing on the inside. It had been inevitable that they would find out, but she had hoped that, before they did, Creighton and his crony Billy Duke would be exposed as Paul's assassins.

"What?" Derek demanded, and when neither she nor Dodge said anything, he repeated it angrily. "Goddammit, *what?*"

Julie tried to speak, but her tongue was stuck to the roof of her mouth. She managed only to stammer his name imploringly.

Dodge heaved himself up and walked to the door. He even took hold of the doorknob before he turned back into the room. "That Tuesday wasn't one of their ordinary afternoon rendezvous. She and Wheeler were celebrating something that day. Right, Ms. Rutledge?"

Still unable to speak, she nodded.

"Sanford and Kimball had to go to their supervisor and ask for his clout. He came down hard on Wheeler's lawyer, and even then, the pertinent file had to be subpoenaed before the lawyer would give it up."

"File on what?" Derek asked.

"Paul Wheeler's will. He'd had it changed. It hasn't been probated yet, but Ms. Rutledge is due to inherit his entire fortune. His share of the business, his property. Every last cent."

The words reverberated like the tolling of a death knell, then were followed by a dense silence.

Derek stared at Julie with a mix of incredulity and barely suppressed rage.

Slowly she shook her head from side to side, knowing that if she said anything at that moment, it was sure to be the wrong thing.

Dodge said, "I'll be outside."

A few minutes later Derek joined him in a courtyard where the hotel served high tea from three to five each afternoon, weather permitting. Shady and serene, it was enclosed by ivy-covered brick walls on three sides and an impenetrable hedge of shrubbery on the street side. In the center was a carved stone fountain, unobtrusively trickling water over a cherub holding a lyre.

They had it to themselves.

Derek sat down at a small wrought-iron table where Dodge had already lit up an unfiltered Camel. For a time they just sat there. Derek watched a hummingbird flit from one hibiscus blossom to another. Dodge stared into space and smoked.

Finally he looked over at Derek. "You've tupped her?"

"Since the plane?"

"Since breakfast."

Derek snuffled. "Essentially."

Dodge nodded as he rubbed out his cigarette. He lit another. "She never mentioned the will."

"No."

"Bad time to find out."

"Tell me."

"What did she say about it just now?"

"Nothing. I didn't give her a chance. I had to get some air, clear my head."

"Is it clear yet?"

"Not even close."

"So what are you going to do?"

"Hell if I know." Derek stood up and began to pace the lichen-covered brick paving.

"Didn't you tell me that she's retained Ned Fulton to represent her?"

"Yeah, and he's good."

"My advice, Counselor, let him have her and stay away from this mess."

Derek continued to pace, Dodge to smoke. Several moments elapsed, then Dodge said, "You're not going to, are you?"

Derek stopped pacing and studied the hummingbird where it hovered above a blossom as large as a bright red parasol. "It's very possible she's being framed, Dodge."

"Sounds awful melodramatic."

"That's the point. Cutting off Maggie's head was melodramatic.

We can't dismiss Creighton and his flair for melodrama. He's devious. He's a goddamn eel. As Julie said, he doesn't have a conscience. He's cocky and one hundred percent confident of his ability to pull off anything he damn well pleases *and* to get away with it."

"And he'd have the same motive for killing Wheeler," Dodge mused aloud. "The inheritance. Maybe he knew his uncle was about to change his will and wanted him taken out before he could."

"Or he could have learned it was a done deal and killed him to get vengeance."

"If that was the case, why didn't he have her capped, too?"

Derek thought about it, thought about Creighton's personality traits and everything Julie had told him about the man. "That wouldn't have been any fun."

"Fun?"

"He likes the inside joke. If he successfully pins his uncle's murder on her, he gets his laugh at her expense, as well as guarantees that she never gets to spend the fortune. If she's convicted, he and his parents could probably have the new will recanted."

"Millionaire duped by murdering mistress. Nephew reinstated as heir."

"Precisely. That would give Creighton a chuckle or two."

Dodge crumpled an empty pack and thoughtfully opened another. "Works. In theory. But there's still nothing tying Creighton Wheeler to Billy Duke."

"There wouldn't be. He's too frigging smart. Something's been bothering me, but I couldn't put my finger on it. But when Julie started talking about his keeping out of the limelight, I realized what it was. That first day he came to my office, and the time after that, he didn't touch anything. Not a drinking glass, not the arms of the chair, not the doorknob. I or Marlene held the door for him every time. He didn't even shake hands."

"He leaves no trace of himself."

"No physical evidence."

"By contrast, they've got a shitload of it on her." The investigator hitched his chin in the general direction of the hotel room where Derek and Julie had spent the night. "They'll have an arrest warrant by lunchtime. Mark my words."

"For killing Billy Duke?"

"Him. Wheeler. Take your pick. Maybe both."

"It's all circumstantial, Dodge."

"They can still hold her for a few days while they gather more evidence."

"There isn't any that wasn't planted. I'm certain of that. She loved Paul Wheeler."

"We're talking about a lot of money, Derek."

Dodge never called him by his first name. And he never spoke that softly or earnestly, either. Derek couldn't miss the significance of his doing so now. He repeated, "She loved the guy, Dodge. Believe me, it gives me no pleasure to say it, but it's a fact."

He stared Dodge down until the older man relented. "Okay. She wouldn't have had Paul Wheeler killed for any amount of money. You can say it till doomsday, but it doesn't solve your problem."

"We'll get nothing from Creighton. The solution lies with Billy Duke." Derek thought a moment, then said, "Julie says he looked ghastly, sick, in need of help. When can we expect the autopsy to be done?"

"Since so much is hinging on it, I'm sure the detectives are pressing the ME to get to it soon."

"Stay in the pipeline, Dodge. Let me know everything you hear."

"It'll cost you."

"Promise that policewoman—Dora?—three fancy dinners. I need information which translates to ammunition. Start with the contents of the duffel bag they found in Billy Duke's car."

"I told you already."

"Get me a complete inventory if you can. And—"

"Am I gonna have time to take a piss?"

"Not today. Check for a rap sheet on Creighton."

"Already have. No such animal. Not even a DUI. He'd been issued a few speeding tickets. That's it."

"Juvie files?"

"I've put out a few careful feelers, but that's the Holy Grail."

"Do what you can."

"Meantime, what are you going to do?"

"Go back upstairs and confer with my client."

• • •

Ariel didn't hear the news about Billy Duke's death until she turned on the TV early that morning. As one report segued into another, each as startling as the next, she tried to call Carol to ask if she'd heard. Of course, since her friend had urged her not to get involved, Ariel would leave out the role she had played in identifying him. And she wanted to remain out of it. All the same, it was exciting to hear repeated references to the anonymous call she'd placed to the police hotline.

It had shocked her to hear that Billy had died in Julie Rutledge's house. The police department spokesperson, a detective named Roberta Kimball, had strongly hinted, although she didn't come right out and say it, that he hadn't died of natural causes, like your basic heart attack, and that Ms. Rutledge had somehow caused him to die.

Ariel asked herself why a classy woman like her, with a million-aire lover, had got tangled up with a hustler like Billy Duke. But then the millionaire had been older than Ms. Rutledge. Maybe he hadn't been able to satisfy her sexually, whereas that was Billy's specialty. He could also be suave, charming, and funny when he put his mind to it. Julie Rutledge would be a target for his kind of hustle.

Ariel became so engrossed in the related reports that, before she knew it, a half hour had elapsed, meaning that she was going to be off schedule for the rest of the day. Today of all days. When she had so much to do!

She wanted to make things perfect for her dinner date tonight.

She didn't get off work until five-thirty, and dinner was sched-uled for seven-thirty, so she wanted to do as much as she could ahead of time.

She dressed for work in a hurry, then went into the kitchen, browned the beef roast in olive oil, then placed it in the Crock-Pot, where it would simmer all day. She would add the vegetables when she got home. And make the salads. And spoon the sorbet into indi-vidual dessert glasses and return them to the freezer.

She had set the table when she returned home last night, tipsy from the apple martinis and drunk with the pleasure of having seen him again, and learning that he hadn't run out on her after all and that he really wanted to see her again. *Alone.* And how many times had she had to assure him that nobody would walk in on them?

If that didn't sound promising, she didn't know what did.

On her way out, she gave the dining table one last glance, wishing that she had a screen or some other means of separating the table from the kitchen. Candles would help to achieve a softening effect. She must remember to pick some up when she bought the flowers and wine. Red. To go with the beef. Tony would know stuff like that, like red wine going with red meat.

And she must remember to buy a package of condoms, too.

A girl could hope.

She turned up her car radio when they did headline news, and sure enough Billy was mentioned. The last time he'd called her, he'd tried to say something before she immediately hung up and then took the phone off the hook so he couldn't call back. That would have been the night before last.

Ariel hoped her neighbor Mrs. Hamilton wouldn't connect the man whose death was making news this morning with the man who yesterday had come seeking Ariel at home mere hours before he died. Which was kinda creepy. Ariel couldn't help but wonder what it was that Billy had wanted to tell her.

"A matter of life or death," he'd said to Mrs. Hamilton. Ariel had thought it was only a figure of speech, but obviously not. Billy's antics had finally caught up with him. He was dead. While she mourned him as a fellow human being, she was relieved she no longer had him to worry about.

She could push him from her mind and daydream solely about her date tonight with Tony.

CHAPTER
24

DEREK RETURNED TO THE HOTEL ROOM TO FIND JULIE ON HER cell phone, apparently talking to Kate. She was admitting to her assistant that having Billy Duke show up at her house and die there had been a harrowing experience.

"Unfortunately, the news reports are correct. He did suffer a knife wound, but . . ." She glanced at Derek, who was slicing his finger across his throat. "It's a police matter, Kate, so I'm really not at liberty to discuss it."

She went on to assure Kate that she was safe and doing as well as could be expected, and then entrusted the management of the gallery to her assistant until further notice. "I hope to be back to work very soon," she concluded.

"Did you tell her where you were?" Derek asked as soon as she disconnected.

"I hedged on that."

"Good."

"Am I officially avoiding arrest?"

"Not yet."

"What about your office? Aren't you going in?"

He shook his head. "I called Marlene and brought her up to date, told her I'd be out all day. She knows how to handle inquiries."

"Evasively?"

"Exactly."

"What about your other clients?"

"You're the one with the urgent situation, so you get my attention."

"Thank you."

"It's not gratis. You'll be billed. You can afford it," he added under his breath.

She frowned. "That's exactly the kind of remark I hoped to avoid."

"Is that why you didn't tell me? To avoid wisecracks? Or did inheriting a bloody fortune just slip your mind?"

"When would have been a good time to drop it into the conversation, Derek?"

"Anytime."

"For instance?"

"When we met."

"That's not something you tell a total stranger."

"Yeah, that would have been awkward. Both before and after we screwed." She flushed red, but he went on before she could come back. "How about the day after, when I showed up at the gallery?"

"You were furious, in no mood to listen."

"You could have told me last night."

She didn't say anything to that. She didn't have to. The look she gave him said it all. He cursed out of frustration, moved to the window, looked out, came back around. "It was bound to come out sooner or later. Surely you knew that."

"I hoped it would be later. I dreaded it. It was the second shoe."

"Then why in God's name didn't you tell me, Julie?"

"Because I knew this is how you'd react. I knew it would change everything."

"You're damn right it changes everything!" he said with heat. "It gives you the oldest motive in the history of jurisprudence. It's criminal law 101."

"I know! I knew how it would look to you. How it would look to Sanford and Kimball. To everybody."

"It wouldn't have looked as bad as it does now."

Her anger evaporated. "I was wrong to withhold it. I see that."

He backed down, too. "I'm as mad at myself as I am at you. I knew all along you were keeping something from me."

"Actually, you're not as angry as I thought you'd be."

"As Derek, the guy you made love to all night, I'm furious with you." He flung his arm toward the French doors separating the rooms. "In there, nothing was . . . We did . . . How could you . . ." His eloquence abandoned him. He swore, then sliced the air with his hands. "We'll deal with that aspect of it later. As your lawyer—"

"You'll still represent me?"

"It would look really bad to the police if I backed out now, after declaring myself your legal representative last night. Anger is an emotion I can't afford. Anger is counterproductive. So is hindsight. You misjudge a juror you thought would favor your side, you miscalculate how convincing a witness will be, your client's lie is exposed to you in open court, there's no do-over. It's done. You deal with it and move forward." He sat down on the ottoman, facing her. "So, first things first. Sanford and Kimball will want to know when this came about."

"Paul changing his will? He mentioned it as far back as a year ago and continued to bring it up. I tried to talk him out of it."

"They'll seriously doubt that, Julie."

"It's the truth."

"Who would turn their back on that kind of money?"

"I would. I did. But Paul wouldn't be dissuaded. He had his lawyer draw up a new will. He had signed it that Tuesday morning before meeting me for lunch."

"Thus the celebration."

"*His* celebration. Not mine. He was pleased. I was . . ."

"Displeased?"

"Dubious. I knew it would cause trouble."

Derek lapsed into thought for a moment, then asked her what the lawyer had thought of the new will. "Did he try and talk Wheeler out of it?"

"I wasn't privy to their conversations. But he was very kind toward me when we met following Paul's death. I made it clear that I was in no hurry to have the will probated."

"Creighton would be."

"The lawyer stalled him."

"So the Wheelers were and still are unaware that Creighton is no longer going to inherit?"

"As far as I know. Paul was emphatic that it remain just between us for as long as possible. I think he feared Creighton would do something. Paul made no secret of his affection for me. Creighton made no secret of disliking it."

"He saw you as a threat."

"Which has made me wonder why I wasn't his target instead of Paul."

"Dodge remarked on that, too." Derek shared with her what he'd ventured to his investigator.

"You're probably right," she said after giving it some thought. "If Creighton had eliminated me, it wouldn't have been nearly the game this has become. I'm afraid he's still playing it." She leaned toward him. "What was Billy Duke doing in my house, Derek?"

He stated the obvious. "Planting evidence linking you to the robbery."

"If we can prove that—"

"We're screwed."

That took her aback. "Why?"

"Because it then would appear either that Billy Duke was acting alone or that he wanted to double-cross you, his partner. Either way, Creighton's clear."

"Billy Duke was doing it on Creighton's behalf."

"No doubt. But don't advance that theory to the detectives, Julie."

"Why not?"

"Because they'd ask why, if Creighton had the jewelry all along, he didn't hide it in your house while he was in there messing with your stuff."

"The police don't know about that."

"They will. They must. That'll be your only explanation for the housecleaning that was so extensive your maid mentioned it to Kate, who told the detectives."

"Who thought it was significant."

"They're not detectives for nothing."

She dropped her head forward.

"Furthermore—"

She groaned. "There's a furthermore?"

"Billy Duke didn't have a weapon. Reasonably, we can't contend that he went to your house to do you harm."

"Making it appear we were friendly."

"At least acquainted."

"But I didn't let him in. He broke in."

"That's something. Not much."

She sighed. "It's bad, isn't it?"

"I won't bullshit you, Julie. Yeah. They've got the motive."

"The new will. But what about opportunity? When was I supposed to have plotted this with Billy Duke? I'd never laid eyes on him until yesterday."

"There's a preponderance of evidence to the contrary," he said. "The phone records. His coming to the gallery. The button in his room, the hair in his car. All circumstantial, but added up and coupled with Paul Wheeler's estate, it's enough to make an ambitious prosecutor salivate."

She got up and went to the bar, opened a soft drink, but set the can down without drinking from it. "Meanwhile Creighton is free of suspicion."

"I'm afraid you're right. His fall guy is dead, and so far nobody has linked the two of them."

"Where would they have got together? Nebraska?"

Playing devil's advocate, Derek asked, "What would a cosmopolitan urbanite like Creighton be doing in Omaha? I can see him shuddering at the thought of even flying over Omaha at thirty thousand feet."

"He went there to recruit Billy Duke."

"To swap murders."

"The widow for Paul."

"Possibly."

Reading his doubt, she asked, "What?"

"First we'd have to place Creighton in Omaha. And if Billy Duke was in jail, where did they meet to strike this bargain? I suppose Creighton could have visited him in jail but—"

"He would be too smart for that," she said. "The jail would have a record of his visit."

"Exactly what I was about to say. If Creighton strangled a woman on a supermarket parking lot, like a 'phantom,' and without anybody witnessing it, he would—"

"Want someone to know."

This time it was Derek who was taken aback. "That *wasn't* what I was about to say. It contradicts what you said about him earlier keeping a low public profile."

"No it doesn't. It would be an inside joke. Which is exactly like him. Going back to the movie, beyond the point where we stopped watching, there's a scene where the millionaire shows up at a party.

"The murder of the tennis player's wife is the talk of the city. In the course of party conversation, this silly old woman questions how one would go about strangling someone to death. The millionaire offers to show her. He places his hands around her neck to demonstrate. Of course no one, except the tennis player, knows he's actually reenacting the murder he committed."

She returned to her seat on the sofa. "Creighton doesn't want to be caught, but I think he'd like to show off, particularly to us, how clever he is."

"He wants us to be in on his joke."

"Yes, and I'm very afraid of what the punch line will be."

Derek stood up and began to pace. "We've got to connect him to Billy Duke."

She picked up the sheet Dodge had left behind, Billy Duke's cell phone records. "The gallery isn't the only number he called numerous times." She pointed the other out to him. "He called it at all hours of the night."

"It could be a pizza delivery."

"It isn't. While you were outside with Dodge, I dialed it and got one of those voice mails with an automated response, not a personal greeting."

"If we noticed it, you can bet Sanford and Kimball did." Derek reached for his own cell phone, flipped it open, and used speed dial to call Dodge.

He answered immediately. "Your ears must've been burning. I was just about to call you."

"Listen, on those phone records—"

"They already checked it."

"And?"

"Ariel Williams. Twenty-seven years old. Working girl. Scared shitless when Kimball showed up at her place of employment, wanting to ask her questions about Billy Duke."

"She knew him?"

"She admitted it was her who called and ID'd him after his picture went out on TV."

"What was their relationship?"

"She hem-hawed on that, but general thinking is that he was a former boyfriend she no longer wanted to lay claim to."

"Where did they meet?"

"Nebraska. She disapproved of his acquittal. Said she wished he'd gone to prison, which is what he deserved. She moved down here and wasn't at all happy when he called and told her he'd followed. She told him to get lost and leave her alone. But he was persistent. Did the call and hang up routine he did with Ms. Rutledge."

Derek had put his phone on speaker so Julie could also hear. He cut his eyes to her when Dodge said that, and she gave him a look of satisfaction.

"The girl swore up and down she hadn't seen Billy Duke since she left Nebraska, and when she heard on the news this morning that he was dead, she wasn't sorry." Dodge paused and wheezed a breath.

"Did she mention Creighton Wheeler?"

"Not to my knowledge."

"Ask."

"Okay. Something else. You ever heard of a movie called *Frenzy*?"

"No." Derek looked at Julie, who shook her head.

"Well, I don't know what it signifies, if anything," Dodge said. "But a DVD of it was in Duke's duffel bag."

• • •

"I can't believe it of Julie," Sharon Wheeler said as she spread butter onto a cheese biscuit.

Doug pushed his plate away, his lunch virtually untouched. "I *don't* believe it."

"I do. I never trusted her." Creighton motioned for Ruby to refill his glass with iced tea. "There was something . . . *off* with her and Uncle Paul."

"Off?"

"Yes, Father. Off. I never could figure what it was. But it was definitely there." Ruby—with undisguised attitude—sloshed tea into his glass. He grabbed her other hand and kissed the back of it. She snatched her hand away and waddled off, grumbling under her breath. "Thank you," he called to her in a singsong voice.

Not even the maid's surliness could affect the lighthearted mood he'd been in since he'd turned on the television in his bathroom this morning and heard that Billy Duke had died in the home of Julie Rutledge, apparently of a fatal stabbing.

The news had given him a hard-on.

Billy Duke had gone to Julie's house. Julie had stabbed him. He was dead, and she was under investigation.

Perfect! Priceless!

Was he brilliant, or what? He had laid the groundwork. The button off her blouse, easily dropped on the floor of the motel room kitchen. The strand of hair placed in Billy's car. He'd planned on the police finding Billy dead in the Pine View Motel, murdered, with the trail leading straight to Julie.

But this was even better. This scenario made her look even guiltier and had much more entertainment value.

From the beginning, Billy's fate had been sealed. Creighton had never intended to let him go on living once he'd held up his end of the bargain. However, he had decided it was only fair to let Billy live long enough to see his former girlfriend die the gruesome death she deserved.

But then Billy had forced Creighton to rethink the timing. First, he'd come to Creighton's building to deliver the note. That was stupid. His heartfelt "She's just a kid. And I wasn't exactly fair to her, either," and so forth, had convinced Creighton that Billy, despite how many times he'd bad-mouthed the girl for testifying against him as a character witness, was, indeed, pussy-whipped. A man in that state of mind didn't think clearly and was capable of doing something rash. Like confessing.

So, bye-bye, Billy, nice doing business with you.

Luckily, Creighton had gone to the Pine View Motel prepared. Billy liked beer. He was too immersed in his misery to notice how long it took for Creighton to uncap the bottles. He hadn't suspected a thing.

Creighton wondered if, later, maybe in the middle of the night, when his insides began to cramp and he started to feel sick and disoriented, he'd guessed.

Maybe he thought the ham had gone bad. Or the cheese. Maybe he thought he'd caught a stomach virus.

But, actually, killing Billy hadn't provided Creighton the least bit of thrill. He hadn't got to witness the end. Maybe if he had, it would have been more exhilarating. As they shared Billy's last meal, he kept telling himself that he was killing the man, that he was as good as watching him die.

When, honestly, it had been a yawn. It hadn't been as exciting as, say, seeing blood geyser from that dog's severed artery.

But it had been effective, and one couldn't have everything.

Creighton had planned on returning to that disgusting motel one last time, before Billy's body started to stink, and searching for the stolen jewelry, because he knew the greedy son of a bitch was lying through his teeth about having thrown it away. The gun he probably had disposed of as he'd said. Because even Billy was smart enough not to risk getting caught with a murder weapon. But the jewelry, there was profit to be made from that, and Billy had enjoyed flashy clothes.

Creighton had been spared the unpleasant cleanup problem when, for reasons that would remain forever unknown, Billy had gone to Julie's house. Creighton would probably never know Billy's motivation for doing it. Obviously Billy had been trying to get rid of the evidence linking him to the holdup and murder. But why take a chance on getting caught?

Ah well, what did it matter now? Billy's dying in Julie's house had worked out in Creighton's favor, and that was all that really interested him. He was in the clear, and Julie looked guilty as hell.

Tee-hee.

This morning, to celebrate this fabulous turnabout, as soon as he was out of the shower, Creighton had placed an emergency call to a madam, who'd sent over one of her girls right away. His father had actually phoned while she was giving him expert head. It was tough to hide his elation when he'd told his father, yes, he had heard the news about Julie, and wasn't it positively dumbfounding?

Doug had told him that it was important that the family maintain a unified front and suggested—make that *ordered*—that Creighton not talk to any media. As if he would anyway. "Rather than going to the office," Doug had said, "why don't you spend the day here with your mother and me? We must regroup and decide the position we're going to take regarding this."

Creighton had had no intention of going to the office, as his father well knew, but he was so full of bonhomie he didn't quarrel with his old man about circling the wagons.

After issuing one brief statement to the reporters who'd assembled on the street in front of the estate, Doug had retreated to his study to go over some paperwork. Sharon had spent the morning planning a dinner party for when "all this is finally behind us." Creighton had worked on his backhand with the ball machine, then taken a swim. Ruby had asked if they'd like lunch served on the terrace, and Creighton had said that sounded like an excellent idea.

It was pleasant outside, not too hot, and they were lingering over the meal.

His mother said, "Creighton, you truly believe that Julie and this Billy Duke plotted to have Paul killed?"

"That's what it looks like, doesn't it? Mmm. I swear, nobody makes chicken salad like Ruby." He looked at his father's plate. "Not hungry?"

"No."

"Julie and I never had much in common," Sharon observed as she absently played with her strand of pearls. "She declined when I offered to put her name under consideration for membership in my garden club, but she was very nice about it. And she did seem to love Paul."

"She did love him," Doug declared. "I'm sure of it."

Creighton rolled his eyes. "You always take up for her."

"I'm not taking up for her. I'm stating a fact. No matter how it looks, I'll never be convinced that Julie conspired with a . . . a *criminal* to have Paul killed. Our stance on this, unanimously," he stressed, looking at Creighton, "is going to be that we hold Julie Rutledge in the highest esteem, that by all indications she was as devoted to Paul as he was to her, and that we're certain that, following a thorough investigation, she'll be cleared of all suspicion. Understood?"

Sharon reached across the table and touched his hand. "Of course, darling."

Having had his say, he pushed back his chair and stood up. "I'll be in the study."

"He's still grieving," Sharon said to Creighton once Doug had gone inside. "Any reminder of Paul sets him off. I'd better go talk to him." She left the table and followed her husband into the house.

Creighton stretched and yawned, looked up through the branches of the live oak that shaded the table, and wondered what he would do with the rest of his day, now that he didn't have to go back to the Pine View Motel and search for his uncle Paul's Patek Philippe.

He even felt a little aimless and downcast now that it was all over. It had been such an intricate plan, inspired by one of his favorite films, and perfectly executed. Pardon the pun.

It began on the day his tennis coach had taken extra time with another player. Initially Creighton was irked by having been kept waiting, but it turned out to be fortuitous. He rarely read a newspaper. Things he imagined were always more interesting than actual events. Real-life drama paled in comparison to what his mind conjured.

But even the country club's practice backboards were occupied that day, and there was nothing else to do while waiting for his coach, so he'd picked up the newspaper that someone had left behind and was thumbing through it when he noticed an obscure story about a young Atlanta woman who'd been subpoenaed to appear in court in Omaha, Nebraska, to testify against a man on trial for extortion.

What Creighton had found most interesting was that the prosecution's case hinged on the testimonies of the Atlanta woman, a former lover of the man accused, and that of the widow he was charged with blackmailing.

Poor sucker, Creighton thought. *I bet he wishes they were dead.*

He didn't stay for his tennis lesson.

Instead he switched out his Porsche for the Land Rover he'd bought on a whim but driven only a few times. He went into a Wal-Mart for the first time in his life and bought the ugliest clothes he could find, a pair of reading glasses with minimum correction, and a package of temporary hair dye.

It took him two days to drive to Omaha, where he checked into a motel under an assumed name. He was at the justice building the following day just as court was convened. The widow was surrounded by local news crews as she arrived. Basking in the glow of her notoriety, she looked bleached, blowsy, and world-wise, and, in Creighton's opinion, poorly cast as a victim of deceit.

Billy Duke wore an unconvincing smirk of complacency.

Creighton pored over the local newspaper stories about the trial and watched every newscast on his motel TV. It was reported that the young woman from Atlanta had blubbered her way through her testimony. She'd been called as a character witness, and the portrait she'd painted of the accused wasn't flattering.

She admitted to having been in a sexual relationship with Billy Duke. He'd led her to believe it was true love that would ultimately result in marriage. All the while he was making matrimonial promises to her, he was screwing the widow.

Billy Duke was a scoundrel and a heel. Whether or not he was a criminal would be decided by the testimony of the widow, and she was coming to court mad as hell and gunning for him.

For two days, Creighton tracked her every move, waiting for his opportunity.

On the evening of the second day, she stopped at a supermarket. When she came out, as she approached her car, Creighton walked up to her and, wearing his most disarming smile, asked if she was the woman he'd been seeing on TV. Flattered, she smiled, fluttered her false eyelashes, thrust out her enormous bosoms, and said why yes, she was.

Stupid cow. She revolted him. He tried to avoid touching any part of her except her throat. Other than that, it was amazingly easy.

By the time the jury got the case, he was sick to death of Omaha, his off-the-Wal-Mart-rack clothes, and his dark hair.

Shortly after Billy Duke's acquittal, Creighton showed up at his front door and introduced himself as the person to whom Billy owed his life. He then told the dumbstruck man what he must do for him in return. Billy was so impressed—or intimidated—by Creighton's audacity, and so grateful for his freedom, he was easily persuaded. The hundred thousand dollars helped mitigate any lingering reservations, moral or otherwise.

Billy had been cunning, in his way, but he wasn't in the same league as Creighton. Not even close. There was also a poignant footnote: Billy had had a soft spot for the "sweet kid" all along. He had pleaded for her life.

"Right up till the bitter end."

"What's that, dear?" Creighton didn't realize that he'd spoken aloud until his mother rejoined him, bringing with her a demitasse cup and saucer. "Espresso?"

"No thanks."

"Your father is on the phone with Paul's lawyer."

She continued prattling, but Creighton tuned her out. He didn't have an attachment to the sweet kid like Billy did. And he didn't like loose ends. If Billy had been calling her house, who knew what he might have said, intentionally or not, about Creighton Wheeler?

"One of the news vans left tire tracks on the lawn outside the gate," his mother was saying. "They have absolutely no respect for other people's property."

Besides, it would be fun. Abruptly he stood up. "Excuse me, Mother. I've got to go."

"Go? I thought you were spending the day with us. Doug expects you to. He'll be angry."

"He'll get over it."

"What should I tell him? What's so important?"

Creighton bent down and kissed her cheek, then, as he pulled back, he winked. "I have a date."

CHAPTER
25

WHILE KIMBALL WAS INTERVIEWING ARIEL WILLIAMS AT the company where she worked, Sanford was at the Fulton County Medical Examiner's Center observing the autopsy of Billy Duke. The detectives had decided to split up for the sake of expediency. A coin toss had determined who would go where.

Sanford lost.

He carried two packs of Doublemint in with him and gave several sticks of it a workout while Billy Duke's organs were removed. When done, the deputy ME left the sew-up to an assistant and moved to a sink to wash his hands. Sanford, glad it was over, asked for a preliminary opinion. "He bled out, right?"

"The knife wound definitely had the potential of being fatal. He'd have bled out. Soon." The pathologist shook water off his hands and pulled two paper towels from the dispenser. "But my understanding is that the EMTs arrived at the scene within minutes of his sustaining the wound."

"That's right. We've got a tight timetable from when the 911 came in."

"If the victim had received immediate attention at the trauma center, he could have survived the stabbing."

"Meaning?"

"Meaning he died before he bled out. He died of something else."

"Like what?"

"I'll let you know."

Sanford arrived at the police station just ahead of Kimball, who carried in a sleeve of saltine crackers and set it on his desk. "What're these for?" he asked.

"You're always queasy after an autopsy. Crackers help."

"Thanks." He ate two right away. "What did the girl have to say?"

Kimball recapped her interview with Ariel Williams. "My impression, she's telling the truth. She's a bit sketchy on the personal aspects of their relationship, but it couldn't have been easy for her to talk about. She hasn't been working at this place for long. All her co-workers were gawking. She looked scared and innocent and said she knew it sounded heartless, but she was glad Billy Duke wasn't around to cause any more grief."

Sanford ate another cracker. "Did she say anything about Julie Rutledge? Had Duke ever mentioned her?"

"Never."

"That would have been too easy," he groused. His desk phone rang, and he answered. "Hey, Doc. That was quick. Yeah, lay it on me." He listened, then said, "He died of *what*?" Leaning forward, he grabbed a pen and notepad, scribbled something, then pushed the tablet across to Kimball.

He listened another full minute without interruption. Then, "Any idea on the time frame? Um-huh. Um-huh. Okay. Will you be around today if we need you to answer some questions? Great. Thanks for getting back to me so soon." He hung up.

"Hepatic necrosis due to toxicity," Kimball said, reading what he'd written down on the tablet. "He was poisoned?"

"The doc's guessing an overdose of acetaminophen."

"Tylenol?"

"More likely acetaminophen combined with propoxyphene, something you can't buy over the counter, like a prescription pain reliever."

"Are you sure?"

"Don't you read the pamphlets we're getting all the time on street drugs?"

"I know you're right about that," Kimball said crossly. "How does the ME know that's what killed Billy Duke? He hasn't had time to do a complete toxicology workup."

"Educated guess. Says he saw this a lot when he worked the ER. Because the drugs are so available, it's a popular form of suicide. He lost one patient to it. A guy changed his mind about ten hours after taking a whole bottle of Darvocet, like thirty, forty tablets. Called 911 and was transported to the ER. He was treated with the accepted antidote, which usually works if administered in time. But this was such a huge overdose, and the guy waited too long. The effects couldn't be reversed. He suffered acute liver failure and died. The ME says he'll put Duke's organs through the required tests, of course, but he's pretty sure he's right."

"So Billy Duke was dying when he got to Julie Rutledge's house."

"Looks like." Sanford flipped open his spiral notebook and read his notes. "According to Graham's team, they found vomit on Ms. Rutledge's bed, on the bathroom floor and commode. Appears Billy Duke was there for a while before she came home and discovered him. Doc said he would have been growing increasingly groggy and generally feeling like shit."

"Was the overdose intentional? A suicide?"

"If so, why'd he drag himself to her place?"

"He must have been compelled by something awfully important." Kimball sighed. "Whatever, she wasn't lying about him looking sick and in need of help."

"All the same," Sanford said, slapping closed his notebook, "I'd like to know if she ever had a prescription for a pain reliever."

"Hey, Linds. Is this a bad time?"

Even dressed in jeans and a baggy T-shirt instead of a beaded gown, Derek's red-haired friend was ravishing. Today her glorious hair had been pulled into a messy topknot. She divided a curious look between him and Julie, then stepped aside and motioned them into the foyer of her house.

Derek kissed her on the cheek. "I would have called first, but we've been sorta busy."

"I heard. You've both been mentioned on the news. You're her lawyer now?"

"As of last night. Lindsay Graveau, this is Julie Rutledge. Julie, Lindsay."

The woman smiled at her, saying, "We met the night of the auction."

"It's unforgivable," Julie said, "our barging in on you like this."

"Are you in trouble?"

"A little," Derek admitted. "But not to the extent that you're breaking the law by letting us inside."

She laughed. "I would let you in if you had a posse after you. Come on back. I was repotting some plants on the deck." They followed her through the house and into a neat but lived-in kitchen.

"Where's Jackson?" Derek asked.

"At a friend's house. I'm supposed to pick him up at five. Would you like something to drink?"

"Nothing for me," Julie said.

"Actually, we came to watch a movie." He held up the plastic bag from the rental store containing the DVD they'd picked up on the way. "Can we borrow your TV?"

"Sure, but what's the matter with yours?"

"I'm reluctant to go home. And we can't use Julie's house because it was searched by the police this morning. I'm sure it's a wreck." He didn't tell his friend that the hotel room in which they'd spent the night together didn't have a DVD player. "It's complicated, Linds, but we think this movie might provide a clue."

"To what?"

"We're not sure," Julie replied honestly.

Julie liked her for accepting the situation without qualification. She indicated a room adjacent to the kitchen and said to Derek, "You know where it is because you had it installed. Help yourself to anything in the fridge. I'll be right outside if you need me."

Julie followed Derek into a cozy den that looked like the room where Lindsay and her son spent a lot of time. There was a Game

Boy on the end table and a pair of sports shoes with cleats poking from beneath the sofa. The jigsaw puzzle on the card table was half finished. Books that appeared well read were stacked on the second level of the coffee table. There was an array of DVDs in the shelves below a flat-screen TV mounted on the wall.

"You gave them the TV?"

"For Christmas last year."

"What did you give them this year?"

"A Wii." Reading her expression, he shrugged. "I spoil Jackson. I know I do. But I enjoy it, and he's not a bratty, demanding kid. Lindsay sees to that."

They sat down on the sofa, and he used the remote to get the movie started. "Ever seen this?"

"No."

"Me neither." During the opening credits, he said, "We're in the back row. Want to just mess around instead?" She looked across at him, and he grinned. "It's been hours, after all."

"Half that time you've been furious with me."

"Doesn't mean I don't want to jump your bones."

He reached for her hand and used his thumb to draw intimate circles in her palm. The sensations traveling up her arm were delicious, but she whispered, "We're missing the opening scenes."

It was another Hitchcock thriller, a chilling story about a serial killer in London. Derek fast-forwarded through most of it, looking for the violent scenes. "I feel like a sicko speeding through, interested only in the violence."

The pivotal scene was cinematic violence at its most shocking. After watching it, Derek paused the DVD. For a moment they were too disturbed by the images to speak. Finally Derek exhaled a long breath. "Did that bother you as much as it did me?"

She nodded.

"Violence without blood."

"Like in *Strangers on a Train*. Brutal. Calculated."

"And like that villain, this one is so—"

"Focused. Cold. Cruel."

Saying no more, they watched the movie till its conclusion. Lindsay came in just as it ended. "It's almost five. I've got to go get Jackson. Anything I can do for you two while I'm out? Pick up some carryout?"

"No, thanks. You're a doll to let us do this." Derek got up, went to her, and gave her a hug. "I doubt we'll be here when you get back."

"As you go, lock up and set the alarm. You know the code."

Julie stood. "I really appreciate this, Lindsay."

"Don't mention it. Next time we meet, I hope things are better for you." She smiled kindly at Julie, then whispered something in Derek's ear and kissed his cheek.

Julie waited until she was certain Lindsay had gone, then asked, "What did she say?"

He removed his cell phone from the holster on his belt and checked the LED. "I had it on vibrate. Dodge has called twice. I didn't want to answer and hear what he might have to tell us."

"Did Lindsay say something about me?"

"She said she was glad we'd got together."

"How did she know?"

"I guess she saw that dreamy glaze in your eyes every time you look at me."

Julie glared at him, and he laughed. "Women's intuition? I don't know." He shrugged indifferently and continued to fiddle with his phone. "Dodge didn't leave a message. Which probably means the news is bad."

"Have you talked to Lindsay about me?"

"Not really. But the night of that charity thing, when I was driving her home, she told me I should wait an appropriate amount of time out of respect for Paul Wheeler and then ask you out."

"She did?"

"Yeah. But I told her I was in no rush because I'd already fucked you, so—"

"*What?*"

He looked across at her and grinned. "Just kidding."

"You didn't tell her about the airplane?"

"Of course not. I'm her kid's godfather, for crying out loud." He speed-dialed Dodge's number. "But she did urge me to call you. She said you were smart, classy, lovely, just the kind of woman I needed."

"How did you respond?"

He shot her a smile. "I mumbled something to the effect that I didn't need a matchmaker, thank you very much. Then I drove straight to your house and almost got shot. Hey, Dodge. Sorry I'm just now—"

Julie could hear Dodge's voice coming through the phone. He sounded perturbed.

Derek interrupted. "No, we've got all our clothes on. We're at Lindsay Graveau's house. We came here to watch the movie that Billy Duke— Okay, hold on." He switched on the speaker. "Talk. We can both hear you now."

Without preliminary, Dodge asked, "Ms. Rutledge, have you ever taken a prescription pain reliever?"

"Why?"

"Just answer."

"Last spring."

"I got the skinny on the autopsy," he said, sounding unhappy about it.

"Did he die of the knife wound?"

"No. But it would've been better for you if he had. You could have pled self-defense."

Holding Derek's worried gaze, Julie sat down on Lindsay's sofa, dreading what Dodge was about to tell them.

"ME's best guess, Billy Duke ingested a lethal overdose of a prescription painkiller."

Dodge stopped there, apparently waiting for a reaction from one or both of them. Derek remained silent, watching Julie.

She made a gesture of helplessness. "Paul got it into his head that I should learn to golf so we could play together. I was terrible at it and not really into learning the game. I was almost glad when I pulled a muscle in my lower back. It gave me an excuse to quit the lessons. The doctor prescribed an anti-inflammatory and a knock-you-senseless painkiller. I was afraid of it. I only took two to get me through that first night. After a day of bed rest, the anti-inflammatory kept the pain to a minimum. I didn't need anything else."

"The police emptied your medicine cabinet during the search. No prescription painkiller," Dodge said. "But Kimball called your pharmacy. You got the prescription in March."

"Did you keep the leftover pills, Julie?"

"Yes," she replied to Derek. "I wanted them on hand in case my back bothered me again. Creighton must have taken the bottle when he was in my house. I wouldn't have missed them, not even the next day, when I was cleaning."

After a short but significant pause, Dodge continued. "Sanford did some research. These overdose symptoms include vomiting, jaundice, disorientation, difficulty speaking and walking, convulsions. And so forth. Exactly how you described Billy Duke in your statement to the police."

"That's inconclusive," Derek said. "Those are symptoms of other ailments, too."

"They'll do a complete toxicology workup. His liver may've been fried by something else. But in the meantime . . ."

"It's another mark against me."

Neither of the men said anything contradictory, so she knew they were thinking the same. "I suppose you think this confirms my guilt, Mr. Hanley."

Dodge's cough sounded wet and gurgling. "No, Ms. Rutledge. In fact, I owe you an apology."

Derek's brows shot up. "Why's that?"

"Creighton did have a juvie file, just as you suspected. It's been in my possession all of five minutes, which is enough time for me to see that she's been right about this guy all along. He's twisted. It's a lot of stuff, and I'm only gonna give you the highlights because, having seen this, I'm real scared we're running out of time."

Derek and Julie were looking at each other, their expressions as solemn as Dodge's voice. Neither interrupted.

"One Jerry Bascomb was a classmate at Creighton's school. A tony prep school in North Carolina. Creighton claimed Jerry solicited sex in the locker room, so he cut off his little finger with a hunting knife. Instead of saying a simple no thank you, he maimed that boy for life.

"The Bascomb kid swore up and down he didn't have one homosexual tendency and no such proposition had ever occurred. Police questioned what Creighton was doing with a hunting knife in his gym locker in the first place. While they were conducting further investigation, the Wheelers went to the other family and said surely they could work out their differences through a mediator."

Derek said, "I'll bet there was an implied threat that if the Bascombs didn't want Jerry exposed as a degenerate who propositioned his fellow students, they should let the matter drop."

"Whatever," Dodge said, "Creighton was never charged. The problem went away."

"Money changed hands?"

"What do you think, Counselor? Roll around to the following summer. Creighton's fifteen and away at camp. One Sarah Walker accused him of raping her. She admitted to getting sloshed on contraband liquor at the wiener roast. Creighton invited her to go for a walk alone in the woods. When she staggered out an hour later, she was bleeding from the vagina. Hysterical. His version was that he hadn't known she was a virgin, that he was following her lead, giving her what she wanted."

"Oh, no doubt she asked to be brutalized," Julie said with sarcasm.

"He called it 'rough sex.' That's a quote from his statement. The girl was a mess. Had to get counseling. Wouldn't leave her room. Her family was pressuring the DA to bring an indictment when, suddenly, several of the other boy campers came forward, ready to testify to hand jobs, blow jobs, and other sexual acts. Said Sarah was a virgin only in the most technical sense, and had they been enticed into the woods with her, they would have responded exactly as their good buddy Creighton had."

"Creighton doesn't have buddies," Julie said.

"Just lots of dough to spread around." That from Dodge, said after a spitting sound.

"Let me guess," Derek said. "It went away."

"Charges were dropped when Sarah Walker refused to testify."

"Were her family's pockets lined?"

"That's not in the file, but I wouldn't bet against it," Dodge said. "There's more. Some minor offenses, dating back to when he was a kid. A man reported he and his wife woke up to find Creighton standing beside their bed, just staring at them. It was attributed to sleepwalking. A manicurist who'd gone to their house to do Sharon Wheeler's nails accused him of exposing himself while 'in an aroused state.' He admitted to jerking off but to having no idea she was watching, which makes one wonder how his semen got on her shoe. But the manicurist suddenly gets a job in a fancy spa on Amelia Island.

"Another girl, an Allison Perry, went on a date with him on his sixteenth birthday. He took her for a ride in his new convertible, where she was sodomized. He said they'd agreed that would be the surest method of preventing pregnancy."

"Christ." Derek dragged both hands down his face.

"Was he ever jailed?"

"Not once, Ms. Rutledge."

"The Wheelers bought off his accusers."

"And probably bribed various and sundry public officials along the way," Dodge said. "Whatever else he's done, the little shit's exhibited deviant behavior. What I'm thinking is, he's graduated to murder."

Julie laughed drily. "He's the deviant, but I'm the prime suspect."

"Keep us one step ahead of them, Dodge," Derek told his investigator.

"I'm on it."

He clicked off. Thoughtfully, Derek tapped his phone against his lips.

"What now?" She gestured toward the TV. "The movie didn't provide a breakthrough."

"I'm not so ready to dismiss it as insignificant." He studied the blank TV screen as though seeing images playing across it, then looked at Julie. "It wasn't like Billy Duke had an assortment of DVDs to help while away the time at the Pine View Motel. He had only one. This one. Why this particular movie? I'd never heard of it before today. Did Creighton give it to Billy Duke? When? And where?" He slammed his fist into his palm. "Goddammit! Why can't we link them?"

"I pinned my hopes on the girl who identified Billy Duke. But according to Dodge, she didn't have anything of use to tell Kimball."

Suddenly Derek stopped pacing. "Remember earlier, when I told you that criminal law 101 was money as a motive?"

"Yes."

"Know what criminal law 102 is?"

"What?"

"Everybody lies."

Creighton left his parents' estate by way of the service gate, in order to avoid the reporters out front hoping for a sound bite. He went to his condo and spent the next hour and a half in his home gym, exercising until his body glistened with sweat.

He toweled off, then got into his tanning bed to even out his skin tones. He followed that with fifteen minutes in his steam shower to sweat any impurities out of his system. Next came a hot, soapy shower, which he followed with a plunge into a tub of ice-cold water that closed his pores. He flossed before he brushed his teeth, cleaning them so vigorously that, when he spat, the toothpaste was tinged with blood.

He clipped and buffed his fingernails. He used an exfoliating mask on his face and followed it with a fragrant toner that made his skin tight and tingly. He took special pains with his hairbrush and blow-dryer.

Before dressing, he paused to admire the infinite reflections of himself cast by the mirrored walls in his bathroom. He could see his polished nude form from every angle. He couldn't find a flaw.

From the back, he looked like a statue of Adonis. He was perfectly proportioned, toned from shoulders to hips. His buttocks were taut, slightly concave on the sides, beautifully curved where they melded into his thighs. Hours spent on the tennis court had shaped his calves.

He appreciated the front view even more. What wasn't there to like? Sun-kissed hair. Aquamarine eyes. A nose that even the most expert, most expensive rhinoplasty surgeon couldn't improve upon. His lips were well shaped and sensual, not too much pigment, not too little. His mouth was saved from being pretty by his angular jaw and square chin.

He didn't have chest hair. If he had, he would have had it removed. Hairy chests reminded him of films about barbarians, hirsute men who gnawed on large animal bones and mated with women with dirty feet. Repulsive.

His chest was smooth and golden. He fingered his nipples, and when they were rigid, he pinched them till the pleasure turned to pain. His penis twitched, then swelled and stretched. The beauty of it brought tears to his eyes.

He masturbated slowly, taking his time, drawing out the pleasure of making love to the endless images of himself surrounding him. His climax left him weak but euphoric.

He dressed in clothes he'd never worn before. It was an important night, and he wanted to look his best. Unfortunately, no one would know about it except him. If only he could share how brilliantly he took a movie plot and turned it into living drama.

Julie was getting the credit for Billy Duke, just as Billy had got credit for Uncle Paul. No one knew, nor could they ever know, that Billy was just a facilitator. Creighton was the mastermind.

It was a shame, really, that he was denied the deserved recognition. But going uncredited was the price he must pay for his particular brand of brilliance. Even as a teenager he'd reconciled himself to the fact that no one ever would—or could—know of his genius except himself.

And his victims, of course.

Tonight's leading lady was particularly naïve. She would die in a state of supreme bewilderment, because never in a million years would she see it coming. The perfect smash cut.

CHAPTER
26

DESPITE THE HARROWING DAY SHE'D HAD, ARIEL GOT EVERY-thing ready for her dinner date by seven-thirty. The roast filled her small house with a scrumptious aroma. The salad was chilling in the fridge. The Cabernet was breathing. A bowl of roses was in the center of the table, flanked by tapers that were ready to light.

So organized was she that twelve minutes had been allocated for her to shower and refresh her makeup before dressing. Her sundress had a halter top and a scandalously short skirt.

She smoothed lotion on her shaved legs and slipped on her high-heeled sandals, fluffed her hair, dabbed fragrance on her bare shoulders and between her breasts, threaded gold wires through her earlobes, and she was ready.

At seven-thirty she put match to candles, then peeped out the window in her front door and scanned the street for the first sign of him, wondering if he would arrive in the Porsche. Imagine what the neighbors would think when it growled down their block of modest houses and parked in front of hers!

At seven-thirty-five she checked the roast to make certain it wasn't drying out.

By seven-forty-five she was concerned, but not really worried.

He could be stuck in traffic. Because of rubbernecking, a flat tire on the shoulder of the freeway could slow traffic, a fender bender could bring it to a standstill.

At ten of eight, she told herself she would just die if he stood her up again. She really would.

What was this, Crap on Ariel Week?

Earlier today she'd almost fainted when she was summoned to her boss's office and he'd introduced her to the squatty woman detective. "She wants to ask you some questions."

That had been an understatement.

For the next half hour, the detective had grilled her about Billy Duke. This not an hour after Ariel had resolved, now that he was dead, to banish him from her mind forever. How like him to continue being a menace.

She'd owned up to placing the anonymous call to the police hotline, believing that would demonstrate to the detective what a solid citizen she was. But she wasn't let off the hook that easily. Roberta Kimball had persisted, asking her questions about Omaha. "Did he ever live with you there?"

"No. Never. He spent the night at the apartment a few times, you know. But that's all."

She'd been particularly interested in learning when Ariel had last seen Billy.

"Not since his trial." She hadn't told the detective about his attempted visit to the house yesterday.

The detective had cited his repeated phone calls.

"But he never said anything, and neither did I. I always hung up."

"What about your roommate? Did she ever talk to him?"

"No. Carol's staying in Athens this summer."

The detective had asked if Billy Duke had ever mentioned Paul Wheeler or Julie Rutledge.

"No. I'm absolutely certain of that. I'd never heard of them until Mr. Wheeler was killed."

Ariel had answered all her questions truthfully, but she hadn't volunteered anything. Eventually the detective had seemed satisfied that Ariel was telling her everything she knew and that to question her further would be a waste of time. She'd thanked Ariel for her co-operation and left.

Ariel had returned to her duties, pretending for the sake of her curious co-workers that she was unfazed by the interview. It certainly hadn't been pleasant, but she'd got through it all right. Billy was dead. His days of preying on women were over. Soon people would forget that she'd had even a passing acquaintance with him.

Again, she'd set her mind on not letting anything, especially the late Billy Duke, spoil her evening with Tony. By the end of the workday, she had pushed the detective and everything relating to Billy from her mind and let herself anticipate the evening to come.

As a precaution, she hadn't answered her phone. It had rung at regular intervals since she got home. She didn't recognize the number, and there was no name to identify the caller. Fearing that Roberta Kimball was calling with another round of questions, she'd let her voice mail get it.

She knew it wasn't Tony. She'd never given him her number—either her cell or home phone—and the oversight had been intentional. She'd avoided that because, secretly, she was afraid he would cancel on her.

When eight o'clock arrived and he still hadn't shown, she was certain he wasn't coming. How could he do this to her *twice*? How could she have been just as gullible the second time? He must think she was the biggest moron ever born. If he thought of her at all.

At eight-fifteen she blew out the candles and went into her bedroom to change clothes. Sobbing, she kicked off her sandals and was just reaching up to untie her halter when there was a soft knock on her front door.

Her heart nearly leaped out of her chest. All the horrible things she'd thought of him, and all the filthy names she'd called him, flew right out of her mind. Giddy with happiness, she ran to her door and yanked it open.

His name died on her lips.

While Ariel Williams was across town anxiously awaiting the arrival of her dinner date, Derek was shouting into his cell phone. "What do you mean she's gotten coy?"

"Don't you know what *coy* means?" Dodge fired back.

"Yeah, I know what *coy* means, but I thought you'd patched things up with her. All we're asking for is an address."

"You're not Most Popular with the PD, Counselor, in case you didn't know. On account of you, too many scumbags have gone free. Now you're trying to get that Connor kid off. You're making noises that the first cops on the scene fucked it up in terms of gathering evidence and that exculpatory information is being buried. Cops haven't been this pissed off at a defense lawyer since the O.J. trial. The first one."

"Are you finished?"

"I'm just saying. Cut me some slack. I got you the juvie file, didn't I? Practically had to suck a guy's dick, and what thanks do I get?"

"I'm sorry. Thank you."

"You're welcome."

"But we need that address, Dodge."

"I understand. But if the rank and file of Atlanta's finest don't care who killed your dog, they sure as hell aren't disposed to give you information, a piece of which is Ariel Williams's address. And I can push Dora only so far. She's a single mom of two. She's got a job to protect. She says if they find out she's the pipeline through which you've got information about the timing of the search of Ms. Rutledge's house, and the autopsy, and—"

"All right." Derek tiredly rubbed his forehead. He looked across the console of his car at Julie, who was also on her cell, talking to Kate. With a shake of her head, she let him know she was having no better luck than he.

Dodge was saying, "Things have really clamped down now that they're officially seeking Julie for questioning into Duke's demise."

"I know you're doing your best. But I'd really like that address. Ariel Williams may be the key to all this."

"Beyond that . . ."

"What?"

"Well, knowing the kind of guy Creighton Wheeler is, I'm kinda worried about this girl. He wouldn't have liked her identifying Duke to the police."

"Even more reason to find her soon. Go back to your lady friend. Promise to let her be on top." Derek slapped his phone shut.

Julie, who had ended her call seconds earlier, raised her eyebrows inquisitively.

"Don't ask," he said. "Kate have any luck?"

"She called the company where Ariel Williams works, but since it's after hours, she got the number for emergencies. She called it but got another recording, asking the caller to leave name, number, and nature of the problem, and someone would get back.

"She's looked up every possible way Ariel Williams could be listed in the phone directory, but there are thousands of Williamses, none of the combinations have been right, and if this girl is getting nuisance calls, it's doubtful she's listed anyway.

"A Google search turned up Ariel's pages on Facebook and My-Space, but neither has her home address, and the most recent postings were two weeks ago. Kate has e-mailed her. No reply. She's still searching." She picked up a French fry that had turned cold, considered it, then returned it to the box with disinterest. "I feel rotten, asking Kate to do this for me."

"She wants to help. She said so. She feels she owes it to you after talking to the police behind your back."

"I know her willingness to help is genuine. But I'm a fugitive. She's aiding and abetting."

"Nobody's asked her if she knows where you are."

"Because she hasn't answered the detectives' calls. She doesn't answer her phone unless she knows it's me. That's a deliberate evasion."

"Which can't be proved. Even if they do ask her your whereabouts, she can tell them honestly that she doesn't know, because she doesn't." He looked through the windshield of his car at the neon golden arches of the McDonald's. They'd ordered at the drive-through, then parked to eat their Big Macs while making their calls.

Derek had thought Ariel Williams might open up to them more easily than she would to a detective as intimidating as Roberta Kimball. It was worth a shot, anyway, so they'd started calling her as soon as they left Lindsay's house, but had got the automated recording each time.

For almost three hours they'd been waiting for Dodge to come through with some useful information, such as her address, but so far he'd come up dry, too. He'd been unable to reach any of his moles at the DMV or tax office who could have accessed her records. And his policewoman had turned coy.

"He's going to try more sweet talk," Derek said.

"I can't feature Dodge sweet-talking."

"It's a stretch."

Julie folded the wrapper around the remains of her burger and replaced it in the sack along with her uneaten French fries. "Meanwhile I'm a fugitive from justice. Do you believe they could actually convict me?"

"No way."

"Are you speaking from the heart, or is that your objective, professional opinion?"

"With what they've got, they can't convict you. I'd stake my career on it."

She gave him a wan smile. "I think you have."

"I'll continue to."

"I'm not as afraid of being tried and convicted as I am of Creighton going free. He's evil, Derek."

He put his scraps into the sack along with hers. "You'll get no argument from me. I've only been back to my house once since I found Maggie. I haven't wanted to go back. I can't picture myself in those rooms without her. It was an act of senseless brutality. He did it out of pure meanness. Evil, if you will.

"Not only did he kill my beloved pet, he also desecrated my home. It won't ever be the same for me. Each time I think about that, this rage boils up inside of me. And whenever Maggie crosses my mind . . ." He stopped, unable to go on.

Leaning across the console, Julie placed her hands on his cheeks and gently kissed his lips.

When she pulled away, his eyes roved over the features of her face. He whispered, "That meeting and falling in love thing I talked about over breakfast?"

She nodded.

"Well, guess what?"

He gazed at her meaningfully, and it held until his cell phone rang. He flipped it open. "Please tell me Dora's come through."

"I may have to marry her."

"Ariel Williams?"

The young woman's elated smile collapsed upon seeing them. The color in her cheeks was high, and it was evident to Julie that she'd been crying. Her mascara was smeared. Except for shoes, she was dressed for a special occasion, not for a quiet night at home. Beyond her, Julie saw wisps of smoke curling from candles recently blown out.

"Ariel Williams?" Julie repeated.

Speechlessly, she bobbed her head.

"My name is Julie Rutledge."

She swallowed visibly. "I know who you are."

"How?" Derek asked.

Her eyes shifted to him. "I've seen her on TV. On the news."

"My name is Derek Mitchell." When she neither said nor did anything to acknowledge that, he said, "We'd like to talk to you."

"About what? If it's about Billy, I already told the police everything I know." Her lower lip trembled slightly. "And this isn't a good time."

"Do you know how Billy Duke died?" Julie asked.

"You stabbed him or something."

"The medical examiner believes he died of liver failure due to a drug overdose."

Ariel's eyes, shiny with recent tears, widened. "I never knew him to do drugs."

"He fell into a knife that I was holding to protect myself, but he died of an overdose of a common pharmaceutical. I didn't give it to him. We, Mr. Mitchell and I, believe a man named Creighton Wheeler did." Julie paused, then said, "Please, Ariel, may we come in for just a few minutes? We promise not to stay long. It's very important or we wouldn't impose on you."

The girl divided a look between then, then sighed. "I guess you'd just as well."

The door opened directly into her living room. She motioned

them toward the sofa, which had a muslin-colored slipcover accented by brightly colored throw pillows. It and a bentwood rocking chair were the two main pieces in the room. There were a couple of mismatched tables and lamps, a leafy, well-tended ficus tree near the window, framed travel posters on the walls. Decorated on a budget but with an eye for color and proportion, it reminded Julie of her first apartment in Paris. It was a pleasant room and very tidy.

Ariel sat down in the rocking chair, and to Julie, it seemed she was indifferent to them and the reason that had brought them unannounced to her front door. The dining table was set with dishes and glassware, flowers and candles. A bottle of wine had been uncorked but was still full.

Julie caught Ariel wistfully glancing at it. "Are you expecting a guest?"

"Yeah, but he . . . he seems to be running late."

That explained the recently extinguished candles and her mascara-streaked cheeks.

Derek said, "He's missing out. It smells great, and that's a knockout dress."

"Thanks." She blushed. "So what do you want to know?"

"Start with how you met Billy Duke."

She rolled her eyes. "I rue the day. My friend and I were out clubbing."

"This was in Omaha?" Derek asked.

She affirmed that with a nod. "Billy showed up at this club we were at. We hung out that night. Then he started coming there regularly. He was cute. Friendly. A snappy dresser, drove a nice car, and didn't mind buying the rounds. He was very boastful, always acting the stud, always flashing money around. But he was never specific about what he did for a living. Now I know why he didn't talk about his work. He was a professional con artist. A swindler."

"You didn't know until later that he was involved with the widow and stealing from her?"

"God no! But by then I had begun to suspect that he was shifty."

"What made you suspect?"

"He broke dates. He avoided giving direct answers to direct questions. He would disappear for days at a time, then show up with flowers and wine but without an explanation as to where he'd been. All signs that he was two-timing." She addressed Julie. "But you know how we women are. We hate to admit what we know in our heart."

Again she glanced at the table, and the disappointment in her expression touched Julie. She seemed like a sweet girl, and she'd been hurt. Coming back to them, she said, "When Billy was arrested, I saw it as an opportunity to make a fresh start. I talked Carol into—"

"Carol?" Derek asked.

"My roommate."

"I talked her into leaving Omaha and going someplace new. She and I moved here. We loved it right off. The food. The way people talk." Her brow puckered into a frown. "I wasn't all that shocked when Billy was charged with extortion. The trial and all. And then they let him go! I couldn't believe it!"

"The prosecutor was sloppy," Derek said. "He shouldn't have based his whole case on the victim's testimony. The minute the widow died, he lost."

Ariel looked at him strangely. Julie said, "He's a defense attorney."

"Oh."

Derek continued, "Billy followed you to Atlanta."

"I couldn't believe that, either. So much for a fresh start in a new place. The first time he called and identified himself, I was furious and hung up immediately. He didn't have my cell number, but he continued to call the house phone."

"We know his MO," Derek said. "He wouldn't say anything to you. You'd hang up."

Sheepishly, she ducked her head. Derek glanced at Julie, and she knew he had sensed a lie. "I told that detective—Ms. Kimball?—I told her that I'd never talked to him. But that's not entirely true. He had called here the same night I called the hotline and gave them his name. I'd had it with his stupid calls. I shouted at him, told him he was pathetic and that these phone games were childish, and ordered him to stop. Of course he didn't. He kept on calling right up to the night before he died. He called from a number I didn't recognize, so I answered. But it was him."

Julie leaned forward. "Did he say anything?"

"He tried, but it was garbled. I didn't—" She covered her mouth with her hand. "Oh, God. Do you think he'd already been drugged? Was he calling for help? I took the phone off the hook," she said miserably.

"You figured it was another prank call," Derek said to her kindly. "That was the last time you heard from him?"

Her gaze bounced between them as she worried her lower lip between her teeth. She couldn't have looked guiltier, and Julie realized that this young woman couldn't lie convincingly no matter how hard she tried. Roberta Kimball must not have asked the right questions.

Derek said her name, softly, as though he was gentling a spooked foal. "Is there something else?"

She hesitated, then blurted out, "Billy came here yesterday. But I was at work." She rattled off a story about an elderly neighbor who lived across the street. "She saw him banging on my door. She yelled at him and asked what he wanted. He said it was a matter of life or death that he talk to me. She said he didn't look right. In fact, she thought he was on drugs. I thought that was just an old person talking, but I guess she was right. Anyway, he frightened her. She ran inside and locked her door."

Tears filled her eyes. "Now, I think maybe he was coming to me for help. Oh, gosh, I feel just awful. I mean, I couldn't stand the guy, he was a crook, but if he was dying . . ." The tears spilled over her eyelids and rolled down her cheeks. "Why didn't he go to the hospital?"

Derek said, "Maybe he didn't know he'd ingested a deadly dosage."

"If he'd gone to the hospital, he'd have been arrested," Julie said. "He didn't want that." She reached across the space separating them and covered Ariel's clenched hands. "But I understand exactly how you feel. He was inside my house. The police think for a time. Hours maybe. I believe he went there to plant evidence to make me look guilty of killing Paul. But he was also dying. I didn't know that. I reacted as anyone would who thought they were being attacked."

"I never thought you meant to kill him," Ariel said. "When I heard on the news what had happened, I knew there must be some other explanation. An overdose. Jeez. Who did you say you suspect of giving it to him?"

"Paul Wheeler's nephew, Creighton," Derek said.

"The name sounds familiar. Has he been on TV, too?"

"No," Julie said, giving Derek a glance. "He ducks publicity. His name is familiar to you because the police did question him several times."

The girl's eyes brightened. "He had an alibi. I remember now."

"However, Julie and I think Creighton conspired to have his uncle murdered."

"With Billy?"

"Yes. We think they struck a deal in Omaha, that Creighton killed the widow who was about to testify against Billy, then presented Billy with an IOU."

"Wow." Ariel pieced it together mentally. "Then once Billy had served his purpose, this nephew wanted him out of the picture?"

"That's what we believe," Julie told her. "Unfortunately, we can't substantiate it. That's why we came to you. We hoped you might provide us with something."

"Like what?"

"Like a link between Creighton and Billy," Derek said.

"I'm sorry. I can't. I never heard him mention anyone named Creighton."

"What about Billy's friends in Omaha?"

"If he had any friends, I didn't know them."

Derek leaned forward. "Ariel, I don't want to frighten you. But Creighton has hurt people. I'm not guessing or making false accusations. The violent crimes he's committed are a matter of record. If he considered Billy Duke a threat he had to eliminate, he may consider you one, too."

"Me?" she squeaked. "I never even met him."

"But you were connected to Billy. You identified Billy to the police. Creighton may fear that Billy told you something about him."

She was looking at them wildly.

"Ariel." Julie reached out and touched her hand again. "As Derek said, we don't want to alarm you. But on the outside chance

Creighton should approach you, get away from him as quickly as you can and call the police."

"If not the police, one of us." Derek took a business card from his breast pocket and jotted down several phone numbers on the back of it before passing it to her. "There are all my numbers, Julie's cell, and my investigator's cell phone. His name is Dodge. He knows about you. He'll respond immediately. Good guy to have on your side."

She took the card and clutched it in her fist. "I don't want to stay here by myself. I'm going to ask Carol to come back."

"Good idea." Derek smiled at her with reassurance. "I truly think if Creighton was going to contact you, he would have done so by now." He looked at Julie. "Anything else?"

"Just be careful, Ariel, and stay in touch. I'd like to know how you're doing."

Somewhat shyly, she said, "It was sad what happened to Mr. Wheeler."

"Yes, it was. Thank you."

They all stood and walked to the door. Derek glanced back at the table. "Did your dinner date stand you up?"

Ariel sighed. "Looks like it. He was due here over an hour ago."

"What's his name? I'll hunt him down and beat him up for you."

She giggled, blushing again over Derek's attention. "His name's Tony. Bruno actually, but he goes by Tony."

"No wonder," Derek remarked. "Whatever his name is, he's a fool for passing up a date with you."

"Thanks," she said, her blush deepening.

They shook hands with her, then started down the walk toward Derek's car. "She's cute. Sweet," he said. "I feel for her, getting mixed up in murder and mayhem and none of it having anything to do with her."

"So do I. On top of that, her date stood her up."

"What a jerk."

"I could tell the moment she opened the door that something was wrong. Then I saw the table and—" Julie stopped dead in her tracks and grabbed his arm. "Oh my God!"

She spun around and ran back toward the house.

"Julie? What?"

"His name," she called back to him. "I just caught it."

"His name?"

"Bruno. That's the name of the killer in *Strangers on a Train*."

"Jesus, you're right."

Julie reached Ariel's door first and began knocking hard on it and shouting her name. The girl opened it, wide-eyed with fear. "What now?"

"Bruno," Julie blurted. "What's his last name?"

"Anthony. That's where he gets Tony."

Julie looked at Derek. "Bruno Anthony."

"Why?" Ariel asked. "What's the matter?"

"What does he look like, Ariel?"

"He's . . . he's very good looking. I mean like superhot."

"Tall? Slender? Blond? Blue eyes?"

She nodded.

"Well dressed? Very debonair."

"How'd you know?"

"That's Creighton Wheeler."

The young woman fell back a step.

"When did you meet him?" Derek asked.

"A few nights ago."

"Where? How? Did he approach you?"

"Yeah. At . . . at Christy's. The bar? I . . . I caught him staring at me. He . . . he came over and started talking and bought me a drink." She told them about his inviting her for coffee, then running out on her. "The valet told me he left with another woman."

"That must have been me," Julie said, addressing herself to Derek. Then back to Ariel: "I might have saved your life that night."

"That's probably why he was so angry when he came to my house after that encounter," Derek said. "You'd thwarted his plans for Ariel."

She whimpered, "His plans for me?"

In a protective gesture, Derek placed his hand on her shoulder. "Damn, I'm glad we found you tonight."

"Yes, thank God," Julie breathed.

Ariel didn't share their relief. "Why would he want to hurt me?"

"Somehow he learned, probably through Billy, that it was likely you who identified Billy to the police. And you said Billy was boastful. Maybe Creighton feared that, in the hope of winning back your affection, Billy had bragged about being in cahoots with a rich guy, about killing his uncle for him."

"In the hope of winning back my affection?"

"After he'd cheated on you with the widow."

Confused, Ariel looked at them in turn. "Billy didn't cheat on *me*. He wasn't *my* boyfriend. He was Carol's."

CHAPTER

27

CAROL MAHONEY?"

Her face—he could see only half of it—was a mix of surprise and wariness. Her eyes darted, looking behind him. "Yes?"

Creighton smiled. "Thank heaven. I had the dickens of a time finding you."

She had opened the front door only as far as the chain lock would allow. He recognized her from the photos accompanying news reports of Billy's trial in Nebraska.

"Who are you?"

"Sorry." He flashed another grin. "Peter Jackson," he said, betting she didn't know one movie director from another, even Academy Award winners. "I'm a feature writer for *The Atlanta Journal*."

Her face, already swollen from crying, became belligerent. "I don't want to talk to a reporter."

Before she could close the door, he said, "Ariel told me you were gun-shy of the press. She warned me you'd probably slam the door in my face."

She hesitated. "You talked to Ariel?"

"Not in person. On the phone." Citing her friend and confidante had helped, but there was still indecision in her moist eyes. "Look, I'll wait while you call her, check me out." It was a bluff, and while she was debating it, he was thinking, *Get me off the porch before someone drives by and sees me.*

"I don't want to bother Ariel tonight," she said. "She has this guy coming over for dinner."

He laughed. "Ah. That must've been why she sounded breathless over the phone."

"She just met him. She's excited."

Am I good, or what? "Then I'm even more glad she took time out to talk to me. I was persistent, I'm afraid."

"I guess you want to ask me about Billy?"

"Billy Duke is big news today. Dying in the home of his victim's mistress. Hell of a thing."

Her expression turned sour. "Not if you knew Billy."

"I didn't. That's why I wanted to ask you a few questions. Get your take on him."

"I don't want to talk about him. I don't want to go through that again."

"Like what you went through in Omaha?"

"You know about that?"

He gave her a sad smile. "I had to do my research, Carol. It's my job."

"I'm sorry then, Mr. . . ."

"Jackson. Call me Peter."

"You seem nice, Peter, and I'm sorry you drove all this way and took the trouble to find me. But I don't wish to comment." Again, she was about to close the door. Of course he could have put his foot to it, busted it and the flimsy chain, but that was not how he wanted to do this. It would be better if there was no sign of forced entry.

Her body would be found days later, and it would remain a mystery who her attacker had been. So far she hadn't noticed that he hadn't arrived in a car. It was parked down the road, in a thicket, out of sight. The cottage couldn't have been better positioned for what he was about to do. If he'd been scouting locations to film a woman-in-jeopardy movie, this would have been perfect. It was off the beaten path, had no discernible address, and the nearest neighbor was half a mile away.

"I understand your reservations," he said quickly, before she shut the door. "Jesus, after all that went down in Omaha, who could blame you? But I want to give you fair warning. One of my colleagues is doing a front pager on Billy Duke that'll run tomorrow. You're mentioned. I read his draft, and it wasn't flattering to you. He's become a card-carrying misogynist since his wife left him."

Lowering his voice to a sympathetic pitch, he said, "My story would take a different slant on you and your relationship with Billy. I'm not out to paint you as one of his whorish—"

"The other reporter called me whorish?"

Creighton shrugged helplessly. "He's an asshole. I'll set the record straight. But I can't if you won't talk to me."

Through the crack in the door, she looked him up and down, and he could see her defenses weakening. "I was having a glass of wine on the back porch. Want to come around?"

He grinned, turned, and started for the corner of the house. If she didn't change her mind and call Ariel to check him out, he was home free.

There was terrific irony at play here. Carol Mahoney had escaped the clutches of the suspected killer Billy Duke, only to be murdered by an unidentified person, seemingly without motive.

He could imagine one of the local cops venturing a guess that she'd been killed by a customer of the sports bar where she worked, where nightly she squeezed her sizable breasts into a T-shirt two sizes too small, where she lifted trays of chicken wings and beer mugs high above her head, providing an unrestricted view of her breasts to a boozy crowd of horny baboons.

She teased and taunted them to get better tips.

It would be concluded that one had got tired of being teased.

Anyone who'd ever seen a scary movie knew that the slut always died. The body count of bad girls considerably outweighed that of their virtuous counterparts. Jamie Lee Curtis's promiscuous friend in *Halloween*. Diane Keaton in *Looking for Mr. Goodbar*. The list was endless.

He'd thought about leaving it alone. He really had. He'd thought seriously about just letting it go and allowing Carol Mahoney to go on living.

But there were problems with that. First, as he'd told Billy, she was a loose end he could ill afford. If Billy had been stupid enough to use his cell phone to place numerous calls to the house Carol shared with Ariel, then God knew what other stupid things he might have done. Creighton hadn't been in a position to ask Ariel if she'd relented and told Billy where he could reach his former girlfriend. But Creighton had to assume that she had. For all he knew, Billy had been pouring out his heart to Carol for days. Weeks, even. At least the problem of the phone had been solved. It was now at the bottom of Stone Mountain Lake, unless a catfish had swallowed it.

Second, he'd promised Billy that he was going to do it, and although Billy was dead, he had been his partner and Creighton felt honor bound to keep his word to him.

Third, he wanted to.

He'd tortured people before and derived enormous pleasure from it, but the ultimate, all-time high had been choking that blowsy widow till he felt the life leave her body. It had been fucking fantastic. Actually, that was inaccurate. It had been far superior to fucking. No food, or drink, or drug, or haute couture, or car, or sex, nothing had equaled that rush of pleasure. That kind of transcendent bliss must be particular to taking another person's life, to playing the god of their being, the dictator of their fate.

Ever since the widow went limp, he had wanted to feel that particular thrill again. Uncle Paul didn't count. Neither did Billy, really. He hadn't got to watch them die. To achieve that certain high, it must be a hands-on experience.

Finally, Carol had betrayed Billy when she testified against him, and she really shouldn't be allowed to get away with that.

Ariel would continue to live only because someone at Christy's might remember seeing her with him. No doubt the poor girl would be devastated when she learned of her roommate's murder. Her loyalty to Carol was plain. She'd gone to great lengths to get her out of Omaha. She had endured Billy's pestering in order to protect Carol from further involvement with him.

Of course she would never connect Carol's murder to Creighton. If ever she was to discover that the heel who'd stood her up twice was not Bruno Anthony, but none other than Creighton Wheeler, there was a simple explanation: He often used a fake name upon meeting a woman, not wanting her to make the connection between him and Wheeler Enterprises. The instant women learned his real name, they latched on; they became leeches with a thirst for the family fortune. So only rarely did he give his real name to a woman he'd just met.

If this discovery concerned Ariel enough for her to take the matter to the police, he could truthfully say that his meetings with her had been random both times. While tipsy on apple martinis, she might have mumbled something about a former alliance with a criminal, but—*my God!*—who would ever have thought she was referring to Billy Duke, his uncle's cold-blooded killer? What were the chances of that?

The detectives might think the chances of that were awfully slim, but they couldn't prove otherwise. He and Ariel had met twice in the same bar by pure happenstance. He'd never phoned her, nor she him. Yes, he'd made a date with her, then later changed his mind. Granted, he was a cad for standing her up. But breaking a date, or even a heart, wasn't a criminal offense.

And now that he knew she was even tangentially linked to the slayer of his late uncle Paul, well . . . Thank God he'd trusted his instincts and had skipped their dinner date.

All this ran through his mind as he made his way around the corner of the house. Carol was waiting on a screened back porch, pouring urine-colored wine into an ordinary drinking glass.

He noticed that the grass gave out several yards away from the foundation of the house and that the bare soil around it was moist. It was begging to have a footprint left in the mud. Not that he hadn't taken a precaution against that. He was wearing the shoes he'd bought before going to Nebraska. They were eyesores and spoiled the perfection of his wardrobe, but if a shoe print was ever discovered, it would be traced back to Wal-Mart, where hundreds of thousands of men in the greater Atlanta area could have bought the shoes. Creighton had paid cash.

Note to self: Get rid of the shoes later tonight. He wouldn't cry over the damn ugly things.

He stopped at the edge of the grass and nodded toward the wine. "How much of that have you had today?"

"Not enough."

"Or too much. You didn't go to work tonight. I went to the bar where Ariel said you'd be." Actually, he'd put on a tracksuit over his clothes and pretended to be a jogger working a cramp out of his calf while he staked out the bar for half an hour. When he hadn't seen her, he'd looked for her at her friend's house, which he'd had to do some detective work to find.

Ariel had helped with the rest.

I haven't been there, but she told me it's at the end of this country road. A really cool place. Sorta old, but charming, you know? Has this giant wisteria vine that covers the whole south side. I think it was this girl's grandmother's place or something.

Thank you, Ariel.

Carol was telling him what he had already deduced. "I called in sick today."

"Who could blame you?"

"Ariel could. I told her I wasn't feeling up to hustling drinks tonight. She urged me to. She'd put Billy out of her mind, and I should, too, she said. She's more resilient than I am, I guess. Anyway, she thought I was going to go to work. But I just couldn't."

He looked around, taking in the scenery. Choosing his spot. He motioned toward the tree line thirty yards away. "Does the property stop there?"

"I'm not sure where the property line is. I know there's a creek back there, and an old Indian burial ground."

"Let's walk."

"Walk? It's dark."

"Which is what makes it so nice. The moon's coming up." Smiling engagingly, he extended his hand. "I think you need to get out of the house. You've been cooped up inside all day, right? Trying to sort out your conflicting feelings about Billy? You hated him, but you were once involved with him, and you can't help but feel bad about the way he died."

She ducked her head. "Exactly like that."

"I could tell right off you'd been crying. If it's any comfort to you, from what I've heard of that guy, he isn't worth one single tear. Especially yours. Come on. You need the fresh air."

And just like that, she was his.

She unlatched the screen door and pushed it open. She was wearing shorts and a T-shirt. Her feet were bare. Her toenails were painted a dark magenta. He gave her legs an appreciative glance. "Ariel told me I'd know you as soon as I entered the bar. She said you were eye candy. I thought she was exaggerating. She wasn't."

She made a self-conscious gesture. "Thanks."

Just then Gloria Gaynor's "I Will Survive" began to play somewhere inside the house. Carol stopped and looked back. "That's my cell."

Fuck!

And no sooner had he thought that than another telephone began to ring. "And that's the house phone. Somebody's trying to reach me."

"Damn him!" Creighton said.

Carol looked at him, startled by his vehemence. "Who?"

"My colleague. The bastard has got the same resources I do. I'm only surprised that I tracked you down first."

"Why would he be tracking me down if he's already written his story?"

"That's how he operates. He writes a story the way he wants it to be, whether it's accurate or not. Then he has the subject dispute it. Of course, what's printed first is what the public believes." Outrage coming off him in waves, he said, "You want to take the call?"

She hesitated, then firmly shook her head and started walking with purpose toward the trees. "No. He does sound like an asshole."

Creighton reached for her hand, and she let him hold it.

With his other hand he loosened his necktie.

"Detective Kimball?"

"Ms. Rutledge?" The detective's voice was surprised, tense, abrupt. "Where are you?"

Julie was riding shotgun. Ariel was in the backseat, sobbing and praying and frantically punching numbers into her cell phone. Derek was driving like a madman.

"Listen to me, please, Detective," Julie said. "There's a young woman in danger."

"We have a warrant for your arrest, Ms. Rutledge."

"And Derek and I have Ariel Williams."

"Ariel—"

"We're on our way to Athens to see her roommate."

"Carol Mahoney," the detective said.

"Creighton Wheeler is going to kill her if we don't stop him."

There was a short silence, then she heard Kimball say, "Pull over," and assumed that she was addressing Sanford. "What are you talking about, Ms. Rutledge? What does Creighton Wheeler have to do with Ariel Williams's roommate? How did you locate her, and what—"

"All that can wait." Derek, who'd been listening on speaker, broke in. "This young woman's life is at risk. Call the Athens PD, the Clarke County SO. Get somebody over to . . . Ariel, where's she work?"

She hiccuped. "The . . . the . . . Red . . ."

"Red Dog?" he said.

"Red Dog," she affirmed.

"The Red Dog," he said loudly enough for Roberta Kimball to hear. "It's a sports bar. Every cop in the vicinity will know it. Get a squad car over there. She needs police protection. Tell the officers to stay with her."

"What the hell are you two talking about?" Sanford's voice came to them as though from the bottom of a well. He was on speaker, too. "I can put out an APB on your car, Mr. Mitchell."

The threat rolled off Derek. "You can. It'll cost time, and then if this girl dies tonight, you can carry the guilt to your grave with you."

"Why would Wheeler want to kill Carol Mahoney?" Kimball asked.

"On the outside chance she can put him and the late Billy Duke together," Julie said. She looked back at Ariel. "Any luck?"

"I've called her cell a dozen times. No answer. But she usually doesn't answer while she's at work. She calls me back when she gets a break. Or we text."

"Did you send one?"

"About eight. She hasn't responded. I suppose her battery could be dead, although we're both conscientious about that."

"Do you have the number at the house where she's staying?"

Ariel began punching in the number.

During this conversation, Kimball and Sanford had been alternately shouting questions and making demands, all of which had been ignored.

Now Derek shouted back. "Are you going to get somebody over to that bar or not?"

"I'm not," Kimball said. "Not till I know there's cause."

"We told you the cause," Julie said.

"You're prejudiced against Creighton Wheeler, Ms. Rutledge," Sanford said.

Looking at Derek, Julie said, "I can tell them about the movie plot."

"Movie? Did you say movie?" Kimball shouted into her phone. "Movie of what?"

"That would only waste time," Derek said for Julie's ears alone. "And it wouldn't accomplish anything. Not in the frame of mind they're in." Speaking louder, he said, "Would you at least see if you can locate Creighton Wheeler?"

"For what purpose?"

"Ask him where he left the body."

"What body?"

"Of the girl he killed while you two were jacking around." Then to Julie, he said, "Hang up." She did. "Let them chew on that for a while, see what they do."

"She doesn't answer at the house, either," Ariel said from the backseat. "I've called five times. The voice mail picks up each time. Did you mean what you said about her body?" she asked tremulously.

"No, Ariel, that was only to shock the police into taking action." But he cut his eyes to Julie, who knew he shared her fear for Carol Mahoney's safety.

Derek's phone rang. "Dodge," he said to Julie.

As they had run from Ariel's house to Derek's car, he had dialed Dodge, told him to drop everything and start driving toward Athens. He told him to call for further information once he was under way.

Derek answered on the second ring. "Where are you?"

"Still about twenty minutes out."

"How'd you get that far that fast?"

"I broke the law. Pushing ninety and ran all the red lights through Lawrenceville. Where am I going when I get there?"

"The Red Dog. It's a bar—"

"I know it. I've been there on game day."

"You're looking for Carol Mahoney. Carol Mahoney. She's a waitress there. Hold on a sec." Looking at Ariel in the rearview mirror, Derek asked her to describe her roommate loudly enough for Dodge to hear.

"Petite. Dark hair. Brown eyes. Pretty. Big boobs."

"Get that?"

"Big boobs."

"She'll be scared of you, so be nice."

"I'm always nice."

"Tell her you're acting on Ariel's behalf. Isolate her if you can, don't take your eyes off her. If she wants to talk to Ariel, call me."

"Why am I doing this?"

"We think Creighton Wheeler is going to try and kill her. But don't tell her that."

"Where are you?"

"Behind you, but past all the red lights in Lawrenceville."

"I'll call," Dodge said and hung up.

Julie made a sudden decision. "I'm going to call the Athens police myself."

"And turn yourself in?" Derek asked.

"I'll let Ariel talk to them. She can tell them that she's concerned about her friend because she hasn't heard from her, and ask that an officer be sent to check on her."

"It's only been a few hours since they talked. That's what they'll say."

"But they have to check it out, right?"

"Worth a try," he said, but he didn't sound hopeful.

Julie got the main number for the Athens PD from information.

"You know," Derek said as she punched in the number, "you've been on your phone almost constantly for hours. The Atlanta PD could locate us that way."

"We'll have to take the risk." Passing her phone back to Ariel, she said, "Mention that Carol was an ex-lover of Billy Duke. They'll recognize his name."

Ariel was tearful and scared, sometimes to the point of sounding hysterical. Julie wasn't sure if that was an advantage or not. She hung up after five minutes. "They said the whole town's turned upside down on account of the fraternities and sororities getting ready for rush week. Everybody's out of place tonight. But they said they'd send somebody to the bar to ask about Carol when they could spare an officer."

Julie looked at Derek. "What else can we do?"

"Nothing except wait till somebody gets back to us."

"How much farther?"

He pressed his accelerator all the way to the floor.

Detective Kimball clicked her phone closed, ending a call. "Sharon Wheeler says Creighton had lunch with them, then left because he had a date. She didn't know who with. Neither she nor his father has talked to him since. She wanted to know why we were calling, asked could she help. You heard what I said."

"Just checking some things out."

"Just checking some things out."

"Impression?"

"The call made her uneasy," Kimball said. "They were informed of the new will today. She started crying, said they dreaded telling Creighton about 'Paul's treachery.' That's a quote."

"Creighton doesn't know yet?"

Kimball shrugged but picked up the transmitter to their police radio. "Let's have somebody drive past his condo building, see if he's there, see if his car's in its parking space." She talked to the dispatcher and asked for a report ASAP.

When she finished, Sanford said, "That talk about a movie. Julie Rutledge mentioned it. Mitchell chimed in."

"Yeah, what was that about?"

Sanford flexed and stretched his right arm as though warming up to catch a Hail Mary pass. "Do you remember the first time we questioned Creighton?"

"The maid served us sweet tea and homemade macaroons."

"That's what you remember?"

"I had to sweat off the calories the next day. What do you re-member?"

"I asked him what his job was at Wheeler Enterprises. And he said, 'I'm the king of the world!' "

"I do remember. He flung his arms out and shouted it."

"Um-huh. Like Leonardo DiCaprio in *Titanic*. My kids have watched that movie a dozen times or more. They love it. I tease them, tell them the ending never changes. The ship always sinks."

"I thought he was just being a jerk," Kimball said. "Flaunting the fact to two underpaid cops that he doesn't have to do squat at the family company."

"That's what I thought, too. Kind of a hinky way of saying it, though. A piece of movie dialogue."

"So what does that signify?"

"Hell if I know."

The dispatcher interrupted to patch them in to the patrol officer presently at Creighton Wheeler's condo building. He said, "His Porsche is in its spot."

"Oh," Kimball said, feeling let down.

"So's his Land Rover."

"He's got a Land Rover?"

"And an SUV. Its spot is empty. One of the other owners in the building was in the garage when I got here. She said Wheeler has a blue and tan SUV. Isn't sure of the make or model 'cause they all look alike to her. It's not here, and he doesn't answer his doorbell."

Kimball thanked him but asked him to stay there and report when and if Wheeler returned. She looked at Sanford and said, "Derek Mitchell's smart, right?"

"Smart as they come. That's why we hate him. And he always covers his ass."

"So he wouldn't make wild allegations just because somebody rubbed him the wrong way."

"Bad for business."

"He wouldn't stick his neck out unless—"

"He was absolutely sure he was right," Sanford said, finishing the thought for her. "However, he might stick his neck out for her."

"*Her* meaning Julie Rutledge?"

"I picked up vibes. Did you pick up vibes?"

Kimball rolled her eyes. "If by vibes you mean like plate shifts in the earth's core, then yeah. And one of the officers who responded to the call about his dog?"

"Yeah?"

"E-mailed me this afternoon. Asked did I know that Julie Rutledge was at Mitchell's house that night, lending support. Didn't know if it was important, but—"

"You didn't tell me."

"All that's happened today, I didn't think of it till just now."

Sanford gnawed on it. "Okay, say they have a thing going."

"Safe to say, I think."

"Still . . ."

"Derek Mitchell covers his ass."

"That's what I'm thinking, too. If he says Creighton Wheeler poses a threat to somebody—"

"I follow you." Kimball snatched up the transmitter again and asked the dispatcher to contact Athens PD. "What the hell?" she said to Sanford while she waited. "Won't be the first time I've made a fool of myself. Or you, either."

Without a word, Sanford slapped the portable light on the roof of the car and stamped on the accelerator, driving in the direction of Athens.

CHAPTER
28

Derek's phone rang. He snapped it open and turned it on speaker. Dodge said, "She's not there."

"*What?*"

"You got a plug in your ear?"

"Did she leave with someone?"

In the backseat, Ariel was freaking out. "He's already got her. I know he does."

"She didn't come to work today," Dodge said. "One of the other girls said she called in sick, and she was pissed off because they couldn't find a replacement and it's a madhouse. Greek rush. Some such bullshit. The place was packed. I think the only person in Athens who isn't in that bar tonight is Carol Mahoney. But there she ain't."

"Then you gotta go to the house. Ariel." Derek glanced back at her. She was clutching her middle and rocking back and forth. "Ariel," he repeated sharply.

She raised her head and looked at him in the rearview mirror.

"Where's Carol staying?"

"At this girl's house."

Derek tried desperately to hang on to his patience. "I know, but what's the address?"

She cut her eyes to Julie, saying mournfully, "I don't know. I've never been there, and Carol never told me the address."

Through the phone speaker, Dodge could be heard chanting derivatives of the F-word.

Julie said, "Ariel, can you remember anything? The name of the street? The area of town? Is it near campus?"

"No. Out a ways. At least that's the impression I got. She said there were woods behind the house. One wall of it is covered by a wisteria vine."

"That narrows it down to half the houses in Georgia," Dodge remarked.

Hearing that, Ariel started to cry.

Hearing her, Dodge swore. Then after a short pause, he said, "I got an idea. I'll call you back."

Dodge reentered the crowded bar and shoved his way through the throng until he found the waitress he'd spoken to earlier. "Where's Carol staying?"

"In Savannah's house."

"Do you know where that is?"

She told him no. He couldn't hear her, but he read her lips.

"Where's your manager?"

"What?"

He placed his lips against her multipierced ear. "Point out your manager."

Perturbed over being bothered when there were tips to be made, she went up on tiptoe, scanned the room, then jabbed her index finger in the direction of the bar. "The one with his cap on backwards. Bulldogs T-shirt."

Dodge bobbed his head in thanks and pushed aside two guys who were hitting on the same coed. When he reached the bar, he leaned across it toward the thirty-something who'd been pointed out to him. "You the manager?" he shouted.

"Yeah. What?"

"Some guys? They're emptying out your storeroom."

"Like stealing?"

"Just thought you'd want to know."

"*Shit!*"

He slid a beer toward his customer, yelled at one of the other bartenders to cover for him, and dashed toward the back of the bar, disappearing through a swinging door. Dodge followed. He found him standing in the center of his stockroom, hands on hips and looking around, baffled.

"You got a waitress named Savannah. I need her home address."

"What the *fuck*? Are you *crazy*? Who *are* you?"

Dodge went up to the guy, grabbed his right hand, and pulled his thumb back until it was almost touching his wrist. "I'm the guy who's gonna break your thumb if you don't give me Savannah's address. You got till two. That's one and a half."

"I should have put on some shoes," Carol said. "I'm afraid I'm going to step in something nasty."

"Would you rather sit down? There's a fallen tree over there."

"It'll have bugs in it. Maybe even a snake."

God, she's a complainer, Creighton thought. He wondered what Billy had ever seen in her. Beyond the obvious. The breasts.

"Let's go back," she said. "It's too dark to see, and it's kinda spooky. That graveyard and all."

"You haven't told me about you and Billy yet."

"I'll tell you over a glass of wine."

"Tell me now."

She stopped and looked at him, and by moonlight he could see the first twinge of apprehension. She tried to hide it with a lame smile. "We'll be much more comfortable on the porch. I've got some good cheese, too."

He forced himself to smile back. "Now you're talking. Lead the way."

Her smile widened. Then she turned and started walking in the direction of the house.

Following, he reached up and slid his necktie from beneath his collar. "Carol?"

"Hmm?"

" 'If I forget to tell you later, I had a really good time tonight.' "

"Okay. It's on Dabney Road, off 441 south of town," Dodge reported through the speaker of Derek's phone. "Know where that's at?"

"I know the highway. Inside or outside the loop?"

"Out, but not too far. I've got it on my GPS."

Since Derek was driving, Julie jotted down the directions as Dodge rattled them off. "Don't wait for us," Derek told him. "We're on the loop now, only two minutes from the turnoff."

"Already on my way."

Derek disconnected. "Ariel, call the house number one more time." She obeyed him without comment. He looked at Julie and could read a worry that matched his over what they might find when they got there.

Julie jumped when her phone rang in her hand. She answered. "Yes?"

"Julie?"

Julie, not Ms. Rutledge. That was a switch from the last time she'd talked to Roberta Kimball. "Yes?"

"Detective Sanford and I have been in touch with the Athens police. An officer at the Red Dog was told by the manager that a man forced him to give out information on Carol Mahoney."

"That was Dodge," Derek said where he could be heard. "We didn't know the address of the house where Carol Mahoney is staying, and we were desperate. Dodge probably didn't say pretty please."

Sanford asked, "Is that where you're headed? To the house?"

Not wanting to be intercepted, Julie hedged. "Ariel is very worried about her friend. She's anxious to make sure she's all right."

"Listen to me." It was Sanford at his most stern. "I remind you that this is a police matter."

"And I remind you that you didn't respond when we first called you," Julie said heatedly.

"Wait for the Athens police," Roberta Kimball said. "They've dispatched a car to the house. Sheriff's office has been notified, too."

"They're late and we're here." Julie disconnected. Ahead, she could see Dodge standing in the glow of the porch light of a small house. As she was watching, he put his shoulder to the front door and broke through it.

Derek brought his car to a jarring stop. The three of them practically fell out of their doors as they shoved them open. They clambered up the steps onto the porch.

Dodge met them at the front door. "Not here."

"Any sign of violence?"

"No. One wineglass on the back porch."

"Her car's here," Ariel said. "She's gotta be here."

She pushed past Dodge and ran through the rooms, frantically calling Carol's name.

As soon as she was out of earshot, Dodge spoke in an undertone. "Didn't want her flying off, going hysterical on you. But I wasn't the only one today asking the bar manager for this address."

"Creighton?"

"Manager said a guy called, passed himself off as a faculty member in the foreign language department who needed clarification on this Savannah's home address. The manager realizes now he was manipulated into giving it to him. He didn't know not to."

Ariel ran back into the living room, appearing to be a hair-breadth away from the hysteria Dodge feared. "She's not here. Where is she? What's he done with her?"

Julie took her by the shoulders. "You mentioned woods behind the house?"

"Dammit!" Kimball said.

Sanford took a corner on two wheels. "What?"

"Officers just arrived at the house."

"No one there?"

"Everyone's there," Kimball reported. "Carol Mahoney's car. Two others."

"An SUV?"

"No. Derek's and his sidekick's. They ran the plates. However, a navy and tan SUV was reported abandoned in a thicket a quarter mile from the house."

Sanford cursed, and Kimball echoed it. They had called this one wrong from the get-go. If Carol Mahoney wound up dead at the hands of Creighton Wheeler, it would be on their heads.

Sanford said, "At least the locals can prevent Mitchell and Ms. Rutledge from taking the law into their own hands."

"*Cars* were there. No sign of the people."

"What?"

"The house is empty."

"Where the hell are they?"

The four ran across the clearing that separated the house from the tree line. Derek was grateful for the moon, but he was in city shoes and the ground was uneven. At least he was in decent shape. Dodge was struggling. Although both of them outdistanced the two women, who had ignored him when he told them to stay in the house. They were behind him and Dodge, but not by much.

"You got a gun?" Dodge shouted.

"No."

"Bad habit, Counselor. You should always carry a piece."

Derek glanced back and saw Dodge slipping a handgun from beneath his jacket. He was licensed to carry a concealed weapon.

"If you get him," Dodge puffed, "what do you expect to do without a gun?"

Derek reached the tree line, but he didn't slow down. He plunged headlong into the darkness of the forest.

Creighton quoted the Julia Roberts line from *Pretty Woman* a mere heartbeat before looping the necktie over Carol's head and pulling it tight around her neck.

She made a shocked sound that turned into a choking gurgle. Her knees buckled, her hands flew to her throat. He pulled the necktie tighter, twisting it against the nape of her neck, and continued to twist it as though trying to wring water from it. She struggled wildly, digging into the earth with her bare heels.

She began to claw at the tie, then reached behind her head and tried to scratch his face, his hands. He'd anticipated she would and was ready. Placing one of his hands against the back of her head, he smashed her face into a tree trunk, dazing her and causing her hands to fall limply at her sides.

But he didn't want to kill her that way. It would be too quick. He twisted the necktie tighter, hoping to provoke a response. In *Frenzy*, the necktie killer was face-to-face with his victim. He got to watch her face as he strangled her. Creighton would have enjoyed that, but the circumstances were different. He wasn't raping Carol Mahoney as he choked her, either. Time and place just weren't conducive for him to replicate the scene exactly.

He also would have liked her to scream. Like Sarah Walker and Allison Perry had screamed when he tore their virgin flesh. Like Jerry Bascomb had screamed when he saw his severed appendage lying in a puddle of blood on the wet tiles of the shower room floor. Creighton figured that the skinny kid had screamed more in horror of the sight than from pain, but it had been exhilarating all the same.

Of course the lack of air prevented a scream from Carol Mahoney, but he would have liked at least a whimper. Like the widow had made on the supermarket parking lot.

"Carol!"

The shout came from a distance, but it caused him to freeze. It roused the girl from her stupor. She moaned and began shifting her weight in a futile attempt to escape him.

"Carol!"

Another voice this time. Julie's. *Julie's?* How in the hell . . . ?

Hearing a sound, he turned his head just in time to catch Derek Mitchell's fist against his chin. The blow was so hard, it sent him flying backward. The necktie slipped from his hands.

Mitchell drove him into the ground, landing on top of him, straddling his chest. "You murdering son of a bitch."

Mitchell slammed his fist into Creighton's jaw just in front of his ear, and pain rocketed through his skull.

"Derek?"

Julie? Her again? That woman is a nuisance. He should have had Billy kill her, too.

"Here!"

Their words were distorted. Creighton was having trouble focusing.

Mitchell was saying, "That one was for all those kids you hurt and got away with. This is compliments of Paul Wheeler."

Another blow to Creighton's chin caused him to bite his tongue with teeth that then cracked.

"And this, this is for Maggie."

Creighton saw the fist coming, but he was helpless to stop it.

He heard his facial bones crunch. The pain was delayed, but when it came it was with the impetus of a pile driver, and it almost caused him to black out. He was aware of Derek Mitchell planting his hand on his chest and climbing off him. But then he heard Mitchell cry out in alarm, "Julie! No! Don't!"

Creighton pried his eyes open. Julie was standing over him, cradling a pistol between her hands, staring down the barrel of it directly into his face. In the most chilling voice he'd ever heard, she whispered, " 'Make my day.' "

And then she pulled the trigger.

"For your hand." Dodge passed Derek an ice pack.

With a nod of thanks, he applied it to his swollen, bloody knuckles.

Dodge had gone out to smoke a half hour earlier and had just now returned. In addition to the ice pack, he'd brought back a Starbucks sack with three coffees in it. He passed one each to Julie and Derek, and kept the third for himself.

They were in the ER waiting room of Athens Regional hospital, where Creighton and Carol had been transported in separate ambulances. Uniformed police officers and sheriff's deputies were milling around trying to look official, drinking vending machine coffee, and getting in the way of the medical personnel. Their plainclothes colleagues were in a huddled conference with Sanford and Kimball.

Dodge slurped his coffee. "Anybody look at it yet?"

"My hand?" Derek flexed and stretched his fingers. "It's okay. No bones broken."

"A wonder, the way you hit him."

"He had it coming, and then some."

"He got some." Dodge shot Julie an arch look.

Derek growled, "What in hell were you thinking, Dodge, giving her your pistol?"

"I couldn't run any farther without collapsing. I didn't want her charging in there after you without a weapon." He gave her a grin of admiration. "Didn't know she was going to pull a Dirty Harry."

"I only wanted Creighton to think I was," she said softly. When Paul had insisted she keep the revolver beneath her bed for protection, he'd also insisted she learn how to shoot it with accuracy.

The blast from the pistol had made Creighton scream. She'd fired the bullet into the ground near enough to his head for him to feel the impact, near enough for him to know what Paul Wheeler's last instant of life had been like.

Dodge glanced toward the detectives. "Have they made noises about booking either of you?"

Derek shook his head. "They're probably arguing jurisdiction."

"They haven't even questioned us to any extent." Julie, who was sitting close to Derek, brushed soil and other organic matter off the knee of his trousers. "I told them Creighton didn't go down easily, and that Derek and I had to do what we could to subdue him until the police caught up with us."

Dodge gargled a chuckle. "Subdue? I'll say."

"Ariel backed me up."

"From what I saw of Wheeler when they put him in the ambulance, his cheekbone was caved in," Dodge said.

"He's in surgery now."

"He won't be as pretty from here on." The investigator snorted. "And I'll bet they had to change his underwear." He looked around. "Where's Ariel?"

"With Carol," Julie told him. "The doctors have examined her. She'll be bruised and her throat will be sore, but she's going to be fine in a few days. Ariel got permission to spend the night with her once they get her into a room. Both are still shaken."

"A few more seconds and we would have been too late," Derek said. "Even if we'd captured him, Carol could be dead."

"But she isn't," Julie said, rubbing his thigh.

Derek turned his head and smiled at her, then as he was taking a sip of his coffee, he nodded toward the entrance. "They're here."

Doug and Sharon Wheeler and a man Julie didn't recognize came through the automatic doors. Spotting her instantly, they walked toward her. Doug looked resolute. Sharon appeared shattered, barely holding on to her composure. Julie had never seen her with a hair out of place. Tonight, she looked ravaged.

"They brought in a heavy hitter," Derek said under his breath, referring to the man who angled off toward Sanford, Kimball, and their Athens Police Department counterparts.

"An attorney?" Julie asked.

"More like the Antichrist," Dodge muttered. "I'm gonna smoke."

The Wheelers didn't give Dodge a glance as he passed them on his way out. Julie stood up to meet them. Derek also came to his feet.

"It's not true!" Sharon shrieked, causing everyone else in the waiting area to turn and stare.

Doug placed his arm around her and pulled her close, but he never took his eyes off Julie. He spoke her name, making a question of it.

"Creighton's still in surgery," she said. "He was hurt—"

"He was brutally beaten!" Sharon cried, glaring at Derek.

"Your son was caught in the act of trying to choke a young woman to death, Mrs. Wheeler," he said.

Julie loved him for speaking to her without rancor. His tone was even kind.

"If I hadn't stopped him," he added, "he would have killed her."

Sharon crumpled against her husband. Derek hastily moved aside and helped Doug guide her into a chair. She covered her face with her hands and began to sob. Doug bent over her, whispered something in her ear as he patted her back, then straightened up and turned to face Julie and Derek.

"We'll do our best for Creighton." His tone suggested that he expected an argument from them. He glanced toward the lawyer who was laying into Sanford and Kimball, both of whom remained stalwart against his tirade.

When Doug came back around to Julie, the pain in his eyes—Paul's eyes—was immeasurable. Her heart went out to him. "I'm sorry, Doug," she said, her voice made hoarse by emotion. "I mean that."

"I know you do." He made a helpless gesture. "Creighton is

a . . . a tragedy. But he's my son. As his father, I must do all I can for him."

"That's what parents do. They take care of their children."

Doug looked at her for several seconds, then said, "Just as Paul did for you. His daughter."

EPILOGUE

I NEED YOU TO HANG MY PAINTING."

"You haven't hung it yet?"

"I had the walls repainted first."

"What color?"

"Same color."

"I see. Well, the painting looked good on the wall it was propped against."

"You think?"

"I assume you still want it in your bedroom."

"Unless you find a better place for it."

"I'll be happy to take a look. Let me know when would be a convenient time for me to come over."

"Okay."

It was a Saturday morning, two weeks after that long night in Athens.

Not expecting him, Julie had answered her door wearing an apron over a pair of jeans and a tank top. He was dressed for a Saturday morning, too.

The conversation died there as they stared at each other across her threshold. She'd been hungry for the sight of him but hadn't dared to contact him. She knew if she was ever to see him again, the move must be his. Her heart was pounding as she wiped her hands on her apron.

"The coffee's still fresh." She motioned him inside, then led the way into the kitchen. "I've been cooking."

"I guessed." He gestured at her apron.

"Coq au vin. Would you like coffee?"

"Sure."

She poured him a cup and managed to pass it from her hand to his without making skin contact.

He glanced toward the oven. "Smells mouthwatering."

"I'm making it for Kate's mom. She's having her Bunco group over tonight and wanted to serve something special."

"Nice of you to go to all that trouble for her."

"No trouble. I enjoy it. Cooking is therapeutic."

"You need therapy?"

She laughed lightly and refilled her coffee cup. "Sit down."

They sat across the bistro table from each other and sipped their coffees in silence. Neither, it seemed, knew where to look. She was the first to speak. "You painted your walls. So you plan to stay in that house. You're not moving."

He looked at her quizzically.

She went on, "You said you didn't think the house would ever be the same for you without Maggie. I thought maybe you'd move."

"She'll always be missed, and every room holds a memory of her. But to move, I'd only be spiting myself. I love the place. Besides, I refuse to give Creighton Wheeler that much influence over my life."

"I'm glad you're staying there. It's a beautiful place."

"Thanks. When you come to hang the painting, I'll give you the grand tour."

"I look forward to it."

Another awkward silence stretched between them.

Finally she said, "Roberta called and—"

"It's Roberta now?"

"She insists. She called and told me that as soon as Creighton was able to speak, he waxed eloquent for almost five hours from his hospital bed. They recorded it all on video."

Derek was nodding. "I was given an account, too. He confessed—proudly and without any remorse—to everything, even to crimes no one knew he'd committed."

"Did they find the bodies of those two other girls he claimed to have killed?"

"Yesterday. Right where he said they would be."

Julie shook her head sadly. "At least now their families know what happened to them."

"He was afraid Paul would marry you, maybe even have a child, and that would usurp him as Paul's heir. According to Sanford, once he started talking, his ego seized control of his tongue. His lawyer was apoplectic, but Creighton wanted to boast about how brilliant he was. In short, he's a sociopath."

"Roberta wanted to see the movie he was emulating with Carol Mahoney. I gave her the DVD of *Frenzy* and told her I didn't want it back. That scene . . ." She rubbed her arms, which broke out in goose bumps. Softly, she added, "That young woman owes you her life, Derek."

"You figured it out, not me. If it hadn't been for you having the hunch about *Strangers on a Train*—"

"I'd still be their prime suspect."

"And Carol Mahoney would be dead. Perhaps Ariel, too. Although Creighton claims he didn't have plans to kill her, I think he had developed a taste for it. Anyway, those women owe their lives to you, too."

"Well . . ." She didn't want to take credit for a fortunate set of circumstances. "One thing I can't figure out is why Billy Duke came to my house to plant the evidence."

"My guess?"

"Please."

"Creighton was trying to sever all his links to Billy. Maybe Billy was trying to sever all his with Creighton. He was trying to shift the blame onto you."

"Then flee and leave me holding the bag."

"Literally."

"I watched him shoot Paul. He killed him in cold blood. But I don't think he would ever have killed anyone if Creighton hadn't coerced him. In a very real sense, he was Creighton's victim, too. He died a horrible death. I'll never forget it."

"There's a lot we'll never forget."

Their gazes held for several seconds. She was the first to look away. Keeping her head averted, she said, "The news about Jason Connor . . . You were right about him."

The story had dominated the headlines for days. It had been Jason's twelve-year-old sister who had committed the double murder in a fit of rage, having been subjected to her stepfather's sexual abuse for years. Out of fear, but more likely indifference, her mother had allowed it. Jason had suspected his sister was being abused, but the instances always occurred when he wasn't in the house, and the girl was too ashamed and too afraid of reprisal to tell him.

He came home from school and discovered her sitting on the floor near the bodies of the two, covered in blood, knife in hand, in a near catatonic state. He cleaned her up and assumed the blame, feeling he was guilty and deserving of punishment for not protecting her. When he was jailed, she was placed in the custody of relatives, to whom she confessed.

"It wasn't my place to argue with you over him," Julie said. "I apologize."

"Usually my clients are guilty, Julie. Some are lowlifes with no redeeming qualities whatsoever. I go to battle for them because it's their constitutional right to have a defense. Some are rich and influential but equally guilty. They, too, are entitled to a defense.

"But occasionally, like with Jason, the accused really is innocent. That's how I can do it. That's *why* I do it. Every once in a while a person *is* falsely accused and in desperate need of someone in his corner, believing in him, fighting for him."

"I'll never ask you to justify or explain yourself to me again. I promise." She took a deep breath. "You, on the other hand, are past due an explanation."

He set his coffee cup down. "Paul Wheeler was your father, not your lover."

She raised her shoulders in a small shrug. "Following her high school graduation, my mother went to spend the summer at the beach with distant cousins. She met Paul at a dance. They were seventeen, the climate was sultry, moonlight on the shore, strawberry wine. You get the picture. I happened."

"Wheeler didn't know?"

"He knew. Mother contacted him and informed him that she was pregnant. My dad, the man who raised me, had been in love with her for years, waiting for her to reach a suitable age so he could marry her. She told him, too. He still wanted to marry her, and she truly loved him.

"Seeing their relationship for what it was, Paul relinquished parental rights, knowing it would be in my best interest for him to do so. He was about to enter the university. He was unmarried. My dad wanted to marry my mother and claim me as his. So Paul gracefully withdrew from my life.

"He offered his financial support, but my mother and dad respectfully refused it. He honored their wishes, but he made Mother swear that if she or I ever needed anything at any time she would send for him. She never did. Until I got into trouble in Paris."

The timer on the stove dinged. She got up, pulled on oven mitts, and removed the cast-iron Dutch oven. She returned to her chair and pulled off the mitts. "Mother was sick and unable to help me out of that mess, so she summoned Paul. Even though it had been years since they'd had any contact, he went to see her immediately. She told him about Henri. What she knew, that is. I'd kept a lot from her, not wanting her to fret over my circumstances, which I'd foolishly brought on myself. Paul dropped everything and, as you said, flew to my rescue."

Derek regarded her thoughtfully. "What did you think when this American millionaire showed up and introduced himself as your father?"

"You'd think I would resent him, wouldn't you? You're my father? Where have you been all this time? But Paul was inordinately kind. He had only the highest regard for my mother, both as the girl she'd been and as the woman she'd become. He praised my dad for the loving, accepting man he'd been. He said that kind of selfless, unconditional love was exceptional, and that he, Paul, was grateful I'd grown up with such a man caring for me."

She gave a weak smile. "Even though his news shook the foundation of my life, I could find no cause to hate him. He made it clear immediately that, although he hated that I'd suffered Henri and the unhappiness he'd caused, he was grateful for the opportunity to do something for me. He said that, although he hadn't been in my life, I had never been far from his mind. He wanted to make up for lost time. Not only did he want to help me out of the crisis situation but he wanted to get to know me, develop the relationship we'd been denied."

"But he didn't claim you as his daughter."

"I wouldn't let him."

"Why?"

"Out of respect for my dad, first of all. And out of respect for Paul's wife, Mary, whom he had loved with all his heart. I didn't want him acknowledging me when Mary hadn't been able to bear him any children."

"Did he tell her about you?"

"Yes. They'd kept no secrets from each other. He said that from time to time she would urge him to contact me, to invite me into their lives, but for all the reasons I've told you, he didn't. Maybe if she had still been alive when he came to Paris, maybe if Mother had lived, we'd have made different decisions about his claiming me publicly. But, as things were, I thought it was better that he and I left the nature of our relationship unspecified, let people conclude what they would."

"You know what they concluded."

"In return for the scorn of people I didn't care about, I had two years with someone I cared about very much. And they were wonderful years, Derek. Taking nothing away from the two dear people who reared me, Paul and I made up for a lot of time missed. He loved me, and I loved him."

"Even Doug didn't know about you."

"Not until Paul's attorney told him in regards to the will. I'm glad he knows now."

"Will he accept you as family?"

"I don't know. If he does, he'll preserve the secret of our kinship. But I hope he and Sharon will accept me on some level. They'll need support now with Creighton behind bars. I understand that most of their so-called friends have deserted them. They're facing this alone. I want to help them any way I can, any way they'll let me."

Derek fiddled with the handle of his coffee cup but didn't pick it up. At last he said, "You could have told me, Julie."

She reached across the table and covered his hand. "I almost did that night we were parked outside the hotel and you kissed me."

"You said, 'Don't do this to me.' "

"Because it was torture. I hadn't been with a man since Henri. I hadn't sought a romantic relationship in all that time with Paul. He encouraged me to date. He wanted to see me happy with someone who loved me. I think he would have enjoyed having grandchildren," she added with a sad smile.

"But what happened with Henri had made me wary. Besides, most men wouldn't have understood my 'friendship' with a rich, handsome older man. So that part of myself had been deprived for a long time. Until that night on the airplane." She glanced across at him, then away. "I shunned your kisses because, even though I wanted you, I knew you were thinking that I was a fortune seeker ready to take up with the next man. Straight from Paul's bed and into yours."

"I wasn't thinking anything that ugly."

"But along those lines?"

He shrugged guiltily. "So it was hands-off because you wanted me to respect you in the morning."

She smiled. "As cliché as it sounds, yes."

"Then why didn't you tell me that night? Or any time? Why did you let me go on thinking the worst?"

"At first, I couldn't trust you with the secret."

"And later?"

"By the time I came to trust you, it had grown into a lie of omission that would have made me look even more untrustworthy than you already believed me to be."

"Whatever I thought, it didn't keep me from wanting you. But am I glad you were Paul's daughter rather than his lover? Yes. Definitely."

"I'm glad you're glad."

He hesitated, then asked, "What about the money?"

"I never intend to touch it. I'm giving it away."

"Nobly said, but be realistic, Julie. It's a freaking fortune. Even giving it away will take a while."

"I've got the rest of my life." She looked at him imploringly. "Please don't let it be an issue with you. Because I swear to you, it's not an issue with me."

He studied her face intently, and when he saw that she was sincere, his features relaxed. "Dodge plans to hit you up for a loan."

"Oh, he likes me now?"

"Yeah, he does." Dropping the volume of his voice considerably, he added, "So do I."

"I like you, too," she said huskily. "Very much. Where have you been?"

"Since I stormed out of the ER? Thinking."

"About us?"

"About how I and my ego felt about being made a fool of."

"I didn't keep my secret to make you look foolish, Derek. I was protecting Paul, my mother, my dad, Mary Wheeler, all of them, from scandal."

"Yeah, that's one of the conclusions I and my ego reached."

"That and what others?"

"That you were Paul Wheeler's daughter and heir when we met. And that had I known that when I touched you for the first time, it wouldn't have made one bit of difference."

"It wouldn't?"

He shook his head.

"You would have still . . . ?"

"Oh, yeah. Nothing would have stopped me from following you into that lavatory."

He stood up and came around the table. Pulling her out of her chair, he placed his arms loosely around her waist. "The final thing I concluded was that I really would be a damn fool if I denied myself years of happiness because of a little pride."

"Years?"

"Starting today. Starting right now."

He touched her lips softly with his, then they fell on each other, kissing hungrily.

When at last he raised his head, he said, "That's all I needed to know. We'll work out the details later."

He bent to kiss her again, but she angled her head back. "One thing."

He nuzzled her neck as he untied her apron strings and slipped his hands beneath her tank top. "Make it short."

"When our children ask how we met . . ."

He chuckled. "We'll think of something."

ABOUT THE AUTHOR

Sandra Brown is the author of numerous *New York Times* best-sellers, including *Smoke Screen; Play Dirty; Ricochet; Chill Factor; White Hot; Hello, Darkness; The Crush; Envy;* and *The Switch*. She and her husband live in Arlington, Texas.

Visit her website at www.sandrabrown.net.